SHAKING TREES

SHAKING TREES

AN ABBY EATON MYSTERY

VICKI STEVENS

BLOODWOOD
PRESS

This is a work of fiction. Names, characters, places and incidents mentioned in this novel are products of the author's imagination or are used fictitiously.

Published by Bloodwood Press in 2018
Armstrong Creek, QLD, Australia

ISBN 978-0-6483831-1-6 (paperback)

ISBN 978-0-6483831-0-9 (ebook)

Quote from *The Perpetual Calendar of Inspiration* by Vera Nazarian Copyright © Vera Nazarian 2010

The Apple Blossom by Charles G Eastman, 1816-1860

Cover design by Predrag Marković: Predra6art

 A catalogue record for this work is available from the National Library of Australia

For Ron & Dawn and Jack & Marj

'Listen to the trees as they sway in the wind. Their leaves are telling secrets.'

— VERA NAZARIAN, THE PERPETUAL
CALENDAR OF INSPIRATION

PROLOGUE

11 January 1958

The train is late. Easing the throttle of his motorcycle, he checks over his shoulder. By now, his Triumph Thunderbird should be racing a locomotive—passengers waving, egging his bike to outrun the rattling beast—but the railway tracks beside the dirt road are empty. A glance at his wristwatch confirms his belief; the morning train bound for Shadow Creek is behind schedule. His hope in putting on a show for his girl is now dashed, and he will have to settle for greeting her at the station instead.

A sound of sirens.

He stares ahead and within seconds a bright yellow ambulance barrels towards him. Swerving the bike to the road's edge, he brakes and plants a foot for balance, letting the engine idle while a police car, a fire engine, and an assortment of vehicles appear through clouds of dust and hurtle past.

A battered Bedford truck smelling of cow manure labours

behind. Two men in grimy overalls are seated on the back tray, their legs dangling.

'What's going on?' he calls above the din.

One man cups his hands to his mouth. 'Train jumped the tracks.'

Fear trails over him. 'Which train?'

'The 10:15!'

He kicks the bike into gear, skids it around and draws alongside. 'How far back?'

'Below Archer's Lookout!' the man hollers. 'A bloody awful mess, so we've heard. They'll need all the help they can get, young fella.'

With a squeeze of the throttle, he accelerates and overtakes the flow of vehicles from Shadow Creek.

Racing over familiar territory, the motorbike slides through thick dust at each road bend and narrowly misses roadside trees. Drawn by the constant scream of a train whistle, he crests a rise and glimpses the rail line, making out the bulk of the derailed steam train—carriages at odd angles like collapsed building blocks. His heart seizes.

Speeding downhill, he veers off the road and aims for a gap in the barbed wire fencing. Tearing across a paddock and through a herd of grazing cattle, he halts near a group of people standing on a knoll. The bike falls to the ground as he leaps from the seat and reefs off his goggles to take in the scene.

The air is filled with noise. Around him are gasps and cries from the onlookers. Below him come screams, shouts, the hiss and groan of the dying locomotive, and the shriek of the whistle's alarm. Dozens of people swarm over the wreckage like scavengers over a carcass. Some carriages remain standing, while others lay crushed and splintered behind the toppled engine half buried in the dirt. Survivors have been marshalled onto a grassy flat where medics conduct a triage, the injured being stretchered to an increasing line of ambulances. In the shade of a large hoop pine is a makeshift morgue. He cringes as he sees the number of shapes draped in white sheeting grow, and turns back to the wreckage.

From what he can make out, the descending train must have taken the horseshoe bend near the bottom of the mountain at speed. Unable to manage the curve, the locomotive jumped the tracks, tipped sideways and ploughed into the side of an embankment, gouging out a huge furrow in the earth before stopping. The carriage following the water tank was destroyed on impact, while the next two had telescoped into one another so that it is now impossible to tell where one carriage ends and the other begins.

He decides he can't stay on the hill gawking like the others. A man carrying a camera and a tripod ducks under the barbed wire fencing and he does the same, sprinting down the embankment. Moving across to the grassed area and group of survivors, he scans the crowd for a recognisable face, only to be greeted by haunted stares from strangers.

A police constable blows a whistle and shouts. 'Excuse me, everyone! We are gathering personal effects found in the wreckage and placing them here, on this tarpaulin. Anything not claimed or identified by the end of the day will be taken to the police station at Shadow Creek.'

He eyes the collection of hand luggage, shoes, jackets, and children's toys already piled on the tarp. Nothing is familiar. He pulls his wallet free from his jacket pocket and draws out a dog-eared photograph of a young woman. Walking amongst the travellers, he flashes it around. Shrugs and shaking heads offer hope at the thought that she may have missed the train altogether and was waiting back at the city's central station.

A tug of his sleeve.

A woman a little older than his mother stands beside him. Her outfit is soiled and tattered. She takes the black and white image from his trembling hands and, pushing her spectacles further back on her nose, squints and asks, 'Is that frock white with pink flowers?'

A memory of the effort it had taken him to undo the buttons and release her from this same dress is still vivid. He answers a fervent, 'Yes.'

The woman nods. 'Then I've seen her. I saw her from the train window. She was on the platform at Central Station. A pretty dress on a pretty girl.'

His heart leaps. 'So she didn't get on the train?'

A coughing fit interrupts the woman's reply. She covers her mouth with a handkerchief and wipes spit from her lips. 'Yes, dear, she did. Just moments before the train pulled away.'

He clutches her arm, easing his grip away when she flinches. 'Where can I find her?'

She turns towards the wreckage. 'There were six carriages.'

His eyes move to study the mangled engine and the mess of timber and iron close behind. Following on are three upright carriages, still linked together and undamaged.

'I was in the fourth from the front, the first one of those still standing. The young lady got into the carriage ahead of mine.' Her face suddenly crumples. 'I'm so sorry.'

His head swims. She would have been in the third carriage behind the engine—its whereabouts now difficult to distinguish.

The woman wipes her nose and returns the photograph. Her fingers linger on his. 'Why don't you check with the ambulance men? She may have only been hurt.'

He makes his way over to a team of white-coated medics working on the injured. She is not there. Approaching an officious looking fellow brandishing a clipboard, he asks after her.

Flicking through the paperwork, the man shakes his head. 'Nope. Not here. Have you been over there yet?' He indicates the temporary morgue where the number of bodies has now doubled. 'We need folk to identify the deceased.'

He stays rooted to the spot. The medic waves a fellow worker over whose coat is smeared with various shades of crimson.

'Looking for someone, are you?' the second medic asks, brushing sweaty strands of hair back from a freckled forehead.

Her name edges out of his mouth, one syllable at a time.

The medic frowns. 'How old?'

'Nineteen.'

'Hair . . . dark or light?'

'Brown,' he answers, with an urge to describe the richness of colour and the way the soft whorls tended to wrap around his fingers. Instead he just adds, 'and curly'. Before he can remove the photograph from his jacket pocket to show him, the medic begins to walk away.

'Come with me,' the man urges.

He hesitates, and then lags behind as the medic leads him over to the large hoop pine.

His skin prickles as they pass a stretcher bearing body parts— severed arms and legs, feet still wearing shoes. Flies swarm, drawn by the smell of blood. He hurries on, his breath catching in his throat at the sight of a woman kneeling before a young child partially covered by sheeting. The child is definitely dead. Past crying, the woman rocks back and forth, her hands pressed to her face. He quickly diverts his gaze and finds the medic has stopped in front of a covered form. Bending, the man lifts a corner of the sheet, peers beneath, and then lets it drop. Moving to the next concealed body, he does the same, yet this time he beckons him over.

His jaw clenches as he takes those last few steps and notices blood has soaked through the lower half of this covering.

'Are you ready?' the medic asks, and without waiting for an answer, peels back the cloth.

He sucks in air. A beautiful, yet ashen face is revealed. Both eyes are closed as if in sleep, though the pale lips and the trickle of red coming from the corners of her mouth imply otherwise.

'Is this her?' The medic asks.

Bile rises. Tears sting. He swallows hard and shakes his head.

The sheet is replaced.

'Where is she then?' he croaks, his throat burning.

The medic swats away a fly. 'They haven't got everyone out yet. It could take a while. Maybe you could help.'

The whistle has now ceased its alert, and men of all ages are rallying around the wreckage—volunteers, police, firemen. He joins them. Another steam engine has arrived and railway workers are busy hooking up the righted carriages for removal. Here there is no panic, only action.

At close range, the horror of the crash surpasses anything he could have imagined. People are still trapped—their bodies caught by the wreckage—and clumps of helpers, or maybe relatives, offer words of comfort to soothe their cries. A quick scan reveals she is not amongst them. He moves on, his chest constricting at the sight of a robed parish priest holding the large hand of a man—the only part of him visible through the crushed timber—and giving the last rites.

He prays once again for a miracle, and wonders how he can be of assistance.

'Need help up here!' comes a shout from a young man standing atop a section of the overturned remains and waving wildly. 'There's a kid inside!'

He scrambles over splintered wood. Another fellow joins him.

As the carriages have tipped sideways, they clamber up to the line of windows that are now at the top. Crouching, all three peer through a gaping window into the shadows. A boy of about twelve stares up from the rubble. He is covered in a thick layer of chalky dust and a leg, twisted at an odd angle, looks to be broken.

'Where'd you come from?' asks one man. 'I thought we'd got everyone out of here.'

'Dragged myself from way back.' The young face contorts with pain. 'I tried real hard ... but I can't move no more.'

'Geez kid, it's a miracle you got this far. Stay strong, we'll get a pulley up here to help you out.' The man turns to the others. 'Poor lad must be hurting like blazes.'

He has to help the kid. He falls on his stomach. 'Grab my legs! I'll get him.' The other men clasp his thighs as he stretches down into the darkness. 'Give me your hands,' he urges the boy.

The boy raises his arms, groaning with the effort.

Clutching the small, trembling hands, he slides his grip past two narrow wrists to take hold of the upper arms. Muscles strain. Slowly, he and the boy are dragged out into the open air.

'You did it, champ,' he says, as the boy is taken from him and laid on a stretcher. 'You're one gutsy kid. Is there anyone else down there?'

The boy nods. Tears make fresh paths through the dust on his young cheeks. 'A lady ... back where I was. She's stuck.'

He stares down into the darkness of the carriage. 'I'm going in.'

'It's bloody unstable,' another rescuer warns. 'Wait till we get some more equipment up here.'

He shakes his head, eases his legs through the narrow opening, and drops.

Timber and glass shatter under his weight.

As his eyes adjust to the gloom, he discovers bench seating has been flattened and steel framework warped by the impact. He strains to hear sounds from within, but hears nothing other than muffled voices and the tapping and wrenching of all manner of rescue tools coming from outside. Crouching in the confined space, he quickly gets to work on the rubble, clearing a way large enough to pass through.

A stream of sunlight cuts through a crack in what was once the roof. It catches a flash of something shiny and red. He shuffles close and pulls a handbag from the shattered mess. He recognises the red vinyl, black bow, and silver clasp. His pulse drums in his ears. She must be nearby.

He calls her name. No answer.

He kicks the wall of debris with his boot, but with little result. Wedging a piece of twisted metal underneath the pile, he levers the panelling. Timber groans and snaps, and he sees movement. Kneeling, and numb to the shards of glass piercing his flesh, he forces his hand through the gap. His fingers touch the softness of bare skin. He cries her name and tells her it won't be long, that she'll be out soon. He withdraws his hand. It is sticky with blood. He wrenches away more timber and reels back as an arm—pale and limp—suddenly flops through the opening. On one finger of the hand is a diamond and sapphire ring he remembers well.

In a frantic attempt to release her, he tugs, pushes, kicks and pulls until his energy is spent. Falling back, a primal cry erupts from his mouth. Before him, still caught in the jaws of the wreckage, is the mutilated body of the woman he loves.

1

2018

Something had woken me. Sticky eyes struggled to open. It should have been morning, yet the lounge room was crammed with shadows. I turned my head to study the wall clock and groaned at the hammering within my skull from too much wine. 7:25 am. Definitely morning.

Junk food wrappers fluttered to the floor as I eased my stiffened body from the sofa and staggered over to the floor-to-ceiling window. Blinking, I took in an abbreviated view of a day boxed in by heavy fog. The valley and the town of Shadow Creek below our ridge were completely hidden beneath a cotton ball shroud, while in the distance the only hint of the surrounding mountain range was a lone rocky peak stabbing through cloud. What had dragged me from drunken slumber back to a reality I didn't want to face? Could it have been the rain tap-dancing on our iron roof, or the wind shoving furniture around on the back deck?

My head jerked at an invasive sound coming from the front door—a pounding from an urgent fist. My breath caught in my throat. This was strange. We didn't get many visitors up here on the mountain, especially on a Sunday morning.

Concerned that someone might be in need of help, I stumbled over empty wine bottles to the smaller window facing the road. Parting the curtains, I snuck a peek. There was no one standing on the porch, however, a cloud of mist in the front yard swirled in on itself as if disturbed by a presence. My skin prickled. Rushing to the front door I snatched a jacket from the coat stand, slipped my feet into a pair of rubber thongs, and swung it open.

'Hello,' I cried, my tongue feeling like a wad of carpet in my mouth. 'I am home!'

A slap of moist air against my cheeks was the only response.

Moving out onto the porch I called again, louder. Still no answer, so I shuffled down the steps and onto the paved driveway.

Cutting my way through dense mist, I tackled the incline and stopped when my feet hit the concrete kerb. Brushing wet tendrils of hair from my face, I strained to listen, hearing only the sound of water streaming down roadside gutters. A breeze momentarily cleared my view in a teasing game of peek-a-boo: a flash of a postbox, a snatch of a garden, a glimpse of the road, a hint of a house. I was all alone—no person, no car, no evidence that anyone had visited.

Fighting to keep the jacket closed over my T-shirt nightie, I continued waiting. Again nothing, only more fog.

'You're going crazy, Abby Eaton,' I chided myself, and then jumped as a loud cackle cut through the air.

Startled by the kookaburra's laugh, I slipped off the kerb and into the flowing gutter. Before the rubber thongs acted like a set of surf skis and sent me skidding down to the road's end, I grabbed hold of an overhanging tree branch and pulled myself back up to the safety of the footpath. Catching my breath, I spied the pesky bird perched on a weathered fence post and gave it a sneer, despite how ridiculous I knew I looked.

Heading back down the driveway to the house, I was certain of three things: I was puzzled, delusional, and should have remained indoors wallowing in self-pity instead of following an apparition into the mist. I contemplated snuggling up in bed with a coffee and a book befitting my mood. There were some horror novels perched like hideous gargoyles on a shelf of my bookcase that I could easily escape into. Carefully manoeuvring up the slippery steps to the porch, something caught my eye. Resting on the wicker chair near the front door was a small, wrapped parcel.

My stomach knotted.

Somebody had been here.

I dropped onto the sofa, my hand trembling as it held the parcel wrapped in brown paper and tied with twine. There was no card or note attached, or any kind of marking to indicate the sender. I wasn't even sure I was the intended recipient. Grappling with the tight knot, I unwrapped the paper only to find another layer beneath. This one was aged newspaper. Reminded of a game of pass-the-parcel, I ripped open the newsprint and gasped as a shiny object fell into my lap. Lifting it by its delicate linked chain, I watched as a heart-shaped pendant dangled before my eyes. It was a necklace. Outlined in silverwork, the porcelain surface was covered in a pattern of tiny flowers in bright shades of pink, blue and green. The design was familiar, and the blossoms stirred pleasant memories.

I leapt up and crossed the room, carefully stepping around broken glass from a vase I vaguely remembered smashing in anger the previous evening. It had been a birthday present from my family. I made my way over to a display cabinet filled with a collection of vintage English china that I'd been adding to over a number of years. Opening the leadlight glass door, I scanned the assortment of teacups, plates, and figurines, and removed a small scallop-shaped dish that had once belonged to my mother. It fitted perfectly in the palm of my hand and had the exact same pattern as the pendant—a James Kent design entitled 'Apple Blossom', a favourite of mine. As I held the two items side by side, I was convinced that the necklace had been meant for me. Returning the small dish to the glass shelving, I lay the necklace on top of the cabinet.

Running my fingers through hair that now felt like dried seaweed, I wondered who else knew of my avid interest in this design. Why would someone take an early morning drive up here to Rosella Ridge and drop off a gift without bothering to leave a note? Whoever it was, I hoped they would make contact soon. In the meantime, I needed a hot shower, headache pills, and caffeine.

The first coffee hardly hit the spot. The second proved much better. As I stood on the back deck, sipping slowly and watching low-lying clouds peel away to reveal a stunning view of the valley, I wished my troubles would disperse just as easily.

Two days earlier, my employment at Huckleberry's had been terminated. Daniel, who'd taken over management of the city bookstore from his early-retiring father, had called me into the newly refurbished office—now all glass and chrome—seated his tight arse on a sleek futuristic-styled desk, and told me he had to let me go.

'Downsizing due to successive financial losses,' he had said with an inappropriate smile, and then thanked me for my seven years of faithful service.

Shock rendered me speechless. I was barely aware of him taking my hand and pumping it wildly for I was thinking how consistently busy the shop had been, and how much effort I had put in over the years generating sales and excelling in customer service. It made no sense. But what could I do, the young upstart had made his decision and I was forced to walk away from a job I loved; a job I needed.

Then yesterday, Shane and I ended up having a rare blazing row when I found out he'd withdrawn our savings for a holiday to celebrate twenty-one years of marriage, and selfishly bought a motorbike. 'A sweet Yamaha V Star 650,' he'd crooned. More confusing than him doing this without consulting me, was the fact that he'd never once shown an interest in motorbikes other than complaining about what a nuisance they were on our winding mountain roads. As far as I knew he didn't even have a bike licence. He'd taken off to his brother's place for the remainder of the weekend to cool down, while I was left reeling from such a horrid fight, hurting from Shane's lack of consideration, and confused as to why he couldn't stay and talk things out like we normally did over less major disagreements.

That afternoon, to expend my frustration, I tackled the task of weeding my overgrown herb and vegetable garden. In the process, I discovered why our clever, obedient, seventeen-year-old son had been so keen a few weeks back to tend the plot for me. In amongst the basil and zucchini I found five young, healthy cannabis plants. If Elliott had been home and not staying over at his girlfriend's place, he would have received an earful of his mother's wrath over his illegal actions. Instead, I'd sent him a text, 'WTF!' with a photo of his cultivation. Not surprisingly, he hadn't replied.

To top the day off, I received a message from my vacationing daughter informing me that she had met a guy in North Queensland. They'd bonded over a sailing and snorkelling adventure around the Great Barrier Reef, and she was already considering throwing in her job as a veterinary nurse back here in Shadow Creek and moving in with him and his two young sons in Port Douglas. What was Gemma thinking? She was barely nineteen! I think that was when I threw the vase against the wall.

Keeping every aspect of my life on track was like juggling balls, and now they'd all come tumbling down around me.

I glanced back into the lounge room, to the china cabinet and the item that was an additional concern. I crossed off a mental list. The necklace couldn't have come from Shane—too soon—we weren't on speaking terms let alone exchanging gifts. I ran a thick imaginary line through his name. My mother? No. My parents wouldn't have travelled up here a day before my arranged visit to their place. Mum was eager to shower love on her youngest, now-jobless daughter—which was Mum-speak for feeding me until my sorrows diminished—and I'd readily accepted her invitation. My sorrows had since multiplied and my life was a train wreck, yet I had no intention of confessing this to them or anyone else. Another cross off.

I thought hard. What about Donna? My friend and her husband owned the antique shop in Shadow Creek, and it was Donna who had fuelled my initial interest in English china. She was aware of my sentiment for James Kent designs and could have come across the necklace and thought of me. Yes, that could be it. Though why hadn't she phoned and asked me to come to the shop rather than driving up to Rosella Ridge to deliver it so early on a Sunday morning?

I phoned the shop. No answer. I phoned her mobile. Just a voice message saying she'd get back to me. I tried again, several times, with the same frustrating result. In the end, I decided I needed to move on to more satisfactory tasks, like cleaning up my mess, watching a backlog of TV shows, and comfort eating.

As night fell, my anxiety grew. Shane had not yet returned, and Elliott wouldn't be home until after school the next day. This meant I was home alone, in the dark. Due to the strange morning 'drop off', I found myself jumping at weird outside noises, frequently peeking through windows to check for lurking strangers, and wishing Shane would hurry home to protect me. When he messaged to bluntly say he needed another night away, my worries increased and I began to regret my volatile reaction to his spending spree and not insisting he stay to discuss the situation. Now he was probably drowning his sorrows with his brother and mouthing off.

Rather than fall asleep on the sofa in a sad, drunken state as I'd done the previous night, I retired to the comfort of my bed, but not before making sure all windows were shut and all doors locked. Still too nervy to sleep, I attempted to take my mind off my concerns by ripping open the bodice of a new gothic romance and plunging headlong into the first chapter.

Three chapters in, I found my concentration waning and my thoughts trailing back to my situation. One of the perks of working in a bookstore was being able to regularly sample recent releases—much to the annoyance of Shane, who was of a rather different ilk and preferred to kick back on a comfy recliner with a cool beverage in one hand, a packet of potato chips in the other, and allow a story to unfold on the widescreen TV. Now I had no job and my husband, who I believed was experiencing some stupid mid-life crisis thing, was sleeping elsewhere.

Dropping the book onto the empty space beside me, I flicked off the lamp and discovered the enveloping darkness somehow accentuated the lack of noise coming from the rest of the house. An ache formed within my chest. It had been a long while since I'd felt so alone. Rolling to Shane's side of the bed, I sobbed into his pillow.

2

Stanthorpe, September 1957

Hurried footsteps on earth. Flashes of yellow and white through greenery.

Poised high on a weathered ladder, he parts leafy branches and watches as the orchard's intruder halts in the shade of the aged apple tree. He frowns. On the verge of making his presence known, an outburst of colourful words assaults the surroundings and convinces him to hold his tongue.

'You conniving bastard! I hate you. I bloody well hate you!'

He decides to wait for the mane of auburn curls to cease shaking before opening his mouth.

A sharp cry pierces the air.

He lurches, his feet slipping from the timber rungs. Amongst a discord of snapping and crashing, he plummets through the foliage and lands heavily on the dry earth just seconds before the ladder lands on top of him.

Rolling out from under the ladder, he wheezes, fighting for his next breath. When the stars disperse, he opens his eyes. Before them appears a pair of white sand shoes. Pushing up onto his elbows, he discovers that the shoes belong to slender legs leading up to a pair of yellow cotton shorts. He tilts his head back, squints against the sunlight, and makes out a white blouse and a face bearing a scowl.

'What are you doing?' is snapped through a red pout.

Wincing, he stands, finding he towers over the young woman by almost a foot. Though, when she lifts her chin and glowers up at him with eyes as green as a tree snake, he sees she is no shrinking violet.

'Were you spying on me?' she says, planting her hands on her hips, and thrusting out her chest.

He is distracted from the absurdity of this question by the tautness of her embroidered lawn blouse. 'What? Spying? Geez, no. Just having a gander.'

'A gander? At what?'

'Buds,' he says, reverting his gaze to her face, which is now sporting sharp, questioning eyebrows. 'In the tree,' he adds, pointing upwards.

She arches her neck to study the branches and he glimpses a snatch of firm round flesh through a gape between two buttons of her blouse.

'Are they apple blossoms?' she asks.

'Well, being an apple orchard, I'd take a stab in the dark and say, yep, they are.'

The scowl returns.

As her eyes move over him, he self-consciously brushes dust from his stained work clothes and twigs from his unruly hair.

'You work here?' she asks with a twitch of her nose, making him wonder if the smell of worthwhile labour had offended her prissy constitution.

'You bet I do. I was working a treat until you came bowling along, disturbing all and sundry with that unholy outburst.'

A surprising blush creeps from her neck to her cheeks. 'You heard that?'

'Every man and his dog for a mile around would've heard it. You sure were spittin' some chips, and that banshee scream ... well that's what knocked me off my perch.'

Her bluster returns. 'Can't a girl show a little emotion?'

'A little? I thought only blokes like me spouted words like that. Not proper young ladies.'

There is that glower again. 'Proper! What is proper? Well behaved? Obedient? Do as commanded? I'm not a dog, you know!'

He takes a step back, holds up his hands. 'Settle down. I didn't say you were.'

Her shoulders sag. Her demeanour suddenly softens. 'Sorry, it's been a rough day. I shouldn't be taking it out on you.'

'Well, I'm not going to argue with that.'

She lets out a sigh. 'Are you all right? That was quite a dive you just took.'

He gives a snort. 'Of course. I'm as tough as old boots.'

'Are you sure?' She points. 'Your face ... it's bleeding.'

His hand moves to his cheek. There is blood on his fingers.

She steps forward and removes a neatly pressed handkerchief from the confines of her blouse, begins to dab at the scratch.

He balks, then realises the proximity simply affords him a closer view of her. He also discovers that she smells like a cottage garden, and bears an intriguing V-shaped scar above her right eyebrow. Their eyes meet. An unusual emotion stirs within—one that is both thrilling and ominous. He gives a shudder.

She notices and pulls away. 'I really don't think it's that serious.'

'As long as it hasn't harmed my good looks,' he jokes.

The green of her eyes intensifies. 'Someone certainly has tickets on himself.' She shoves the bloodied cloth into his hand. 'You can keep it. I have more where that came from.'

He gives her bodice another curious peek.

She peers over her shoulder. 'So, how do I get out of this orchard?'

'Well, if you're looking for the road, it's that way,' he indicates with a nod to the left. 'Just follow the fence line over the hill. You can't miss it.'

'Thanks,' she says, and rushes away, disappearing behind a row of budding apple trees.

Like the dropping of a stage curtain after the first act of a play, tranquillity instantly returns to the orchard.

He shakes his head. 'Well I'll be blowed.'

Lifting the handkerchief to wipe away a trickle of sweat snaking its way under his collar, his eyes are drawn to the fancy stitching on the linen. Next to a bright smear of blood, is an embroidered letter 'M'.

3

The drive down the mountain was always a pleasant one. On the western side of Rosella Ridge, where I lived, lay the valley and village of Shadow Creek. While the eastern side revealed the distant shimmer of Moreton Bay and further south, the crop of skyscrapers belonging to the city of Brisbane. With extra time to kill before I was expected at my parents' place, I pulled over at the road's edge to admire a scene that never failed to captivate.

Stepping from my bright yellow Volkswagen Beetle—the colour chosen for its liveliness, rather than ease of detection by nervous drivers as Shane had once intimated—I walked over to an escarpment safely edged by fencing and sucked in a breath of clean country air. The overcast sky of the previous morning had been replaced with a vivid expanse of blue; a contrast to the rich green of undulating hills and tree-lined gullies. Wind rippled over grassy slopes in waves, and on one verdant knoll a small herd of cattle munched unperturbed in the warmth of the sun. A currawong trilled a 'good morning' and I closed my eyes in an attempt to practise 'mindfulness', which I'd heard was supposed to ease tension. Accepting the depressing thoughts, I tried to focus on more positive ones.

It was October, spring here in Australia—my favourite season of the year. I thought on the free time I now had to enjoy it. I focused on the rumble in my stomach and how, having skipped breakfast due to fearing another early morning knock on the door, I was looking forward to Mum's cooking. I pondered on the pretty china necklace and the mysterious morning visitor. Then my thoughts veered to the ominous task of looking for another job, to Shane's cold-shouldering of me, to my kids and their troubled futures. Frustration bobbed to the surface. Anxiety kicked into life. Anger reared its dreadful head. My eyes flew open and my meditative bubble burst spectacularly. Damn!

Returning to the car, I wrenched open the door and flopped behind the steering wheel. Reaching back to retrieve my seatbelt, I heard a 'ping' as a button in my shirt broke free and ricocheted off the dashboard. A yawning gap between stretched fabric now flashed more than a hint of cleavage. Great, just what I needed. Searching for the stray button without success, I realised that if I didn't want anyone gawking I would need to locate a safety pin. As I continued my journey down the mountain, I hoped the loss of a button wasn't a forerunner of more bad luck to come.

Passing several large properties, and noticing that they had recently been divided and were being sold as acreage lots, I wondered what an influx of 'tree-changers' would do to the small-town ambience. Maybe it would help boost the economy and create diversity. Coming to a T-junction, I went left down a winding tree-lined road leading into the village.

Only a thirty-minute drive from suburbia, Shadow Creek was like an island of yesteryear in the midst of modernity. On weekends, city folk visited in droves to pass their time visiting the quaint shops, eating wholesome food, and downing a cold one at the heritage-listed pub. Being Monday though, it wasn't difficult to find a parking spot right in front of Fine 'n' Dandy.

The vintage doorbell tinkled as I entered the antique store. As usual it was chock-full of nostalgic treasures—both antique and reproduction—bringing back memories of a simpler, more refined past. It was like stepping through C. S. Lewis's legendary wardrobe, but discovering you'd entered the world of your forefathers instead of Narnia. I hung back watching as Donna related the history of a delicate piece of carnival glass to a group of elderly customers.

She acknowledged my presence with a nod of her short bob. 'Abby! Be with you in a moment.'

'That's fine, no hurry,' I said, and waited at the shop counter.

Fingering a fancy embroidered tablecloth, I admired the intricate handiwork and imagined an industrious pioneer woman dressed in sepia colours, toiling by the light of a kerosene lantern. The price tag was attached to the cloth by a safety pin. I stealthily undid the pin and used it to fasten my gaping shirt.

Donna took her place behind the counter. 'Sorry, we're flat out this morning.'

'It's okay. I thought I saw the mini bus outside. The grey parade in town today?'

'Yep.' She grinned. 'I sure do appreciate pension day.' Her smile disappeared as she leant forward to squeeze my arm. 'How are you doing? Found a new job yet?'

'It's only been three days, Donna. Let me recover from the shock first. Anyway, I do have some back pay to tide me over.'

Her eyes flicked to my chest, and the fleeting scrunch of her brow indicated she'd seen how I was keeping my decency intact. 'You know, if we were making more money I'd offer you a position here.'

'I know, thanks. So, how come you didn't answer my phone calls yesterday?'

'Yesterday?'

'Yeah. I phoned both your shop and your mobile several times. I even left messages. Where were you?'

'Oh ... we shut the shop to attend an antique fair in Toowoomba. I left a note on the door.'

'Well, I couldn't see it from Rosella Ridge, could I?'

She grimaced. 'Sorry. My phone died. Forgot to charge it. What did you want so urgently?'

I placed a small velvet jewellery bag on the counter and undid the drawstring. Lifting out the necklace, I studied Donna's face for a response.

Her eyebrows arched, and her generous mouth formed a perfect circle as she let out a long 'Oooh', followed by, 'Where'd you get that little beauty?'

I frowned. 'You didn't drop it off yesterday morning?'

'Dropped it off? Where? Your place?'

'I found it on my front porch around half past seven. It was wrapped in old newspaper.'

'7:30? In the morning?'

I nodded. 'I heard someone knocking, but they were gone by the time I answered the door.'

She shook her head. 'It wasn't me.'

'So you haven't seen this necklace before?'

'No, I certainly have not.' She took it from me and dangled it by the chain. 'It's made from a piece of china.'

'I know that.'

'It's the Apple Blossom design you like.'

'I know that too.'

She stared at me, through me. Her eyes squinted. 'Well who gave it to you?'

'I don't know,' I groaned. 'I was hoping it might have been you.'

'Hmm ... Shane?'

'No!' I said, a little too strongly. I wasn't about to fill her in on my marriage woes—or any of the others. Not yet, anyway.

'O-kay. Your mother, then?'

'I guess it could be a long shot. I'm seeing her soon, so I'll find out.'

Donna's finger caressed the pendant. 'A heart is a pretty intimate gift, Abby. Is there something going on that you haven't told me?'

I blinked. 'Like what?'

'Oh, I don't know.' The dimple near the corner of her mouth deepened. 'A secret fling, perhaps?'

'God, why would I be having an affair? It's hard enough keeping track of one man, let alone two.'

'Excuse me,' a voice interrupted from behind. It came from a white-haired lady in a blue kaftan. She was standing in front of a tall display cabinet. 'Can I make an offer on this adorable Japanese vase?'

Donna handed back the necklace. 'Gotta go. Keep me in the loop, Abby. I'm keen to hear how you get on.'

As she hurried around the counter and made her way over to the woman, I slipped the necklace back into the velvet bag and headed for the door.

Before leaving Shadow Creek, I stopped at the bakery and bought a packet of apple turnovers dusted with icing sugar as a token offering towards Mum's morning tea.

∽

'We're moving to the country for some well-earned peace and

quiet,' Dad informed us eight years ago when selling the suburban family home at Kedron.

Soon after, they bought an original 1910 cottage set on two acres amidst farmland at Tulipwood, ten minutes outside of Shadow Creek. It had needed major renovations and was now a delightful example of early 20th century architecture with 21st century mod cons, including a TV satellite dish and ducted air conditioning.

I made my way up the front stairs, blinking against the sunlight bouncing off the iron lacework verandah trim. Breathing in the heady fragrance of jasmine wafting from the creeper wrapped around the bannisters, I plucked a sprig and tucked it into my hair out of habit.

The screen door flew open and my father rushed out; wispy, white hair fluttering from the top of his freckled scalp. 'Aberdeen, sweetie!' he cried. 'How are you, you poor thing?'

Dad was the only person who called me by my birth name. Being of Scottish ancestry—and proudly descended from a convict transported for sheep stealing—he'd remained loyal to his roots by naming his offspring after towns he'd only ever sighted on a map of Scotland. My two older sisters, Skye and Paisley, were the fortunate ones. My father, rather inebriated from celebrating my birth—or drowning his sorrows on once again missing out on a son—had randomly chosen my name from a wall map in a game akin to 'Pin The Tail On The Donkey'. Mum, in her postnatal exhaustion, had given her agreement, though vowed to only ever use a shortened form—Abby—for which I will be forever thankful. I sometimes wonder what she would have done if Dad had drunkenly chosen Dumfries, Cumnoch or Lossiemouth.

'Getting by,' I sighed, without confessing that things had gone from bad to so much worse.

I was enveloped in a smothering bear hug. Being the runt of

the litter had its pitfalls—like being at the same level of my father's armpits.

'Terrible news about your sacking,' he said.

I pulled out of his tight embrace. 'I wasn't sacked, I was made redundant.'

'All the same, it's bloody shocking. Come in, your mother's been cooking up a storm.'

Following him inside, I was led to the sunroom where a table had been set with embroidered linen and English china. I placed my packet of apple turnovers between a large serving of freshly baked pikelets and a stack of homemade biscuits, and found Mum in the kitchen spooning jam and whipped cream into cut glass dishes.

'Oh, Abby,' she said, taking my face in her hands. 'So sorry to hear about your job. Don't worry. You're clever. You'll get another one soon enough.'

I gave her a hug, and tried not to let the moisture forming in my eyes turn into full-blown tears.

'Some home cooking will make you feel better.' She handed me the dish of cream. 'Did you know you're missing a button?'

I glanced down. The safety pin was no longer holding my shirt together. It too must have shot off into the ether.

'I'll sew a new button on it before you go. Can't have you advertising your wares to all and sundry.' From out of nowhere, she produced a clothes peg and fastened it to the front of my shirt. 'There, that'll do for now.'

We joined Dad in the sunroom. While Mum proceeded to load up my plate, Dad eyed my chest and frowned.

'I popped a button,' I said, before he enquired as to the peg's purpose.

He nodded his understanding of the situation and plonked a

bulging manila folder onto the table. 'Now you're here, let me give you an updated printout of our family tree.'

My father's obsession was genealogy. He relished the wonders of the Internet, and was forever searching for new information regarding our ancestors. I was interested—for the most part—like when he'd discovered we were related to his idol John Wayne. What a commotion he made about that! Then there'd been the time he discovered we had a very distant connection to both JFK and Elvis. Talk about six degrees of separation.

'If you keep shaking our tree you might be shocked by what falls out,' I'd warned a few years back. This had only encouraged him further.

Mum slapped her hand over the folder. 'Not now Bobby, leave the poor girl alone. She's just got here. How are Shane and the kids?' she asked, turning my way.

'Good,' I lied, and quickly changed the subject. 'Oh ... a strange thing happened yesterday.' Reaching into my shoulder bag, I took out the velvet drawstring pouch and withdrew the necklace. 'This arrived on my doorstep,' I said, holding it aloft.

I waited for either parent to give me the answer I was hoping for—that they knew all about it. It didn't come. Instead, their eyes followed the sway of the pendant. Back and forward, back and forward. I let the necklace slip to the table top before they both went into a hypnotic trance.

'Who sent it to you?' asked my mother.

'It wasn't sent. It was left on the chair on the porch. A small paper-wrapped parcel.'

Dad reached over and slid the necklace across the tablecloth towards him. 'No note?'

'No, just this.'

'It's very nice. Clever silver work.' He passed it on to my mother.

'It's made from a piece of china,' said Mum, stroking the pendant with fingers as slender as mine, though more aged.

'Yes. James Kent's Apple Blossom.'

'Aahh ... yes. I had a pin dish in this design. Have no idea where it is now.'

'I have it.'

She looked up, eyes wide behind her glasses. 'You do?'

'You gave it to me. Don't you remember? A couple of years ago.'

She shook her head. 'Who would have wanted you to have this?'

'I have no idea.'

'It's all rather odd, isn't it?' She handed the necklace back so she could pour the tea.

I took another pikelet from the pile. 'Mum, that pin dish you gave me, where did it come from? Did you buy it or was it given to you as a gift?'

She returned the teapot to the trivet and passed me a steaming cup of Earl Grey. 'No, not a gift. Not really. It was my cousin Marion's.'

'Marion? The one Nana always said I looked like? We had the same large eyes or something.'

'Yes, and similar wavy hair, and slight build.'

I spooned a dollop of jam onto my pikelet, followed by another of whipped cream. 'Remind me again. Whose daughter was she?'

'Aunt Ruth's, Nana's sister. Her father, Uncle Owen, gave it to me along with a suitcase of Marion's belongings.'

I swallowed my mouthful. 'Why would he do that? Didn't she want them?'

'No,' Dad answered. 'Marion died.'

I gasped and almost choked on my mouthful. 'When was that? I don't remember going to her funeral.'

'You weren't even born,' said Mum, 'and I was just a teenager.'

Dad removed a sheet of paper from the manila folder and tapped a spot on the page. 'Eleventh of January 1958, to be precise. She was … let's see … nineteen at the time.'

'Yes, that's right,' agreed Mum.

'How did she die?'

A breath drifted from my mother's lips. 'A train crash. It was terrible.'

'The crash wasn't far from here as a matter of fact,' added Dad. 'Shocking it was. Over a dozen people died. The train was filled with people coming out from the city to picnic at Shadow Creek.'

'A train … to Shadow Creek? You're kidding me. I didn't know there'd ever been a train line out this way.'

'The line ran over the range. As it wasn't used much once the road with a more direct route from Brisbane was built, they ripped it up; in the sixties, I believe. The crash details appeared in all the newspapers. With a little research, you should be able to find out more.'

'It was so sad,' said Mum, 'because Aunt Ruth, had just died from breast cancer.'

'That's terrible. Were you close to Marion?'

She smiled. 'When we were kids. Marion was four years older than me, but we got along fine. She stayed with us when Ruth had surgery to remove her breast. The cancer returned years later.' She took a sip of tea. 'I hardly saw Marion once we got older.'

'So Uncle Owen gave you the dish as a remembrance of Marion.'

'Yes. There were also photos and books, and some trinkets like the little pin dish. I think they was just too painful a reminder for him to keep.'

I checked the sheet of paper lying on the table between my father and me. 'Marion never married.'

'No,' said Dad.

'But I think she was engaged to some fellow at the time,' added Mum. 'I didn't know much about him. She and her parents had moved to Stanthorpe.'

I sat back in my chair and glanced out the window to the backyard and the large apple tree loaded with blossoms. 'If she was living in Stanthorpe, what was she doing up here, 250 odd kilometres from her home?'

Mum gave a shrug. 'She'd come up for her mother's funeral and was supposed to be heading back to Stanthorpe. The next thing we hear she'd died in the train crash near Shadow Creek. A mystery that's for sure. Maybe she wasn't ready to return.'

Dad's chair creaked as he pushed himself up to his feet. 'I've got some photos of her, if you're interested.'

Mum pulled him back down. 'Don't worry about that now, we're eating.'

'Later will be fine,' I said. 'Though, I'd love to see them.'

'Righto,' he nodded, sneaking a second apple turnover while Mum gave her attention to me.

'What are you going to do about the necklace?'

I stared at the pendant resting on the tablecloth. 'I don't know. Wait a little longer I suppose. I guess someone will eventually come out of hiding to make contact.'

'You'd expect so,' said Dad, brushing pastry flakes from his chin, and sliding the manila folder in front of me. 'Don't forget to take this with you when you go.'

'I'm not going yet,' I balked. 'I've only had one cup of tea, and haven't really made a start on all these goodies.'

As I reached for a cornflake biscuit, an idea struck me. Instead of being consumed by worry and frustration, I could direct my energy into solving the mystery of the necklace. At the very least, it could prove a helpful distraction.

4

Stanthorpe 1957

Her legs hang leisurely over the edge of the jetty. She chews on a lock of hair and eagerly turns another page of the book recommended by her mother. *Jamaica Inn* is proving to be an enjoyable read after all, and on her next visit to the library, she intends to search out other titles by Daphne du Maurier.

A chirping of wrens breaks the silence. She glances up and scowls. Someone is breaking through the reeds on the edge of the waterhole; an intruder to her seclusion. She recognises the face and closes her book.

The young man reaches behind his back, pulls his shirt over his head, and tosses it to the ground. Quickly unbuttoning his shorts, he lets them drop to his ankles and then kicks them aside. Dressed only in white boxer shorts, he clambers onto a granite boulder. Stepping back, he runs forward and leaps, tucking his knees to his chest. His bomb dive causes a huge eruption of water. Surfacing, he floats on his back, bobbing to the rhythm of the restless pool. Here is a body that is obviously not a stranger to hard work. The wide shoulders and long sinewy arms frame a broad chest. The olive skin —tanned a shade darker on the limbs—glistens in the sunlight.

From her vantage point on the timber jetty shielded by reeds, she wonders if she should let him know he isn't alone. A dragonfly beats her to it and chooses that moment to perch on his broad nose. He first opens his eyes and then gives his head a shake. The insect flees but returns seconds later to hover and then plunge again. This time the young man swings both arms to swat it away. Losing buoyancy, he sinks below the waterline.

When he emerges, she calls out. 'Well hello there, Johnny Appleseed. Enjoying the wildlife?'

His head twists around. 'Hey, who's the one spying now? Why didn't you say something?'

She places her book on the decking. 'I didn't want to interrupt. You looked so ... peaceful.'

He swims over and hoists himself up onto the jetty, plonking down beside her. Shaking his head, dark, wiry curls sparkle with liquid jewels. She edges away from the puddle he is making and safely hides her library book under her straw hat.

Brown eyes squint down at her. 'You're trespassing on private property you know.'

'Private property?' She shades her eyes with her hand and scans the surroundings. 'No, it isn't.'

'Yep, it sure is. It's my uncle's property. You know, the one with the apple orchard?'

'Oh ... I thought this waterhole was for public use.'

'Nope, and shrieking banshee women are especially not welcome.'

She glares at him and leans back, her towelling robe falling wide open. She catches him eyeing her new sky-blue bathers, and is pleased with her purchase.

'Alright,' he says, 'I admit it. You don't actually look like a banshee. But geez almighty you sure sounded like one yesterday. What a god-awful screech that was.'

'I had my reasons,' she says with an edge to her voice.

He stares down at her. His eyes have an intensity that makes her feel edgy ... exposed, like he can read her mind. She pulls her robe closed and looks away.

He breaks the resulting silence. 'What does the 'M' stand for?'

She turns back. 'I beg your pardon?'

'It was on the hanky you gave me. I've been trying to work it out.'

'Oh, have you now?' she says with intrigue, feigned as indifference.

'I reckon you look like a Martha.'

She raises her eyebrows.

'Okay, how about ... Mimi?'

She rolls her eyes.

'Mehitabel?'

Her nose wrinkles with distaste.

'Hmm ... I'm not having much luck, am I.' He taps his chin with a finger. 'Wait there. I've got it. Medusa!'

'Now that's just rude!' she snaps.

'Then give a fella a hand. Spit it out. What is it?'

Stretching her legs, she dips her toes into water. 'If you must know, it's Marion.'

He gives a bow. 'Pleased to meet you, Maid Marion. The name's Banjo.'

'Banjo?'

'Yeah, it's Aussie for Benjamin,' he grins, revealing a slight gap between his top front teeth.

'No, it isn't,' she scoffs.

'It is if your surname's Patterson.'

Marion tilts her head. 'Oh, I get it, a nickname. You're not really related to that renowned bush poet, are you?'

He shakes his head. 'Nah. My mates gave me the moniker and it's stuck. Mum still calls me Ben ... or Benjamin if I'm getting up to mischief.'

'Which I gather is often, right?' The glint in his eyes stirs her. She sits forward. 'Maybe I should be wary of you.'

'You should,' he says, elbowing her sharply.

The rough jab to her ribs causes her to lose balance. Toppling sideways over the edge of the jetty, she plunges headfirst into the murky depths.

Thrashing under water, Marion eventually rises, spitting muddy liquid from her mouth.

'Strike,' the young man says, kneeling on the jetty and peering down at her. 'I don't know my own strength. Sorry about that. Here I'll give you a lift up.'

He reaches down and Marion eagerly grabs hold of his hand. Then yanking hard, she watches him plummet into the water beside her.

She is in a fit of laughter when he surfaces.

'Oh, so you do have a sense of humour,' he says, brushing hair from his eyes.

'I have a lighter side, just like anyone else.'

Shrugging free of the sodden robe, she hurls it onto the jetty and ducks under the ripples. Resurfacing moments later in the middle of the waterhole, she places two fingers between her lips and lets out a sharp whistle.

'Hey, Benjamin!' she calls. 'Let's see if you can do more than dog paddle. Race you to the edge.'

He ploughs towards her in a perfect freestyle.

She swiftly swims away and is already standing in the shallows when he comes up for air. As he struggles to his knees amongst the reeds, Marion plants her hands on her hips.

'You're obviously ... not as good a swimmer ... as this mere slip of a girl,' she pants, her chest heaving with each intake of air.

He opens his mouth to answer back, but remains silent as his eyes trail over her.

Marion glances down and notices that her wet, strapless bathers are now clinging to her like a second skin. A blush warms her cheeks, and she turns on her heels.

Hurrying back to the jetty, she collects her belongings. 'I think I'll just call you Ben!' she shouts.

'And I'll call you Cheat,' she hears as she makes her departure through the bushy scrub.

5

A phone call interrupted my drive home. It was Julie, another friend I'd made since moving out this way three years ago.

I pulled the car over to the road's edge and turned the engine off.

'Where are you, Mrs Eaton, lady of leisure?' she asked.

'I'm driving home from my parents' place.'

'Great. Want to join me for a coffee at Serendipi-teas to drown your sorrows?'

'Hang on. I know I'm jobless, but why aren't you working at the medical centre today?'

'I've just had day surgery for recurring onychocryptosis.'

'Oh my God!' I gasped. 'What the hell is that?'

I heard Julie sigh, and visualised her head shaking at my lack of understanding of medical terminology. How was I to know what it meant? I hadn't studied nursing like she had.

'Ingrown toenail,' she stated. 'I just had one removed.'

'Ouch! That sounds painful.'

'Drugs help. But the dressing is a bit of a nightmare. They should've let me put it on. So, are you up for a coffee?'

'Well, normally I'd say I'd love to, but I'm stuffed to the gills from my mum's cooking, and I'm half way up the mountain.'

'What a shame. Anyway, I'll see you Friday night. Are you guys all set?'

Julie and her husband Graeme were hosting a fancy-dress dinner party to celebrate Halloween. Shane had intended on going as an Egyptian mummy and had bought a truckload of bandages, while I was still to put together a 'goth' outfit for my costume as Morticia Addams. A thought hit me. Would we still be going to the party? I guess we could still attend, even if we weren't going as a happily married couple.

'Yeah ... we will be,' I answered hesitantly.

'Great. Graeme reckons I don't need much to add to my wicked witch costume. Says I am almost there anyway.'

'How dare he! That's an awful thing to say.'

'It's okay,' she chuckled, 'I told him all he needed was a couple of bolts to add to his thick neck to become Frankenstein.'

'Frankenstein's monster, actually,' I corrected.

My comment was met with silence. Julie may have been fluent in medical terminology, but she was not on a par with me when it came to literary knowledge.

'Are you still there?' I asked, wondering if she was madly searching the Internet to see if I was correct.

'Sure am,' she replied.

I lowered the window to release the warmth building inside the car and was greeted by a shrill chorus of cicadas announcing an increase in temperature. A hot breeze drifted in.

'Being a local and all, Julie, do you know anything about a train crash near Shadow Creek? Sometime in the late 1950s?'

'Well, there was a station here. My mum used to talk about

catching the train when she was young. It was demolished years ago. Most of the track ripped up and used for fencing, I believe. But I don't know anything about a train crash. Why?'

I related a little of what I'd just heard from my parents, and told her about the necklace.

'You're not having a sordid affair, are you?' she asked bluntly.

I groaned. 'Really? You actually think I'd do that?'

I heard Julie slurp, what I presumed, was her usual mochaccino. 'Nah. S'pose not. Anyway, you should talk to Beryl Erbacher from the Historical Society about the train line. She volunteers in the local craft shop most days.'

Agreeing to pay Beryl a visit, I said I needed to go because it was too hot sitting in the car.

A view out the rear-view mirror, showed a car labouring uphill; an old, light coloured ute. If I didn't drive off before it reached me, I knew I would be stuck behind that piece of junk most of the way home.

6

Stanthorpe 1957

The hours drag in the orchard. For a spring day it is a scorcher, making the men's task of spraying trees with insecticide an arduous one. Shirts cling to lean bodies soaked with sweat, and the lively banter of earlier on has all but ceased. Working diligently alongside others, Banjo's mind drifts elsewhere. He yearns for the coolness of the waterhole. This in turn reminds him of the captivating Marion—her feistiness; her bathers. He wonders if he will ever see her again.

When knock-off time comes around, he doesn't join the group heading into town to the pub, but races down to the creek.

The waterhole is undisturbed and the jetty is vacant. The strength of his disappointment is unsettling and he toys with the idea of retreating to catch up with his work mates.

A crunching of dried leaves. Movement in the long grass.

Marion appears.

'Great minds think alike,' she calls, casually walking over to the granite boulder Banjo used as a diving board the previous day, and laying down a towel.

He hurries around the water's edge and doesn't hesitate in sitting alongside her.

'Has your uncle always lived in the Stanthorpe area?' she asks, kicking off her scuffs.

'No. He came here for work after the war. Then once he'd saved up enough dosh he bought his own property.'

'And you work for him?' Her gaze has no rough edges today.

'I help out when I can. I actually live west of Brisbane. Have you heard of a village called Shadow Creek?'

'No.' She shades her eyes with her hand. 'Do you have family up there?'

'Just my mum.' He unbuttons his shirt, and uses a corner to wipe sweat from his face. 'Dad died in the war.'

'I'm so sorry,' she says, and he believes her.

'That's alright,' he shrugs, 'he was a rat.'

'Oh ...' Marion falters, drops her hand. A frown puckers her forehead. 'Well ... that's not good.'

He smiles. 'You know, as in Rats of Tobruk. You have heard of them, haven't you?'

'Ahh ... right,' she nods, 'of course. That's what the Germans called Australian soldiers in the Middle East, after seeing them scurrying around in the desert digging tunnels. I knew that ... I just didn't catch your meaning.'

He chuckles. 'My dad and uncle were in the same battalion. The 2nd Fifteenth.'

'Really? Brothers serving together?'

'Well, mates actually. Uncle Marty is my mum's brother.'

Marion swivels around to hang her legs over the edge of the rock. Her toes wiggle well above the waterline. 'I see. You must've been young when your father died.'

Banjo also drops his legs over the edge, though his feet sink well below the rippling surface. He feels his usual guard peeling way. 'I'd just turned five. I don't have a strong memory of him, just bits and pieces ... like snapshots. I can remember how he smelt though.'

Marion studies him. 'Really? What did he smell like?'

Her eyes are large, inquisitive, jade green—like the elephant ornament his mother keeps on her dressing table at home. Under their gaze, words tumble out easily. It's as if his mouth has a mind of its own. He tells her that his father smoked a pipe and smelt like tobacco. He also mentions that he played a mouth organ.

'He could play all kinds of songs. I have this beaut memory of him playing 'Happy Birthday' to me. I'd woken up early, it was barely light, and there he was sitting on the edge of the bed playing away.'

'That's sweet.'

'It was my fifth birthday.' Banjo nudges her knee with his. 'He died from a Kraut bullet the next day.'

Marion's mouth gapes. 'But that would mean he was still over there.' Her hand grips his arm. 'Now that's spooky.'

'I dunno. I take it he must have been thinking pretty strongly of me that day.' He eyes the fingers clutching his arm, so pale and slender against his tanned skin. He flexes his bicep, just a little.

She nods slowly. 'A way of telling you how much he loved you. Sending his spirit across the waters to convey a message.'

'Yeah, something like that, I reckon.'

Her hand drops and as she leans forward, curls of hair fall over her face. 'What's it like growing up without a father?'

Banjo rests back on his elbows. No one has ever asked him that question before. And if they had he probably would have changed the subject. He delves deep for an answer.

'I guess I've gotten used to it. Mum's always been great, and then there's Uncle Marty. He's always got a yarn to tell about the mischief he and Dad got up to. From what they both tell me, I reckon he must've been a pretty good bloke.'

Marion sighs loudly. 'I wish it was my father who'd gone to war and not come back.'

She must have heard his gasp for she looks over her shoulder at him, her expression far from bright.

'Well, how would you feel if you discovered your father and his work partner had decided to cement their business relationship?'

He squints. 'I don't get it.'

'My father and Cameron Duff think a union between the two families would be a highly satisfactory career move.'

'Cameron Duff? From the property next to this one?'

She nods.

'Whattaya know. So, what kind of union?'

Marion swivels around. 'Are you really that dim? A union between me and Donald Duff.'

'Donald?' He chokes on a laugh.

'You know him?'

He shakes his head, and spurts out another laugh.

'It's not funny,' Marion chides.

'Sorry,' Banjo grins. 'Donald Duff. Good friends with Mickey, is he?'

'Mickey? Mickey who?'

He rolls his eyes. 'Now who's the dim one. Mickey-flaming-Mouse.'

She gives a chuckle. 'You know, I've never thought about that.' The smile quickly disappears, as if she's suddenly replaced one theatre mask for another. 'It still doesn't change the fact they want me and Donald to marry.'

'Marry?' Banjo cries, pushing up.

'Yes. Can't you follow a story?'

A heavy lump forms in his gut. 'Well ... are you?'

'Going to marry him?' She pulls a face. 'Cripes, no! That's why I was so angry ... in the orchard. My father had just spilled the beans about their wonderful plan. He didn't even ask for my opinion, just told me how it was to be.'

Banjo nervously clears his throat. 'And do you have feelings for this Donald?'

Marion folds her legs to her chest. 'I don't even know him that well. Mum and I have only been here in Stanthorpe for a few weeks. Anyway, Donald is always following my father around, talking crops and yields and the like. I'm not sure he even knows I exist. So, in answer to your question, no. None, what-so-ever.'

He lets out a breath he wasn't aware he'd been holding. 'Have you told your father?'

'I sure did. I reminded him that I was nineteen and could choose for myself, thank you very much.'

'That's the ticket.' He gives her shoulder a playful punch. 'It's not the bloody 1800s for Christ's sake,' he says, quickly adding, 'Sorry, 'scuse the French.'

'As you can imagine, Dad's not happy with me at present and we're not talking, which suits me fine, so ...'

Banjo waits, but Marion doesn't continue. She just drops her head onto her knees.

He takes the opportunity to admire the way the sun lights up her hair, amazed at the number of shades of brown and russet red that live in those shoulder-length curls. His fingers ache to touch the whorls, to see if they'll spring back if tugged. He hears a sniff, and sees Marion rub her eyes. What should he do if she begins to bawl like a baby? He gets to his feet, peels out of his shirt, and leaps into the waterhole before he needs to decide.

When after a few minutes Marion still hasn't stirred, he swims over and splashes her. By the irritated look she gives him he expects her to get up and rush away. Instead, she lifts her loose cotton dress above her head and reveals those welcome blue bathers. Slipping gracefully into the water, Marion paddles towards him, obviously leaving her worries to sizzle and evaporate on the hot granite.

7

The loft study was my favourite room in the house—a true bolthole and refuge from life and family. A wooden staircase led up to this inviting space of exposed beams and timber flooring that gave it rustic appeal; while a multi-coloured rug, floral upholstered sofa, and whitewashed bookcase added cottage-style charm. Most precious of all, and positioned in front of a wide casement window boasting glorious views, was a restored silky oak writing desk. It once belonged to my grandmother, Gloria—an avid letter writer—and I often pondered on the encouraging words and titbits of news that were penned on its surface until Alzheimer's robbed her of the desire and ability to communicate.

That afternoon, I sat at the desk engrossed in my latest discovery. An Internet search had directed me to a surprising number of websites with varying information on the train crash of 1958, including archived newspaper articles, reports from Queensland Railways, and even transcripts from those involved in the rescue.

The information I gleaned said the crash occurred on the morning of Saturday 11th January 1958 on the Shadow Creek train line, in the vicinity of Archer's Lookout. I knew the lookout well for it had a northerly view across the countryside, incorporating the area where my parents lived. The train had been hauling six passenger carriages between Brisbane and Shadow Creek, and was filled with day-trippers looking forward to spending time at the picnic spots along the waterway. Records showed that excessive speed, due to the inexperience of the driver, had caused the derailment in which the engine and three carriages were destroyed. Nineteen people had died, and twenty-three were injured.

I was at a loss as to why so few people these days were aware of its occurrence. Sixty years had passed. Were people still coming to terms with their grief, or waking from gruesome dreams of what they'd witnessed? The various reports and vivid descriptions had turned my stomach, but not as much as the graphic photographs contained on one site, which brought home the true devastation.

A crowd watching from a distance as rescuers—ambulance men, police, and local farmers still in their regular work clothes—tried to free people trapped amongst the debris; a rescuer lifting a boy smeared with blood up through a broken window of a wrecked carriage; a pair of twisted limbs sticking out from beneath an unhinged carriage door; sheet-covered bodies of all sizes being carried on stretchers to a line of dark vehicles.

The wreckage was immense, and the faces of those helping looked tired and dispirited. Strangely, in the background of many photos a herd of cattle grazed unconcerned in a paddock, only metres from the wreckage. I choked up. A beautiful summer's day had been transformed into a horrid nightmare.

Footsteps broke through my despondency.

My heart kicked up a notch. Someone was in the house.

I grabbed a letter opener with one hand, and a paperweight with the other and spun around to see Elliott appear at the top of the stairs.

He looked as guilty as when he was a toddler and had been caught with his hand in the biscuit barrel.

I let out a breath of relief. 'How'd you get home so early?'

'Bree's dad dropped me off. The bus was running late.'

I returned the improvised weapons to the desk. 'So, you've come home to face the music, have you?'

'I guess so,' he murmured, screwing up his face and scratching his backside.

Sometimes he looked so much like his father.

I jumped up from the chair and, as he towered over me, once again realised that at seventeen Elliott was almost a man. His size eleven feet, legs longer than mine, and shoulders broadening by the minute made me feel less superior.

I pointed to the sofa. 'Sit!'

He did. It was easier for me to wield authority when Elliott was seated.

I planted my feet, crossed my arms, and cleared my throat. 'So, young man, what the hell are you playing at? I thought you were a good kid. Now this. Growing drugs?' I threw my hands in the air. 'Geez, Elliott, what were you thinking?'

'Well, it's like this ...' He rubbed his hands over his knees. 'Bree's step-mum was in a bad car accident last year.'

I cocked an eyebrow. 'Yes, I know that. What's it got to do with—'

'She's always in pain, Mum! It's not good. They say smoking weed helps with pain ... I thought I could do something to help.'

My jaw dropped. I certainly wasn't expecting that for an excuse. 'Really? Are you sure that's the only reason you were growing the stuff?'

He nodded without blinking. For the time being I had to trust he was telling the truth.

I dropped onto sofa next to him, pushed out my chest and raised myself as high as I could to fill more space beside him. 'Where did you get your hands on the plants?'

'A kid at school. His brother has a ... a kind of nursery.'

'For growing marijuana?'

'Yeah.'

'So, he's a supplier?'

'Nah ... not exactly. He mostly grows it for himself. The kid at school got me some seedlings.'

'How much did they cost?'

'Nothing.'

'Nothing? Really?'

'Yeah. His brother's got a good heart.'

I laughed. 'A drug dealer with a good heart, that's a first. You know it's illegal.'

Elliott grimaced. 'Mum, I'm not stupid.'

'But you're growing an illegal substance. Police have drones, you know. They use them to check on things like marijuana crops. You could get caught, end up in juvenile detention, or jail with hardened criminals. How would you like that?'

He shook his thick, dark mane, the fringe falling further over his eyes. 'You've been watching too many TV shows, Mum. Who's going to send out a drone to Rosella Ridge to check on five measly plants?'

'You never know. They might find them by chance while on another recon mission.'

He blew air through lips as thin as Shane's. 'So, what did you do with them?'

'Nothing ... yet. I just covered them with shade cloth until we work out what best to do.'

His face took on a more sombre expression. 'What did Dad say?'

I gave a shrug. 'He doesn't know.'

Now it was Elliott's turn to raise a sole eyebrow—one much bushier than mine. 'How come?'

And it was my turn to look sheepish. 'We haven't spoken since Saturday. We had a bit of a ... a tiff. You know I lost my job, right?'

'Yeah, you sent out a group message. I sent you back a sad face.'

I remembered now. Here was a young man with loads of compassion. 'Well I wasn't in a good place, and then your Dad told me he'd ...' I quickly stood. 'Never mind. I was angry, he was angry. He left to stay at Uncle Paul's for the weekend.'

'So, he'll be home tonight?'

'I ... um ... I'm not too sure.'

Elliott leapt up. 'You're not thinking about getting a divorce, are you? That's stupid! I don't want to be one of those kids who have to choose which parent to live with. It sucks.'

'No! Of course not. Don't jump to extremes. It was just a fight. We'll work things out soon enough.'

He glared at me, raised his chin. 'So, what's my punishment?'

I hadn't actually thought that far ahead. I'd assumed Shane would be back by now and we'd have made a decision regarding our son's fate together.

'Let's see what Dad says. In the meantime, you should destroy the plants. I'm sure there are other drugs, prescription ones, that could help Bree's step-mum. Anyway, it's not your responsibility. You're a good kid. You have your whole life ahead of you. Remember our family motto?'

'Be safe. Stay safe.' he said, robotically.

'And you can make pizzas for dinner.'

'Sure, no probs.' He waited. Cocked his head. 'Is that all? No being grounded? Privileges taken away?'

'Well, not just yet. We'll see what Dad comes up with.' I wrapped my arms around him. 'So, enjoy it while you can.'

He hugged me back. 'I will ... er ... but not too much.'

'Good. Now go and change. You smell like a classroom of stinky teenagers.'

Instead, he followed me as I returned to my desk.

'What's all this?' he asked, leaning over my shoulder. 'Is that a train crash?'

'It happened near Archer's Lookout back in 1958. Nana's cousin was one of the fatalities.'

He reached for the mouse and scrolled through the images. 'Pretty graphic stuff.'

'I'm thinking of finding the exact location of the crash. Pay a visit.'

'That sounds creepy.'

'Not really. I thought I could pay my respects to the victims. To Marion.'

'Was that her name?'

'Yeah, Marion Douglas. She would have been your ... let's see ... third cousin. She was about Gemma's age when she died.'

Having someone else show an interest—even if he was my wayward son—was appreciated. I filled him in on what I knew so far. Then I led him down to the lounge room, to the china cabinet and allowed him to hold the necklace while I told him about the mysterious visitor.

He pulled a face like the one I'd seen on Shane after he'd sucked on a lemon before a Tequila shot. 'Hell, Mum, you don't have a secret admirer, do you?'

I drew back. Why did people jumped to this conclusion? 'Don't be silly. Who'd be interested in an old married woman with two annoying brats?'

'You'd be surprised Mum. There's a lot of desperate losers out there.'

I winced. I wasn't sure if these were words of warning, or a put-down. Did he really think that all I could attract was a hopeless desperado?

The house phone rang.

I answered.

It was my dad telling me he would leave the photos he'd found of Marion at Fine 'n' Dandy the next morning, on his way to the doctor's.

'Don't worry. Just a check up,' he assured me.

When I hung up, Elliott was holding out my mobile phone. 'Dad just texted. Says he's still not ready to come home yet.'

'Still not ready?'

I wrenched the phone from his hand and checked the message. Those were Shane's exact words. Before I tapped out something I'd later regret, I threw the phone back to Elliott and trudged away.

Elliott found me on the back deck. He passed me a glass of cola, while he took a seat next to me with the can in his hand.

'I'm guessing Dad told you about the motorbike.'

My head snapped around. 'You know about the bike?'

He nodded and took a long guzzle from his can before answering. 'I went with him to view it.'

'You did what!' I jumped up, spilling cola over both of us. 'That's another secret you've been keeping from me.' I leant back against the railing. 'I don't understand it. He's never been interested in bikes. Never!'

Elliott wiped his arm and eyed me cautiously, as if weighing up whether to chance speaking or not. 'He said it was you who didn't like bikes. You, who was scared of them. He's been wanting one for ages.'

My whole body slumped. 'You're kidding me.'

He shook his head.

'Well I'll be damned. He's never told me that.'

I was even more perplexed. Why now? Why did Shane feel he had to blow our savings on a bike right now?

8

Stanthorpe 1957

B anjo steps out of the town hardware store, a Stillson pipe wrench wrapped in butcher's paper in his hand. The number of people in town startles him. The local population looks to have doubled in size while he was doing a deal inside the store on behalf of his uncle. With just two days to go until the Apple Blossom festival, the town is throbbing with anticipation, hinting that once again it will be well attended.

Each spring for the last three years, Stanthorpe has celebrated their famous fruit growing by hosting this festival. Beginning with a grand ball on the Friday night, and the announcement of the Miss Apple Blossom Queen, celebrations continue the following day with a street procession. Marching bands, decorated floats, and pavements lined with stalls selling delights made from locally grown produce are usually the go. Banjo has experienced all but the first festival and is looking forward to enjoying the party atmosphere.

As he edges his way through the throng of shoppers, he spies Marion studying the display in the drapery store's window. He winds his way over.

'Morning, Maid Marion,' he says over her shoulder.

She spins around. Her crimson lips—the exact shade of her cherry red dress—curve into a smile. 'Ben!'

In heeled shoes, she is taller. Yet standing alongside, Banjo finds that Marion's eyes still only come level with his chin.

He returns her smile. 'I almost didn't recognise you with clothes on ... I mean ... so many clothes on ... oh, bugger.' He slaps the side of his head with his free hand. 'You know what I mean.'

She laughs. 'I think I do.'

He views the shop front. 'Window shopping then?'

'Shopping? Oh, no. I've spent the entire morning dressing this window. I was just making sure the fabric display looked presentable.'

'You work here?'

'Didn't I mention that the other day?'

He shakes his head.

'Well I do, part-time anyway. I was lucky enough to pick up some work soon after we arrived here.' She taps the window glass with a painted fingernail. 'So, what do you think?'

Banjo stares at the headless store dummies draped in colourful cloth and surrounded by a scattering of artificial flowers and packets of paper patterns. He tilts his head one way, and then the other. 'It looks to me like someone's been practising their wood chopping skills. The milliner up the road could probably lend you a few fake noggins if you asked him nicely.'

'I think I'll keep it just the way it is, thanks.' Marion says, checking her wristwatch and then searching the steady stream of shoppers.

'Am I keeping you from something?' Banjo asks.

VICKI STEVENS

'I'm waiting for my father to meet me for lunch. He had an appointment at the bank and should've been here by now.'

Banjo joins her in scanning the busy sidewalk, even though having never seen him before, he has no idea how he'd recognise the man. 'So, you're talking again.'

'Well, barely.' She checks her watch again.

He clears his throat and acts on a whim. 'Um ... Marion ... would you like to come with me to the Ball tomorrow night? It's a bit of a shindig and lots of fun ... if you like dancing that is.'

'Oh,' her gaze drops to her feet, 'sorry, I can't.'

'You can't dance? Well I don't mind teaching you. I can do a mean foxtrot, and plenty of girls have told me I am—'

Her hand on his shoulder interrupts him.

'I know how to dance. I just can't go with you to the Ball.'

Banjo's stomach knots. He must be crazy to think that anyone with film star looks would step out with the likes of him. A chinwag at a waterhole is one thing; an invite to a dance is another. He catches his reflection in the window glass—grimy overalls, stained shirt. He probably reeks too. Brushing greasy hair back from his forehead, he wishes he'd at least shaved this morning.

'I see,' he says, with a clench of his jaw. 'My mistake. I shouldn't have bothered you.'

'Don't be like that. It's just that I'm ...' She lets out a sigh. 'I'm already going with someone.'

Relief trickles over him. Of course, someone as gorgeous as Marion would have received dozens of invitations by now. He'd just missed his chance, pure and simple.

'It's already organised.' Marion gives him her full attention. 'I'm obligated, you see.'

He balks. 'Obligated? Geez, that doesn't sound like a fun way to

56

spend an evening, I'd hate for any girl to feel duty-bound to go out with me.'

Her lips purse. 'And you've never gone out with someone for a greater cause other than your own enjoyment?' Her tone is curt.

'Nope. It's about having fun and knowing how to give a girl a ripper of a good time.' He chews the inside of his cheek. He'd shown more defence than intended.

Marion glares back. 'Who do you think you are? Errol Flynn? Do you actually think you possess the ability to show any girl a good time?'

'Too right!' he answers with even more bluster. 'No problems there.' She is starting to rile him up good and proper.

Her hands go to her hips. 'What about me? Do you think you know how to show me a good time?'

He's about to answer when a wayward pram slams into him from behind. His knees buckle and he falls forward, pinning Marion up against the display window. Crushed together—thigh against thigh, her arms around him, her face pressed into his neck —is quite thrilling, and he wonders if she can feel the blood thumping through every part of him.

Her breath is hot and laboured against his throat. 'So, do you?'

'Do I what?' he says, easing off slightly.

'Think you can show me a good time?'

Leaning down, he presses his mouth against her ear. 'I think I have a pretty good idea how to tickle your fancy.'

Her breath catches, and she shoves him away.

He stumbles backwards, just as a voice booms above the din of the crowd.

'Marion!'

They both turn. Striding towards them is a hefty, middle-aged man with thinning hair and a stern look on his ruddy face.

'Come on, girl! We're late!'

Marion frowns. 'I've been waiting ages for you, Dad. You said you'd be here at twelve. That was twenty minutes ago.'

'I'm a busy man, and now we have to pick your mother up from the doctor's. Damned inconvenient.' He takes her by the elbow and, without even a glance in Banjo's direction, steers her away.

Marion struggles to match the pace of her father and twists around just long enough for Banjo to glimpse the disappointment in her eyes.

'Rude bastard,' Banjo mutters, and pushes his way through the throng to the kerb.

His work mates from the orchard are sitting in the front of his uncle's truck where he'd left them, though now they are sharing hot chips wrapped in newspaper.

'By crikey, who's that corker you were talking with?' asks Mal, stuffing a handful of chips into his mouth.

Banjo throws the pipe wrench behind the bench seat. 'None of your bloody business.' He shoves his buddies over to give him room behind the steering wheel.

'How come I haven't seen her before?' Mal winks. 'Is she new to town?'

Tony snatches the greasy parcel from him. 'She's staying at the Duff's farm next door to Marty's.'

Mal eyes Tony. 'Now how the hell do you know that? I thought I was the one with the dolly radar.'

'My mum told me. She does a bit of cleaning for Mrs Duff, and she's met the family. Douglas, I think their name is. They've blown in from Brisbane. Staying in the worker's cottage.'

'Well you're a right fount of knowledge.' Mal turns back to Banjo. 'So how do you know her then, Banj me old mate?'

Banjo turns the key in the ignition. The motor rasps into life. 'I ran into her the other day at the orchard.'

'What was she doing there?' asks Tony.

'I think she was lost.'

'And you showed her the way home, did you?' smirks Mal. 'Like a good little boy scout.'

Banjo's fingers curl hard around the steering wheel. 'Something like that.'

Mal gives a sharp whistle. 'Maybe you showed her a little something else too, you old sheik. I reckon I should get to know her too. I'd enjoy leading her up the garden path.'

Banjo slams a fist against the dashboard. 'Bloody leave off, will ya!'

'Geez, keep your hair on. Only having a dig. Anyway, she seems a bit too hoity-toity for my liking.'

'Good. Now let's get back before Marty sends out a bleedin' search party.'

He thrusts the gearstick into place and jerks the Dodge out from the gutter. With a wrench of the steering wheel the truck staggers down the main street, smoke billowing from the exhaust pipe in thick, grey clouds.

9

Back in town the next morning, I found Fine 'n' Dandy devoid of both customers and shop owners. I waited for a bit, coughed loudly a few times, and when neither Ross nor Donna had appeared I pressed the counter bell. It dinged sharply.

Thick curtains dividing the shop from the back rooms suddenly parted and Ross stumbled out. In his haste to greet me, he side-swiped a mannequin dressed in a 1920s Great Gatsby styled flapper outfit and knocked her off her stand. Swiftly righting the plaster woman before she face-planted on the stained timber floorboards, he straightened her bobbed wig and brushed down the black fringing of her strappy dress.

'Sorry, Abby. Donna's over at the bank and I'm in the middle of re-upholstering an uncooperative genoa lounge. Have you come for the stuff your dad dropped off?'

'Yeah, I got his message.'

He moved around me and extracted a woven shopping bag from behind the shop counter. 'Are you sure I'm not party to a drug deal?'

'Of course not. Just photos,' I assured, taking the bag from him.

'Er ... blackmail then?'

'That's right, Ross. My dad's really a sleazy P.I. and I'm the go-between. No, it's just family history stuff.'

'Good old Mr Gordon. He's certainly addicted, isn't he?'

I rolled my eyes. 'That's for sure.'

He folded his arms over a shirt stained with furniture polish. 'I should spend more time working on our family tree. I'm sure there are a few skeletons in the family's closet. Or a few relatives needing to come out of one,' he added with a weird snort. 'Crap news about losing your job. You didn't see it coming?'

'Nope. No warning at all. I thought the business was going well. We had regular customers and I was always kept busy selling and re-stocking. Apparently, they've been struggling to cover costs for a while now and needed to make some sacrifices—me being one of those, so it turned out.'

He nodded. 'It's a tough time for small businesses. Believe me, I know.' Then he eyed me strangely, like a magpie eyeing a rubbish bin filled with scraps. 'How's Shane doing?'

'Shane?' I cringed. 'Why do you ask?'

He gave shrug. 'He's just seemed a little odd of late. Phoned me Saturday night and invited me to go clubbing with him in the city.'

'Clubbing?' I was stunned. 'With DJ's and techno music?'

'Well, maybe not clubbing ... more like go hang out at a whisky bar.'

'A whisky bar? In the city?'

'Yeah. I didn't take up his offer, of course. Not my thing.'

It wasn't Shane's thing either. He was more at home drinking beer around a barbecue sizzling with steak and sausages. I shook my head and sighed loudly. 'Beats me what's going on with him.'

Ross checked the clock on the wall. 'Oops! I better get back to tackling the lounge before the boss lady returns, otherwise I might be out of a job too,' he said with a wink.

Outside was warm and humid. A storm was brewing. I checked the sky and noticed a thin line of cloud coming in from the west. It didn't look too ominous. I walked along the sun-drenched pavement towards the pub, not to drink alcohol—too early even for me to be doing that—but to sit and think.

On my way up to the top of town, I caught sight of a vinyl banner hanging from the verandah railing of an old Queenslander. According to what I'd recently read in the local newsletter, the house had originally been home to a pioneer family and then, over the last fifty years, a number of varied businesses. For weeks now, this building had been transforming into a new restaurant. In huge red lettering, I was now informed that their grand opening was this coming Saturday. 'A unique dining experience – guaranteed to transport you back in time,' it read. I hoped this didn't mean listing bread and dripping, or bully beef on their menu. This thought of food reminded me that I needed to buy groceries, but that could wait.

Stepping around a woman with a stroller containing a squealing toddler, I collided with an old man carrying a hessian sack filled with potatoes. I apologised and returned a potato that had toppled from the pile. He mumbled something and gave me a gummy grin. His speckled, craggy face bore as many wrinkles as the number of years he'd chalked up, which I presumed was hitting around one hundred and twenty by the look of him.

I continued walking, then stopped as a weird feeling of being watched prickled my skin. I spun around. The old guy and the woman were still roadside, but standing in the shadow of a shop awning was a figure. A man. Was he looking my way? Was it Shane? I raised a hand to shield my eyes from the sun, but the figure suddenly swivelled and ducked around the side of the building before I could get a better look. Odd—very odd. I turned away.

Purchasing a bottle of iced tea from the bar inside the pub, I came back out to sit at a vacant table on the verandah that was shaded by one of the large fig trees. Clearing the table of dried leaves, I laid down the bag from my father and withdrew a paper packet. Turning it upside down, I gave it a shake. Excitement stirred as black and white photographs tumbled out. I was relieved to discover Dad had attached Post-it notes to each photo, saving me from having to decipher the faded handwriting on the back.

The first one I viewed was of a group standing at the water's edge of a shelly beach. I recognised my grandfather standing in the centre of the group and brandishing a fishing rod. On one side of him was my mother—about eight or nine years old by my guess—and on the other side, her little brother Stevie. Next to him was a girl of about twelve. She had large eyes and a fine-featured face surrounded by a mass of dark curls that fell to her shoulders. Turning over the photo, the yellow Post-it informed me that the girl's name was Marion.

The second photo, taken in a backyard with a swing set, showed Marion spraying my mother with a spurting hose; both were in swimwear. Mum's hair was plastered flat on her scalp, while Marion's hung in wet coils. I deduced that this and the previous photo had been taken around the time Marion's mother, my great-aunt Ruth, was in hospital having surgery.

The others were from years later. One showed Marion now in her mid-teens and standing with her parents, Owen and Ruth Douglas. Having grown as tall as her mother, Marion only reached her father's chest. He looked rather surly, whereas both mother and daughter—their arms around each other's waist—were smiling for the camera. They both had the same large eyes, though on Aunt Ruth they seemed quite haunting. She was an average-looking woman, and her sharp features gave evidence of her struggle with ill health.

The final photo was of Marion by herself; smiling, dressed in shorts and buttoned blouse, and holding a tennis racket. Though still petite, she now had the fuller figure of a woman. She was beautiful.

I took another lucky dip into the green bag. A carved wooden trinket box came out next. A sticky note attached indicated that this was one of the items from the suitcase passed on to Mum after Marion had died. I opened the lid, sniffing in the scent of camphor wood. More photographs.

As I began to sort through them, I heard my name being called.

With a start, I looked up. Hurrying across the road—and holding down his perfectly styled, black coiffure—was Lester Schilling, real estate agent and friend. I reluctantly snapped the lid shut on the camphor wood box and returned it to the bag.

'I saw you from the office window,' Lester said, reaching my table.

His real estate office faced the pub, and I imagined if you peered carefully between all the property ads adorning the large pane of glass you'd have a pretty good view of anyone taking time out on the verandah. I wondered how long he'd been watching.

'What are you doing in town today?' he asked. 'Got a day off work?'

I couldn't bear the thought of once again bringing up the pain of losing my job, so I just left out a few specific details. 'Yeah, they didn't need me in the shop today.'

His eyes were drawn to the strewn photos. He fingered one. 'What've you got here, old snaps? Hey, is this you as a kid?'

I flinched. 'I'm not that old. They were taken with a box brownie. She was a cousin.' I returned the photos to the paper packet, away from prying eyes.

Lester checked his Rolex wristwatch. 'I've got some spare time. I can sit with you for a bit, if you like.'

He promptly seated himself on the opposite side of the table and loosened his tie—navy with pink stripes—which co-ordinated well with his mauve business shirt. He let out a long sigh, and a sudden hint of garlic was released into the air. Somebody had eaten Italian for lunch.

'It's a hot one, isn't it?'

I nodded and took a gulp from my bottle, wishing Lester hadn't bothered to step out of his air-conditioned office to interrupt me at such an inopportune time. A light breeze fluttered by and now a strong scent of Hugo Boss wafted in my direction.

'So, you and Karen still coming to the Halloween party?' I asked.

He leant forward. 'Well I certainly am. Got my costume organised. Don't know what Karen's up to though. I've hardly seen her this week.'

'Been that busy?' I said, trying to sound interested.

'You don't know the half of it.' He shook his head, and then checked that his hair had stayed in place. 'Now that she's taken on the role as acting school principal, I've had to play Mr Mum every evening while she's locked away in the study.'

I shrugged. 'Well it's a fast-growing school. The responsibilities must be enormous.'

Lester's Julius Marlows shuffled on the timber decking as his legs began to jig under the table. Along with all ten of his fingers tapping the top, no one would've been blamed for thinking he was channelling Peter Allen and about to break into a lively rendition of 'I Go To Rio'.

'I can't remember the last time Karen and I had a decent conversation,' he scowled. 'She's either too busy or too friggin' tired. And intimacy ...' The tapping and jigging suddenly ceased. 'Well let me say it's not just gone out the window, it's shot off into outer space.' He banged a hand on the table, and both I and the packet of photos jumped. 'I am SO frustrated!' he yelled.

I glanced around. Not one pair of eyes from the adjacent tables had looked our way, which was surprising considering the level of Lester's voice. I felt a bead of sweat trickle down my neck and caught Lester's eyes following the drop as it slowly made its way down to the top edge of my singlet shirt and headed for my cleavage. I swiped the trickle away and covered my chest with my arms. No need to tempt a starving man.

Lester's eyes went all red and veiny. 'Abby, what if Karen doesn't love me anymore.'

God, I didn't need this. 'Don't talk rubbish,' I cajoled in my friendliest of tones. 'Her career has just taken priority. I'm sure she just wants to do her best with her new role and hasn't realised what it's doing to you and the kids.'

'You reckon?' He sniffed, loudly.

'Of course, Lester. Why wouldn't she still love you? Look at you. You're a successful, sensitive, good-looking man with impeccable fashion sense. A real catch in my opinion.'

He dabbed his eyes with the corner of a well-pressed handkerchief. 'You believe that?'

'Of course I do.'

His sudden grin revealed overly-whitened teeth that if caught by a shaft of sunlight would have blinded me for sure. 'I never knew you thought that, Abby.'

'Well, there you go.' I forced a smile.

He took my hand in his. 'Thank you. You don't know how much your words have helped.'

I slid my hand free. 'I'm sure things will improve. You'll be doing the samba in no time.' I shook a pair of invisible maracas.

His head cocked to the side. 'What?'

'Never mind. Just have hope and ... and believe in love.'

He grinned again. 'You're the best. This has really brightened my day.'

A buzzing sound came from under the table. Lester removed his phone from his trouser pocket and checked the screen. Tightening his tie, he got up. 'Got to call a client back. See you Saturday night?'

I nodded, and as I watched Lester saunter across the road, a sense of unease washed over me. Like Karen, had I taken my husband for granted? Had I also been so occupied with my own job and interests that I allowed our marriage to drift into mediocrity? Is that why Shane went looking for excitement elsewhere?

I checked my phone. I hadn't heard from him since his brief message last night. Why did he need more time? What else was he up to?

Dropping the bag of photos off to my car, I went to the craft shop to see if Beryl Erbacher was available for a chat and found the shop closed. Of course, it was Monday. They were always closed on Mondays. Standing on the shop steps and looking out at Main Street, my eyes were drawn to the street sign directly opposite. Station Road. Funny how I'd never wondered before why this short bitumen road that ended abruptly in a grassy paddock had such a name. Now I knew.

That must have been where the Shadow Creek train station once stood.

I hurried across the street and followed the almost deserted road. Two old Queenslanders shaded by tall palm trees were all that stood on the left hand side, while on the right was a storage shed and a fenced field containing a Shetland pony and two white goats. They stopped mid-chew and watched with interest as I walked by. At the end of the bitumen was an open paddock. Stretching in from the road was a very level grassy rise, incongruent to the flat surrounds. It was roughly a metre wide and continued until I lost sight of it in the distance.

The other hint that a train line had been hereabouts was a weathered timber stand part way along. It would have once held an iron water tank used for replenishing steam trains. I was fascinated. Somewhere in this vicinity, a small wooden building and platform would have stood. What excitement the station must have generated on its construction—a true link to the 'big smoke'. Now there was nothing. No station, no rail tracks, and not even a plaque to state that the station had ever existed, just a long grass covered mound.

I stood there awhile, imagining this section of town in its heyday with people coming and going, boarding and disembarking. This was probably where Marion was headed on that fateful day, or at least one of the sidings along the route. Was a picnic beside the creek the purpose for her visit, or something more enticing?

Retracing my steps, I crossed Main Street and followed a cement path until I came to a park edging the creek that gave the town its name. It was much cooler in the shade of tall hoop pines, spreading eucalypts, and Moreton Bay figs with wide buttress roots. High above, amongst leafy branches, lorikeets chatted noisily; their feeding frenzy causing small seedpods to sporadically plummet to the earth like heavy raindrops. The creek was flowing due to the recent rain and I was tempted to wade in or strip off and have a quick swim. Instead, I leant back against a paperbark gum and breathed in the day, almost believing I had nothing to be concerned about and that this time next week my life would be back on track.

A dog bark disturbed the serenity.

I spun around and froze. A small, muscular animal with a broad head and brindle coat bearing a flash of white down its barrel chest was less than a metre away. Brown eyes fixed on mine. Bared teeth dripped with saliva. Furry, athletic legs flexed in readiness to pounce. It cocked its head at the strange squeak that crept from my dry mouth. Then, narrowing its beady eyes, it growled menacingly.

I waved my hand and cried 'shoo' in a pathetic attempt to scare the beast away.

The strong jaw snapped at air, sounding like a steel trap being set off.

I jumped back.

The dog lowered its body. Muscles rippled as its paws took a firmer hold in the dirt.

I knew what would come next. I reached for a fallen tree branch at my feet and raised it high above my head. 'Don't you dare!' I snarled, preparing to smash the demon's brains out if a fight for survival was necessary.

A whistle suddenly came from the vicinity of a thick hedge.

The dog's head jerked, and we both eyed the dense shrubbery. I expected a head to pop up and give a face to the whistler, but it didn't come. A second, sharper whistle did though. This time the dog bolted towards the hedge, forced itself through the dense greenery, and disappeared.

I stood open-mouthed, heart racing, the branch still held high and shaking in my grasp. When nothing else occurred, and no one made an appearance, I dropped my arm and let the branch slip from my fingers. It fell to the ground with a thud and I rested against the tree for support.

What the hell was that all about?

The whistler had to be the dog's owner. Then why hadn't he shown himself? My shoulders tensed. The whistle had come only when I'd taken up a weapon in defence. What if the owner was just protecting his dog from being hurt, not calling it away before it attacked? A crack of thunder added to my alarm. I yelped. The sky was now swirling with dark, threatening clouds.

I hurried back along the path to the street, frequently checking behind in case I was being followed. I made it safely to the grocery store and, after some quick purchases, I found my car and swiftly drove away.

On my way home, I had to pull over to the side of the road to read a phone message sent by a bookstore customer I'd come to know quite well. Rather than offering her condolences, she informed me that when visiting the store that day, she had met two lovely young ladies 'fresh out of high school by the looks of things' serving behind the counter. They told her they had both just started working there and were still learning the ropes.

'Shit!' I yelled. Daniel had lied, the bastard!

I was under the impression that I was let go because the shop was having financial difficulties. Now he'd employed two inexperienced teenagers to take my place. His real reason for ousting me was because I was too old and didn't fit in with the new décor.

I slammed my fist against the car window. In response, the heavens opened.

Boiling with rage, I was amazed I was able to drive home without injuring myself or anyone else on the slippery, wet roads.

10

Stanthorpe 1957

The Dodge is parked amongst a growing line of vehicles across from St Joseph's Hall. Banjo pulls the keys from the ignition and pockets them into his suit coat before sliding from the seat.

Mal is already out and standing on the gravel parking lot. 'Hurry up you two. Nothing worse than having to choose from the bruised fruit.' He rubs his hands together. 'I like 'em ripe and juicy.'

'I think you've been around them apples too long,' Tony remarks, slamming the car door.

Mal checks himself in the side mirror, licks his palm and presses his hair down flat on his scalp. Blowing himself a kiss, he gives a wink. 'Bloody handsome devil, if I say so myself.'

Banjo rolls his eyes. Mal never seems to have any trouble getting the girls, though it has more to do with his charm rather than looks. Well below average in height, and with a nose that's been the target of more than a few angry fists, he knows how to make a girl feel like a princess—at least until his excitement wanes. Mal is a rogue, and watching his creative attempts to crack on to a new girl, or narrowly escape strife, was always good for a laugh. Tonight should prove highly amusing.

Banjo brushes down his navy pinstriped suit and straightens the snazzy red tie. He'd spent a good deal of hard earned cash on this new outfit and feels very dapper. A shame though, that he can't get his hair to slick back no matter how much Brylcreem he uses. It has a life of its own and keeps falling forward over his forehead in unruly strands. Still, he notices several girls turn their heads as he lopes up the hall's timber steps.

The interior is gaily decorated with thousands of white apple blossoms. Spectacularly, six huge, living apple trees in full bloom have been replanted in large pots and stand at intervals around the hall. Smartly dressed men, and women in ball gowns so dazzling they would rival any film star, are standing in groups or rushing around greeting one another. A dance band is warming up and the excitement is palpable.

The trio spy a vacant wooden bench against one wall and rush to claim their seat.

'There she is!' Tony calls, waving wildly.

A cute, bubbly blonde pushes through a curtain of people and plants a kiss on Tony's flushed cheek.

'Hi Marjie,' greet the other two.

'Hi, fellas. You're all looking spic and span tonight.' Her yellow organza gown rustles as she flops down on Tony's lap.

'Where's Christina Civello?' Mal asks, his eyes perusing a bevy of beauties grouped nearby.

Banjo laughs to himself. So, Mal is considering taking a chance with Christina, the Sophia Loren look-alike who has every male wanting her but very few brave enough to give her a try. He'll certainly be biting off more than he can chew with that one.

Marjie lights a cigarette and dangles it elegantly between her fingers, 'Oh, she's here. I saw her outside, wrapped around Sandro Manzoni. Lost your chance there, buddy.'

Mal stands. 'That's what you think, sweetie. That wog's no competition for a stunner like me. Anyway, I reckon I'll try some appetisers before the main course,' he quips, and strides over to girl in pink sitting by herself. Bowing graciously, he takes the girl's hand and gives it a kiss.

The band strikes up a Glenn Miller classic, and 'Moonlight Serenade' brings Tony and Marjie to their feet. They join Mal and the girl, and fifty or so other couples on the dance floor, while Banjo stays sitting on his own.

He glances around for a suitable dance partner and his eyes do a double take when he sees Marion entering the hall. The bodice of her gown is a snug lavender, while the black taffeta skirt falls wide from a tiny waist to the floor. Her hair is piled neatly on top of her head, accentuating a slender neck encircled by a black ribbon choker. Banjo is certainly swept off his feet by her beauty tonight.

A man appears at her side. He is tall, clean cut, and young, with a generous mouth and fair hair slicked down successfully from a middle part. Banjo's hackles rise. Following behind comes Marion's father. Holding firmly to his arm is a thin, pale woman. The resemblance to her daughter is obvious, though this woman seems to have had life sucked from her. He is surprised. Marion hadn't mentioned that her mother was so unwell.

Banjo watches as this foursome join another couple at a table across the room. He recognises a second middle-aged man as his uncle's neighbour, Cameron Duff. With relief, he now realises that Marion's date is his son, Donald. Accepting the seat he pulls out for her, she stiffens her back and clasps her black-gloved hands in her lap, very proper like. There is no smile on her lips, and her attention is not with those seated around the table.

'What's with the dilly-dallying, Banj, me old mate?' says Mal, stepping out of the crowd with a buxom redhead now at his side. 'Need some Dutch courage?'

He reaches into his back trouser pocket, and produces a silver hip flask. When Banjo shakes his head, Mal deftly takes a swig before returning it to its hideaway.

Tony and Marjie spin by and Tony unclasps his girlfriend's hand to slap Mal on the back. 'Hey, don't play silly buggers Mal. You don't want to spend all night in the clink.' Then they twirl back into the squirming throng.

Banjo grips his friend's shoulder. 'Yeah, mate. You don't want to be doing that in here. You know the rules. At least sneak a drink outside like the rest of the blokes.'

Mal holds up a thumb. 'She'll be apples. Haven't been caught yet.' He then scuttles off, the girl giggling in his arms.

Banjo's view of Marion is now completely blocked by dancers. He catches the eye of a plain looking young woman standing on her own not far from him. An unflattering dress festooned with multi coloured bows doesn't do any justice to her already unremarkable looks. Persuaded by her forlorn expression—and Marion's recent remark about his selfish behaviour—Banjo decides to ask her to dance. She flashes a set of large teeth and follows him across the floor for the Progressive Barn Dance.

While everyone takes up their position, Banjo arches his neck in search of Marion. He finds her. She is still on the far side of the room, though she is now standing in the circle and being clasped by Donald Duff. Banjo's heart soars when he sees that she is smiling over at him. He grins back. The tune starts up and, as the dance needs partners to repeatedly change, he eagerly awaits Marion's arrival.

When she is finally standing in front of him, he gives her a gracious nod. 'Marion,' he says politely, though his heart is doing somersaults.

'Benjamin,' she replies, just as courteously. 'I almost didn't recognise you with clothes on.' She flashes a smile and turns sideways, raising her arms at the elbows. 'You scrub up quite well. I am impressed.'

'So you jolly well should be,' he laughs, taking her hands in his. 'This get-up cost me a pretty penny. Though I reckon you must've raided Grace Kelly's wardrobe for your frock.'

'Oh, no,' she responds, as they promenade forward. 'I whipped this little number up myself just the other day.'

'Is that a fact? Now it's my turn to be impressed.'

They give a kick, and then take backward steps. Turning to face each other, they cross their arms out in front, while their left feet cross over their right, followed by their right crossing over their left.

'I gather your date is the one and only Donald Duff?'

'Yes,' Marion answers as their feet repeat the crossing steps. 'My father had arranged the whole thing earlier.'

'He's quite a catch.' Banjo says sarcastically, dropping one of Marion's hands and raising the other high.

Marion's face contorts as she spins under his arm. 'Sure, if you like sweaty hands and two left feet.'

'He's no Fred Astaire like me then?' Banjo says, giving Marion an extra twirl before passing her on to the next fellow.

After this dance, there is a trumpet call, and the Master of Ceremonies appears on stage. One by one, the Queens from each district enter the hall and are led across the dance floor and onto the stage. There are eight girls in total this year, and each take their turn to answer pertinent questions about themselves and their district.

Eventually a judge steps forward to announce the name of the Charity Queen. The winning amount is revealed and everyone applauds. But it is the announcement of the Miss Apple Blossom for 1957 that receives the most response. Shouts of jubilation erupt from those from her district. As the ornate tiara is carefully placed on her head, an even louder round of clapping greets her. Her gloved hand trembles as she grasps the heavily jewelled sceptre, yet her face glows with delight.

Marion is standing alongside her parents. To Banjo, watching from a distance, she outshines every other woman in the hall, including the newly crowned Queen. He wonders how he can catch some time alone with her.

After another few dances, including a lively Quick Step and a Pride of Erin, the MC invites all attendees to take refreshments in the adjoining supper room. People quickly file in, though Banjo waits for Marion to escape the attention of Donald Duff before following her along the covered tables piled high with baked goods. As she fills a plate, he leans over and asks her to partner him for the Fox Trot.

She surprises him by declining. 'Sorry, but I need to dance some more with Donald. It's only fitting seeing I came with him. And besides, Dad has been giving me the evil eye so I'd better do what's right.'

'Okay, give the poor bloke another sympathy dance then. But you have to promise to join me for the waltz.'

Marion agrees. 'I have to take this over to my mother. I'll talk again later.'

Banjo watches her leave, and then proceeds to stack treats onto his own plate. At one point, near the sausage rolls, he sees Marion's father and considers on a whim to introduce himself.

The opportunity is missed when the woman he assumes is Mrs Duff whisks the older man away for an intense conversation by the punch bowl. Banjo redirects his attention to his plate and almost drops the contents when his arm is yanked.

Tony's eyes are as large as the jam drop biscuit Banjo was about to bite into. 'Quick Banjo! Mal's outside getting his arse kicked!'

Before he can respond, Banjo is shuffled through the crowd and out the doorway.

From the top step, he makes out a crowd of men standing in a rough circle on the other side of the street. They are cheering and punching their fists in the air as two bodies roll in the dirt in the midst of them.

'See,' cries Tony, 'Mal and Sandro are having a right royal blue.'

'Hell,' Banjo groans, 'has this got anything to do with Christina Civello?'

Tony nods. 'I'd bet a full wage it has. With Mal's track record you'd think he'd have learnt not to pinch another bloke's girl.'

'Well by the looks of things, he sure as hell hasn't. C'mon.'

They hurry down the stairs and cross the road, narrowly avoiding being collected by a shiny blue Ford Zephyr. Muscling through the rowdy mob, they each take hold of a collar and attempt to separate the tussling pair.

'Break it up will ya!' Banjo yells, and is rewarded with a slog in the face by a random swinging fist.

'Bloody well stop it before the cops come,' Tony demands, tugging Sandro off Mal by his hair.

At the same time, Banjo grabs Mal by the ankles and drags him over to a clump of grass. He plants his shoe on Mal's chest to stop him from crawling back towards the seething Italian. 'Leave it Mal. Your brains are in your arse. She's not flaming worth it.'

Sandro Manzoni shrugs off Tony's effort at holding him by his shirt. 'That slimy mongrel moved in on Christina!' he shouts, spitting blood from a cut lip. 'You're a dingo turd!' he fires over to Mal. 'Find your own girl if there's any left that'll have ya.'

Mal wipes his bloodied nose with the back of his hand and glares across at his opponent. 'I thought she deserved the attention of a real man, not a fumbling wog like you.'

'Why you …' Sandro is on his feet, but before he can take a stride over for another go, he is tackled around the neck by the strong arm of Martin Baxter.

'C'mon you clowns, enough of these shenanigans. You keep this up and you'll be spending the night at the watch house in the loving arms of some lousy drunk.' He hands the squirming youth over to his companions. 'Now everyone get back inside! Except for you,' he adds clipping Mal over the head. 'You're a dead-set idiot getting involved like this. You've been on the turps, haven't you?'

Mal's bloodshot eyes look away.

'Well you can get on home then. I'm your boss, not your nursemaid. If this happens again you can shove off back to wherever it is you came from. I don't need any galahs working for me.'

Banjo pulls Mal to his feet. 'I'll get him home, Uncle Marty.'

'You'd best do so before I lay my own boot into him.'

Martin Baxter heads back to the hall, while Banjo and Tony push the crumpled heap of humanity towards the utility.

Once there, Tony shoves Mal onto the back tray. 'You smell like a bleeding brewery. Thanks for messing up a good night.'

Banjo clutches Tony's shoulder. 'Go on, Tony. Get back inside. You don't want to let Marjie down.'

'You sure?'

Banjo nods.

Tony slaps him on the back, 'Your blood's worth bottling, Banj,' and then bolts away.

Mal groans and rises, his head in his hands. Banjo notices that the earlier bravado has vanished and all that is left is a miserable Lothario. 'I'll be back in a tick,' he informs him, 'so don't bloody move.'

Mal responds by lurching forward. Banjo has just enough time to step aside before being covered in vomit.

Entering the hall, Banjo brushes down his suit and combs his hair with his fingers. He spots Marion standing against the far wall and races over.

Her hands clutch her face. 'My God, what have you been up to?'

'Nothing,' he says with an air of innocence. Then seeing the horror in her gaze, he examines himself with an eye that is starting to swell. His navy suit is streaked with dirt, and down one trouser leg is a splatter of chunky spew. He raises a hand. His fingers are dripping red.

'Is that blood?' Marion gasps.

'Oh, it's not my blood,' he assures her. But there is no relief in the eyes blinking back at him.

'Well whose is it?' she cries.

'My mate, Mal's. He had a bit of a stoush and we had to break it up. It's all good now.'

Banjo flinches as Marion's father appears like magic at her side.

He studies Banjo with a derisive glare. 'And who might this be, Marion?'

'Dad, this is Ben Patterson. Martin Baxter's nephew.'

This is not the way Banjo expected to officially make Owen Douglas's acquaintance, but there is nothing he can now do about it. He thrusts out his hand. 'Pleased to meet you, Mr Douglas.'

He sees a further look of disgust from the man. Rather than responding to the offer of a bloodied handshake, Owen Douglas takes a step back.

'There was a bit of trouble outside,' Banjo explains, hiding the offensive hand in his trouser pocket.

'I see.' The stony face turns away. 'Marion, come. I hear the waltz starting up.' He holds out an arm for her to take.

Marion glances from her father to Banjo. 'I'm ... not sure I can,' she falters.

Banjo sees the man's eyes bulge, and realises the quandary she is in. 'It's all right, Marion, I came to say goodnight anyway. Mal's got a busted nose and I've got to take him home.' He gives her a weak smile.

There is no reciprocation. Marion feeds her arm through her father's and is once again whisked away.

Banjo's jaw clenches.

11

I made it into the house without getting soaked. Dripping water onto the floor, I put the groceries away, then changed into drier clothing. My nerves had not yet settled so I poured myself a tall rum and ginger ale. To take my mind off almost being mauled to death, and then being stabbed in the back by a deceitful employer, I headed up the stairs to the loft.

Removing the wooden box from the bag of photos, I opened the lid and lifted out a photo of a group of people at a party, or a dance of some kind. They were all well dressed and sitting around a table. Marion was wearing an exceptionally stunning ball gown. She looked like a classic movie star.

Another photo—an outdoor shot this time—showed Marion in more casual clothes standing on the porch steps of a cottage. Her flower print dress had a wide collar and buttons right down to the hem. Her eyes glistened in the sunlight as she smiled. I wondered who the photographer had been. I flipped this photo over. 'December 1957'. A month before her death.

The next photo, marked with the same date and showing a

wider view of the same cottage, gave a hint as to who had been behind the camera in the other. Sitting astride a motorcycle in front of a picket fence with the cottage behind, was a young man. He was tanned, broad shouldered, with dark hair hanging over his forehead in wiry curls. He was also grinning, and I noted he had a gap between the top front teeth. The more I studied it, the more I felt I'd seen this handsome young man before.

'Who are you?' I asked, looking into his dark eyes.

The silence of the house was broken by the sound of the front door being opened. This was followed by something heavy being dropped to the floor.

My body tensed. 'Hello!' I called, my voice quavering.

'Hello, back!' cried Elliott.

I checked my watch. 4:00 pm already?

'There's an iced bun in the container on the bench if you're hungry!' I shouted.

'I sure am!' came the expected response. He was a growing boy.

I returned to the photo of Marion on the steps. She looked happy. She could have even been laughing. My heart took a tumble when I saw a thin chain around her neck and, hanging from it, a pendant. At least that's what I thought it must have been as only the top of it peeked out from the edge of her collar. I brought the photo up for a closer inspection.

A few seconds later I'd descended the stairs, sidestepped Elliott's school bag sprawled in the entry, and was hurrying into the lounge room. Pulling up in front of the china cabinet, I let out a cry. The necklace I'd left on top of the cabinet had disappeared.

I scanned the room. No sign of it. I raced to my bedroom and checked the dressing table and then my jewellery box on the off chance I'd moved it without thinking. Nothing. Where could it have gone?

With increasing desperation, I rushed to Elliott's bedroom. Music pumped from behind his closed door. I knocked hard.

'What d'ya want?' he yelled.

Rather than strain my vocal chords I turned the knob and struggled with opening the door. Heaving back what I found out was a barricade of dirty clothing, I peered into the dimly lit room. The carpet was littered with CD and DVD cases, and assorted footwear. As usual the bed was unmade with the quilt twisted into a ball at the end of the mattress. I found Elliott comfortably entrenched in his beanbag. A black-haired girl was curled in his lap.

'Hi, Mrs Eaton,' Elliott's girlfriend said, with a wave.

'Oh ... hello, Bree. I didn't know you were here.'

'I came on the bus with Elliott. Hope that's okay.'

They must have been caught in a downpour between here and the high school for she was wearing an old 'The Killers' T-shirt of Elliott's, while his school shirt had been replaced with a black 'Thirsty Merc' one. At least I hoped that was the reason. 'Do your parents know you're here?'

She nodded. 'Yep, Mrs Eaton.'

'You can call me Abby, remember.'

'Okay, Abby,' she giggled, playing with her nose ring. An adornment I'd only recently got used to.

'Alright if she stays for dinner?' asked Elliott.

What could I say? The poor girl couldn't leave without eating. She already had the figure of a waif-like catwalk model. 'I guess so. It's nothing flash, just pies and chips.'

'Thanks,' Bree said, untangling herself from my son.

I was about to broach the subject of the necklace, when I spied it hanging around her neck. 'The necklace. You're wearing it.'

'Sorry, I was showing it to Bree,' Elliott said, lifting it over her head. 'She thinks the mystery is pretty cool.'

'Yeah, way cool,' the girl nodded, now sitting cross-legged on the floor, and stretching the hem of the T-shirt over her knees.

'Give it here!' I demanded.

Elliott glowered. 'Settle down, Mum. It hasn't come to any harm. Here you go.' To my horror, he drew back his arm and threw the necklace.

It flew towards me in an awkward, tumbling motion. Startled, I stumbled forward, tripped over a mountain of clothes, and landed amongst a pile of dirty socks and underwear. Meanwhile, the necklace soared overhead and clattered on the hallway floor.

'NO!' I shrieked.

Scrambling on hands and knees I saw the necklace sprawled on the floorboards and broken in two. 'Elliott!' I screamed, too shocked to move. 'You killed it!'

He came rushing out and picked the pieces up off the floor. 'No, I didn't.'

'It's broken!'

'I don't think it is Mrs ... Abby,' said Bree over Elliott's shoulder. 'I think the back just came off.'

I got to my feet, and watched as Elliott tried to clip the flowered front piece into the silver backing.

'It should go in,' he said pushing harder.

'Hey, don't force it!'

'I think there's something in the way.' Using a fingernail, he scraped the back of the floral heart.

I gripped his arm. 'Be careful.'

His fingers peeled away what looked like a tiny wad of paper, the size of my thumbnail. As he dropped it into my outstretched hand it began to unfurl like the petals of a flower.

Carefully separating the delicate folds of some kind of tissue paper, I let out a gasp. 'Oh my God. There's writing on it.'

12

Stanthorpe 1957

The Apple Blossom Festival is in full swing. Hundreds of excited folk line both sides of Maryland Street cheering along the colourful procession of marching bands, decorated floats and cheeky clowns that form The Grand Parade. The sun has a bite to it, an assurance for drink stall owners that they will be kept on their toes.

The Apple Blossom Queen float passes by. It is covered in masses of pink and white imitation apple blossoms and carries the 1957 Queen, seated proudly on an elaborate throne and flanked by the other contestants still dressed in their fancy ball gowns.

Amongst the crowd stands Banjo. Next to him are Tony and Marjie, who is waving madly.

'Greta, over here!' she yells. A girl, standing on the float amidst the other runners-up, smiles back and nods demurely. Marjie turns to Tony, 'She should have won you know. She worked real hard raising lots of money.'

'I'm sure they all did.' Tony adds, lifting the brim of his hat to wipe sweat from his forehead.

'Greetings and salutations!' shouts a voice.

The three spin around. Mal is pushing through the horde to join them. 'I've been looking all over for you guys.'

He is looking worse for wear. His injured nose is taped with white adhesive, and both eyes are ringed with purple bruising. The accompanying gashed lip doesn't stop a huge grin from spreading across his face.

Banjo squints. 'You look like the cat that's swallowed the canary. What's with that?'

Behind Mal, and taller by a head, appears the glamorous visage of Christina Civello. Banjo stares. She is stuffed into an orange dress so taut that her ample bosom spills over the low neckline much like Niagara Falls, while her cleavage is as deep as the Grand Canyon.

'What you see when you haven't got a gun,' says Marjie.

'Well bugger me,' Tony blurts out.

Banjo just gives Mal a questioning glare.

Mal beams back. 'What's wrong with you lot? Christina decided after all, that I, the Great Mal had so much more to offer.' He grabs her around the waist and pulls her close. 'Isn't that right, doll face?'

Banjo expects Mal will lose an eye at any moment if he isn't careful.

'My little dynamo,' Christina purrs, bending down to kiss him.

'That's a nice frock,' Marjie says, though Banjo can tell the smile on her face is forced.

Christina smooths down the front of her dress, and puffs her chest out even further. Tony's jaw drops. Marjie notices and digs him in the ribs.

'Thank you,' Christina says, 'my papa bought it for me on his last trip to Milan.'

Marjie's eyes widen. 'Well lucky you, Christina. Most of us girls just have to make do with throwing something together ourselves.'

'And you look smashing,' Tony whispers into Marjie's ear.

Mal stands on his toes to peer over heads and view the road. 'So, have we missed anything good?'

'Sure, but there's more to come. Check out the line up back there.' Tony points to the queue of cumbersome vehicles moving down from the top of the street.

'Strewth! I've just got here and feel like a drink already. Hey Banj, isn't that the girl you're sweet on?'

Banjo follows the direction of Mal's pointing finger. He sees Marion. This time she is dressed in a pink blouse and white pedal pushers. Standing either side of her are her father and Donald Duff, whose nose is buried in a festival programme. Banjo waves, but Marion doesn't notice. She seems too busy laughing away the amorous advances of a unicycle-riding clown.

'Give us a lend of this, will ya, mate,' Banjo says, plucking Tony's hat from his head and waving it enthusiastically in the air.

When there is still no response, he places two fingers in his mouth and whistles sharply. Marion finally looks his way, and Banjo signals her to come join them. She eyes the two men beside her and then shakes her head. Banjo struggles with knowing what to do next, and loses sight of her as a school band proceeds to march past in lines of six abreast.

Marion peers hard between rows of parading children. Ben's friends are there, but now there is no sign of him. Suddenly a small chubby boy brandishing a pair of cymbals breaks through the ranks. He rushes over and hands her a piece of folded paper before falling back in line with the rest of the band members. Marion cautiously opens a white paper bag, now devoid of the lollies it once held. Scrawled in bright red lipstick is a brief message. 'Meet me at the post office,' it reads. She glances up, but Ben is still nowhere to be seen.

Turning to her father she shouts above the noise of the street. 'Dad, I'm feeling a little faint, I think I'll try to find some shade.'

'Do you want one of us to come with you?' he yells back.

'No, don't do that,' Marion insists, 'It's just the heat. I'll get myself a drink, and if I don't feel better, I'll make my way home.'

'I can take you back if you like?' Donald says, leaning in.

She shakes her head. 'You two stay here and enjoy the parade. I'll be fine.'

'If you say so.' Her father's attention is drawn away by a bevy of dancing strawberries blowing kisses into the crowd. He pretends to catch one and slip it into his shirt pocket.

Marion edges her way through the masses, keeping her eye on the post office clock looming overhead. Once clear of the crowd, she hurries along the pavement. In the shade of the stone building waits a young man in a white shirt and beige trousers.

He waves and rushes forward to meet her. 'Thank God, you got my note. I thought I might be left standing here like shag on a rock.'

'Yes, your carrier pigeon successfully delivered the message. How much did that cost you?'

'Two bob. But you're worth it.'

Marion touches his bruised cheek. There is swelling around his eye. 'My word, that sure is a shiner you've got there.'

'Oh, yeah, I almost forgot about that. Thanks for reminding me.'

'It makes you look tough.'

'Stupid more like it. I should've kept my distance.'

'How's your friend?'

'Mal? Happy as Larry.'

Marion is baffled. 'Didn't he get his nose broken?'

'Yes ... but he also got the girl. Anyway, enough of him, let's get out of here.' He takes her arm.

She smiles. 'You know, I had to pretend I had the vapours to get away.'

'Well don't faint on me now. I don't think I could manage carrying your hefty weight around.'

'Hey!' She pulls her arm free.

'Just joking.' He takes it back, and leads her away from the bustling town centre.

'Where are we going?' she asks, as he steers her down a vacant side street.

'I have an idea that I think you'll enjoy.'

They halt beside a dusty utility. The passenger door creaks as he opens it.

She shoots him a curious glance, 'Are you abducting me?'

He grins, 'Maybe.'

Marion is puzzled. They have been driving for over fifteen minutes and are now turning onto a familiar dirt road. 'You're taking me home?'

He squints, 'Not quite.'

She watches as the Duff property passes by. The vehicle slows, and they enter the adjacent property through a set of open rusty gates. A weathered farmhouse comes into view.

'Your uncle's place?'

'You hungry?' he asks, pulling the car up near the front porch.

'Starving.'

'Good.' He opens the car door.

'Wait,' she calls. 'I haven't met them yet, and they may not want —' but he has already leapt out and is taking the porch steps two at a time.

Marion wonders if she should follow, then decides to wait and see if she is welcome. Moving along the bench seat she stretches up to check her reflection in the rear view mirror, fluffing her hair, and evening out the colour on her lips. What is taking him so long? Leaning back, her hand grazes the depression in the worn upholstery where his body rested. It is warm and damp. She casually lifts her fingers to her mouth and tastes the saltiness of him. A yearning stirs. A prayer is sent up requesting that this day will not rush to its end.

The screen door bangs.

Marion quickly returns to her side of the seat as Ben races down the stairs. He is carrying a large cloth bundle, which he places in the back tray before climbing behind the wheel.

'Did you miss me?' he grins.

Marion rolls her eyes, 'Hardly. What's in the bundle?'

'I raided the kitchen. I'm sure Aunt Gina won't mind us finishing off some leftovers.'

She peers out of the window. 'They aren't home?'

'Nope. They're at the parade, like all the good folk. Aunt Gina has a stall.'

He starts the motor and steers the car around the side of the house. They follow a well-worn track alongside a healthy vegetable garden, and eventually reach another wide gate. This one is closed.

Marion flings open her door. 'I'll get the gate, but only if you tell me where it leads.'

He nods. 'To the best picnic spot around.'

She waits for the vehicle to pass through, then hoists herself back inside.

They bump along the dusty corrugation and crest a rise with a view of the vast apple orchard edged by the creek. Driving down, and past row upon row of budding trees, they come to a stop in a clearing.

Banjo steps out and retrieves the bundle from the back. Marion follows close behind as he chooses a perfect spot in the shade of a large, old apple tree and places the bundle on the grass. Untying the huge knot, the checked tablecloth falls back to reveal an array of delicious looking goods.

'*Voila!* Madame, lunch is served.'

Marion claps her hands. 'Oh, this is wonderful.' Dropping to her knees, she inspects the food. 'Salami, fruit, olives ...' She sniffs a wedge of yellow, '... an incredibly mature cheese ... and a jar of tomato relish, I believe.'

'Aunt Gina's specialty.' He twists off the lid, scoops out a blob, and sucks it from his finger.

Marion lifts a breadstick to her nose. 'Mmm ... fresh sure is best. This is a feast.'

'Remarkable what you can do in a jiffy.' He prods the cloth with a foot. 'Damn, I forgot the plates ... and the silverware. There should be a knife here somewhere.'

'Who needs them when we have God-given utensils right here.' She waves her fingers in the air.

Banjo hurries back to the utility and returns with a brown glass bottle in each hand. 'Didn't forget the Vino though!'

He sits on the grass. Uncorking a bottle with his teeth, he takes a swig and passes the bottle on. 'You've gotta try this. I'm usually a beer drinker but this is top shelf. Gina's family are making some pretty good wine on the side. A lot of Italian families are, these days.'

She places the bottle to her lips and takes a sip. 'Not bad. Spicy and fruity at the same time.'

He gives his fingers a noisy kiss. '*Buonissimo!*'

With only half the bread and a small number of treats remaining, their hunger is well and truly satisfied.

'Is it true that Stanthorpe was once known as Quart Pot Creek?' Marion asks, lifting the second wine bottle to her lips.

He nods. 'Too right. It was changed sometime back in the 1800s when tin was discovered and thousands flocked here to stake their claim. Some bright sparks got it in their heads to change the town's name to a combination of the Latin words for tin, which is 'Stannum', and 'Thorpe', meaning village.'

'But there's no tin mining here now, is there?'

'Nope. When the tin petered out, they realised the climate in the area was perfect for growing fruit, especially apples. So, boosted by the arrival of hardworking immigrants like Aunt Gina's family, the new venture worked a treat.' He spreads his arms wide. 'As you can see.'

'Well thanks for the history lesson, Mr Patterson,' Marion says, raising the bottle in a salute and then taking another swig. 'This is so good. Though I think I might be getting a little tipsy. I'm starting to see double.' She shakes her head and rubs her eyes.

Banjo takes the bottle from her. 'Woah there, Nelly. I don't think I'd like to drop you off home drunk as a skunk. I'm betting your father wouldn't be too pleased.'

She rises unsteadily to her knees and wags a finger in the air. 'Oh no, I must never put a foot wrong. Don't want to give the family a bad name now, do we? You know, Ben me old mate, I'd love to do something shocking. Something that would force them to see me as my own person, not just a chattel to be bartered around.'

He cocks an eyebrow. 'Would you now? And what do you think would knock them sideways?'

'Oh, probably anything out of the ordinary. They are so prim and proper. I'm sure if I just bleached my hair white they'd have a fit.'

'C'mon, you can do better than that,' he goads.

She taps her chin. 'Let's see. Maybe if I took off all my clothes and danced naked in the moonlight spouting Shakespeare they might take notice.'

'I know I sure would,' he says, raising the bottle to his lips, 'Just let me know the time and the place.'

'Oh you ...' Marion pushes him hard and the bottle slips from his grasp, spilling red wine down the front of his white shirt. 'Oh bugger ... I'm so sorry.'

He dabs the wetness with a corner of the tablecloth. 'No harm done, I'm sure it'll come out.'

'Give it here.' Marion leans forward and starts to undo the buttons of his shirt. 'We'd better wash it out before it stains.'

He grins. 'My, you're keen.'

She stops. 'Well, do it yourself then.'

He holds up his hands. 'Hey, I'm not complaining.'

Marion completes the task and takes the shirt from him. Kicking off her sandals, she hurries through the grove to the creek's edge.

Once there, she quickly steps into the running water. Washing the shirt as best she can, she wrings it out, and holds it aloft. The stain has completely disappeared. She lifts her eyes and her breath catches in her throat as she sees Ben on the bank grinning back her. His bare chest glimmering in the sunlight reminds her of caramel toffee. Her heart twists and she nearly loses her footing.

He holds up both thumbs. 'What a good washerwoman you are. A real scrubber.'

Marion scowls. 'How dare you. I am no such thing.' Stomping out of the water, she shoves the sodden material into his hands. 'It will need to dry now.'

A warm breeze picks up as she struts back through the grove. It swishes through leafy branches causing blossoms to drift down like colourful snowflakes. Reaching out, she captures them in the palms of her hands. They are as light as gossamer and as soft as silk. She follows the wave of air to collect more.

Banjo reaches the picnic spot and squats to bundle up the leftovers. Hearing footsteps, he feels a surprising coolness on his back. Peering over his shoulder, he finds Marion smiling down and showering him with petals. As she comes around to sit in front of him, he notices that her cheeks are flushed from the wine, or the sun—or both—and her eyes are alight. Her beauty is all-consuming. He reaches out and removes stray apple blossoms from her hair.

> 'Here's an apple blossom Mary,
> see how delicate and fair.
> Here's an apple blossom Mary,
> let me weave it in your hair.
>
> Ah, thy hair is raven Mary,
> and the curls are thick and bright,
> And this apple blossom Mary,

is so beautifully white.'

Marion's eyelids flicker. 'Where did you—'
He presses a finger to her lips and continues.

'There, the apple blossom, Mary,
looks so sweet among your curls.
And the apple blossom Mary,
crowns the sweetest of the girls.

But the apple blossom Mary,
you must have a little care,
Never tell your mother, Mary,
that I wove it in your hair.'

He hands her the petals. Normally this would be the moment when a fellow would take a girl in his arms and plant a kiss on her lips. But Marion's expression is now peculiar. Her eyes search his. She seems bewildered; scared even. This is not what she wants from him.

He looks away, only to turn back when his shoulders are seized, and lips soft and urgent assault his mouth. He readily succumbs, finding that Marion's mouth tastes pleasantly of herbs and red wine.

When he is finally released, he lets out a gasp. 'Hey, I was going to do that.'

'Well, why didn't you?' she says. 'I got tired of waiting.'

'I was trying to be a gentleman.'

'Well maybe a gentleman isn't what I want right now.'

She pushes him backwards onto the grass and sits over him. Her hands explore his naked torso with fingers light and teasing.

He blinks hard. 'Geez you're a surprise. Are you sure this isn't just the grog spurring you on?'

'Yep,' she nods, and then hiccups loudly. 'I'm very clear headed.'

Banjo laughs and circles her waist with his hands. She is so narrow that his fingers almost meet. 'I've wanted to kiss you since the moment I first clapped eyes on you.'

'Is that a fact,' she grins. 'Then you do have a thing for banshees.'

'Seems like it.' He moves his hands up to the small of her back and eases her down. Just as their lips meet, she hiccups again.

'Sorry, I'm not use to so much wine.'

'I don't mind. I've never been attacked by a drunken trollop before.'

'Hey,' she scowls, feeding her fingers through his hair and gripping tightly. 'I may be a little tipsy, but I'm no trollop.'

Her tongue slips into his mouth and he accepts it eagerly.

After a few joyous moments, he rolls to the side, taking Marion with him. Brushing hair back from her forehead, he fingers the faint scar on her brow, the one he noticed back when they first met.

'How did you get this?' he asks.

She turns her face away. 'I ... fell out of bed ... as a child.'

'It must've hurt.'

'I survived,' she says, laying on her back, looking upward.

Banjo trails his finger over her cheek and jaw. She doesn't flinch this time, so he continues down to the dip at the base of her throat. He hears her sigh, and moves his hand lower. The skin just above the neckline of her blouse is warm, and flushed. She takes in a deep breath and her blouse strains over her rising breasts. His fingers tremble. Before he can make another move, Marion covers his hand with her own.

'That poem. Did you write it?' she asks.

He can feel her heart pounding through his fingertips. 'Oh, it's not mine. I just memorised it.'

'I didn't know you liked poetry.'

'There's a lot you don't know about me, Maid Marion.'

Her face is dappled by sunlight falling through the overhead branches of the apple tree. She is perfect. A lone flower spirals down to settle on her cheek. He moves his hand to flick it away, but stops. Jumping to his feet, he raises his arms and grips hold of an overhanging branch. As he shakes it, more blossoms shower down. In seconds Marion is covered in a scattering of pink and white.

'I'm so glad I ended up in the orchard that day,' she says, with a giggle. 'I might never have met you otherwise.'

He kneels and brushes flowers from her face. 'Well, you caught me at the waterhole too, remember.'

'Oh yes,' she smiles widely, 'it was destiny.'

'What do you think your father would say about this? About us.'

'Right now, I don't care.' Petals slide off to cascade around her as she sits up. 'Hopefully he'll get over this silly notion of pushing me and Donald together and let me see whoever I want.'

'Like me?'

'Yeah,' she nods, 'someone like you.'

Banjo takes her hand, feels how small it is in his and has a strong urge to protect her—from what, he isn't sure.

'Where's your shirt?' she asks, looking around.

'On that bush over there.'

'Which one?'

He points, only to see that the shrub is now unadorned. 'Geez, the wind must have blown it away.'

They both rise and run through the grove, searching.

Venturing down to the creek, something white is seen bobbing in the water.

'Well, Benny boy,' Marion says with a wink, 'I guess we'll just have to wait for it to dry again.'

Making his way to the water's edge, he glances back. 'Now that we've gotten to know each other better, you can call me Banjo.'

'Really?' she calls back. 'Does that mean we're mates?'

'Too right,' he answers, wading out into the swirling stream.

13

Hurrying back into Elliott's room, I shoved a chair draped with two damp school shirts away from his desk and switched on the desk lamp. Pushing aside his laptop, I carefully pressed the thin piece of paper out flat and leant in for a closer look.

Under the bright light, it was easy to see the four lines of finely written words. It looked like a stanza from a poem.

Elliott came alongside and also read the wording that had something to do with a girl named Mary with apple blossoms in her hair. 'Whoever owned the necklace must've really wanted to keep this safe. I don't recognise the poem.'

I elbowed him. 'And you're a connoisseur of poetry, are you?'

'Hey, I've read a bit in my time. Remember, I did get a Distinction in English last semester.'

I peered again at the piece of paper. The cursive script was a dull brown, with strong strokes slanting forward. 'I wouldn't be surprised if this was written by a man.'

'And you're a handwriting expert?' Elliott chided.

'Have you seen your grandmother's handwriting? It's flowery and curly and feminine. People took pride in their writing skills back then. Not like your drunken ant scrawl.'

Elliott gave a shrug. 'Why bother? We type everything these days anyway.'

I turned the paper over and eyed a couple of scribbled words above a smudge of ink.

'What does that say?' said Elliott.

Lifting it up to the light, I let out a cry. 'Oh ... my ... God!'

'It says that?' Elliott took it from me. Holding it up, his eyes grew large. 'Woah! Does that say ... Banjo Patterson?'

I nodded slowly.

Bree said from behind, 'Wasn't he a famous person?'

'A famous Australian writer,' I replied a little taken aback by her lack of literary knowledge. 'Most people are familiar with his poems about bush life.'

I read the verse again and had to agree with my son; I didn't recognise it either. Maybe it was something that had never been published. I mentioned this.

Elliott chewed the inside of his cheek. 'You mean we could have stumbled across a real find ... like an original never-before-seen poem by ol' Banjo? That'd be worth a bit, wouldn't it?'

Bubbles of excitement fizzed in my stomach. 'Maybe.'

'Well, let's see if we can find it online,' suggested Bree, handing the laptop to Elliott, who sat on the edge of the bed with it resting on his knees.

He began typing, while I remained at the desk, studying the piece of paper. Should be wearing gloves, like they do in museums when handling ancient artefacts? What if we'd opened it up to our toxic atmosphere and it rapidly disintegrates right before our eyes? I cautiously placed the piece of paper on the desk and stepped away.

I watched Elliott scroll through Internet sites giving information on the famous Australian poet and his writings.

'I didn't know he was named after a horse. I thought he played a banjo?' he said, amused.

'Yes,' I replied knowingly, '"The Banjo" was the name of a horse he once owned. He took it on as a pseudonym when he started writing for the Sydney Bulletin.'

'Well ... I can't find anything written by him about Apple Blossoms.' He rubbed his hands together. 'This could be good!'

I was doubtful. 'It doesn't actually sound like him, though, does it? It's not quite ... I don't know ... bushy enough.'

'Okay, I'll type in the first line and see where it takes me.'

It didn't take long for him to discover that it came from a longer poem in a book of collected works penned, not by Banjo, but one Charles G. Eastman.

I was disappointed and confused. 'That's weird. Why would someone add Banjo's name to this, then?'

Bree leapt from the bed and went over to the desk. 'How many t's are there in Banjo's last name?'

Elliott studied his laptop. 'One.'

'Well there are two in this surname.'

'So?' said Elliott, unperturbed.

Bree crossed her arms. 'Just saying. It was an observation that's all. What if the poem was written on the paper by someone else with the same name.'

Elliott chimed in, 'Yeah, people do it all the time, name their kid after someone famous. I know a Jesse James ... and a Clark Kent.'

'My friend Zoe McDonald has a cousin called Ronald,' nodded Bree.

I agreed. 'And what about that girl in your pre-school class, Elliott? Alice Cooper.'

'What's strange about that?' frowned Bree.

Elliott's and my eyes met. 'I'll fill you in later,' he said.

Now it was Bree's turn to pick up the piece of paper and hold it close to the lamp—a little too close for my liking. I cringed, hoping it wouldn't catch alight and burn to a crisp.

Her eyes narrowed. 'You know ... I think there are words within that smudge on the back.'

'There are?' I moved over and looked with her. 'I can't see anything.'

Bree reefed a magnifying glass out of Elliott's pencil caddy and handed it to me. 'Here, this might help your old eyes.'

She was right, there were another couple of words. I sucked in air. 'No way!'

'No way, what?' She snatched the magnifying glass and read it for herself. 'Does that say Shadow Creek?'

I nodded. 'I think so.'

'But what does that mean, Abby? That Banjo #2 came from around here?'

I looked over at Elliott. 'Can you do another search?'

Elliott typed and reported back. 'Unless it's referring to a Golf Course in Las Vegas, there is no other town called Shadow Creek other than ours. Wasn't your cousin Marion heading out this way when she died?'

My head hurt. 'Supposedly.'

'Well that's it!' squealed Bree. 'She was coming out to see this Banjo. The one with two t's.'

My brain felt like an unmatched Rubik's Cube. 'Well, who was he then?'

'Someone who liked Apple Blossoms, I guess,' jeered Elliott.

'And secrets,' I added, staring at the last line of the verse.

~

We sat at the dining table amongst the remains of our pie and chips.

'So, what do you think?' The necklace and an enlarged picture of Marion lay side by side in front of us. I pointed to the chain around her neck. 'Are they the same?'

Elliott brushed his fingers through his hair. 'Well ... the links in the chain are similar, and the silver edging on the heart is a close match. We can't really see all of the flowery pattern, but I'd say there's enough evidence.'

I held my hand up for a high five that didn't come. I dropped it again. 'This is exciting!'

'Well this isn't.' Bree appeared, carrying a local phone book. 'No Pattersons in the Shadow Creek area, and that's with one or two t's. If someone by that name ever lived around here, they don't now.' She dropped the book on the table and flopped into a chair. 'Is the necklace a match?'

'Yep, pretty much,' said Elliott.

'What does that mean?' she asked, twizzling her nose ring.

'Let's see,' I said. 'We now have proof that Marion wore this necklace, and that at some stage, the poem verse was hidden inside.'

Elliott wiped gravy away from the side of his mouth. 'What if Marion owned the necklace but didn't know what was hidden inside? Maybe she wasn't the original owner, or someone owned it afterwards and hid the poem there. Old stuff gets passed around all the time. Just look at all that junk in your china cabinet, Mum.'

'It's not junk,' I said, annoyed.

'Or sold,' Bree chipped in. 'Just look on eBay. People get rid of things for all sorts of reasons.'

I didn't like that train of thought one bit. Just when I was beginning to put this puzzle together, these two clowns come along and upend it all with alternate, yet plausible, scenarios.

'Hang on a minute.' I sat forward. 'Don't forget the connection to Shadow Creek.'

Elliott got up from his chair. 'Oh well, Mum. I guess you've got more work to do on this then. I should be doing some homework. You coming Bree?'

'In a minute,' she said, studying the enlarged photo. 'Did your cousin Marion have a birthmark?'

'I don't know, why?'

She slid the photo across the table. 'What's that on her neck?'

I picked it up. There was a blemish on the side of her neck, below her jawline. 'A shadow? Maybe a bruise?'

'Or,' her eyes grew large, 'a love bite.'

I looked more closely at the suspicious marking. 'Really? Given by who?'

She sighed loudly. 'That's a no-brainer, Abby.' She tapped the photograph with a black painted fingernail. 'I'm betting that hot guy on the motorbike wasn't there just to take photos.'

Elliott and Bree were supposed to be doing homework together, though I couldn't see how that was possible with all the loud music and giggling coming from the bedroom. I should have checked on them, but I preferred to clear my head outside on the back deck.

The storm had long passed. The night air was pleasant, with only the light streaming out from the kitchen to break the darkness. I glared at the phone in my hand. The text I'd sent minutes before, informing my absent husband that I was worried about him and needed to talk, hadn't been responded to. Was Shane having another session at a whisky bar? I contemplated calling his brother. I didn't want to be one of those annoying, harping wives, yet there was so much I needed to tell him.

A 'beep' sounded. My hand jerked. A message had come, though not from Shane, from Gemma. It was an irksome picture of her and Max, the old guy she was planning to ruin her life for. They seemed to be having a fun time snorkelling the shores of a sandy island. I stared at his smarmy, sunburnt, thirty-something-year-old face and wished him the hell away from my daughter.

A dog barked. A large, angry dog by the sound of it, and it was coming from the side of the house.

The phone slipped from my grasp and clattered to the decking. Flashes of the afternoon's run-in with a slobbering beast dashed through my mind. I listened anxiously, my breath coming out in ragged bursts. Retrieving the phone, I held it tightly against my chest. Would an emergency call for protection from an angry bull terrier and its menacing owner be acted on at this time of night? Probably not.

I hurried inside, flicking the lock on the sliding glass door.

A knock on the front door.

'Shit!' I cried.

After some hesitation, I eased my way through the lounge room to the door. Grabbing a potted plant from a timber stand for protection, I braced myself, turned the handle and flung open the door.

'Hi Abby, sorry I'm ...' Bree's father's words hung in mid-air, just like the philodendron I was brandishing.

I saw the surprise in his eyes, and quickly lowered my arm. 'Oh, hello, Brad.'

'Dad!' cried Bree, rounding me from behind. 'You're a little late.'

'Yes, sorry about that, kiddo.' He looked my way. 'Been out

trying to find a 24-hour chemist. Mel's had a difficult day. Ran out of pain killers.'

'That's not good,' I said sympathetically, feeling an elbow nudge me in the ribs as Elliott appeared at my side. I knew what that jab meant but had no regrets about my decision to have him destroy his little plantation.

Bree and her dad soon left and Elliott retreated to his room.

I made myself a mug of decaf coffee. My heart had already had enough stimulation for one day.

14

Stanthorpe 1957

After weeks scattered with stolen moments, Banjo is keen to spend more time with Marion. He parks the Dodge outside the drapery store, just as the shop lights go out and Marion and Lucy, a colleague, step through the doorway.

Banjo leans out of the window and gives a whistle. Both girls look his way. 'Anyone need a lift?' he calls.

Lucy shakes her head, while Marion hurries near. Banjo stretches over and opens the passenger door for her.

She climbs in. 'Well this is a surprise. I was going to catch a lift with Lucy.'

'Feel like a hamburger?'

'Sure do. I'm famished. Seems like ages since lunch time.'

'Good.' Banjo drops two paper packets onto her lap. 'Hang on to these. Want to take a little trip?'

'Where?'

'Not far, but certainly worth the drive.' He looks over his shoulder and backs the truck out.

They rattle down the main street, passing darkened shop fronts and workers ambling along the footpaths, making their way home.

Marion kicks off her shoes and unpins her hair. 'We've had a really full day of sales. I've hardly had a break.'

'There must be a lot of ladies dressmaking at home, then.'

'Not just ladies, you know. We do have a few men who regularly buy from us as well.'

He chuckles. 'They make their own clobber?'

'And curtains and bedding. You'd be surprised whose hobbies include a little fancy work on the side. But my lips are sealed.' Marion pretends to sew her mouth shut.

'Not really my thing I'm afraid,' he shrugs, 'I'll gladly leave that to you women folk. I have more manly pursuits.'

'Like poetry?' Marion scoffs.

'Don't knock it. I'll have you know that nothing stirs the blood in us hearty blokes like a good dose of prose.'

'Better than a spoonful of castor oil, then?'

'Bloody oath.'

They turn into a narrow signposted road.

'Mt Marlay Lookout? 'I've been this way before,' Marion remarks.

Banjo grins. 'But not with me.'

'It's almost dark. We won't be able to see much.'

'Stop your whinging. Who said we were going to look at the view?'

She smiles and shakes her head. 'And I thought you were a nice boy.'

The truck labours uphill and winds its way to the summit,

stopping in the car park near the lookout. They remain seated inside and eat the hamburgers by the fading light.

Banjo glances at Marion. 'I have something for you.'

She wipes her mouth with the back of her hand. 'What, more food?'

He switches on the overhead light and reaches behind the seat, withdrawing a paper wrapped parcel. 'I saw these the other day and thought of you.'

Marion crumples up the hamburger wrapping and takes the parcel from him. She peels away the tissue paper to find two matching china dishes decorated in a colourful pattern of dainty flowers. 'Oh ... how sweet. Are they pin dishes?'

'I don't know. They just looked nice. Turn them over.'

She does so and reads the inscription. '"Apple Blossom by James Kent".'

'I thought they'd remind you of our picnic in the orchard.'

She beams. 'Of course, they do.'

'There's more,' he says, pointing.

Marion smooths out the tissue paper, holds it closer to the light. 'There's writing on one corner. Your apple blossom poem?'

'Well not mine, actually. I thought you'd like a copy.'

'It's lovely.' She stares down at her gifts. 'They're all lovely. Thank you.'

'You're welcome,' he smiles, pleased with himself.

As she carefully bundles up the pin dishes, he steps out of the truck and walks over to the railing at the edge of the lookout. Below, streetlights twinkle in the cooling air. The lit windows of houses lined up in strategic rows hint at life within.

'It looks like Fairyland, doesn't it?' says Marion, moving in her stockinged feet in front of him.

Banjo's arms surround her and she leans back against him. He feels the warmth of her body and the steady rise and fall of each breath taken. He's as happy as he's ever been.

'I could stay here forever,' she sighs, as if reading his mind.

'At the lookout?' he jokes.

'No, in your arms.'

He lifts his head and studies the night sky. 'Can you see Sputnik?'

She looks above. 'Is the satellite up there?'

'Somewhere, looping around for the zillionth time. Did you know it only takes about an hour and a half for it to orbit the earth?'

'My goodness, that's fast.'

'Yep. 18,000 miles per hour, so I read.'

'The Russians are pretty clever.'

'America won't be far behind. Just you wait, those Yanks will be shooting their own satellite up there in no time. Maybe even a rocket ship. Then the race will be on. Outer space is just begging to be discovered.'

She swivels around. 'You're very knowledgeable, aren't you?'

'I like to think I am,' he says, kissing the top of her head. Rising on her toes she offers her mouth and he takes it readily.

'Missed me today, did you?' she chuckles, reefing his shirt from his trousers and sliding her hands underneath.

It doesn't take much for his passion to be stirred. Clutching her by the arms, he shuffles Marion backwards until she bumps against the grill of the Dodge. In one swift movement, he lifts her onto the bonnet. She pulls up her skirt and wraps her legs around his waist.

He kisses her more deeply. His hands move to her breasts. Things have progressed somewhat since the day of the picnic, and he tries to move things along a little further. Sliding the fingers of one hand between the buttons of her blouse, they touch the cool satin within. Buttons ease from their holes, giving him more access. His fingers find the smoothness of her flesh and Marion arches back. Banjo kisses her throat, discovering her pulse throbbing against his lips matches his own heartbeat. He moans softly. He wants more.

His other hand slides up her leg until it reaches a suspender clasp. Skilfully, he unfastens it and then the others until he is able to peel the nylon down to her ankle. He squeezes Marion's bare thigh and his heart hammers in his ears. Her heels dig into his back, and he moves his fingers up to the lace edging of her underwear. She rasps his name and he lifts his head, and freezes. In the moonlight, he sees a trickle glisten and roll down her cheek.

'Don't,' she groans, 'please don't—'

Banjo reels back, slapped by an unseen hand. 'Oh God, I'm sorry ... I didn't mean to ...'

Marion slips from the bonnet, and wipes her eyes. 'Banjo ...' she gulps.

He tugs at his hair. 'I was moving too fast. I'm so sorry. I'm such a louse.' He walks around to the side of the truck.

She follows; grabs him by the shoulders. 'Banjo! Listen! I wasn't upset.'

He frowns. 'You weren't? But you told me to stop.'

She shakes her head. 'I was about to say, don't stop.'

Banjo's mouth gapes. 'Don't stop?'

She nods. 'I've never felt like this before, it's deep'. She takes his hand and presses it against her breast. 'Can't you feel it? You set me on fire.'

A staccato rhythm dances beneath his fingers. His breath eases with relief. 'I know what you mean. It's only been a few weeks, but I'm going crazy inside. I want you so much.'

'Me too,' she says.

He kisses the top of her head, her face. As their mouths meet, a sound of an engine startles them. Before they can break apart, they are caught in the headlights of a car as it reaches the summit.

Banjo stuffs his shirt back into his pants. Marion buttons her blouse.

The lights go out. A car door slams and footsteps approach.

'Nice night for it,' a deep voice says from behind the burning tip of a cigarette.

Banjo stops himself from uttering, 'You got that right, mate,' as the man passes, heading for the lookout.

Marion scrambles in the dirt, searching for her stocking.

'C'mon,' Banjo says, peeling it off the grill where it was caught and handing it to her. 'I had better get you home before your father thinks you've scarpered.'

The truck pulls up outside the Duff's property. Banjo opens his door. 'I'll walk you down.'

'No,' Marion protests, 'I'll be okay.'

'It's pretty dark.'

'It's just down the drive. I'm not a little girl, you know.'

'That's a fact,' he laughs, and then adds in a more serious tone, 'You don't want your father to know you were out with me, do you?'

She remains silent.

'We'll have to tell him sometime.'

She clutches his arm. 'Not tonight. I don't want to spoil our evening.'

'It's already been spoiled,' he grins, and pulls her close. 'Give me another cuddle before I head back to my lonely, old bed.'

She does, then hands him her stocking. 'Take this with you. A little keepsake.'

Banjo slips it into the pocket of his shirt. 'Nice. I'll add it to my collection.'

'Of stockings?'

'No, of things that belonged to Marion. I still have your hanky, remember.'

She smiles. 'That's right, you do. Well now you have something more personal. You can put it under your pillow and dream of me.'

'I don't need anything to help me dream of you. Hey, want to meet at the waterhole tomorrow afternoon? Around four o'clock? Swimwear optional,' he winks.

She gives him a quick kiss. 'I'll see what I can do.'

Collecting her belongings, she steps from the truck and hurries down the drive.

Banjo leaves when she disappears from view, hoping that the shadow moving near a hedgerow was just a trick of the moonlight.

15

I felt a little uneasy about staying home alone the next morning, so I dropped Elliott off at the bus stop in town and waited safely in my car outside the craft cottage until it opened. Walking inside, I found a tall, robust woman stacking shelves with jars of homemade jam, chutney, and relish. She was dressed in mauve and wore her grey hair short. I put her somewhere in her late seventies. She greeted me with a friendly, 'Good morning.'

'Beryl Erbacher?' I asked.

'That's me,' she smiled, her eyes crinkling behind large purple frames.

'My name's Abby Eaton. Do you mind if I ask you some historical questions?'

'Did you say historical or hysterical?' she chuckled. 'Sometimes they end up being the same thing.'

I followed as Beryl moved over to the serving counter. She went behind, took a seat on a stool, and eyed me with a confident what-I-don't-know-isn't-worth-knowing sort of look. 'Ok, fire away.'

I blinked, a little nervous under her inquisitive gaze. 'I'm looking for someone who may have lived in the area quite a while ago. I think his name was Patterson, Banjo Patterson.'

Her eyes narrowed reptilian-like. I almost expected her to spit in my face for attempting to pull her leg. She cocked her head. 'Paterson? THE Banjo Paterson?'

'No, no. Not that one. Someone else by the same name. Maybe it was a nickname. I'm not sure. But this Patterson had two t's not one like the real Banjo Paterson.'

'Oh,' her brow furrowed, her lips pursed, and both eyes flickered.

That's it, I thought, I have her stumped—an unusual experience for Beryl, I presumed.

She finally cleared her throat. 'I ... er ... can't recall anyone by that surname, at least not from any of the well-known local families. What years would you be looking at?'

'I don't really know. Possibly the '50s. Around '57, '58 or thereabouts.'

'Hmm ...' Beryl dropped from her perch and disappeared from view.

I heard her fumbling around and leant forward for a better look, only to jerk back when a large, leather bound book was thumped onto the counter in front of me.

Beryl sprung back up, patting her hair into place. 'We had this book published about ten years ago. It's Shadow Creek's history— from the white man's point of view, anyway. No history worth knowing until the pioneers settled here, they used to say. I personally don't agree, but it's difficult researching indigenous tribes when there aren't any descendants living in these parts anymore.'

'I guess they were run off long ago,' I said.

'Some still lived around here in the early 1900s. My mother-in-law spoke of an old fellow she saw when she was a child. He lived in the caves up on Rosella Ridge.'

'Is that so? That's where I live.' Her strange expression caused me to add, 'Oh, not in the cave. In a house, on Rosella Ridge.'

'You'd know Tickle Bridge, then.'

I nodded. I drove over it every time I came and went.

'Above it there is a rocky escarpment, and if you look closely you'll see some clefts in the rock. That's where the cave is. The old fellow lived there for quite a time. My mother-in-law said she used to fear him. Though by all accounts, all he ever did was just sit up there on the rocks and watch people.'

'Probably wasn't very happy with all the changes going on.'

'I'm sure he wasn't. Maybe he was just passing through. I guess we'll never know.'

Beryl flicked the pages until she came to the rear of the book. Using a long-nailed finger, she skimmed an alphabetical list.

'Patterson, you say. No record here. But if he was just in town for a short time it may not have been listed. A lot of people came and went. Life wasn't always easy out here. Earlier on, during the Depression, there were a lot of itinerant workers happy just to stay long enough to earn a little cash.' She closed the book and peered over the rim of her glasses. 'I only moved here in 1964. Now the Erbachers, my in-laws, have been here since 1887. Let me ask someone who's lived here all his life.'

'Sure,' I said, preparing to take my leave.

'Stoney!' she yelled.

Startled, I knocked into a display of crocheted coat hangers. They landed every which way on the floor like a set of pick-up-sticks.

'You still back there?' Beryl shouted, as I squatted to retrieve the hangers. 'Can you come here a minute?'

A gruff voice swore from a distance.

Staring down at me from the counter, Beryl groaned. 'He's probably sneaking a ciggie. He knows I don't like folk smoking in here. It smells the place out and no one wants to buy craftwork reeking of cigarette smoke, do they now?'

I shook my head and stood to re-hang the hangers.

Strange noises came from a back room, and then an elderly man, sporting a vivid Tam O'Shanter cap and an impressively long moustache, entered through an internal door.

'What in God's name do you want me for this time, Beryl?' he growled. The flushed face exploded into a huge grin when his eyes clapped onto mine. His puffy cheeks rose high, swallowing two beady eyes. 'Oh, hello there,' he said sweetly, and sauntered over to join us. Strong scents of cigarette and pine air freshener followed in his wake.

'You've been smoking, haven't you, Stoney?' Beryl accused.

'Hell's-bloody-bells, I have not.' He looked highly offended. 'I told you, Beryl, I've given it up.'

'You're lying! I can smell the blessed stuff!'

'Never.' He gave me a wink. 'It must be my musky aftershave.'

Beryl pinched her nostrils together. 'Well I think it has passed its use-by date. It reeks.'

He gave a grunt. 'What did you want anyway, tearing me away from unpacking all those bibs and bobs?'

The only pack he'd been opening, I thought, would have contained finely cut tobacco rolled in paper.

'This is Abby Eaton,' Beryl said, with a flourish of her hand. 'She's trying to find someone who might have lived here in the 1950s. I thought you might know something.'

The likeable larrikin bowed graciously. 'Gladstone Maloney, at your service. Now which bludger are you looking for?'

'A man called Patterson,' I replied.

'Patterson ...' he fingered his yellow tinged moustache. 'In the '50s you say. I would've been a young buck then. First name?'

'Ban-jo?' I said with hesitation.

He let out a raucous laugh. 'Yeah that's a good one. Oh ... hang on a sec ... that rings a flamin' bell.'

'It could have been a nickname,' I urged.

'Well that's what I'm a-thinking. I worked at the timber mill for a while. There was a young bloke with that name, I'm sure if it. It gave us a bit of a chuckle.' He fingered his whiskers with both hands. 'Or was it Henry Lawson? Who wrote Waltzing Matilda?'

'Banjo,' I answered.

'Yeah, well that's what it was. He had a little dog we used to call his Matilda. Lovely dog it was ... a real bitser, but real smart. Used to do all sorts of tricks. Banjo ... that wasn't his real name.'

'What was it?'

'For the life of me, I can't remember. Beryl, have you still got some photos of the mill?'

'Of course I have. There's some in here.' Beryl re-opened the leather-bound book.

'See if you can find them. I know I'm in a couple.' He gave me another wink.

She flicked the pages until arriving at a section on the history of the Shadow Creek timber mill.

Old Stoney examined the pages of black and white photos. 'There ya go!' He spun the book around and pointed with nicotine stained fingers to a group of men standing in front of a large timber shed. 'There I am, that handsome devil there.'

I saw a stocky man with a mop of wild hair and a jaunty grin on his face. His moustache—though a more decent length—was still full and impressive. He was wearing a light-coloured shirt with sleeves rolled up. Across his broad chest was folded a pair of remarkably muscular arms. The other men posed similarly.

'There,' he moved his finger, 'that's the Banjo fellow on the end, if I'm not mistaken.'

I eagerly perused the line-up until I came to the last person on the right. My heart skipped more than a beat as the face of the handsome motorcyclist stared back at me. 'That's him!'

'Bloody ripper!' exclaimed Stoney, clapping his hands together.

Beryl just smiled, 'That's good news, then.'

I stroked the page. 'You bet. I can't believe it.'

'Well that was pretty easy,' Stoney grinned. 'Is he a relative?'

'No ... at least I don't think so. I'm sure he knew a relative of mine though.'

Stoney suddenly let out a whoop. Beryl and I both jumped about a metre in the air.

'Ben! That's his name! I remember now. Ben Patterson. His mother worked at the bakery. He'd bring pastries over for smoko and his dog would do tricks for pieces of cake. See, my brain's not pickled after all.'

'That's what you think,' Beryl hissed.

I was elated. Coming here was a good move. 'When was this photo taken?'

Beryl swung the book around and read the paragraph beneath. 'It says ... 1957.'

'That'd be right,' Stoney nodded. 'We had our photos taken around Christmas time, just before having a huge nosh up. We'd finish work early and they'd line us up for a snap before we stuffed ourselves silly. Oh ...' he patted his swollen belly, 'that brings back memories. They put on a mighty good spread in those days.' He leant over my arm to view the photo again. 'And they were top blokes. Jolly hard work all right, but by jingo we had some good times.'

'Does this Banjo ... Ben ... still live around here?'

Stoney shook his head. His Tam O'Shanter slipped backwards, but kept its balance. 'If I remember correctly, he only worked at the mill for a few years, and then pushed off. He probably moved to the big smoke like most young blokes did.'

'Is it possible to get a copy of this photo?' I asked Beryl.

'Certainly, we have a photocopier out the back. It comes in handy sometimes. Stoney, do you mind?'

'Your wish is my command, Beryl dear.' He took the opened book in his large hands and slow-marched back through the dark doorway as if carrying an ancient and precious item, like the Gutenberg Bible.

I was on a roll. 'I guess his parents would be long gone now. Is there any way I could find out some information on the family?'

'Well, I could look up some records for you.'

'Could you? That'd be great.' I hoped my chances were good. I wasn't ready to come to an abrupt halt in my search.

Stoney returned and handed me a sheet of paper. 'I had another squiz, but can't find him in any of the other photos. Must've been a shy one.'

'Thanks so much. If either of you remember anything else about him, or discover any leads, I'd appreciate it if you could give me a call.' I took two craft shop business cards from the holder on the counter, and wrote my name and mobile phone number on the back. Then I handed one to Beryl and the other to Stoney.

'I'll put my thinking cap on then,' he said, patting the tartan on his head, and shoving the card into his trouser pocket.

A clatter on the wooden floorboards, made us all look down.

A blue plastic lighter spun in circles at Stoney's feet.

'Well stuff me with the rough end of a pineapple. Will you get a load of that!' He quickly crouched to retrieve the incriminating evidence. Standing, and without flinching an eyelid, he stared at

Beryl. 'I've been looking for this jolly lighter for weeks. Ever since I gave up the dreaded tobacco.'

He was good, I thought. Very good.

Beryl grunted and snatched the history book from Stoney, giving him a glare that would bring snow to the Outback. Directing a sweet smile at me she said, 'Well Abby, I'll call you if I find anything.'

'So will I,' announced Stoney with a salute, before scurrying back into the antechamber, probably to light up another cigarette.

Before leaving, I bought a large jar of tomato relish.

Beryl leant forward to whisper, even though there was no one else present. 'I tell everyone the recipe was handed down to me by my grandmother, but between you and me and the gate post, I copied it from an old Shadow Creek Country Women's cook book.'

'The secret is safe with me,' I assured her.

'He looks familiar,' I said, studying the photocopied picture of the mill workers.

I'd bumped into Julie and we were grabbing a bite, alfresco, at Serendipi-teas before she went to work at the medical centre. Now that her toe was on the mend, she was returning for only an afternoon shift. I'd quickly brought her up to date with the necklace mystery.

'Of course he looks familiar,' she said, taking a mouthful of her Thai Beef Salad. 'Didn't you say he was the guy in the photograph you have at home? The guy with the motorbike?'

'I know that,' I said pointing my fork at her, 'I meant from somewhere else.'

'He was pretty cute, wasn't he?'

'Yeah,' I grinned, 'the best of this bunch.'

I viewed the line-up once more. All these faces. Some sun-tanned and well worn, others fresh and eager. What dreams had these men had? Did their lives pan out as they'd hoped? Were they still alive? I knew one rascal was for sure, and hoped we'd soon discover that this Ben Patterson hadn't yet kicked the proverbial bucket.

Unearthing Marion's story was like viewing an image through a telescope—with each new discovery, her likeness became clearer. Though she was still far from being in focus.

Julie pushed back her plate and wiped her mouth with a serviette. 'Do you think this guy, Ben alias Banjo, is the one your cousin Marion was engaged to?'

'That's what I'm hoping. I'm going to contact my mum and see if she recognises the name.'

My mobile rang. I was surprised and excited to discover that it was Beryl who was calling. Unfortunately, she didn't have any productive news, but I thanked her all the same.

'Well, c'mon,' said Julie, eyes wide with anticipation, 'what did she say?'

'Not a great lot. According to the electoral rolls there wasn't ever a Patterson registered out here, and school enrolment archives say no Patterson kids ever went to the local school. Even cemetery records don't list anyone by that name for Shadow Creek.' I took a long slurp of my iced coffee.

Julie suddenly nudged my elbow.

Coffee coloured froth leapt from my glass and onto my white linen shirt. 'What the hell!' I cried.

She pointed over my shoulder. 'There he is!'

I spun around. All I could see was a black 4WD passing by. Emblazoned on the side were the words 'Schilling Real Estate' with a cheesy photo of Lester. 'You mean Lester?'

'No. Over at the new restaurant.'

I squinted, catching only the back of a tall young man with dark hair before he disappeared through the front entrance of the building.

'Oh, you missed him,' she whined.

'Who?'

'The guy from the new place.'

I hadn't seen anyone connected with the new restaurant, other than some local handymen. 'And how do you know him, pray tell?'

Julie sat back in her chair, crossed her arms. 'I've seen him around town. At the grocery store ... the fruit shop ... the post office.'

'What's his name?'

'I don't know,' she shrugged, 'I haven't spoken to him.'

'Okay, you're a stalker. What would Graeme have to say about that?'

'I'm not. It's just hard not to notice someone who looks like Kit Harington.'

I leant forward over the remains of my frittata. 'Who?'

She rolled her eyes in the same way my kids did when exasperated over my lack of knowledge of what was on-trend. 'Geez Abby, you know, he plays Jon Snow in Game of Thrones.'

'Oh ... him. Really?' I turned again, hoping to catch another glimpse. 'Well, in that case he'll surely give these country boys a run for their money.'

'Sure will.' She gave a sigh. 'If only I were twenty years younger.'

'Yeah ... same here.' I used a serviette to pat the froth from my shirt, only to leave a brownish smear over the linen. 'Anyway, back to my dilemma.'

'I guess you're feeling like you're struggling with a jigsaw puzzle that has pieces missing from the box.'

I was impressed with her insight. 'Absolutely!'

'I have an idea that might help you sort things out.'

'Great. Out with it.'

She gulped down the last of her mochaccino. 'An investigation board.'

I screwed my face up. 'A what?'

There was that eye roll again. 'You've watched crime shows. You know the board on the wall they use for police briefings, with photos and information regarding the investigation pinned to it.'

'Oh ... right.'

'Give that a go. It might help you arrange your thoughts.' She checked her watch. 'Must away.'

Julie pushed herself up from the table, being careful not to bump her recovering toe. As she hobbled off, I held up the picture of the mill workers and stared into the eyes of the man at the end of the row on the right.

If this was around Christmas 1957, then it must have been taken a few weeks before the train crash. Sadness washed over me. If he and Marion had been as close as I presumed they were, how had her death affected him? Had those smiling eyes eventually turned to another ... or had they grown hollow with grief, leading him to become a bitter, resentful man?

I now realised that my quest was not just about the necklace, or Marion, but the fateful entwining of two lives. I had to find out what had happened to Ben Patterson. I also needed to prove to myself that I was competent at something.

16

Stanthorpe 1957

M arion's heart thumps hard in her chest. 'Dad! You scared me.'

Owen Douglas bends to collect the coat he'd just dropped on the dirt. 'Well, you startled me. What have you been up to?'

'I could ask the same of you, lurking in the dark like that.'

'I had a meeting at the Duffs.'

'This late in the day?' Marion follows him up the porch steps. 'Where's Mum?'

'She's inside, where you should be. How'd you get home?'

'I got a lift with a friend.'

'And which friend would that be now?' he asks gruffly.

Though the porch light is dim, she is aware of her father's eyes boring into hers. Knowing full well what his reaction will be, she steels herself and answers truthfully. 'Ben Patterson.'

She is surprised when her father's only response is a calm nod of his head. This is not like him at all. She was expecting a tirade, or at least a sign of disapproval at spending time with someone other than Donald. Her hopes rise. Maybe he is softening. Then she sees it; the clench of his jaw, the flaring of his nostrils. They remind her of a bull preparing to charge. She cringes, readies for an attack. But it still does not come, which is even more disturbing.

'It's rather late,' he says stiffly, 'I guess you've already had dinner.'

She nods and moves towards the front door.

He steps in her way. 'Then you've either been working back, or didn't come straight home.'

Marion's heart picks up speed. She swallows hard.

'Judging by the evidence, I would say it was the latter.'

Following his gaze, she notices her blouse is untucked and her buttons have been fed into the wrong holes. Also visible is a leg minus a stocking. She holds her breath as he leans closer, his face just inches from hers.

'What else did you remove for his benefit?'

'Dad, I need to tell you—'

He holds up a hand. 'Don't tell me the sordid details! I just want this nonsense to stop!'

'It's not what you think.'

'You'll ruin everything!' he hisses. Drops of moisture land on her cheek. 'You've had your bit of fun, now finish it. Think of us. Think of the Duffs.'

She wipes the spit away. 'The Duffs?'

'You wouldn't want them finding out what you've been up to, would you?'

'I don't know what you mean? What have they got to do with anything?'

He drapes his coat over the railing, paces the porch. 'We'll have to get you and Donald engaged as soon as possible. That's what we'll do. I'll go see him tomorrow. We'll meet with his parents and make arrangements. Katherine and your mother will be thrilled. They'll be all a-flutter with planning the wedding.'

Marion clutches his arm. 'But I've told you, I don't want to marry Donald.'

'Oh, you will,' he sneers.

'I will not!' she cries, not the least bit concerned at how easily her voice carries in the night's stillness. 'I want Banjo!'

Her father's head tilts. His eyes narrow. 'Who?'

'Ben!' she shouts, stamping her feet like she'd done so many times as a child when quarrelling with her father. 'Ben Patterson!'

A slap sends her reeling and knocking into a wicker plant stand. The potted plant overturns. Her handbag slips from her wrist and tumbles to the floorboards spewing out its contents. She hears the tinkle of broken china and rights herself, but her father is in her face again.

'You will have nothing to do with that Abo! Do you hear me?'

Marion holds her hand to her stinging cheek. 'What did you say?'

Her father gives a smirk, and her nerves squirm like worms beneath her skin. 'He hasn't mentioned that, has he?'

'I don't understand,' she says, squinting through a haze of pain.

He laughs. 'Oh... so he hasn't told you he's a boong?'

'Banjo's Aboriginal? No, that's ridiculous. You've got it wrong. His mother's Martin Baxter's sister.'

'And his father? What do you know about him?'

She recalls the conversation at the waterhole; the Rats of Tobruk. 'He was a soldier. He served in the Middle East with Martin.'

'We had Abo soldiers there too, didn't you know? Better to use them as cannon fodder than our good white boys.'

Marion gasps.

Bulging eyes glare into hers. 'I guess he didn't tell you he's also a bastard.'

Her chest crushes in on itself. Was her father goading her for his own sick pleasure?

'What a catch, hey. A lying, black bastard. What do you think of that?'

She holds her head, tries to stop the whirling inside. Her father's making it all up. It can't be true. Banjo would have told her.

Her arms are seized. She is shaken like a toy in a dog's mouth.

'Come to your senses, girl! He's no good!'

Marion is too stunned to fight back. Her body slackens. Her father's grip strengthens and the ache throbs down her arms to her wrists. 'How do you know this?' she groans.

'I saw how googly-eyed you were with him. It was my duty to ask around, get some background on this young upstart. It seems he's not a patch on Donald.'

'I don't care about bloody Donald, I've told you that!'

'How dare you defy me!' He shakes her again. 'You will have nothing to do with that dirty mongrel! Do you hear me? Do you?'

His screech reminds Marion of a barn owl in search of prey. Her father has found his, and it is her.

'Owen!' A thin voice calls from inside the cottage. 'What's all that racket?'

He releases his hold and Marion slips to her knees. 'It's okay, Ruth,' he replies cordially, 'nothing to worry about.' Then placing a thumb under Marion's chin, he lifts her head, forcing her to look him in the eye. 'Do as I say,' he snarls, 'or there'll be hell to pay.'

Retrieving his coat, he opens the door, slamming it behind him as he enters the cottage.

Slumping sideways, Marion pulls her knees to her chest and sobs.

17

Stanthorpe 1957

The floorboards creak even though Banjo is trying hard to walk lightly through the farm house. It is only nine o'clock, yet his uncle and aunt are already in bed. 5:00 am starts are usual on a working farm and they would be fast asleep by now. He opens his bedroom door and almost loses his balance as he slips on the small mat guarding the entrance, one of many that Aunt Gina has positioned outside each room. Floor polishing must have been one of her many chores today, he surmises.

His bedside lamp has once again been left on, and the chenille bed cover and starched white top sheet have been turned down. His newly pressed pyjamas lay neatly on top of the pillow, which Banjo considers a waste seeing he prefers to sleep with hardly a stitch on. Though he isn't about to inform his aunt of this fact because, firstly, she'd probably hyperventilate with shock, and secondly because she likes to fuss whenever he stays and he secretly enjoys it.

He kicks off his shoes, untucks his shirt, and removes Marion's stocking from his breast pocket. Holding the sheer nylon up to his face he breathes in her scent. Maybe tomorrow at the waterhole they could continue where they left off. He imagines Marion in her wet swimsuit and the joy of peeling her out of it. Excitement stirs. He shoves the stocking under his pillow. A growl from his stomach tells him he is peckish. A cup of tea and, if good luck prevails, a sample of home baking should do the trick.

He deftly heads back to the kitchen. Lighting the gas stove, he places the well-used kettle over the blue flame and searches within the containers lined up along the bench. He is indeed fortunate. Jam tarts, Anzac biscuits and melting moments are available for the taking. He chooses one of each and turns the gas off just before the kettle screeches. Scooping tea into the pot, he hears a shuffling noise and glances over his shoulder. Uncle Marty is blinking in the bright light. His grey hair and pyjamas are both in disarray.

'Hey there, sleeping beauty,' Banjo jibes, 'did I wake you?'

'Not sure. It was either you fumbling around out here like a blind monkey or Gina's ravioli. I have an inkling she was a tad heavy-handed with the garlic tonight.'

'Feeling a bit crook then?'

'Yeah, not real flash.'

'Want a cuppa?' Banjo takes two cups down from a shelf and pours hot water into the teapot.

'Maybe, after I have a glass of Eno,' his uncle says, removing the lid from the wide mouthed bottle of antacid powder, and mixing a teaspoon of it into a glass of water. He waits until it fizzes then gulps down the lively liquid. A satisfying belch soon follows.

Banjo moves the teapot and cups to the table. Taking a jug of milk from the refrigerator, he sits and stuffs a whole jam tart into his mouth.

'I see you found the stash of goodies,' says Marty, pulling out a chair.

Banjo offers up one of the baked delights.

'No mate, don't want to upset the guts any further.' Marty pats his flat stomach and burps again.

Banjo marvels at the trimness of a man married to such a zealous cook. Hard work has its advantages.

'Been out on the town with the blokes, have you?' his uncle says, pouring himself a cup of tea.

Banjo nods. 'I've been out, but definitely not with the fellas.'

'A young lady, then. And may I fathom a guess which one?'

Banjo raises his eyebrows.

'That cute little Douglas lass,' Marty grins.

'Her name's Marion.'

'Taken a bit of a shine to her, have you?'

'Yep. I guess you could say I'm smitten.'

'Wacky doo.' His uncle reaches for an Anzac biscuit and takes a bite. 'Can I give you some careful advice?'

Banjo shakes his head, 'Please Uncle Marty, you're not going to launch into another birds and bees talk, are you? Give me some credit.'

'Good God no! It was hard enough the first time, if I remember rightly. That's when I found out you knew more about it than I did.' He chuckles, then adds more sternly, 'I'm serious. Be careful. Owen Douglas can get as mad as a cut snake if you rub him up the wrong way. He's not known for his sweet nature, that's for sure.'

Banjo sticks out his jaw. 'I can handle him.'

'I hope you're right.' Marty licks crumbs from his fingers. 'Anyway, she seems a nice sort of a girl. Right soothing to the eye.'

'So, you've noticed, you dirty old codger.'

'Hey, I can still pick out a good filly. It doesn't mean I'm interested in putting in a bid though.'

'I hope not!'

Marty grins, 'You're Aunt's plenty enough woman for me, I can tell you.'

Banjo holds up both hands, 'Please, no! I don't want any scary stories before bedtime.'

His uncle reaches over and musses up Banjo's hair. 'Cheeky bugger. Anyhow, I'm back off to bed.' He drains his cup and pushes up from his chair. 'See ya at the crack of dawn, young fella.'

As his uncle pads off towards the main bedroom, Banjo hears a stumble followed by cursing. He smiles. A floor mat almost claimed a victim. Pouring himself a cup, he lingers long enough to imagine knocking Marion's father down to size.

18

Driving home on autopilot—yet with an unconscious ability to manoeuvre the many sharp bends hugging the mountainside—I snapped out of my daydream when I reached Tickle Bridge.

Officially known as Private Arthur Tickle Bridge, it had been named in the memory of the eldest son of a farming family who had lost his life in the Battle of the Somme. The small bridge spanned a stream that trickled down a watercourse from the ridge. Insignificant as it seemed, this man-made structure came into its own during times of rain when the wash became a waterfall. Cascading into a ravine further below, it is joined by other streams to form Shadow Creek.

As I passed over, I glanced above. Beryl's story of the lone Aboriginal man and the cave intrigued me. Curious as to where this might have been, I pulled over on the shoulder and studied the escarpment.

Steep grassy slopes, wind-blown bushes leaning at awkward angles, and perilous cliff faces brought to mind Charlotte Bronte's classic tale, and it was easy to imagine Cathy and Heathcliff scurrying lovelorn around the boulders scattered over the hillside. Sharp rocky outcrops high up revealed shadowy crevices. From my position in the car it was difficult to ascertain whether these harboured deep caves or not, so I decided to take a closer look.

Leaving the car, I crossed the quiet road with ease. Then carefully threading myself between strands of rusted barbed wire and jumping a narrow stream, began my ascent. Spiky grass, prickly castor oil plants, and clinging cobbler's pegs hindered my progress, yet I was determined to find the cave. Normally, I have a fear of heights, but the undulating slope gave me a false sense of security. It was only when I was halfway, and stopped to catch my breath, that I saw how far up I was. My head swam. I redirected my attention to my legs, rubbing muscles that burned from not being quite as young, fit, and carefree as those wild Yorkshire lovers.

The sound of a labouring engine forced me look back down to the road to see a weathered grey Holden ute round the bend and struggle with the incline. Was this the same ute as the one I'd seen the other day puttering uphill behind me? It groaned and spluttered and eventually came to a halt just before the bridge. An elbow leant out of the driver's open window, followed soon after by a hat-covered head. The wide brim tilted as the driver looked upwards. The face was in shadow, but I knew I'd been spotted on the hill. I gave a little wave, expecting the driver to do the same. But no, he just stared—or at least that's what I guessed he was doing. I gave a 'thumbs up' in case he thought I was in trouble.

When no acknowledgement came, I felt uncomfortably exposed. Searching the view for a sign of oncoming traffic, I willed someone to come hurtling around the bend to defuse the unsettling situation. If it was the weekend, the road would have been busy with day-trippers and cyclists and death-defying motorbikes, but not this day. No one appeared. It was just me and the strange driver out here in the wilds.

I peered above and wondered if I should resume climbing; find refuge in one of those clefts. Then again, the scrub leading up to them looked thicker and more difficult to tackle, and if the man decided to leap from his ute and follow my ascent, he might reach me before I found safety. He might even know where the cave was; an ideal place to hold a person captive. Horrible thoughts sprang to mind of what could be done by an abductor fuelled by evil intent.

I looked below. It would be better to head back down and make a run for my car. But what if the man jumped from his ute and got there before I did, or even worse, tried to run me over? I searched the pockets of my skirt. Damn, why did I leave my phone in the car? I decided to stay where I was. Two could play at this game.

A cicada chorus started up. A hot breeze blew. Dry grass whipped against my legs and sweat dripped down my face. This was ridiculous, yet I wasn't going to be the first to give in. A winged insect of unknown origin landed on my knee, and proceeded to crawl up and under my skirt. I whacked at it and it stung me with its last burst of energy before dying. I lifted the skirt to check on the bite, then dropped it again when I realized I might be showing too much flesh for the driver in the ute. This was humiliating. I studied the ground for a suitable weapon amongst the sticks and stones. A weighty branch could prove helpful, or a sharp wedge of rock. Even a boulder would be useful if I had the muscle to unearth one and send it rolling downward to knock my attacker off his feet.

I was saved from putting my ingenuity into action by the arrival of a miracle in the form of Graeme Roper, Julie's husband. His blue Yamaha motorbike heralded its arrival with a deep-throated rumble moments before it tore around the bend. The sight of him was a huge relief, especially when he skidded to a stop next to my car.

Graeme has a solid build. He wears leather, has a shaved head, an unruly beard, and both arms covered in tatts. He looks just like a member of a biker gang—which he was, until he exchanged his colours for a master's degree in Theology and Philosophy. Wisely he'd dropped the nickname Groper before accepting the position as the minister of Shadow Creek Community Church.

He removed his helmet and peered through the window of my VW. Then he looked up and down the road. Stepping from his bike, he took a couple of strides towards the ute. It suddenly spluttered into life, made a U turn, and then rattled back the way it had come. Graeme pulled at his beard and changed direction, ambling back towards my car. I shouted his name. He twisted around, glanced up, and spotted me standing like a sentinel amongst the spinifex.

He cupped his hands to his mouth. 'What are you doing up there?' he yelled.

'Looking for a cave!' came my reply.

He cocked his bald head. 'Need any help?'

'Not now!' I answered, starting my descent.

He waited patiently as I made my way back down the hill, forded the stream, straddled the barbed wire fence, and rushed over.

'Thank God ... you arrived ... when you did!' I panted, giving him a hug. He was so tall and so wide it was like embracing an ogre—minus the green tinge and funny ears.

'What's this about a cave? Were you looking for somewhere to hibernate or something?'

I slapped a solid arm. 'Don't be rude. I heard a story about an old Aboriginal guy living in a cave up there somewhere and decided to check it out.'

He scanned the hillside. 'Is he still there?'

'I hope not. He'd be about 150 years old if he was. Anyway, thanks for coming to my aid. That creepy guy had been watching me for ages.'

'The guy in the old EH Holden ute?' Graeme nodded towards the bend in the road. 'Maybe he was just wondering what a lone female was doing scaling the heights without a guide rope.'

'Nah ... he was perving for sure.'

Graeme laughed, which I found a little annoying. 'Whatever. Glad I was of service. So, Abbs, what did you think of Shane's latest acquisition?'

I scowled. Bloody hell! Was I the only one who hadn't known about the bike? 'Let's just say I was not impressed.'

Now it was Graeme's turn to pull a face. 'Why not? I thought it was cool. I helped him pick it out.'

'Of course you did,' I said, eyeing his Yamaha gleaming in the sunlight. 'What were you thinking? Shane hasn't even got a licence?'

'A licence? Why would he need a licence?'

'Well he can't legally ride a motorbike in Australia without one, can he.'

'A motorbike?'

'Yes, a motorbike.' My scowl turned into a frown. 'That Yamaha V Star ... or whatever it was.'

Graeme's jaw dropped. 'Shane's bought a V Star 650?'

I nodded. 'Isn't that what we're talking about?'

He shook his head, then scratched his thick neck. 'Sweet! I can't believe Shane's finally lashed out on a bike. He's talked about it, and now he's gone and done it. Good on him.'

'No, not good on him!' I growled, stamping a foot in the gravel.

'He spent our holiday savings on a friggin' toy for himself! How selfish is that? I was fuming when he told me … still fuming. Now he's scarpered off and doing God-knows-what while I'm having to hold the fort and deal with all sorts of dramas on my own.' I counted them off on my fingers. 'A love-struck daughter, a son involved in an illegal activity, a mysterious morning visitor, rabid dogs, and now a pervy stranger. Oh … as well as having my job whipped out from under me.' I kicked a large stone at my feet and sent it flying, only to see it hit the side of my car with a loud 'ping' and leave a dent in the rear panel.

I doubled over, hands on knees, feeling ready to explode … or at least vomit.

Graeme's hand was on my shoulder. 'Take deep breaths, Abbs. Breathe in … breathe out. Seems like you've got a lot on your plate right now.'

I slowly straightened. 'Yeah, I sure have.'

'How can I help?'

I tilted my head back to stare into his eyes. He was serious. 'You can contact Shane and tell him to contact me. He's not answering my calls. Not properly, anyway.'

'Sure,' he nodded. 'I'll do what I can. What are you doing now? More mountain climbing?' He was grinning.

'No way, I'm off home. Bugger the cave. It can stay in folklore for all I care. Where are you headed?'

'Was just out for a spin.' He eyed the road further up. 'Might visit a parishioner.'

'One that offers afternoon tea, I bet.'

'Well,' he tugged his beard, 'it'd be rude to knock it back, wouldn't it?'

He swung his leg over his bike and turned the key in the ignition. The bike purred seductively. 'You sure you're okay, Abbs? Don't need another hug?'

I gave a weak smile. 'I'm fine ... now.'

'Good.' He dropped his visor, and waited while I opened my car door and stepped in.

He and his Yamaha had disappeared uphill before I'd even fastened my seat belt. I checked the rear-view mirror before gripping the steering wheel and easing away from the verge. It'd just be my luck to drive into the path of some lunatic zipping around that bend and be charged with causing a serious accident.

As I continued my drive home, I replayed my conversation with Graeme. What did he mean by 'Shane's latest acquisition' if it wasn't the bike? I added this concern to all the others weighing me down.

19

Stanthorpe 1957

The Soldiers Memorial stands on a hill, amongst granite boulders—a lone watchman guarding the rugged park below and the avenue of pine trees leading to the street. Unveiled just over thirty years ago to celebrate the end of The Great War, the white-painted pavilion is visible from several locations around the township of Stanthorpe. On this hot Saturday, its concrete walls reflect the brilliance of the midday sun, while in contrast, the arched windows and entryways reveal the shady protection within. Townsfolk and visitors venture up here to take shelter, or to ponder the bravery of those who served and died in both world wars. Though for Banjo, his purpose in being here this day is for an entirely different reason.

Perched on the cement steps below the ornately gabled roof marked with '1914-1919' in raised lettering, he rubs sweaty palms over trousered thighs, and takes shallow, nervous breaths. The strong scent of pine fills the humid air, yet he hardly notices.

Kicking a brittle cone at his feet, his mind races backwards and forwards, recalling the confusing events of the last few days. Just when he thought their relationship was blossoming into something tangible, a wall has suddenly risen between him and Marion. Her unexplainable avoidance has become obvious and he needs answers.

He first noticed something wasn't quite right when Marion failed to meet him at the waterhole the day after their visit to Mt Marlay Lookout. He'd waited for her until the sun had dropped behind the trees and the cool of dusk began to fall. Putting her non-appearance down to a busy afternoon at the drapery store, he'd forced his worries aside. Then the following day, as he, Mal and Tony quenched their thirst at the Commercial Hotel, he saw Marion pass by. He was sure she'd heard him call her name through the open window, yet she'd hurried across Maryland Street without glancing back. He'd tried to catch her at the store before heading back home, but Lucy told him Marion was busy ordering stock and couldn't be disturbed.

A similar incident happened this morning when he'd intentionally walked past the store, glanced through the display window, and saw her serving a customer. She'd averted her attention from the length of material she was measuring and their eyes had met. Rather than giving a smile, Marion had quickly retreated to the rear of the store, leaving the woman alone and bewildered at the counter. Frustrated by this strange behaviour, Banjo had entered the shop and given Lucy a message to pass on, requesting that Marion meet him at the memorial after work to give him the courtesy of an explanation for her actions.

Now he sits—his stomach in knots—hoping Marion will show up.

A crunch of pine needles. The clip of heels on pressed earth.

He looks up. Relief turns to despair when he sees her

expressionless face. Brushing past, she hurries up the steps into the darkness of the alcove. He quickly follows.

'What in God's name is going on, Marion? Have I done something wrong?'

She moves to an arched window flanked by brass plaques bearing names of fallen soldiers. Balancing her handbag on the ledge, she faces him. 'I couldn't tell.'

He steps closer. 'Couldn't tell what?'

The scar on Marion's forehead buckles in on itself as she frowns. 'I thought you had Italian in you. Or something Mediterranean, at least.' She wrings her hands. Her eyes dart around the vestibule. 'Maybe even Greek ... or Spanish. I met someone from Barcelona once. You look a little like him, he had—'

He clutches her arm. 'What the hell are you talking about?'

She pulls her arm free. Her eyes fix on him. They remain steady; studying, examining.

Banjo looks away. The backdrop behind Marion is darkening. The sky has clouded over and a distant rumble hints that a storm is imminent. The hairs on Banjo's arms stiffen.

Marion releases a sigh. 'How much?'

He drops his gaze back to her. 'What do you mean, how much?'

'You know. How much ... are you?'

His innards twist painfully. 'How much Abo blood do I have? Is that what you're asking?' He knew this day would come but he'd imagined he would be the one to inform her, not answer questions in an interrogation. 'I also have Irish, Welsh and a bit of Dutch thrown in too, but no one cares about those, just the black bits.' Rage stirs. He forces it down, stops it from rising. 'Why the bloody hell can't we just accept everyone as people first?'

Marion chews on a lip, looks at her feet.

'Who told you?' he asks.

She raises her head. He sees her swallow hard. 'My father.'

'Of course! And what else did he tell you? That I'm a bastard? Is that what he said? I bet he enjoyed telling you that.'

She flinches.

'Well it's true,' he says with resignation, 'all of it.'

A sudden gust of wind whips through the alcove. There comes a 'bang' followed by a 'clatter' as a pine cone hits the roof and then rolls.

Marion holds her billowing skirt down. Her hair dances around her face. 'How did it happen?'

'What?'

'With your parents. How did they ... you know?'

He laughs, though not from mirth. 'It wasn't rape, if that's what you're thinking. He wanted her. She wanted him. A moment of desire and whacko, there I was.'

'Why didn't they marry?'

'Marry?' Banjo gives another derisive chuckle. He takes a seat on a slatted bench under an opposite window arch, and leans back against the hard cement wall. 'Are you really that thick in the head? A mixed-race marriage back then was even less encouraged than it is now. Mum's parents threatened to bring charges against my father. Her mother even offered to help get rid of the mistake. A hot bath and a knitting needle, I believe, was suggested. Or was it a shove down the stairs? I can't remember.'

Marion claps a hand to her mouth. Her eyes widen.

'My parents took off. Moved from one place to another until Dad joined up to serve this mighty country of ours.'

A clash of thunder startles them.

Marion comes closer, her voice trembling. 'Why didn't you tell me all this before? Why did you lie to me?'

'I didn't lie,' he snaps.

'Well you kept it from me. That's as good as lying.'

He shrugs. 'I don't agree.'

Her hands go to her hips. A scowl hardens her face, and he notices beads of sweat lining her top lip. The rage he witnessed at their first meeting in the orchard has returned, though now it is directed at him.

'What kind of relationship doesn't have honesty?' she snarls. 'How can I trust someone who doesn't tell the truth!'

Banjo hears the shower of rain making its approach over the rocky terrain. He inhales the earthy scent of wet dirt that normally brings with it a promise of regeneration; not today though, it is more like an ill omen. He returns his attention to the fired-up woman in front of him. He used to like that about her—the fervour, the determination—now it causes a bitter taste to form in his mouth.

'Maybe I was unsure of how you'd react. It's obvious now what you think.'

Marion shoots back, 'And what is that?'

He's seen it before, in plenty of other faces—judgment, intolerance—and he hates it with a passion. 'You're just like your father. A self-righteous prig.'

Her mouth falls open. 'How dare you! You don't know me at all.'

'Is that right?' He springs to his feet. 'I think I know you better than you know yourself.' He shortens the distance between them; bends down, smells the fragrance of roses on her skin. 'Tell me the truth, Marion. If you'd known I had blackfella in me, would you've come after me the way you did?'

She blinks. Frowns.

Her hesitation gives Banjo the answer he expected, yet also feared. He grasps her by the shoulders and shuffles her backwards until her body slams against cement. Air is forced from her lungs. She wheezes, yet he keeps her pinioned.

'Would you've let my black hands touch you if you'd known?' he growls. Marion squirms, kicks out. His fingers bite into her flesh. 'How about my black mouth on yours?'

She glares up at him and his heartbeat drums in his ears. Even in anger she is beautiful. He yearns to show her how much she means to him, how much he needs her in his life. Desire surfaces. He could so easily make love to her, right here in the pavilion while a storm rumbles overhead. He covers her mouth with his. Crushing his body into hers, he feels the prod of her breasts against his chest, the scratch of her fingernails down his arms. A moan bubbles from his throat. It is swiftly followed by a yelp as her teeth clamp onto his tongue.

He pulls away, tasting blood. Marion shoves past.

He spins around and finds her pressed against a brass plaque on the opposite wall, her face pale, her hands shaking.

'You're wrong!' she yells above the racket of heavy drops battering the roof like bullets hitting their mark. 'You are the one who is like my father!'

Banjo spits out red, wipes his mouth on a sleeve. 'Me? I'm not the one who's prejudiced! That'd be you Marion!'

Tears stream from her eyes. 'You're a brute, just like him!'

His head snaps back, repulsed at being compared to Owen Douglas.

Another crack of thunder and the rain falls in a torrent, the crescendo matching the intensity inside the cement structure. Water sprays in through every opening.

Banjo rushes towards Marion.

She cringes and holds up her hands, warding him off. 'I ... I loved you Banjo. I really did.' Her eyes never leave his as she sidles over to the window ledge. 'It was a mistake, you and I; a big one. I wish we'd never met.'

The stab of pain in his heart could just as well have come from the thrust of a bayonet. He watches in disbelief as Marion retrieves her handbag and slips out of the alcove. Scurrying down the steps, she disappears behind a sheet of thundering grey.

He turns away and catches sight of a paper bag resting on the ledge. Lunging for it, the soggy bag tears open. In his hand lay shards of a broken floral pin dish. He smashes a fist into concrete and falls onto a bench seat. The throb of injured fingers is nothing compared to the ache within his chest.

20

I took a step back and viewed the wall in the loft—the one that, until an hour ago, held a framed collage of family photos. It was now blue-tacked with photos and sheets of printed paper linked together by lengths of coloured twine, successfully resembling an investigation board at a police briefing.

Elliott appeared at the top of the stairs, a bowl and fork in his hands. 'I made my own dinner. Couldn't wait any longer.'

'Two-minute noodles?'

'Yep,' he nodded. 'Woah ... what's this?' He moved over to the wall.

'Well, to aid my investigations, I've laid out what I know so far to see if it makes any sense.'

'Looks impressive.'

The top row included photos of Marion: one with her parents; another of her in a swimsuit; and the one taken outside the cottage wearing the pendant necklace. The row below had the Apple Blossom poem—now safely contained in a plastic zip lock bag—and the necklace hanging from a picture hook. Beneath these, on the third row, were two photos of Ben Patterson—one of him on the motorbike at the cottage, and another with the line-up of mill workers.

I motioned for Elliott to take a seat on the sofa. 'You can help.' Using a plastic ruler, I pointed to the photographs of Marion. 'What do we know about her? No suppositions now.'

He lounged back, settling himself amongst the cushions. 'She was Nana's cousin. Your second cousin and my third.'

'Yes, born in 1938 in Brisbane.' I tapped the photo of Marion's parents, 'Daughter of Owen and Ruth Douglas. What else?'

'She died in a train crash in ...' He gave shrug.

'January 1958.'

'On her way to Shadow Creek,' he added.

'A presumption, but I'll let that one go. Why was she taking the trip?'

'To meet with him.' Elliott pointed towards the photo of Ben sitting on the motorbike.

'Hang on,' I wagged a finger, 'now that's a supposition. A good one though, I must admit.' I moved over to the poem. 'Now, what do we know about this?'

'It's part of a poem about apple blossoms. It was scribbled on paper most probably by Benny boy, and was hidden inside a china heart pendant most likely worn by her.' He indicated the photo of Marion leaning against the cottage railing.

'And we know he gave her the poem because his name is on the back of the paper,' I confirmed. 'What else do we know about him?'

He finished a mouthful of noodles before speaking. 'Well, according to what you told me earlier, Ben Patterson, aka Banjo, lived in Shadow Creek for a time and worked at the timber mill.'

'Right, and this was proven by one Gladstone Maloney.'

'And to back this up, we also have hard copy evidence,' he nodded towards the photo of the men at the timber mill.

'We also have proof that Marion and Ben/Banjo spent time together, as seen by the photos from 1957.' I pointed to the two photos taken outside the cottage. 'Where this meeting took place we don't know as, prior to her death, Marion was known to be living in Stanthorpe with her parents.'

Elliott leant forward, raised his eyebrows, and stabbed his fork in the air. 'I'm guessing those photos outside the cottage were taken near Shadow Creek.'

I scowled. 'Really?'

'Maybe that was where they met.'

'Shadow Creek? How? What brought her here? I wish there were some relatives still alive who could tell us.'

'Marion was engaged to some dude before she died, right? Who was her fiancé then, Banjo?'

'Probably,' I answered, plonking myself alongside Elliott. 'There were no other photos of young men in her collection, so it makes sense to believe he was. Though there's the problem that no one seemed to know why she was taking a train to Shadow Creek. If he was her fiancé and lived out here, then the family would know why she was travelling to Shadow Creek.'

'Maybe people didn't know he was working out there at the time.'

'Or maybe,' I stood again, 'Ben Patterson was someone other than her betrothed.'

'Like who?'

'If we believe that Ben gave Marion the poem hidden in the heart necklace, and gave her a love bite like Bree suggests, then there must have been a romance between those two. According to the photos taken at the cottage it was as late as December 1957. If she was heading out to Shadow Creek, without anyone's knowledge, then something illicit had to be going on. That's why all the secrecy.'

'Like a booty call,' Elliott grinned. 'Maybe they wanted to get it on for one last time before she got married to some boring old fart. I reckon sex had something to do with it. I mean look at her.' He got up and rushed over to the wall. Stabbing a finger on the photo of Marion in her swimsuit, he added, 'She was one hot babe.'

'You know, my grandmother always thought I looked like her.'

Elliott looked at Marion's photo, looked back at me, and pulled a face. 'Really?'

'Yeah, maybe it was the hair.'

He studied the photo again. 'Could be the eyes ... but definitely not the body.'

'Hey, I'd have you know I looked pretty sexy in my heyday. Just ask Dad.'

'Speaking of hay,' said Elliott, 'I reckon Marion looks like she would've enjoyed a good roll in some. Benny boy was one lucky dude.'

'Lucky?' I cried. 'She died on her way to meet him. I wouldn't call that lucky.'

'Well ... no, but he must've had a bit of fun before that. Remember the hickey?' He tapped his finger on the photo of Marion outside the cottage. 'A pash fest at the love shack,' he grinned.

'Have some respect for the departed,' I joked.

'Hey, seeing he isn't here, can I finish off Dad's tub of salted caramel ice-cream?'

'Sure, go for it. You can eat his block of Rum 'n' Raisin chocolate too while you're at it.'

'When's he coming home?' Elliott asked, his smile now gone.

My shoulders sagged. 'Your guess is as good as mine.'

I left Elliott watching TV while I retreated to my bedroom to read, or attempt to read as it turned out. My concentration kept veering from the action penned by Michael Connelly to the scrambled mess in my head. I dropped the book in my lap, picked up my phone, and opened Facebook.

Finding Shane's profile, I scrolled through his recent posts in the hope that I'd find something that would help me understand what was going on. I didn't. Nothing had been added since he'd uploaded a photo of us as a family, taken two weeks earlier at a steakhouse restaurant in the city—his choice for his forty-third birthday. Forty-three. My God, where did all those years go?

I studied his face in the photo. He was still the good looking labourer I fell in love with the first moment I saw him at a barbecue back in the mid-1990s. I smiled as I remembered turning up at the friend's party overdressed in a short cocktail dress, high heels, high hair, and too much makeup. He reckoned it was my hearty appetite for sausages that drew his attention, not the fact that my dress barely covered my bottom or my perky young breasts. The mature Shane was also fit, due to the physical labour needed for his line of work. Sure, he had several lines on his face, a receding hairline, and a scattering of silver in his goatee, but overall, he was in pretty good shape.

Other than this pic there were only infrequent posts about how busy he'd been at work, how well the Brisbane Broncos had played, and comments on the weather. I then searched through his other photos—which weren't that many—and found a number of shots of long, lonely, winding roads. Had he been imagining what it would be like to travel them on a speedy motorbike?

I returned to Shane's home page. He'd just been tagged in a photo added by someone named Cherry Love. Cherry Love? Who in the hell was that? And why was his name tagged in a picture of a woman's bare buttock tattooed with the words 'No regrets'?

My hand began to tremble. What had he been up to?

A knock on my door disturbed my concerns. I flipped the phone face down on my lap.

The door opened slightly. Elliott's head poked in. 'I'm off to bed now, Mum.'

'Okay. I'm about to turn in too,' I lied.

He lingered. I waited. He coughed. 'Heard anything from Dad?'

I shook my head.

He sucked in a lip. 'Me either. He isn't replying to any of my texts. Should we be worried?'

I was also asking that question in my head. 'I don't know.'

'Maybe you should call Uncle Paul. He might be able to tell us something.'

I nodded and Elliott shut the door.

Turning the phone face up, I glared at the tagged photo. 'You cheating bastard,' I snarled, then fearfully tapped on Cherry Love's name.

Her Facebook page instantly opened. One look at her profile pic told me she was young, blonde, gorgeous, and her butt cheek was not the only place she'd had inked. Artistic designs were also tattooed on the side of her neck, her right shoulder, and across the top of two very shapely breasts. Where had Shane met such a sleaze? Cherry's cover photo gave me a clue. It was a picture of a shop front. The decorated sign on the large window read, 'Love Ink'. My eyes darted to the side margin for more info. Cherry Love was a ... Tattoo Artist?

Nervously scrolling through her photos, I found a portfolio of her work; body parts of all shapes and sizes showcasing her talent. One picture caught my interest. It was of a tanned and muscled upper arm being tattooed with an intricate, steampunkish design —a vintage fob watch with a face bearing roman numerals and sleek decorative hands pointing to a quarter to twelve. Flying out from the top of the clock was a flock of birds. It was beautiful and intriguing. Above the arm was the side view of a man's face. A man I knew intimately, until a few days ago.

I couldn't drag my eyes away. A tattoo? Shane had gotten a tattoo? Once again, I was stunned. I couldn't have been more surprised than if my fleeting suspicion of him having a torrid affair with Cherry had been proven correct. I was shocked. Then confused. Then angry. How dare he! I threw the phone onto the mattress. It bounced twice and then slid off to land on the floor. A 'ding' sounded.

Scrambling across the mattress, I leant down to retrieve the phone. A message dashed across the screen. Hope rose, until I saw it was from Gemma. I forced myself to open it. More pics. A rainforest walk, a riverboat cruise, a sunbaking crocodile—all with bloody Max somewhere in the shot. A selfie of them kissing made me want to vomit. In this one, I could even see the grey hair at his temples.

'Wake up girl! He's not for you!' I yelled, slumping down, and pulling my pillow over my head.

21

Stanthorpe 1957

The farmhouse door opens and Martin Baxter appears, shirtless. Tufts of grey hair break above the neckline of his white singlet like frothy waves. He squints. 'Hello. Marion, isn't it?'

She nods. 'Sorry to disturb you. I know it's Sunday afternoon and you were probably taking it easy.'

'Just reading the paper,' he says, eyeing her directly and taking a suck on the half-smoked cigarette wedged between his fingers.

Her pulse kicks up a notch. She'd spent the previous night locked in her bedroom, her heart aching with the enormity of what had occurred that day. Her mind had become a confusing mess of despair and regret and her sleep had been restless. She'd stumbled from her bed to the bathroom to take penance in a tub filled with scalding hot water. It was there she'd decided she didn't want to lose Banjo. She couldn't live without his smile, his support, and his touch. Yes, he'd shocked her with his anger, and scared her with his forcefulness. But it had dawned on her as she soaked, that it must have come from a defensive place of hurt. They could work things out, start over again. As soon as she'd breakfasted, she'd gone for a walk and her feet had led her to the Baxter's front porch.

'Is Banjo around?' she asks. 'I really need to talk with him.'

Marty turns his head to blow a cloud of smoke over his shoulder. 'I'm sorry luv, but Ben's not here.'

Her breathing stops. 'He isn't?'

'He's heading back home to Shadow Creek. Bit of a sudden move, but he said he had to leave.'

Marion's legs weaken. She grips the porch railing for support. 'When did he leave?'

'He caught a train to Brisbane at the crack of dawn.' He gives a dry cough and studies her coldly. 'You wouldn't know what the fuss was all about with him shooting off like that?'

As Marty's eyes penetrate hers, Marion's discomfort grows. What had Banjo told him? She shakes her head. 'He didn't say anything to me about leaving.'

He takes another drag of his cigarette. 'It must come as quite a shock then.'

'Yes ... yes it does.' Marion stares at the man's face; tries to see Banjo in his uncle's features, and fails.

When he drops the cigarette at his feet, grinding it to mulch with a bare heel, she notices feet and ankles much whiter than the exposed skin above. Below a pair of baggy, khaki shorts are sturdy knees and muscular calves shaped exactly like Banjo's. A tear rolls down her cheek. She brushes it away and lifts her sight.

'Would you like an address to write to?' he says with a hint of a smile, and she catches another resemblance in the gentle lines fanning out from the corners of his eyes.

'Yes, I'd like that very much.'

He gives a nod. 'I'll get it for you. Back in a tick.'

Marty retreats into the dimly lit house while Marion waits in the sunshine; hope budding within.

Minutes later, she is hurrying back along the road's edge, a folded piece of writing paper clutched to her chest. As she nears the Duff's property, she catches sight of Katherine Duff standing on the grassy verge. She sees Marion and runs to meet her.

'Marion! Thank God you've returned. Your mother's collapsed.' Her heavily powdered face has taken on an even paler shade, and her crimson lipstick is patchy where she has nibbled her shapely lips. Her long fingernails are as sharp as talons as she grasps Marion's arm. 'She's in agony, poor thing. The ambulance men are with her now. I came for a visit and she just collapsed on the floor right in front of me.'

'Where's Dad?' Marion asks, removing Katherine hand.

'He's out with Mr Duff and Donald.'

'He needs to know.'

'I've telephoned and left a message with the girl at the office. I'll phone around further if I don't hear from him.'

As Marion is ushered down the drive to the cottage, she spots the ambulance. The rear doors flung open remind her of a screaming mouth. She rushes up the stairs and across the porch, almost colliding with the men as they manoeuvre a stretcher through the doorway. Her mother's thin frame is covered with a blue blanket.

'Mum!' she calls, taking up a clammy hand. Her mother's eyes blink and then open. There is a glassiness to them. 'What's wrong with her?' she asks the men.

'Acute abdominal pain. She's fine for now,' one of them assures. 'We've given her something to take the edge off. It may be appendicitis, but we'll know for certain once we get her to the hospital. You can come with her if you like.'

'Yes, of course,' she says.

Running inside to collect her handbag, Marion realises she's still clasping the scrunched note. Dropping it onto her dressing table, she hurries outside to join her mother in the ambulance.

22

S leep eluded me. I'd tossed and turned most of the night and at 4:30 am I gave up and got out of bed.

Stabbing out a phone message to Shane, I told him how I felt about his childish antics. I told him that not only was I worried sick, I was mad as hell that he'd been out drinking in bars, fraternising with questionable women, and getting himself a tattoo without consulting me. I aired my views on his lack of parental responsibility and in not being around to help counsel the kids while they washed their lives down the drain. I shared my disappointment in him not being a supportive husband in my times of need—one being almost having my throat ripped open in a vicious dog attack. I told him if he didn't call me as soon as possible, I may have to rethink our marriage. Then, just as I was about to press send, I deleted everything I'd written except for the words, 'worried sick ... call me ASAP'.

By the time Elliott had left to catch the bus to school, I was beginning to fade. I nodded off in the armchair amid the drone of morning TV, and could have stayed there for hours if it wasn't for my phone heralding that a message had arrived. At last, Shane had responded. My drowsy brain instantly came back to life.

I rubbed my eyes and read his words. 'OK let's meet up. Wilmot's Reserve. 11:30 am. My lunch break.' That sounded ominous. Why couldn't he have said, 'Sure thing. I'll be home tonight, so we can talk then.' My worries grew.

I jolted as the phone rang while still in my hand. I didn't recognise the number but answered it anyway. It was Stoney Maloney, from the craft shop, and he had news.

He had been in touch with an old girlfriend of his from way back, Doris, who he remembered had worked at the bakery with Ben's mother. He'd asked if she could recall the lady in question and fortunately she could, but more for having a good-looking son than much else.

Doris told him the woman's name was Fran and she was very pleasant to work with. She couldn't shed any light on where this Fran and her son had lived at the time as Doris worked at the bakery for only short spell before meeting a passing rodeo rider and running off with him to pursue an exciting life on the circuit. This hadn't worked out as planned, and she'd returned to Shadow Creek a few years later with two small children, a broken marriage and a resolve to never be led by her heart again. By this time, Ben Patterson had disappeared from the area and Fran no longer worked at the shop. Doris thought she'd heard Fran had stopped working due to illness.

I thanked Stoney for this information, and he in turn thanked me. He said that as he had reacquainted himself with Doris, he was hoping to work his charm and ask her out on a date. He had fond memories of Doris and hoped he could rekindle a long-lost romance. I wished him all the luck in the world, and we said our goodbyes.

It wasn't much to go on, but at least I had another name to

work with. Taking a cup of coffee with me, I made my way up to the loft and gave the wall display another glance. Drawn to the photos of Ben, I once again had a suspicion that I'd seen this face before—not just in these recently found photographs, but elsewhere. The more I looked, the more his dark eyes dared me to discover the truth.

As I scrolled through the derailment images I'd saved on my computer, the urge to physically visit the crash site increased. How easy would it be to find after sixty years? I would need to search the Internet for the exact location or, if that failed, pay another visit to Beryl. As I continued scrolling, I came to a picture that caused me to choke on a mouthful of coffee. It was the scene of the injured boy being lifted from the wreck of an overturned carriage.

I jumped up and unstuck a photo from the wall. Holding it next to the computer image of the youthful rescuer pulling the boy free, I let out a 'woo-hoo'. That's where I'd seen him before. The dark, curly hair and tanned face that smiled in one picture and grimaced in the other, definitely belonged to the same person —Ben Patterson.

My elation quickly turned to sadness. This meant that he'd been at the crash site and had been part of the rescue team. Had he known Marion was among the casualties? Instinct led me to believe he was driven by a need greater than most of the other rescuers. The raw anguish easily seen on his grease-smeared face hinted at the truth. He must have been searching for Marion. My heart took off like a mouse on a treadmill. I was now confident that she'd been on her way to see him when she died.

An alert sounded on my laptop. An email had arrived. It was from my father. 'FYI re Marion Douglas' was typed in the subject field.

23

Marion re-reads the freshly written letter in her hands to make sure she has conveyed the truth of her feelings.

Dear Banjo, I know this must be a surprise receiving a letter from me, of all people, but your uncle was kind enough to give me your address. It is with a heavy heart that I write to you.

Firstly, she told him about her mother's illness, and how shocked they were that test results proved the cancer had returned and was spreading quickly. She shared how tiring it had been caring for her mother, and how worrying it was not knowing how much time she has left. Then came the words that were even more difficult to write.

Regarding our last meeting, how do I begin to tell you how sorry I am? It was wrong of me to react the way I did. I know you believed I was judging you, but in fact that was not the case. The truth is, when my father told me those things about you, I was shocked, then annoyed that you hadn't told me yourself. I thought it was because you hadn't trusted me. I was confused and hurt and that's why I avoided you, as well as having my father forbid me to ever see you again. Then when we did talk, your anger frightened me and I had to get away. Having had time to ponder on things, I realise that you acted out of a fear, that me knowing who you really are would make a difference to our relationship. Unfortunately it did, but not for the reason I am sure you assumed. I am offering you my sincere apology and hope you will see it in your heart to accept it.

She finished the letter by saying that she missed him greatly and wished they could wipe the slate clean and start over.

Tears drip from her lashes. She blows air to dry where they fell on the fine paper, but some words have already disappeared. Lifting her pen, she finds her hand is shaking. Then, with a sudden fear of Banjo's rejection, she scrunches the sheet of paper into a tight ball and tosses it across the bedroom. It bounces off a wall and lands directly at her feet.

Not game enough to trust fate, Marion defiantly picks it up and drops the balled-up letter into the waste paper basket near the door.

24

The attachment to my dad's email left me dumbfounded. It was a scan of a newspaper clipping he'd found among my grandmother's keepsakes; an engagement notice with a photograph of Miss Marion Douglas and Mr Donald Duff. The date given was 16th November 1957. I was surprised beyond belief. Who was he? I continued reading the article. Donald Duff was the son of Cameron and Katherine Duff of Stanthorpe. Mr Duff senior, so it stated, was a wealthy property developer.

I went over to my wall display. Removing the photo of Marion outside the cottage, I returned to the desk and added it to the matching one I had of Ben. Flipping them both over, I read the scrawled wording on the back of each photo. 'December 1957'. These, then, were taken after Marion's engagement to Donald Duff. What did this mean? Had she and Donald Duff broken up by then? Or was it that while betrothed to one man, Marion was slyly seeing another? I tried to wrap my head around this thought.

We assumed that on the day of the fateful crash, Marion was on her way to meet with Ben. Was this for a platonic visit, or a secret liaison? Or did she have intentions of telling an eager Ben to leave off and let her continue a future with Donald Duff? Something horrid crossed my mind. What if Ben wasn't the romantic hero I'd made him out to be? What if he was a crazed psycho, or even a stalker? I studied his face. Maybe it wasn't joy that caused him to smile into the camera outside the cottage. Maybe it was victory at bagging his catch. I shuddered. No, it couldn't be. Marion's image wasn't glaring into the lens with fear … or was it? Could what I took for sultry passion, be a pose forced on demand?

I again studied the newspaper clipping. Marion looked happy in the engagement photo. Was it possible that she was in love with this Donald at the time, and then met Ben afterwards? Life can take sudden turns, some good and some bad. I hoped I wasn't going to discover anything sinister down the track.

Another thought caused me to pick up the brown paper bag left for me by my father and rifle through the photos. Finding the one of Marion in a ball gown and seated with others around a table, I examined it more intently. The group consisted of her parents, another middle-aged couple, and a man I now recognised as Donald Duff. Yet this was not what drew my attention. It was the scene in the background that newly captured my interest.

While the photograph pictured Marion seated at the table with the others of her group, in the background was a huddle of young men enjoying refreshments. Among them, and eying the seated party with what looked like a grimace on his face, was Ben Patterson. My insides flipped, twisted, and popped like a hip-hop dancer. He was there, in Stanthorpe. I turned the photo over. No date, just the words 'Apple Blossom Festival'.

An Internet search revealed that the mentioned festival was held in Stanthorpe during the spring season, in October, and included a Ball on the Friday evening. Could this photo have been taken as late as 1957? Is this where Ben had met Marion, at the dance? I was puzzled. What had brought him to Stanthorpe when, that same year, he was working at the timber mill in Shadow Creek? Was he in Stanthorpe for a holiday or other work? Beryl Erbacher had mentioned that in tough times people went where they could to find jobs, so maybe he was an itinerant worker and travelled around.

I collected all the photos I had of Ben and laid them side-by-side on the desk, placing them as best I could in chronological order. Then I sat back and tried to unscramble this riddle.

October—Marion and her parents have moved to Stanthorpe and, together with the Duff family, attend the Apple Blossom Ball. Also in attendance is Ben Patterson.

November—Marion is engaged to Donald Duff.

December—Marion spends time with Ben. He could have been her secret lover. Then again, he could have just been an acquaintance, and Donald was indeed the one who gave her the love bite. Damn. The poem. I'd almost forgotten about that. Therefore, Ben had to be the lover. She could have met him at the dance and ditched Donald sometime before January without her family knowing.

January—Her mother dies. On the fateful day of the train crash, Marion was heading out to Shadow Creek to find consolation in Ben's arms. Or was she planning another tryst to satisfy her lustful need of him? Then again, maybe she was heading out to break it all off and continue with her marriage to Donald. This was becoming even more complicated. Whatever the case, things don't go to plan. Before Marion even gets to see Ben, her train derails and she dies. Or, just maybe ... he was on the train with her! Why hadn't I thought of that before?

So, Ben meets her in Brisbane and brings her home with the intention of meeting his dear old mum. Along the way, disaster happens and Marion dies, leaving him so distraught that he disappears to live a new life without her—or die a broken, miserable man who finds solace in the shapely form of a bottle.

Though, what if Ben wasn't the nice guy we thought he was and Marion had been travelling against her will? Ben, the handsome, sweet-talking stalker, coerces her out to Shadow Creek with the intention of doing evil. That would explain why no one knew of her trip beforehand. His plan comes undone when the train crashes, and he disappears into thin air to carry on as usual ... or find another victim!

It was getting to feel like a 'Choose Your Own Adventure' story or a sci-fi novel dealing with alternate realities. I was close to admitting defeat. It annoyed me that I cared so much for something that had already taken place. I couldn't change anything anyway, so why was I bothering to dig it all up? Then I remembered the necklace. Damn that necklace for dragging me into this mystery. I imagined it tightening around my neck, strangling me with its desperate need for revelation.

I needed a stronger drink, and some Rolling Stones. I certainly wasn't getting any satisfaction with my search for answers. Sensibly, I substituted a couple of painkillers for the alcohol to ease the pounding in my head.

25

Brisbane 1957

Could it really be only four days until Christmas? Marion has trouble comprehending this fact. For her, time seems to have flown by: each horrid day melding into another. Scores of shops line Brisbane's city streets offering an abundance of gift choices, yet she is at a loss. What does a person buy for someone whose life is nearing its end?

Staying with her aunt and uncle for a much-needed break from caring for her mother, and being persuaded to spend the day in town, has not eased her emotions as she'd hoped. So far it has only led to frustration. After hours of traipsing around crowded department stores like McDonnell & East and Allan & Stark, and searching through smaller shops and boutiques, she wonders if she will ever find anything suitable.

Blinking away tears, Marion numbly peruses yet another window display. Her eyes are drawn to a charming red vinyl handbag with a black plastic bow and silver clasp. She glances down at the worn bag in her grasp and decides it needs replacing —a treat for herself. Maybe this will help lift her spirits.

Minutes later she steps out of the shop with her shiny new purchase already slung over her arm. Though feeling guilty for spending money on herself, she also feels brighter. Where should she head next? A row of picture theatres beckons from across the street. From the four on offer, it is the winking lights of the Regent Theatre that tempt her the most. She yields and chooses to see a movie.

Crossing busy Queen Street, she aims for the building with the Art Deco stonework façade. Through the doorway Marion finds herself in an impressive entrance hall. Tilting her head back, she takes in the high vaulted ceiling, decorative plasterwork, and painted murals. Ahead are stairs leading up to the elaborate grand foyer boasting blind balconies decorated with velvet curtaining, and a white marble staircase with ornate balustrades. She marvels anew at the Hollywood inspired elegance. Gothic, Neo-classical, Baroque, and several others design styles she can't remember were used in the theatre's creation. The last time she was here was when Aunt Gloria had brought her and cousin Rose to see *Rebel Without a Cause,* and Marion had fallen in love with both James Dean and Natalie Wood. So much has happened since.

She moves towards the ticket booth to study the colourful billboards. One poster features Elvis Presley eyeing her with salacious intent through the bars of a prison cell, while Gary Cooper and Audrey Hepburn smile back from another gaily advertising *Love in the Afternoon.* Excitement awakens, so does her appetite.

She quickly purchases a large container of warmed popcorn from the confectionary bar before lining up to buy her ticket. While she waits her turn, Marion tucks into the buttery morsels and watches the crowd pouring down the stairs from an earlier movie session. She suddenly gags on a mouthful. Separating himself from the group is a familiar figure. A longer hairstyle and fashionable black leather jacket do little to hide his identity.

Swiftly turning away, she bumps into an elderly gentleman standing behind her. The container is knocked from her hand and spurts out its contents in every direction before upending on the terrazzo floor. She apologises and crouches to clean up the mess while the annoyed man brushes popcorn from his coat and steps around to take her place in the queue.

'Need a hand?' a voice says from above.

Marion's hands pause, so does her breathing.

Banjo squats beside her and returns popcorn to the cardboard container. 'Hello Marion.'

She responds with a glance; her fingers and heart rate as unsteady as each other.

'How are you?' he asks.

'Fine thanks,' she lies, retrieving the last of the strewn popcorn and rising to her feet. Banjo stands with her, yet she is unable to summon the nerve to look him in the eye. 'How are you?'

He slips his hands into the pockets of his jacket. 'Getting by. I'm working back at the mill.'

'That's good,' she nods, fingering the crushed container and staring straight ahead, noticing beads of sweat trickling down Banjo's neck into his shirt collar. She wonders if he is perspiring from the warmth of the foyer or unease.

'You going up?'

She frowns. 'Pardon?'

He indicates the group of people climbing the stairs. 'Into the theatre.'

'Yes ... yes I am. Oh ... I have to buy a ticket first.'

She goes to walk around him, but Banjo blocks her way.

'Wait.' He reaches out.

Marion's heart jolts, anticipating his touch. Instead, he points above her ear.

'You have popcorn in your hair.'

'Oh, do I?' She lifts her left hand to locate the greasy object caught in her curls and hears him gasp.

'You're engaged?'

She cringes, and hides her hand behind her back. She'd forgotten all about the ring. The taste of popcorn in her mouth sours. She feels sick.

'To who?' he asks, his voice rasps.

A word is forced from her mouth. 'Donald.'

'Donald Duff? What the hell made you do that?'

Marion looks at the floor, despising Aunt Gloria for talking her into coming into the city. 'It's complicated,' she says.

Banjo's voice is now a whisper. 'Can we go somewhere to talk?'

Marion surprises herself by giving a nod and following him out the entrance and onto the footpath.

She is taken to a nearby cafe. Finding a table near the window, Banjo asks if she would like a cup of tea. She most certainly does. While he makes his way to the counter, Marion takes a seat, placing her hands on the pink marbled laminate. They are trembling. Her nerves are shot. She eyes the engagement ring and her emotions rise to the boil. Overriding them all is terror. This is not going to be easy.

Banjo returns, sliding the cup across the laminate so roughly that tea spills into the saucer. 'Talk to me,' he urges, sitting opposite.

Marion focuses on the rippling liquid in front of her. 'I wrote you a letter.'

'I didn't get any letter!' he snaps.

'I know, I never sent it. I chickened out.'

'Why?'

'I thought you ... it doesn't matter. I said I was sorry.'

'You did?'

She raises her head and dares to finally look him in the eye. 'I understand the reason you didn't tell me all about yourself. I was a fool ... but my dad ... he reacted badly.' She takes a deep breath. 'After that day at the Soldier's Memorial ... I realised I still cared for you.'

'Yet you agreed to marry Donald!'

She nods. 'Mum's dying. The cancer has returned. I've finished working at the store to look after her.'

His eyes soften. 'I'm sorry. I hadn't heard.'

'Knowing it was over between us ... and what with Dad pushing for the marriage and Mum eager to see me settled, I caved in.'

'But, I didn't think you liked Donald in that way.'

'I could do worse. He really isn't that bad.'

Banjo pushes back; chair legs screech on the polished linoleum. 'Do you love him?'

Marion wavers. The power of Banjo's presence and the anguish written on his face cause her to regret not sending that letter. She should have told him what had been in her heart and what she now realises is still true. She shakes her head.

'Is this the type of marriage you want? One of convenience?'

She shrugs. 'What choice do I have?'

'Your own!' he yells, 'Not that of your parents ... or Donald. Bloody hell, Marion, why do you let them push you around? I thought you had more guts than that.'

She glances away. A child outside is pressing his face against the window; his nose squashed flat, his tongue licking the glass. She would normally have found this amusing. Now she just wants to smack her hand on the window and scream for the boy to get lost. Banjo coughs. Her eyes return to him.

'You deserve so much more Marion. What about happiness, what about passion … love?'

She bites her lip. She has no answer.

He slams his fist on the table. Marion jumps. Cups rattle in their saucers. 'Damn it Marion! What do you really want?'

Her chest tightens. She grips the edge of the table.

'Tell me!' he pleads.

Tears seep between clenched eyelids.

'Please, Marion,' he urges more tenderly, 'tell me.'

She wipes trickles from her face. 'I … I want … you.'

Banjo's chair scrapes sharply as he stands. His arms surround her; she is pulled to her feet. She burrows her face into his chest, hears him whisper in her ear. 'Come with me.'

Marion takes his hand and is guided past startled customers.

Once outside, Banjo leads her down congested streets. They weave through shoppers and wide-eyed children; pass a Santa Claus or two. Marion clutches him, desperate not to let him go as they dodge between trams and offloading passengers. She has no idea where he is taking her. She only knows that having found him again, she isn't ready to leave his side.

They turn down a narrow lane and came to a halt in front of a shiny, black motorcycle.

'Hop on,' Banjo demands.

Marion falters. 'What, on this?'

'Yes, this'.

'Whose is it?'

'Mine. It's a '54 Triumph Thunderbird. I bought it to help me get over you.'

'And did you?' Marion wishes she had the courage to ask.

A helmet hangs from the handlebars. He places it on her head, flattening her hair. Before she can object, he tightens the chinstrap. Swinging his leg over the bike, he shuffles forward on the leather seat and motions for her to take her place behind. 'On you get,' he demands.

'Abducting me again?' she says, hoisting her full skirt, and clambering on board.

Banjo fastens a pair of dark goggles over his eyes. 'Maybe,' he nods, and starts the engine.

Marion clutches him around the waist, her new handbag swinging from her arm. With a burst of power, they speed down the lane and enter the flow of traffic travelling out of the city centre.

26

Three hours until our meet up. I used my anxious energy to do a quick clean of the house just in case Shane decided it was time to return home.

Going from room to room, I emptied waste paper baskets and assorted rubbish into a large black plastic garbage bag. Slinging it over my shoulder like a Santa sack, I made my way out the back door and down the stairs. Walking around the side of the house where the wheelie bins were kept, I noticed a difference in the array of unused plant pots stacked against the fence. One pot had a plant growing in it. Dropping the rubbish bag, I went to examine it more closely. Just as I thought, a marijuana plant. So, Elliott hadn't gotten rid of all the plants like he said he would.

I ran back inside and returned with my phone. Taking a selfie of me scowling while holding up the 'pot' plant, I then sent it on to my recalcitrant son. Upending the pot into the garbage bag, I noticed a piece of newspaper—yellowed with age—sticking out of the rubbish. I recognised it as the news page Marion's necklace had been wrapped in. What I didn't recall was the bold wording just below the top edge: 'RAIL CRASH'.

I eased the paper from the refuse and shook it free of potting mix and food scraps. Pressing it out flat on the wheelie bin lid, I saw that it was an original front page of The Brisbane Telegraph, dated 12th January 1958. I swallowed hard. It was the initial report of the Shadow Creek rail disaster—Marion's train crash.

The information given below the headline was the same as what I had gleaned from my recent Internet searches. In my haste to open the strange gift the other day, I hadn't bothered to study the newspaper in which it was wrapped. Now I re-read it—twice. Beneath the report was a photo of the derailed train taken within hours of the crash. I had already seen one just like it. I carefully folded the page, dropped the garbage bag into the bin, and went back inside.

The wall clock told me I had one hour until my meet-up with Shane, which meant—minus travel time—I had fifteen minutes to get ready. I threw on a shirt and skirt. The shirt was too tight. I undid the top three buttons to ease the tension but this made me look too tarty, so I replaced the shirt with another—same problem. I changed my skirt for a lime green dress, a loose cotton one. Then chose a sleeveless denim jacket to wear over it. Why was I so concerned about what to wear? It was only Shane, for God's sake. Maybe it was because I felt a need to compete with Cherry-the-lusty-tattooist. A little make-up, my hair caught up in a hair-clip, and I was out the door. A minute later I was back again to spray on some perfume, then I was in the car.

As I drove along the ridge to the T-junction and took a left towards suburbia, I flitted between practising my lines for my encounter with Shane, and wondering why someone would wrap Marion's necklace in newsprint reporting the rail disaster in which she'd died. I couldn't help but speculate that the mysterious visitor wanted to send me a message. But what it was exactly, I had no idea. Not yet, anyway.

27

Tulip Wood 1957

Tall city buildings have now been replaced with tin-roofed cottages and houses perched high on wooden stumps. Marion isn't taking the least bit of notice for all she is able to do is cling onto Banjo and wrestle with her emotions.

Disbelief at the sudden turn of events jostles alongside hope and fear. She is unsure if the trembling she is feeling is the result of vibrations from the motorbike or heightened nerves. Panic takes hold. She has no idea where he is taking her or what his intentions are. She still doesn't even know of his feelings for her.

Slowing behind a heavily laden truck, Marion takes the opportunity to lean forward and yell above the noise. 'Where are we going?'

Banjo's head turns. 'Home.'

Marion eyes the unfamiliar housing lining the road. 'Whose?'

'Mine.'

'How far away is that?'

'About thirty-five minutes,' he says, accelerating.

As they lurch forward to overtake the truck, Marion squeezes her eyes shut and grips even more tightly onto his leather jacket.

Houses gradually dwindle in number, and bitumen becomes dirt. The view changes to a more rural landscape. Ascending a bushy mountain range, they ride along winding roads in the shade of dense forests. The aroma of eucalypts and damp leaf litter is strong here. Rounding a bend, a wallaby darts out in front of them and Marion squeals. The motorbike swerves and skids sideways through the dust, narrowly missing the startled creature.

Eventually they descend into a lush valley where farming properties are more prevalent. Bumping over a railway crossing, they follow a dusty road. Signposts show that they are nearing the town of Shadow Creek, though before Marion sees any sign of its existence, the bike slows and enters a fenced property. Nailed into the wooden gate is a sign bearing the painted words 'Tulip Wood'.

A long dirt drive brings them to a halt under the spreading branches of a large poinciana. In front of them, and balanced on short wooden stumps, is a white timber cottage surrounded by a picket fence.

'Here we are,' Banjo announces, turning off the engine.

Marion undoes the helmet and shakes her hair free. Stepping from the bike, she brushes down her dress and views the cottage, taking in the empty porch and shut casement windows. Except for a distant dog bark, all seems quiet.

She hands the helmet to Banjo. 'Is your mother home?'

He removes his goggles and pushes hair back from his forehead. 'No. She left a couple of days ago to visit Uncle Marty.'

Marion is disappointed. She would have liked to have met his mother. She is also apprehensive, for this means they are alone.

Banjo unseats, props up the bike, and clears his throat. 'I ... ah

... do want to introduce you to someone, though. She's a beaut girl and she means the world to me.'

Marion's heart grips. Has she been replaced so soon? She looks away before he can see the pain in her eyes.

A flash of tan and white.

Marion hastily steps aside as a furry torpedo speeds past and leaps into Banjo's outstretched arms. A little, shorthaired terrier licks his face with a darting tongue.

'Marion, meet Honey.'

Marion grins with relief and reaches out to pat the squirming bundle. A pink tongue swipes her cheek. She laughs. 'Well hello to you, too.'

Banjo drops the dog to the ground. 'Settle girl,' he commands, raising his hand.

Honey sits, her whip-like tail thumping excitedly in the dirt. Cocking her head, she waits expectantly. Banjo digs his hand into his jacket pocket and produces a piece of dried beef jerky, which he uses to draw a circle in the air. Honey stands on her hind legs and pirouettes like a canine ballet dancer. When the treat is thrown high, she leaps and catches it in her snapping mouth; gulping it down by the time her paws hit the ground.

Marion claps her hands. 'What a clever girl!' The dog rolls onto its back and offers her freckled belly to be tickled. Marion complies, glancing up at Banjo. 'Your place is called Tulip Wood?'

'The property is. The main house was up there.' He points to a grassy hill a few hundred yards away. The stumpy remains of a sizeable house are barely visible. 'It burnt down about twenty years ago, and the owner decided to pack it all in and leave. Now he just rents out this workers' cottage and offers the land for agistment purposes.'

Marion shields her eyes. 'It's much greener here than Stanthorpe. Not as many boulders.'

He laughs. 'That's for damn sure. Let me show you the house.' He heads up the porch steps, followed closely by Honey.

Marion joins them. 'What's that beautiful smell?' she asks, inhaling deeply.

'That'd be the jasmine bush.' Banjo indicates the creeper growing around the porch railing and laden with white, star-like flowers. 'At dusk the smell is so strong it'll make your head spin.' He goes to the door and turns the knob. 'Stay,' he commands, and Honey lowers her rump on the coir doormat, while he and Marion enter a cool, dark hallway.

Banjo disappears through a doorway on the right, which Marion discovers leads into a sitting room.

Lifting a blind, he opens a window. 'Nothing flash here, but it's neat and cosy.'

Marion takes in the bright yellow curtaining and floral-patterned armchairs. Thriving plants rest in an assortment of brass pots dotted around the room, while in one corner is a laden drinks trolley, and in another an aged radiogram with a new record player resting on top. On the walls hang framed oil paintings of sweeping landscapes.

Placing her handbag on a coffee table, Marion inspects the artwork, recognising scenes from her ride out. She also notes that the artist's signature in the bottom corner of each one is the same. 'Frances Baxter,' she exclaims. 'Any relation to your Uncle Marty?'

'Yes ... his sister.'

Her head turns. 'Your mother?'

'Yep,' he nods.

'Your mother painted all these? They're spectacular.' She fingers the dried brush strokes on a painting of a field of sunflowers. 'Does she sell them?'

'Sometimes,' he says, from over her shoulder, 'but it's really only a hobby.'

Banjo's nearness, and the warmth of his breath in her hair, is unsettling. She moves away. 'Your mother never married?'

He shortens the space between them. 'There have been one or two interested parties, but none worth their salt.'

Marion distances herself this time by rounding the oak coffee table.

'I was a Baxter too, for a while,' he comments from the other side.

Marion is surprised. 'You were?'

'It was easier us having the same name. It stopped having to answer difficult questions.'

Marion stiffens. Was there a bristled edge to his tone?

'Do you like home-made ginger beer?' he asks, slipping from the room before she can give an answer.

Her breathing steadies. Questions stab like knives. Why did Banjo bring her here? What does he want from her? She wishes he would blurt something out—anything—rather than leaving her in limbo. She'd rather have the Band-Aid ripped off in one swift movement.

Shaking her arms free of tension, she approaches a collection of framed photos standing on a wall shelf. Taking down the largest frame, Marion studies the image of a man dressed in the heavy serge uniform of an Australian infantryman. Though lightly tanned, his features reveal his Aboriginal origins. His slouch hat is proudly perched, and the badge of the Rising Sun pinned to the side is polished to a glimmering shine. He looks young and 'gung-ho', as if eager to head off on a new adventure.

'He was a handsome bugger, wasn't he?'

Marion jolts. Banjo is right behind, holding a full glass in each hand. His eyes search hers. If he is looking for signs of distaste, she knows he won't find any.

'I think you have his smile,' she says, and returns the photo to the shelf. 'He looks like a larrikin.'

'Yeah, a bit of a rascal I'm told.' Banjo grins, proving the resemblance to his father.

He hands her a glass and Marion eagerly takes it from him, surprised by the dryness in her mouth. After a long sip she asks, 'Where did your Dad come from?'

'Somewhere near Rockhampton I think. When he was about fourteen he went to work as a jackaroo on a sheep station at Ilfracombe, out Longreach way. That's where he met Uncle Marty.' He nods towards another photo. 'That's all of us just before Dad left for the Middle East.'

In this one his uniformed father is standing next to a young, fair-haired woman with a slender nose and square jaw, just like her brother's. Banjo's mother is outfitted in a belted dress with pin tucks across the bodice. Her expression is strained. Marion wonders at the enormity of farewelling a loved one heading off to fight in a distant war. Such heartache. Their future would have been an unknown quantity at this stage.

Banjo points to the toddler on the woman's hip. 'Check out that little tacker.'

The boy is smiling at the camera, innocently unaware of the events unfolding around him. Dark hair frames his head like a fuzzy halo. He is wearing a buttoned-up shirt and short pants with braces. His socks sag around skinny ankles, and clutched in one pudgy fist is a small tin soldier.

'You were adorable,' she sighs.

'Were?' he responds, a glint playing in his eyes.

The mood in the room has changed and Marion is optimistic.

Banjo lifts his glass to his lips and gulps the contents down in one go. 'Good stuff, eh?'

'Just what I needed,' she says, sinking into the soft cushioning of an armchair, and taking another sip.

There's an awkward silence as Banjo watches her while fidgeting with his empty glass, repeatedly passing it from one hand to another.

Marion finally speaks. 'Why did you bring me here, Banjo?'

He drops himself down on the coffee table. 'Cute handbag,' he says,' sliding it aside so that he can take his place directly in front of her. He shrugs. 'I haven't a clue.'

Placing her glass on the table, she catches him studying the diamond and sapphire ring on her finger. She hides the offending hand in the folds of her skirt.

'Maybe I wanted to take you further away from ... them,' he says, nodding towards her lap. 'Maybe I wanted to show you something of me.'

Marion glances up at the photos on the shelf. 'You don't have to prove anything, you know. I've already told you what I want.' She suspects, by his deadpan expression, that he's yet to be convinced, and focuses on the floral pattern of the rug at her feet. 'I shouldn't have broken things off so abruptly.'

'No,' he says sternly, 'you shouldn't have.'

Woven rose buds quiver before her eyes. She forces back tears. 'I'm so sorry ... I really am. Like I said, I was a fool. I reacted badly.'

He lets out a groan. She looks up.

His voice trembles as he speaks. 'I'm sorry, Marion, for not trusting you with the truth ... and behaving like a monster. You were right, I was a brute, and I'm bloody ashamed of what I did. I shouldn't have let my anger get the better of me.'

There, at last. She sees it now—remorse, exposure, Banjo unmasked. Her heart warms.

He continues. 'I was determined to get by without you. I shut the door on us and was getting on with life ... at least I thought I was. Then seeing you today, all those feelings rushed back ... the feelings I had before ... before all the mess, and I realised nothing had really changed.'

Marion's pulse races. She glances down, sees the buttons of her dress jumping right where her heart is.

Banjo lifts her chin with his hand. His eyes are moist.

'I realised there was no way on earth I could live without you, Marion. I still want you too.'

Then he leans in and kisses the tremor from her lips.

28

Wilmot's Reserve, a picnic ground located on the northern outskirts of Brisbane which held nice memories for us. We used to take the kids there when they were young and we still lived in the suburbs. I drove into one of the many parking spaces available and climbed out of the car. One quick perusal of the parking area told me that Shane had not yet arrived, so I made my way over to a picnic table in the cover of a shelter shed and sat on the bench seating.

Other than a woman walking her dog, and another pushing a toddler on a swing in the playground area, the forested park was empty. Good, I thought. An ideal time and place for a showdown. I checked my watch. He was late. I took in a deep breath of forest air and allowed the ghosts of the past to drift by.

I saw us as a happy family: choosing a shady picnic spot; commandeering a barbecue to cook sausages; playing with frisbees in the clearing. I saw a young Elliott riding his skateboard along the path and Gemma chasing a water dragon around the trees. I saw Shane tugging a book from my hands and pulling me up to walk with him as he identified native flora. Those were the days, all right. A much simpler, more relaxed time.

After ten minutes of waiting, I opened my bottle of water and gulped it down in one go. Another five minutes and I ate the salad bread roll I'd brought along in case I got the munchies. If Shane didn't arrive soon, I would need to take advantage of the toilet block.

Tyres on gravel.

I looked up. A white ute with 'Eaton Landscaping' printed in red on the side panel had pulled into the car park. Shane had arrived. I stepped out into the light and watched as he walked over.

He was in his work clothes. Red polo shirt, grey shorts, and steel-capped boots. Damn, he looked good. I brushed down the front of my dress, smoothed my hair, and licked my lips, feeling as nervous as a woman on her first Tinder date.

He stopped about a metre away. 'Hi,' he said, stony-faced.

'Hi,' I said back, trying to play it cool and keep the upper hand.

His eyes dropped. He tugged at his goatee and kicked the ground with his boot. So that's how it was going to be. I sat back down.

He plodded over and slid onto the bench seat on the opposite side of the table. His blue eyes looked everywhere but in my direction. His fingers drummed on the table. The collar of his shirt was stuck up on one side and I felt an urge to lean forward and fold it down.

'So,' I said, crossing my arms. 'You've no lunch.'

'No, not hungry,' he answered, his fingers picking at the worn timber on the table's surface.

His unfamiliar reticence was doing nothing for my anxiety, so I jumped right in. 'How's your tattoo?'

His eyes found mine, and narrowed. 'What?'

'I said, how's your tattoo?' I pointed to his left arm.

He gripped the shirtsleeve. 'How did you know?'

'A little birdy told me.'

Creases lined his forehead. 'Graeme?'

I pulled a face. 'Graeme?'

'Yeah. Graeme Roper told you, didn't he?'

Of course. Now Graeme's comment made sense. *Shane's latest acquisition.* He'd said he'd helped Shane choose it. 'No, actually it was Cherry Love.'

Shane's eyes widened and a shade of crimson crawled up his neck. 'How did you ...'

I smiled triumphantly. 'I have my ways. Give us a look.'

'What?'

'Show me your tatt!'

He hesitantly slid his sleeve up, revealing the tattoo bit-by-bit until it was entirely visible.

I leant in. 'Impressive.'

He scowled, as if trying to comprehend whether I was telling the truth or joking. 'It's a bit crusty now. But that will soon peel away.'

I pointed to the wording that hadn't been noticeable in the photo I'd glimpsed. 'Tempus Fugit?'

'Time Flies,' he said, dropping his sleeve.

I rested back, studying him. 'What's going on, Shane?'

He stared, his mouth clamped shut.

My hands balled, and my anger broke free of its moorings. 'Bloody hell, Shane! Out of the blue you buy a bike, go drinking at bars, get a friggin' tattoo from Miss No Regrets and don't respond to my phone calls.' I slammed a hand down on the table. 'What is wrong with you?'

Instead of rising up and lashing back as I expected him to, he dropped his shoulders, spread his hands out on the table, and sucked in a mouthful of air. 'I found a lump.'

My rage dropped like a popped balloon. 'A lump? Where?'

'In my ... um ... right testicle.'

Concern took over. 'Oh God, Shane! You should have it checked.'

'I have. Saw the GP on Tuesday. Had an ultrasound yesterday.'

My jaw dropped. This could be devastating. I reached out, covered his hands with mine. 'And?'

He gave a shrug. 'Don't know anything yet.' His eyes reddened. 'Dad died from testicular cancer.'

'Yes, I know.'

A tear dripped from one eye and rolled down the length of his nose. 'He was forty-three.'

I flinched. Shane had just turned forty-three. I tightened my grip on his fingers. 'You're scared it's happening again ... with you.'

He sniffed loudly.

I reached for my bag, found a tissue, and passed it to him. 'Is that what all this has been about?'

He nodded, and blew his nose. 'Dad only had a few months after he found out. It spread too bloody quickly.'

'But things have changed. Technology has advanced.'

'What if I have to have surgery ... have my ball chopped off?'

'Well, you do have another one,' I said, immediately regretting making light of the situation. 'Anyway, there's radiation treatment, chemo, right?'

He shrugged again.

'When do you get the results?'

'Maybe today. Maybe next week.'

'Well, once you find out, you'll know what you're dealing with ... *we'll* know what *we're* dealing with.' I got up and wrapped my arms around him. 'You should have told me. I could have gone with you to the doctor ... to the ultrasound.'

He leant his head against my chest. 'I'm so sorry. I got the spooks. Had to do things I've only ever dreamed about doing, like a Bucket List.'

I gave a small laugh. 'Secret things you've never, ever mentioned ... like buy a motorbike. That was a huge surprise.' I sat next to him. 'Now, the tattoo ... I quite like it, actually.'

'You're not still angry with me?'

I touched his face with my hand. 'No. Confused more than angry. Why couldn't you trust me with the truth? I'm your wife ... for better or worse, remember?'

'It's stupid, I know, but I didn't want to worry you. I wanted to wait until I had all the facts before I said anything.'

'Yet, I was worried, and you pushed me away. That really hurt.'

'Believe me, Abby. I truly am sorry. My mind's been all over the place. I've been a wreck.'

I pushed his hair back from his face, kissed his forehead. 'Like I said, I could have helped. A worry shared is a worry halved, or something along those lines. I missed you.'

He nodded, and suddenly his mouth was on mine and we kissed like reunited lovers after months apart. It was nice, very nice.

Shane peeled his lips from mine. 'Paul isn't much of a bed mate, you know.'

'What about Cherry Love?' I said, with maybe a touch of spite.

He pulled away. 'Shit, Abby! She's nothing! Graeme's known her for ages. He put us together for the tattoo, that's all!'

I had to believe he was telling the truth. 'How long do you have for a lunch break?'

He looked at his watch. 'Crap, better get back. Old Mrs Tucker wants her garden edging finished this afternoon and I'm not sure if Thommo and young Lucas are up to the task.'

'Are you?' My gaze dropped to his groin. 'Does it hurt, this lump?'

'No, not much. I don't know if that's a good sign or not.'

I fed my arm through his and walked with him to the car park.

'You're coming back home tonight, aren't you?'

'If you'll have me.'

'Of course. I might even make it worth your while ... if you're up to it.'

He grinned down at me. 'What are you getting at, Mrs Eaton?'

'I'm feeling a little compassion coming on. Stay tuned, that's all I'm saying. Make sure you let me know if you hear anything from the doctor.'

His face was serious again. 'I promise I'll let you know as soon as I find out something.'

'Good. And there's stuff I want to talk to you about too. You'll be surprised to hear what's been going on in your absence.'

'Will I now,' he said, arching his eyebrows.

I watched as Shane got into his ute and drove away. Please God, I prayed, let the ultrasound results bring good news.

29

Tulip Wood 1957

Locked in an embrace, Marion and Banjo stumble down the hallway. In their urgency, they trip over each other's feet and knock into a wall, almost freeing three porcelain ducks from their brass hooks. Gripping the nearest doorknob, Banjo turns it with impatience. Eagerness propels them through the doorway. Slipping on a rug, they tumble to the floor.

Banjo eases Marion off him. 'Sorry,' he wheezes, 'have we met before?'

Her eyes roll. She kneels over him and proceeds to undo his shirt buttons. 'I so love your chest,' she says, parting the fabric, and bending to kiss each taut muscle.

Her tongue tickles and leaves a moist trail as it travels upwards to his neck. He tries to kiss her, but she teasingly moves away, her green eyes alive with play. His excitement increases and Marion utters his own thoughts.

'This is a dream come true.'

'You bet it is,' he says grasping her around the waist.

'I couldn't be happier,' she smiles.

'Oh yeah? Let's see what I can do about that.'

He thrusts her aside and stands. Pulling Marion to her feet, he pushes her against a tall cedar wardrobe. Stroking her cheek, he then trails his fingers down to the collar of her flowered frock. Peeling back the fabric he leans in and kisses the hollow at the base of her throat. Marion lets out a strangled breath. He proceeds to undo the buttons that line the dress from neck to hem, but fumbles with the fourth one.

'Damn, woman,' he groans, 'how many buttons are there?'

'About ten,' Marion giggles, and deftly undoes the remainder herself. Pink satin and a net petticoat skirt are revealed. With a shrug, the dress slips to the floor.

Banjo scoops her up and carries her to the double bed. Dropping her onto the mattress, she bounces, the petticoat netting fluttering around her. He is relieved to see that there will be no grappling with stockings and suspenders this time.

Marion lays back, spreading her arms wide. A fingernail catches in the stitching of an embroidered pillowcase. She eases free, lifts the pillow and studies the intricate, floral craftwork. A frown wrinkles her forehead. 'This isn't your bedroom, is it?'

'No, it's my mum's,' he says, tugging the petticoat netting down to her ankles and slipping it over her sandled feet.

'And this is your mother's bed.'

'Yes.' He pulls her shoes off and drops them on the floor. Leaning over her, he fingers a bra strap, sliding it from her shoulder. Then does the same with the other.

Marion touches his cheek. 'I don't think we should be doing this here.'

He stops. 'Why not? It's not the first time this bed's been used for such a thing,'

She sits up. 'What do you mean by that?'

'It was my parent's bed,' he quickly adds. 'I'm sure they used it for more than just sleeping.'

'Oh ... but what if your mum finds out?'

'Well, I won't be telling her, that's for sure.' He kisses her bare shoulder. Sneaking a hand around her back, he undoes the clasps. As the garment loosens, something falls from the satin confines and lands in Marion's lap. He laughs, collects a piece of popcorn, and stuffs it into his mouth. 'Well look at that, it's still warm.'

Marion smiles, shakes free of her bra, and falls back onto the mattress.

Banjo's hands tremble as they glide over her bare midriff and cup her breasts. When his fingers roam and tease her flesh, she writhes and turns her head.

'Stop,' she cries, grabbing him by the wrists.

He scowls. 'What the hell! Not this again?'

Marion pushes his hands away and covers her bare chest. 'Your mother's watching us.'

Banjo jerks around, checks the doorway, and relaxes. 'No she's not. There's no one there silly.'

'Not the door. Over there,' her eyes motion to the left.

He turns. Hanging on the wall is a painting of a woman. She has cropped blonde hair and a curious expression on her face. He gives a chuckle. 'You recognised her, did you? It's a recent self-portrait.'

'Well it's making me rather nervous. I can't tell if she's concerned or annoyed.'

'I can fix that.'

He reaches for the petticoat and flings it across the room. It flutters and drapes over the portrait, covering it completely.

'Thank you,' Marion says, 'That's much better.'

'Now, where were we?' he asks.

She places his hands on her breasts. 'I think we were about here.'

'I so love your chest,' he grins, and replaces one hand with his mouth.

She laughs, and lifts her legs, easing his boxer shorts down with her toes.

Never in his wildest imaginations did Banjo think he would be spending his afternoon making love to the girl of his dreams, right here on his mother's chenille bedspread. Once again, fate has brought them together. What knucklehead would argue with destiny? Not this one, that's for sure, he thinks, as Marion wriggles out of her satin knickers.

Walking down the hall from the kitchen, Banjo almost collides with Marion as she steps out of the bathroom wrapped in his mother's lavender towel. A blush colours her cheeks as she eyes his bare chest where her fingernails had scored his flesh. He recalls the exact moment this happened, and knows she is doing the same. She rushes past.

He follows her to his mother's bedroom and leans against the doorframe as Marion collects her strewn clothing.

'I need to get back to Brisbane,' she says, removing her petticoat from the picture frame and her bra from the bed's headboard. 'I wasn't planning to stay out all day, and Aunt Gloria will be frantic if I don't turn up for dinner.'

Banjo checks his wristwatch. 'I guess if we leave soon, I could get you back in time.'

She kneels to search under the bed. Retrieves the engagement ring. At another thrilling point in their love making, Banjo sucked it from her finger and spat it onto the floor.

Straightening, she examines the room. 'What did you do with my knickers?'

He glances high. 'On top of the wardrobe.'

'How'd they get there?'

'Beats me,' he smirks, and reaches for the garment. Marion holds out her hand, but he refuses to pass them to her. 'I could keep them for my Marion collection. They'll go nicely with the stocking and hanky.'

She snatches them from his grip. 'Sorry, but I'm not travelling back to Brisbane without underpants.'

Before she can gather up her dress and sandals, Banjo steps in her way. 'I don't want you to go. Stay the night.'

'And how would I explain my absence?'

'I don't know. You're a clever girl, I'm sure you could come up with some excuse.'

She shakes her head. 'It wouldn't be right.'

'Oh, well,' he moans, 'let's have a bite to eat before we head off. I can make sandwiches. Corned beef with pickles.'

'Great. I'm starving. I'll just get dressed first.'

He grins. 'You don't have to, you know.'

'Yes, I do, you devil.'

'Devil? Not me.' He gives the towel a tug.

Marion grabs it before it slips away. 'Hey, get me something to eat.'

'Okay, you party pooper. I'll give Honey her tucker first. Meet you on the front verandah.'

They share a plate of sandwiches on the porch steps.

Marion touches Banjo's arm. 'I'm going to tell my parents the engagement is off.'

He gives her a nudge with his elbow. 'So you should. Especially after what we've just done. How will you handle the flak? I'm guessing it won't be easy.'

'I'll think of you,' she smiles, 'that'll give me strength.' She leans back against the railing. Closing her eyes, she takes in a deep breath. 'I see what you mean. The jasmine scent is glorious.'

'So are you.' He moves his hand up a bare leg. 'What can I do to convince you to stay?'

'Hmm ... how about a kiss. That should be sufficient.'

'A kiss? But I thought you said you couldn't—'.

She covers his mouth with hers.

Banjo pulls away. 'What about your aunt? You said she'd be worried.'

She gives a coy smile. 'I hope you don't mind, I used your telephone to call her when you were out feeding Honey. I told her I had bumped into an old girlfriend and was staying over for the night. She was fine about it.'

He plants a kiss on her forehead. 'Wacko. I knew you could do it.'

The remainder of the afternoon is spent walking the property and taking photos with Banjo's Box Brownie camera. As the sun sets, they cook a simple dinner together and drink their way through two bottles of cold beer.

Afterwards, while listening to his collection of records, Banjo reminds Marion that she owes him a waltz from the Apple Blossom Ball. She tells him that it wasn't her fault he'd gotten himself involved in a stoush and had missed his chance. He chides her for ditching him for her father, and she argues that Banjo seemed only too relieved to give in to her dad's wishes, probably due to not being able to waltz satisfactorily. She seems impressed when he finds appropriate music and succeeds in proving her assumption wrong.

They round off the evening by toasting the day that had brought them back together with a few glasses of Fran Baxter's sweet sherry, and a little poetry. Banjo had hoped to follow this with a repeat performance of the afternoon's adventure—this time by candlelight—but when he finishes reciting 'The Man from Snowy River', he discovers Marion has fallen fast asleep in his arms.

Marion wakes. She is in Banjo's bed, alone. Sometime in the night he'd carried her here rather than his mother's room, but she only has a hint of that memory. Another memory—one she can recall with clarity and doesn't ever want to forget—she lingers on, smiling as she realises they had acted out their own version of *Love in the Afternoon*.

He'd been so gentle, yet so intuitive, understanding exactly what her body craved before she'd even worked that out herself. Obviously he was much more experienced than her in the art of love making, but she didn't want to dwell on that, only that she'd been the eager recipient of his affection. A desire for a repeat performance surfaces. Maybe this time Banjo will let her take the lead. Wondering where he has gone, her answer comes with the smell of toast and the sound of something sizzling on the stove. Her mouth waters. Breakfast first, then she'll see what transpires.

Marion rolls onto her side. For the first time in a long while, she is happy. No, not just happy, ecstatic. Ecstatic and safe and excited about the future. Her eyes are drawn to a dark curl of hair lying on the pillow. It is Banjo's. She touches it and it comes to life, wrapping around her finger. Blowing a puff of air through her lips, she watches the curl lift off the bed and float away.

Now this, she notes, is the bedroom of a male. Olive green and brown tones decorate the stark but tidy room. A bookcase dominating one wall is filled with an assortment of classics. Amongst them are books on poetry, C.S Lewis's 'The Lion, the Witch and the Wardrobe', and on the bottom shelf, a pile of adventure comics. Such diverse tastes, she muses. That's what makes him so intriguing to her—so many facets. She throws back the bed covers and discovers she is dressed only in her underwear. Unable to locate her dress, she improvises with what is on hand.

A smile plays on her lips as she saunters into the kitchen wearing Banjo's oversized leather jacket. Zipped up, the sleeves hang past her fingertips and the hem almost reaches her knees. 'Good morning,' she says, rising on her toes to give him a peck on the cheek and run a hand over his bare chest.

'It certainly is,' he responds, with a grin.

'I can't seem to find my dress.'

'It's hanging up in the laundry. It was creased. I ironed it for you. Are you hungry?'

'I'm starving!'

'That's what I like in a girl. A healthy appetite.'

He scoops four rashers of bacon and two fried eggs onto each plate, followed by grilled tomatoes and a piece of buttered toast. Handing a plate to Marion he leads her out the back door.

A short pathway brings them to a sunny courtyard shielded by flowering shrubs and edged by a garden filled with colour. In the centre are two seagrass chairs and a table set with cutlery and glasses of orange juice. Banjo pulls out a chair and waits for her to sit before seating himself. In the warmth of the morning sun, and surrounded by birdsong, they share their first breakfast together.

'I'm thinking of catching the train back to Brisbane,' Marion says.

Banjo wipes his mouth with the back of his hand. 'I don't mind taking you to your aunt's. It'll give me another opportunity to ride the bike.'

'I don't want to put you out, and I could do with some time to think.'

'Are you sure?'

She nods. 'I can catch the train from Shadow Creek this morning, can't I?'

'Yep, there are a couple of trains today.'

'I'll catch one to the city, and head back to Stanthorpe tomorrow.'

Banjo stretches, placing his hands behind his head. His eyes squint. 'I think you're a little underdressed.'

Marion checks her outfit, 'It's all I could grab in a hurry.'

'Eager to see me, were you?'

She grins. 'Eager for breakfast.'

'Close your eyes.'

'Why?'

'Trust me,' he says, rising.

Marion does as she is told. She hears Banjo moving around behind her. Her hair is lifted from her neck, and there is a cool sensation against her skin. Her eyes flick open. A silver chain disappears below the leather collar. She unzips the jacket until a heart-shaped pendant is revealed.

'Hey,' she exclaims, 'this has the same pattern as those china pin dishes you gave me.'

'Apple Blossoms.'

'Yes, apple blossoms. Where did you get it?'

Banjo rests his hands on her shoulders. 'I had it made from the broken dish you left at the Soldier's Memorial.'

Marion cringes. 'Oh, that's where I'd left it. I was going to have the dish repaired. I dropped it the night my Father told me about … well … about—'

'I thought you'd smashed it on purpose,' he interrupts, his grasp strengthening on her shoulders.

'But I hadn't . . . honestly, I wouldn't.'

He leans down, his mouth against her ear. 'It doesn't matter now.'

His grip eases. Fingers brush over her skin, following the line of the chain until they reach the pendant. 'Even though I was damn sure we were over, a shred of hope remained. I had a piece of the china cut into this heart shape. A silversmith set it for me. I've been keeping it, just in case.'

Her hand touches his. 'It's beautiful. Thank you.'

He moves around and squats before her. 'I love you, Marion Douglas. I'm not afraid to say that now.'

She smiles. 'And I reckon I might just love you back, that's why I want to leave here as soon as possible. I need to tell my parents about us. I want to get it over and done with so I can be free to live my own life.'

'That's with me, right?'

'Of course, silly. Though before I go, there is one thing I need to do.'

Rising from her chair, she unzips the jacket fully and slips out of the leather. The only thing she is now wearing is the heart necklace.

30

Taking a detour on my way home from the park, I deviated into Shadow Creek to do some shopping. Feeling guilty for thinking the worst of Shane over the last week, I planned an early evening picnic. From the bakery, I bought Shane's favourite chocolate brownies and a rustic bread loaf. I also bought cheese, olives, hummus dip and crackers from the grocery store, and visited the bottle shop at the pub to buy a bottle of cabernet. As I walked back down the road to my car, I bumped into Lester Schilling. He was all smiles.

'Abby! Nice dress. Brings out your eyes. What have you been up to?'

The last thing I wanted was to be caught up in another awkward conversation about his marital woes. 'Oh, this and that.'

'Need someone to share that with?' He indicated the wine bottle sticking out of the paper bag.

'No ... all good, thanks.'

He nodded, but did not move out of my way. I stepped to the side to walk around him.

He grabbed my arm. 'Hang on, what's the rush?'

I looked down at the hand gripping my elbow. 'Lester, what are you—.'

'Sorry,' he released his hold. 'I have something for you.' He rolled his eyes. 'Well not actually for you, for your dad.'

'My dad?'

'Yes, it's in my office. C'mon over. I'll get it for you.'

'How about I stay here while you dash over and get it'.

He frowned. 'Okay, I won't be long.'

He took off across the road while I waited in the shade of a shop awning wondering what he had for my father. Dad wasn't buying another house, was he?

A motorbike zipped around the corner and suddenly pulled up in front of me.

Graeme Roper flipped up the visor of his helmet. 'Hey there, Abbs! Need any more rescuing?'

I glanced across the road to Schilling Real Estate. 'No, I'm fine.'

'Goodo. I hope you're not going to drink that all alone,' he said, eyeing my purchase.

'No. In fact, I'm intending to share it with my husband.'

'Shane?'

'Well that's the only husband I have at present.'

He combed his fingers through his beard. 'He contacted you? Good. I left him a few messages telling him to do so. Is he back in town?'

'He will be. Oh ... and I now know about his tattoo.'

His eyes lit up. 'You do? What do you think? Brilliant design isn't it? Cherry is one talented chick. She's in hot demand right now.'

Her profile picture flashed into my mind. Yep, I'm sure a lot of guys were baying for her attention. With what I had planned for the evening, I was going to make sure Shane was not one of them.

I wasn't sure if Graeme knew about Shane's testicle lump, so I didn't mention it. He said goodbye and sped away, just as Lester returned.

He handed me a large cardboard document wallet. 'It's information about your dad's house. Some old photos from when it first went up for sale in the 1960s. I found them the other day while searching our archives for something else. I told your dad I'd keep them for him, but seeing you're here, you may as well take them and pass them on.'

I said I would, and told him I had to go before my cheese warmed. He let me go this time.

Passing Fine 'n' Dandy, I remembered I still needed to find a black shawl to go with my outfit for the party the next night. I retraced my steps and went inside.

Donna was counting cash from the till.

'Hiya Abby. How's things?'

'Rolling along. Hey, do you have a black shawl anywhere that I can add to my costume?'

'A black shawl ... you know I think I might have something.' She pointed to a far corner. 'Have a look over there on the rack near the handbags.'

I dropped my shopping on the counter and went over to scrounge. Amongst a collection of fur stoles smelling of mothballs, I found a black knitted shawl with a fringe. Just what I needed.

'All this for the party tomorrow night?' Donna said, as I returned to find her rifling through my shopping.

'No, I have something romantic planned for tonight.'

'Ooh ... putting the sizzle back into the schmizzle, hey?'

'Something like that,' I said, with a half-smile.

She looked at me oddly. 'This is with Shane, right?'

'Of course!'

'Good ... just checking. Found your secret admirer yet?'

'No ... and don't call him that. That is even if it is a him.'

She leant over the counter. 'Now that'd be a turn around. A secret female admirer.'

'I'm going,' I said, grabbing my shopping before she started getting any other ideas. 'See you tomorrow.'

'There are several gay women here in town, you know,' I heard her shout as I walked out the door.

I arrived at my car to find something on my windscreen. It was wedged behind a wiper blade. I tugged it free. It was a lady's shoe —old, black, and with a buckled ankle strap, like one my mother might have worn in her younger years. It was for a left foot. Very strange. Who would put such an item here? And why?

I spun around. No one suspicious seemed to be lurking nearby, just the usual type of people found frequenting town on a Friday afternoon—mums with kids, middle-aged couples out for coffee and cake, elderly folk buying their weekend supplies before the tourist rush on the weekend, a few council workers. Nobody seemed to be taking any interest in me holding up a lone shoe like Prince Charming looking for the perfect fit. Maybe it was some strange Halloween prank.

I scanned across the road. Two teenaged boys in school uniforms were sitting outside 'Merv's Fish 'n' Chippery' slurping on bright blue slushies. Could they have been the pranksters? No, they seemed to be too busy coping with brain freezes to have had me in their sights. Puzzled, I threw the shoe on the back seat along with the groceries and got behind the wheel.

31

Stanthorpe 1957

The bus drops Marion off half a mile from the Duff's property. She has to walk the rest of the way in the afternoon heat; the weight of her suitcase increasing with each difficult step.

Her arm aches and her knee throbs from being buffeted by hard leather. Having spent the travelling hours summoning up the courage to speak to her parents about Banjo, she now makes excuses for postponing the inevitable showdown. It would be best to leave informing them of her decision till after dinner that night. Or tomorrow morning before the stress of the day has taken its toll on her father. Then she imagines the long night ahead with lack of sleep due to an anxious wait. No, she needs to get it over and done with; the sooner the better.

She drops the suitcase from her stiffened grasp and rubs her sweaty hand over her skirt. Taking in a deep breath, she prays for the strength to proceed as planned. Her parent's reaction may well surprise her. For all she knows, they might show compassion and see the importance of her happiness—especially when there are graver things to be concerned about. Taking hold of the worn handle with her other hand, she continues.

Inside the cottage, Marion is greeted with silence. The lounge room and kitchen are devoid of life, though there is evidence that lunch has recently been eaten. A plate, two soup bowls, and cutlery are stacked unwashed in the sink. Half a loaf of bread is sitting uncovered on the bench, and so too is a dish of melting butter. Peeking into the small room her father now uses as his bedroom, she finds it also unoccupied. The bed is made, though the cover is crumpled on one edge as if it has recently been sat on, possibly while putting on shoes. Relief comes with the knowledge that the altercation will now be delayed.

Coming to her mother's room, Marion eases the door open and looks inside. The interior is dark and less tidy. This bed is unmade, which is expected seeing her mother spends most of the day resting. The coverlet has been pulled back, and the overstuffed pillows lay askew on the wrinkled sheets. Mustiness fills the air. Marion drops her suitcase by the door and inches her way across the room, stepping over a pile of strewn clothing to reach the window.

Her nose crinkles at the sour odour coming from this side of the room. She draws aside the curtains, forces the window catch, and heaves up the frame as far as it will go. Both sunlight and a breeze rush in. She takes a lungful of fresh air and turns, hearing a metallic ring as her shoe clips an object on the floor. Bending, she discovers that it is an enamel bowl. Then she gags when she sees that it contains congealed vomit. She holds her nose and picks up the bowl.

A moan comes from the floor at the foot of the bed. Marion moves aside folds of material and is shocked to find that what she thought was a pile of clothing, is actually her mother.

'Mum, are you alright?' The moan grows louder as she lifts her mother's head and uses the edge of the bed cover to wipe away a smear of bile from the paled lips. 'Can you hear me, Mum? What happened?'

Veined eyelids flicker. Her mother gives a phlegmy cough, and Marion bends lower to hear the rasping voice.

'I was sick.'

'I know, Mum, it's okay.' She strokes a clammy cheek.

'My head ... the pain.'

'Where's Dad? I thought he'd be home.'

Bloodshot eyes squint against the light. 'He was ...' She coughs again, and a glob of spit slides down her chin. 'He said he needed to go out ... just for a while.' She winces and tries to lift a shaking hand to her head, though her arm just falls onto her chest.

'Can you sit up?' Marion tries to lift the frail body, but the shriek that follows, stops her. 'I need to call the ambulance. I'll go over to the Duff's to use their telephone. Okay?'

Her mother nods and closes her eyes.

Marion takes a pillow from the bed and eases it under the sagging head. She carefully rolls her mother onto her side and positions another pillow behind her back for support. 'I'll be really quick.'

Making her way through the gap in the bottlebrush hedge, she crosses the yard to the main house and notices her father's black Buick is parked in the drive. 'Thank God, he's here,' she says.

Stepping up to the wide, open verandah she pounds on the wire screen door. No one answers so she opens it and walks into the foyer. The sitting room to the left is vacant except for quality furniture and expensive decor. An impressive mahogany sideboard holds a tall oriental vase filled with long stemmed roses. A single petal drops onto the polished surface next to her father's felt hat. She calls out for him, just as the mantle clock chimes the half hour. Checking the parlour on the right, she is disillusioned at finding there is nobody there either. Her head twists as a murmur of voices comes from deeper in the house.

She hurries down the hall, past empty bedrooms, and enters the kitchen, only to discover that the sounds are coming from a room off from this. Created when the side verandah was closed in, and made into a sleep-out, it is now Katherine Duff's personal retreat. Marion has never ventured in here before, but knows it is where Mrs Duff likes to read, or do handiwork, or relax in the quiet. The French doors are slightly ajar and the noises now coming from within spark her curiosity. She creeps closer and peers through the gap, instantly wishing she hadn't.

Two bodies are bent over a table scattered with an array of colourful gerberas. Water dribbling over the edge from an overturned crystal vase, is forming a puddle on the linoleum. This doesn't deter the pair as they rock in unison, the timber creaking beneath them. The wild flapping of a white shirttail gives glimpses of flabby, pale buttocks, while rumpled around the ankles of the thick legs, are a familiar pair of navy-blue trousers. Marion's mouth falls open, then is covered by her hand as she catches sight of the second person's flushed face, quivering long-lashed eyelids, and full lips parted to release a high, extended moan.

Marion pulls away and retreats through the kitchen, bumping

against chairs and cupboards in her haste to distance herself from the horror. Sprinting up the hallway, she fights off a wave of nausea to reach the wall mounted telephone. Fingers fumble as they dial, and the voice that requests an ambulance be sent does not sound like hers.

Returning the receiver to its cradle, she hears her name called. She spins around. Her father stands in the kitchen doorway looking startled. His trousers are now pulled up though his shirt, hurriedly tucked in, has a corner caught in the clumsily fastened fly. Marion looks away.

'What are you doing here?' he wheezes.

'Mum's bad ... I came over to call for an ambulance.'

'You should have knocked,' he growls. 'It would have been polite.'

'I did,' she says, forcing her eyes to meet his.

He gives a fleeting sideway glance into the kitchen. 'We were ... busy.'

'I could see that,' Marion snarls, watching his eyes widen with the realisation that his betrayal is no longer a secret.

Without another word passing between them, Marion heads for the front door and races down the stairs. Her eyes sting, and her heart kicks hard against her ribs as she crosses the yard towards the cottage.

32

A picnic spot along the creek just outside of town, towards Tulipwood, was where I'd chosen to have our rendezvous. I'd messaged Shane and told him to meet me there rather than head straight home. He sent back a smiling emoji. I then informed Elliott that he would be looking after himself for dinner as his dad and I were eating out. He seemed quite pleased with this arrangement, especially when I informed him that his father was returning home.

On my way, I remembered I needed batteries for the lanterns I was taking, so I stopped at the grocery store to purchase some. When I returned to my car, I noticed a vehicle parked two spaces over. It looked like the dusty grey ute that had stopped that day at Tickle Bridge. I couldn't tell whether the driver was sitting behind the wheel or not. I stared back at the store. Maybe the creep was in there doing a little evening shopping. Had I passed him as I darted around looking for batteries? I tried to recall if I'd seen anyone in the store wearing a wide brimmed hat. I didn't think I had, but then he could have removed it before entering. The thought of hanging around and meeting him face to face unnerved me. Anyway, I had other things to do. I got into my car, locked the door, and drove away.

The picnic ground was just off the main road, but nestled in bushland along the creek. A short walk led to a lovely rock pool which was quite popular on hot days when the water was flowing. I knew Shane wouldn't be far behind, so I quickly collected my basket of goodies and hurried over to a table inside a covered shelter, setting it with the wine, glasses, a cheese platter including salami and olives, and the chocolate brownies. I then placed the batteries into the lanterns. The sun hadn't yet set, but it was dark here all the same; lots of shadows. I switched the lanterns on.

Kicking off my shoes, I dropped them along the dirt path leading to the creek. Then slipping out of my dress, I hung it over a shrub in easy view. Now wearing only a pale blue lace bodysuit that Shane had bought me a couple of Valentine's Days ago, I hid amongst the bushes.

A splash came from the water nearby. I'd heard that platypus frequented this part of the creek and, being shy little creatures, to catch sight of one was rare. While I had a little time, I thought I'd have a quick peek.

I tip-toed to the water's edge and stood still on a rock trying to blend in with the scenery. Another splash, and then ripples in the water. I leant down for a closer look, and slipped. Losing balance, I fell ungraciously into the rock pool. It wasn't very deep, but aquatic weeds wrapping around my flailing limbs threatened to keep me captive. As I struggled to extricate myself from their grasp, I heard a car arrive.

Eventually finding my footing, I stumbled from the water.

Light flashed amongst the bushes.

'Great, you found me!' I cried, dripping with creek sludge.

A blinding LED light illuminated my soaked condition. What could I do but spread my arms wide and give a bow.

'A water nymph, just for you,' I announced.

A murmur came from the foliage but the light didn't move away.

I shivered from the dampness. 'What are you doing? Oh ... I get it. You want a raunchy little show.' I slowly slipped one shoulder strap down. 'Is that what you want?'

The light shook a little.

I slid the other strap down and gave a little shimmy. Deciding to bust a few energetic dance moves to aid my nervous stripping, I attempting to channel Shakira, or Beyonce, but ended up looking more like a writhing Mr Bean. The trouble with wet lace is that it clings so very tightly, making it difficult to slide down. The only way I could release myself from the bodysuit was by tugging and wiggling until my breasts were freed from their entrapment. I jumped and wriggled some more, but without further success. Getting the lingerie past my waist and over my hips proved impossible.

'Sorry,' I said, holding up my hands and gasping for air, 'I'm pooped. The show's over.'

That's when I heard the sound of another vehicle arriving. I froze, surprised and horrified that this spot was so popular after sunset.

Shane took off, crashing through the bush as he made his escape.

'Thanks heaps!' I called after him.

Pushing through scratchy bushes, I peered out at the clearing. A vehicle was pulling out of the car park. Both our cars were still there, which meant Shane must have shooed them away or something. I was now free to walk out into the open.

Finding my dress still hanging from the shrub, I wrapped it around me and walked up to the picnic shelter. Shane was already hoeing into the cheese and drinking the wine straight from the bottle.

'Well, that could have been embarrassing,' I said, flopping onto the bench seat.

He turned around and almost choked on a mouthful of Brie. 'Bloody hell, what happened to you?'

'I fell in the creek before you showed up and forced me to strip.'

'You did what?'

'Fell in the creek.'

'No, I meant the other bit.'

'The stripping? You saw me. It was pathetic, I know.'

He shook his head. 'I didn't see anything. I've been eating.'

'Yeah, now you are. But before, you were down there with me.'

He frowned. 'What do you mean? I only just got here.'

'Liar. You were shining the light and watching.'

He eyed me quizzically. 'Ah ... nope, I was running late. I arrived just before that guy left.'

'What guy?'

'The guy in the ute. Didn't you see him?'

A shudder worked its way up my spine. 'Did you say a ute?'

'An ancient EH Holden ute.'

I held my breath. 'What colour was it?'

'I don't know ... blue ... grey.

My hands went to my face. 'OH MY GOD!'

The wine bottle slipped from Shane's grasp, but he caught it before it hit the ground. 'What's wrong?'

'He must have followed me here from the store. It was him watching me, not you.'

'Taking your clothes off?'

I stared, unable to muster even one little blink. Then Shane leant over and ripped my dress away. His laugh was way too raucous.

I jumped up and punched him in the arm. 'It's not funny. It's creepy and embarrassing, and I could've been ravaged.'

'Well you must've given him a whopper of a fright because he sure took off in a hurry.'

I stabbed a finger into his chest. 'You should contact the police.'

'Do you know the ute's registration number?'

'No.'

'Would you be able give a description of the guy?'

I thought for a moment. 'Not really. Could you?'

He shook his head. 'Well, that doesn't give much to go on then.'

He was right. What else could I do? I covered my nakedness with an arm, and poured myself a glass of wine, downing it in one go.

'What are you smiling at?' I growled. I'd expected Shane to wrap me in his arms and offer some sympathy, but no, he just stood there with a silly grin on his stupid face.

'I'm feeling pretty damn happy because, other than seeing you in next-to-nothing, I have some good news.'

'The doctor phoned?'

He nodded. 'Yep. It seems I'm in the clear. The lump is just a cyst. A hydrocele. If it doesn't go away by itself, it will just need draining or minor surgery. I should be as right as rain.'

'That's brilliant! No ball removal.' I hugged him like I'd never hugged anyone before.

Pulling away, I looked down at my skimpily clad self, and groaned. 'It really doesn't leave much to the imagination, does it?'

Shane shook his head. 'Shame to let it all go to waste.'

Grabbing the cheese knife from the platter, he gave one quick slash and the blue lace dropped to my feet.

My anguish soon vanished. For, unlike the lingerie, my original plan had not come undone.

33

Stanthorpe, January 1958

Raindrops chink and splatter against window glass. Marion traces them with her finger as they slither down the pane to sneak under the frame and drip onto the hospital room floor. Perched on the wide window ledge, she wipes a tear from her cheek and rests her head against the cool glass. Her gaze moves across the room to the wrought iron bed, and the frail body partially covered by starched white sheeting.

On being admitted to this ward, her mother's health has quickly declined, and her body—riddled with tumours—is shutting down. Her lack of response, her laboured breathing, and the unpleasant odour drifting around the room indicate that death is imminent. It could be a matter of hours. Marion clings to the assurance that her mother feels no pain; that it will be a peaceful end and she'll just slip away.

Since being told the bad news, Marion's emotions have found new heights. She has spent the precious time left, holding her mother's hand, stroking her hair, and holding a one-sided conversation. When her mother had been more lucid, she'd nodded and stared as Marion gabbled on, reminiscing. On Christmas morning, Marion had the room filled with vases of poinsettia cuttings, and red and white carnations. A nurse brought in a portable record player and played Harry Belafonte's beautiful new song, 'Mary's Boy Child', three times over. Her mother had smiled that day. But on New Year's Eve, just as the sound of fireworks and revelry from the streets outside heralded the birth of 1958, her mother had lapsed into unconsciousness. That was three days ago, and all Marion can do is wait.

Once again, she opens the Christmas card Banjo had sent her. They haven't seen each other since their time together at Tulip Wood. He had wanted to come to Stanthorpe to be with her, but she'd talked him out of it. Things were already difficult here without him turning up to complicate them further. A sprig of jasmine and two photos had been inserted in the card. Marion lifts the jasmine and breathes in its redolent scent as she studies the pictures of herself and Banjo taken at the cottage. How happy they were that day. She aches for the comfort of his arms.

The door opens noisily, and her father appears.

Marion watches him as he walks to the foot of the hospital bed. She's hardly spoken to him since the disgusting incident at the Duff's, and has even orchestrated her visits to the hospital so as not to coincide with his. Staying with Lucy at her flat here in town has given her easy access to the hospital, and distance from her father. She observes him with loathing. His suit is damp around the shoulders and his hat, now held at his side, drips water onto the floor. Marion's eyes follow the drops, notices his navy-blue trousers. She cringes at the horrid memory of those same trousers crumpled rudely around his ankles. When he moves to the bedside and leans forward to murmur into his wife's ear, Marion's anger rises. She cannot remain silent any longer.

'What are you doing, seeking her forgiveness?'

He turns in surprise and catches her sitting on the ledge. 'Spying on me again, are you?' he says.

'Spying? Is that what you thought I was doing at the Duff's?' Marion fervently shakes her head. 'I would rather rip my eyes out than watch you at your dirty games.'

His eyes narrow, and he heads for the open door.

Boldly, Marion drops from the ledge and slams the door shut before he can walk out. Her father eyes her coldly, his lips press together so tightly she can see the quiver of his jaw.

She returns his glare. 'How could you leave Mum alone in the house like that?'

He takes his time to answer. 'Your mother was asleep when I left.'

'With no regard for your sick wife, you decided to go next door for a 'quickie'. Is that it?' He reaches for the knob. Marion leans against the door, keeping it closed. 'It wasn't the first time, was it?' she snaps.

His face reddens.

'Where else did you do it?'

'I am not talking to you about this,' he growls, and tries the knob again.

Marion slaps his hand away. 'Did Mum know?'

'Of course not! Now move away.'

Her courage grows. 'Was it consensual ... or did you have to use force?'

A sickly grin spreads across the sweaty, florid features. 'You tell me, you were there.'

Marion's skin crawls. The scene she has tried so hard to erase from her mind comes flooding back. With vivid recollection, she sees her father's face distorted in ecstasy—eyes bulging, face blotched with patches of pink—and then the parting full red lips of Donald Duff as he bends forward over his mother's table and releases a rapturous moan.

'You're depraved!' she cries.

He slaps her face. She stumbles sideways.

'Don't you dare judge me!' he shouts, shaking the brim of his hat in front of her face. 'You're not so perfect yourself, missy.'

Marion's hand trembles as she lifts it to her stinging cheek. She recoils when her father leans in.

'We all have our little secrets, don't we?'

Her tenacity returns. 'I think Cameron Duff needs to know yours. I'm sure he would be interested in hearing why you really wanted me and Donald to marry.'

The hat falls from her father's hand. He seizes her by the arms, his fingers squashing her flesh to the bone.

She winces, but doesn't move. 'I don't know which is worse. You using me to guarantee a close connection to Donald, or using poor Donald to gain access to the Duff's wealth.'

'You little bitch!' He rams her hard against the door. 'And what will people think when they find out about you and a certain music teacher?'

Marion flinches.

'Mr Mercer, wasn't it? The one who was almost twice your age?'

'H-how did you know?'

'You'd missed the afternoon school bus, so I came looking for you. I'd assumed you'd forgotten to tell your mother about choir practice or netball training or whatever. From what I witnessed you seemed to be getting some interesting, private tuition.'

Marion slumps. In her last year at high school she'd had a crush on the handsome music teacher, like most of the girls in her year. It had been an especially difficult few months between her and her father, and Mr Mercer had been the only one to notice her unhappiness. That afternoon, when everyone else had left class for the day, he'd shared his concern. Her hunger for attention messed with her emotions, and one thing had led to another.

'It was just a kiss,' she says through clenched teeth.

Her father stares accusingly. 'Do you really expect me to believe that's all you did?'

'Yes. I was only fifteen. What did I know?'

'Plenty, from what I saw. It sickened me. I had to get away.'

Her father releases his hold but the ache doesn't cease.

She recalls the way she'd quivered when Richard Mercer had taken her face in his hands and kissed her. It was her first, and it felt incredible. It had been gentle, romantic—like in the movies—and she'd found herself reciprocating. He'd laid a hand on her breast and she'd liked that too, pressing into him, wanting more, letting him guide her hand down to feel the strength of his own desire. But that's as far as it went. He'd pulled away. Told her to go before it progressed further. Urged her not to tell anyone what had happened, that it was an error on his part. She'd been confused and then embarrassed, and had never told a soul, believing it was her fault for tempting him.

'It only happened the once,' she murmurs.

'Yes, because I put a stop to it.'

Marion frowns. 'What do you mean?'

'Why do you think Mercer tended his resignation soon after?'

'They told us he'd accepted a better position at a private school.' But she'd secretly believed it had much to do with her, and the guilt he'd felt, and she'd spiralled into a deeper depression for causing him to leave.

Her father sneers. 'Not before relieving me of a hefty sum.'

'You offered him money? A bribe?'

'Let's just say that when I confronted him about what I saw, he didn't hesitate in taking the bundle of bills I offered if he promised to leave the state. I guess he didn't like the idea of being charged with indecent dealings with a minor.'

Marion's mind whirled. 'You did that for me?'

He grins. 'Don't be stupid. If word got out about my slut of a daughter, I'd be a laughing stock. Mercer had to leave before he blabbed his mouth off. I do whatever it takes to keep my reputation intact. You should know that by now.'

'Reputation?' Marion laughs. 'You have sex with men. You can't keep that a secret forever.'

He blinks. There is a flash of unease in his eyes. His face loses its rigidity. 'Donald won't say a word.'

'What about the others? You don't expect me to believe he's the only one you've rutted.'

Her father lunges. Marion moves, but not fast enough. Her jaw is grabbed between strong fingers and her head is slammed against the plaster wall.

'You think you're such a smartarse, don't you?' he hisses. 'Well you're no match for me. There are people out there who'd be more than shocked to hear what you got up to.'

These words hurt as much as her throbbing skull. She'd accused Banjo of not trusting her with the truth. How would he react if he found out about her adolescent misconduct?

'I am a powerful man, with influence,' he snarls, gripping so tight she fears her jaw bone may snap. 'You may be my daughter, but when push comes to shove, I won't hesitate to ruin you!'

The door beside them bursts open. Marion is released as a nurse rushes in.

The starched white veil shudders as the nurse eyes them suspiciously. 'What's going on in here? I've heard all sorts of noises coming through these walls. Do you think Mrs Douglas needs to witness such a commotion? If you have any personal issues to sort out, do it somewhere else for, pity's sake.'

Marion glances over at the prostrate figure of her mother and doubts she can hear anything from the depths of her unconscious state.

Her father bends to retrieve his hat, and strides from the room, but not before turning to give his daughter an icy glare.

The nurse checks on her mother and then gives her attention to Marion. 'Are you all right, dear?'

Marion nods and moves towards the window, hardly aware that the rain has lessened and the clouds are now dispersing. Her heart pumps wildly. Tears form. If the nurse enquires any further she knows she will break down and blubber like a child. Placing her forehead on the cold glass, she closes her eyes.

After a few silent moments, she hears the door shut.

'I'm sorry Mum. Sorry if you heard all that.' Marion takes her mother's swollen hand in hers. The fingers are cool and the skin is paper-thin.

How had she survived living in a loveless marriage? Had she any inkling about her husband's ways? Marion knows that sometimes people choose to feign blindness, afraid to face the truth. Is this how her mother had coped? A lot of things made sense now. She and her mother—and to some extent, Donald—had been pawns in her father's game.

She gently combs her fingers through her mother's sparse, grey hair, just as her mother had done with her when she'd lay awake in bed as a child, afraid of the dark. It always had a soothing effect, and she hopes her touch is now doing the same for her. A sigh escapes the pale lips, and a great love swells within Marion.

She rests her own head on the pillow alongside her mother's and closes her eyes.

'Mum, I want to tell you more about the man I've fallen in love with.'

A few minutes later, a noise stops her mid-sentence. Someone is in the room. Her eyes flick open.

'Banjo!' she gasps, jumping to her feet. 'What are you doing here?'

'I came to see my girl,' he smiles, hurrying over.

Marion wraps her arms around him, presses her face against the warmth of his chest. 'I've missed you so much. I've just been talking to Mum about you.'

'I know. I heard.' Their lips meet briefly. 'I hope she doesn't mind you gabbing on about us. How's she doing?'

'They say it won't be long.'

He looks over at the bed. 'It must be so hard ... this waiting.'

Marion sniffs. He tilts her chin to wipe away the fresh tears, and she lets out a cry.

He eyes the welt on her face and studies her jaw. 'What the hell? Who did this?'

She drops her head. 'It doesn't matter.'

'By God it does! Your father did this, didn't he?'

'Forget it. It's no big deal.'

Banjo's hands are on her shoulders. 'This has happened before, hasn't it? The scar on your forehead. He caused that, didn't he?'

She lifts her face and sees pain in his dark eyes. She nods.

'What a bastard! Wait till I see him!'

'Please, please don't do anything,' she begs.

'I can't let him get away with it, Marion. It makes my blood boil to know he hurts you like this.'

'Please, Banjo, just forget it.'

'I don't understand. Why would he do this, especially now?'

Marion is touched by his concern. 'How long are you here for?'

'Just the afternoon. I caught a lift down with a delivery. We have to be back in Brisbane tonight.'

'I have some things to tell you.' Marion glances over at her mother. 'Let's go for a walk.'

The sun shines unhindered. Droplets sparkle from flowering shrubs and shimmer over newly mown grass like scattered diamonds. Banjo and Marion are seated on a concrete bench in a quiet corner of the hospital grounds. A half-eaten meat pie rests on its paper packet on Marion's lap. She has spent the last five minutes relating the details of the discovery of her father and Donald.

Banjo shakes his head. 'Well blow me down! You're definitely off the hook now.'

'Pardon?' Marion screws up her face.

'Your father can't expect you to marry Donald now that you know what they've been up to.'

'That's right, I'm free. Once Mum has ... has passed, I'm leaving Stanthorpe and returning to Brisbane.'

'Brisbane?' Banjo frowns, 'Or Shadow Creek?'

'Wherever. As long as I can call on you whenever I like, and vice versa.'

Banjo takes her hand. 'Marry me, Marion.'

Her mouth gapes. 'What did you say?"

'Let's get married. Let's make it official before someone else decides to snap you up.'

'But I'm ... complicated.'

'I like complicated. Haven't I proven that all ready?'

She thinks on her secret, the one her father is bound to expand on if word about his affair gets out. 'You don't know everything about me. I may be a disappointment.'

'Hardly,' he laughs. 'Now stop giving me the run around. You know I love you, so give me your answer.' He squeezes her hand. 'C'mon, don't leave a poor bloke hanging.'

'I love you Banjo, I really do. But there's Mum and ... and everything. I can't get my head around it. Can we just put it on hold until ...' Her throat tightens.

He pulls her to him. 'I'm sorry Marion. I'm a louse, I wasn't thinking. Of course, we'll talk about it later. When you can think more clearly.'

'Thank you,' she mouths.

'At least it's not a no, right?'

She nods and buries her face into his chest.

Ruth Douglas dies in the early hours of the next day. Marion is at her bedside.

'Don't be scared of the dark, Mum,' she whispers, caressing her mother's already cooling cheek. 'Soon you'll wake to a beautiful new day. One that will last forever.'

In the afternoon newspapers, it is reported that the Sputnik satellite burned up that day on re-entry into earth's atmosphere. Marion wonders if her mother had passed it on her way to heaven.

34

Home from our 'evening adventure', and now showered and changed into more suitable clothing, I made my way up to my loft study to find Shane examining the wall display.

'Well, you're certainly organised, I can see that much,' he said. 'Maybe you should be looking for a job with the police force, or consider starting up your own business as a private investigator.'

'Now that's an idea.' I handed him his coffee cup and took mine with me to the sofa. 'Though I can't say I'm successful yet. I still can't make heads or tails of it all.'

He sat beside me, putting his feet up on the wooden blanket box I used as a coffee table. It was nice having him home again. It felt normal, in a good way.

'Well from what you've told me,' he said, 'you've had a time of it while I was out of action. What do you make of these?' His foot nudged the black shoe and the newspaper page, now within a protective plastic sleeve.

I shrugged. 'Well the newspaper has a connection, but the

sandal ...it could be someone's idea of a joke ... or maybe someone was just throwing their rubbish my way.'

'Let's consider the hard evidence, other than those photos up there.' He counted on his fingers. 'A necklace with a heart pendant. A piece of paper with a poem. The front page of a newspaper reporting the crash. A shoe. Am I missing anything?'

I settled back, took a gulp of my coffee. 'That's about it.'

'You believe the necklace was cousin Marion's, and the poem was discovered inside, so,' he drew a tick in the air, 'a connection. She died in a train crash, the same one reported on the front page of a newspaper.' Another tick. 'You said you did some research and found the shoe was consistent with styles from the fifties and sixties. Well, the crash was in 1958.' He traced a third tick in the air.

'Okay, smarty pants, if they are somehow connected to Marion, or the same event, why were they passed on to me?'

'I have a theory,' declared Elliott from the top of the stairs.

'Welcome, Sherlock,' I said, giving him a nod. 'Eavesdropping, were you?'

He seemed to have settled down from the serious conversation he'd had earlier with his father. As expected, Shane hadn't been pleased with the news about the marijuana crop and had given his ruling on Elliott's punishment: two weekends, without pay, assisting him with a landscaping job for a neighbour down the road. The erection of new fencing and the laying of a sandstone path were on the agenda.

Elliott wheeled my desk chair over and took a seat in front of us. 'Nope, just coming up to ask if Bree can stay over tomorrow night while you're boozing it up at that freaky party.'

'Firstly, we won't be boozing it up, and secondly, only if Bree sleeps in Gemma's room. No funny business under my roof, buddy.'

'Our roof,' corrected Shane.

'Sorry,' I patted his leg, 'I got used to not having you around.'

He gave an exaggerated sigh, and then turned to Elliott. 'So, what's your theory?'

Elliott rested his elbows on the chair's armrests. 'Well, I was talking with Bree, and we reckon someone must have found the shoe and necklace at the crash site ... maybe even on the day of the crash and, you know, kept them as souvenirs.'

'But why would they have now passed them on to me?' I asked.

'Somehow they found out you were related to Marion?'

'Are you saying that both the necklace and the shoe belonged to Marion?'

He nodded.

'Well, how would they know that?'

Elliott looked at me, looked at his father, came back to me. 'Either this person knew her personally, or was there at the train crash and took them from her.'

I cringed. 'You mean, like, snatched them from her dead body? That's horrible.'

'Or while she lay dying.'

I gasped. 'No! Now that's disgusting. No one would have done that.'

Shane dropped his feet to the floor and leant forward. 'Okay. Let's just say all this is true.' His eyes stared into mine. 'What would be the purpose of passing them on to you? 'What would someone be trying to tell you, Abby?'

I got up, went over to the pictures tacked to the wall, and studied them all again. I tapped the picture I'd printed of Ben lifting the boy out of the wrecked carriage. 'He was at the crash site.'

'What if he found her,' said Shane.

'What if he took some of her things,' added Elliott.

I focused on Ben's handsome face. Such sadness in those eyes. 'He could have just wanted something to remember her by.'

'Or he was a ghoul,' said Elliott, 'and snatched them to add to some macabre collection of his.'

I twisted around. 'You can be one sick puppy at times.'

He just grinned.

Shane stretched back on the sofa, locked his hands behind his head. 'Didn't you say that your grandmother always thought you looked like Marion? That there were similarities?'

I nodded.

'What if this Ben fellow is still alive? My guess is, he'd be in his early eighties, late seventies at least. Let's say he's seen you. You remind him of Marion. Maybe he's even found out you're related. Now, after all these years, he decides to pass Marion's stuff on.'

'That would mean he's visited Shadow Creek. That he's been hanging around here.'

'Have you seen anyone strange lurking around, Mum?' asked Elliott, 'Noticed anyone following you?'

My eyes fixed on Shane. He was staring hard at me.

'Oh, shit!' I groaned.

Shane handed me a glass of Johnnie Walker on ice as we sat together on the loft sofa. He assured me it would help. I guess after one night at a whisky bar he felt he knew it all. I took a swig and it burned its way down my throat.

'I can't believe the driver of that old Holden ute could be our Ben Patterson,' I whispered to him. 'It's too disturbing.'

'Remember, it's just speculation at this stage,' offered Shane. 'Your yellow VW must stick out like a sore thumb. I haven't seen another one around here ... not regularly anyway. That's how he could have followed you.'

I took another fiery gulp. 'You might be right there.'

Elliott twisted in the desk chair, causing it to squeak annoyingly. 'I can hear you, you know. Why didn't the man speak with you at the picnic area, Mum? He was close enough, wasn't he?'

I glowered at Shane, shocked that he would mention my embarrassing striptease to our son.

He gave me a wink. 'I told Elliott, when you went to the loo just now, that a man followed you tonight. That he hid in the bushes and saw you fall into the creek fully clothed, then hightailed it out of there when I arrived.'

Fully clothed, hey. So, my humiliation was safe. 'Yes, he was close—too damn close. And I don't know why he didn't just speak with me instead of ...' I bit my tongue.

'Maybe he's demented,' said Shane. 'You know ... a few roos loose in the top paddock, a few beers short of a six-pack, a few sandwiches short of a—'

'I get it!' I growled, stopping him before he carried on any further.

These guys might have been trying to help, but they were now getting on my nerves. I'd had a big day emotionally. 'Still, he creeped me out. What am I going to do?'

'Talk to your parents,' urged Shane. 'They're the only ones around here who know your connection to Marion. They could have somehow dropped that information into a conversation with someone.'

'They didn't mention anything about it the other day when we spoke of Marion.' I looked over at my desk, and the document wallet lying on top. 'I do have to pass something on to Dad from

Lester. I could visit tomorrow.' I also had plans to find the crash site, which I'd discovered was not far from Tulipwood.

35

Brisbane 1958

As the black coffin is lowered into the freshly dug grave in Lutwyche Cemetery, Owen Douglas steps forward and drops a single white lily onto the polished lid. Honking into a large handkerchief, arms pull him back into the crowd of mourners.

Marion stands with her Aunt and Donald on the opposite side of her mother's grave. She glowers at her father. Her mother hated lilies, especially white ones. She proudly leans over and scatters an armful of her mother's favourites onto the coffin. Roses, carnations, and gerberas of every colour cover the lone lily.

Collective sounds of grief are heard, but Marion has done with crying—for the time being anyway—and she silently thanks God that her mother is now at peace; enveloped in a pure and limitless love.

~

The wake is held at her aunt and uncle's house, only a few streets away. Marion steps away from accepting well-meaning condolences and corners Donald on the back veranda, where a lattice partition shields them from those inside eating finger foods and downing cold beverages.

Donald fidgets with a plate of curried egg sandwiches, unable to make eye contact. 'I'm sorry you found us like that, Marion.'

'So am I,' she sighs.

He clears his throat. 'It must have been a shock for you.'

She nods strongly.

'You may find this hard to believe, Marion, but I really did want to make a go of it with you. I would have treated you well, you know.'

She frowns. 'As my husband? It would've been a sham.'

'It would've been legal.'

'Yes, but not a real marriage.'

'I guess not.' He balances his plate on the railing, and loosens his tie. 'Though I'm pretty sure I could've cut the mustard with you. Even if it was on the rare occasion.'

Marion laughs. 'Cut the mustard? Now that sounds romantic.' Seriousness returns. 'You mean you would've gone through with the marriage even though your feelings are ... are elsewhere? Did you ever think about me? Did you consider the fact that I'd want more than what my mother had to put up with for all those years?'

He gives a shrug. 'Obviously not. I'm sorry. It sounds ludicrous, but I was prepared to do anything for your father.' His eyes find hers. 'I have such affection for him, you know.'

Marion throws her hands up. 'Why Donald? Why? He's a self-centred brute and I can't for the life of me understand how anyone could love him. Man, or woman.'

'All I can say is that he makes me feel ...' His fingers rake through his perfectly slicked-back hair. 'I don't know ... needed. Like my existence matters.'

'He's using you Donald, I'm sure of it. He's a puppet master. He manipulates people for his own selfish gain. I reckon he's working on getting his hands on your family's money.'

'Well if that's the truth, then he's welcome to it. It's never given me much happiness.'

Marion glimpses sadness in those pale blue eyes and is touched. She hadn't noticed Donald's torment before. She'd assumed his introspective nature was due to a sombre personality, not a life of discontent. Shame surfaces. She'd also been selfish. To be truthful, the betrothal had been an answer to her own woes, a means to make her mother happy and get her father off her back. What a mess. They'd all used each other.

'I'm sorry, Donald. I'm just as much to blame. I really like you, but it's never been love.'

'Let me guess. You're in love with that Patterson fellow.'

Her eyes widen. 'How did you know?'

He grins. 'Well firstly, your sneaky trysts weren't very secretive; and secondly, you had eyes for no another when he was in spitting distance. Even after he left Stanthorpe and you accepted my proposal of marriage, I knew your heart belonged to someone else. But that's okay, so does mine.' He stares past her to the house, and the commotion within. 'I'll tell my parents the engagement is off as soon as I can.'

'What will you say?'

'I have no idea. But I'll make sure it's a believable lie.'

'Tell them I broke it off. Tell them things have changed now that Mum's gone. Tell them I'm depressed ... grieving ... or something.'

'Don't worry, I'll work it out.' He lifts her hand, notices her finger is bare. 'And you can keep the ring. I used my father's money to buy it anyway. Sell it if you like.' His full lips form a wide smile. 'Take it as recompense.'

Marion gives him a hug. 'Thank you, Donald. I hope we can still be friends, even though I'd much rather you find someone other than my father to ... to pass the time with.'

'We'll see,' he says, giving her a peck on the cheek.

A rasping cough interrupts them.

Her father steps from behind the partition. 'Donald, your mother is asking after you.'

Donald nods and gives Marion a smile before walking away.

The older man stays, his powerful presence unsettling as Marion drums up the courage to speak her practised words.

She takes a deep breath. 'I'll be returning to Stanthorpe to collect my things, and then I'm leaving.'

Her father face is expressionless. 'And where on earth will you be going?'

'I don't know yet. Away from you, anyway, that's for sure.'

His jaw clenches. 'Donald won't go. I know that for a fact.'

'Donald? What's he got to do with it?'

'You can't be newly married and live in separate towns. It wouldn't look right.'

Marion steps back. 'You've got to be joking! You don't really expect us to continue with the charade.'

'Of course I do. We had a pact ... or have you forgotten?' He clutches her arm and yanks her close. 'You tell and I tell, remember?'

She shrugs him off. 'I don't need to marry Donald to keep my mouth shut.'

'You have to.'

'Why? I don't intend to live in a loveless marriage like Mum did!' she yells.

'Keep your voice down,' he growls.

'Tell me, Dad. If you prefer men, how was I ever conceived? Unless, Mum had some sense to find a real man to sleep with.'

He raises his hand. It trembles mid-air, then drops. 'Your mother didn't have the nerve. She wasn't a slut like you. You got that from your grandmother.'

Marion is confused. 'Nana Bourke? She was a saint.'

'Not her.' His hands curl into fists. 'The bitch that was my mother. My father wasn't perfect, but he didn't deserve to have a tramp for a wife. I was only a boy, yet I saw what it did to him. He shrivelled up before my eyes.' An ugly sneer appears. 'I was glad when she ran off. I was even happier when I heard she'd been beaten to death by a jealous lover.'

Marion is shocked. Her father has never talked about his mother. She'd realised early on in life that the subject was taboo, so he must have a few drinks under his belt to be talking about it now. She reaches out. 'Dad, I didn't know ... I'm—'

He slaps her hand away. 'She revolted me. So do you. You tease men with your beauty. You play on their affection, lift your skirts high, and draw them in. The poor suckers don't have a chance.' His face comes close and the smell of alcohol is strong. 'How about I go inside and tell everyone what you're like? Maybe I could save a few other poor sods.'

Though sickened by his words, Marion reins in her anger. This was neither the time nor the place for a full-on fight. 'You're drunk. Let me take you back inside for a coffee. You're talking nonsense.'

'Am I? I don't think so.'

She sees menace in those bloodshot eyes. 'Don't be stupid, Dad. I'm nothing like your mother.'

'No, you've stooped even lower. You've acquired a taste for blackfellas. What's next? A bloody Jap?'

Marion strikes her father across the face. A greater pain replaces the discomfort from a stinging hand when he grips her by the throat and crushes the breath out of her. Not strong enough to loosen his hold with her hands, she lifts a leg and stomps onto his foot, feeling the stiletto heel of her shoe pierce expensive leather and flesh.

He squeals like a pig and releases his grasp.

Marion tugs the heel free and takes pleasure in watching her father suck in gulps of air while holding his injured foot. The cheek where she struck him is turning a deep crimson.

'On ... second thought,' she wheezes, her throat aching from being squashed, 'maybe I should marry Donald. With my tempting ways, I'm sure I could entice him back to the right side of the bed. Then where would you be, you fat old pansy?'

'Bitch!' he screeches. 'You'll pay for this. Your life won't be worth shit.'

'No, it will be worth much more,' she says, quickly stepping around him. 'For unlike you, you selfish bastard, I know how to love and be loved.'

Fleeing down the back stairs and around the side of her aunt's house, Marion vomits into a flowerbed. She stays there until her stomach is emptied and her trembling has ceased.

36

Sleeping well due to having Shane back in his rightful place beside me in bed—or the Jack Daniels working its magic—I'd woken the next day in a much better frame of mind. Eager to make a start on the day, I set the ingredients for making pancakes out on the kitchen bench, and left a note: 'Help yourselves.'

As I drove to Tulipwood, I kept my eyes peeled for an old grey ute.

This time there was no lively greeting when I skipped up the stairs of their front porch and plucked a sprig of jasmine. After knocking a few times with no answer, I opened the front door and stepped inside. My parents were home because I'd seen their car parked in the carport, yet all that could be heard was the ticking of the wall clock in the lounge room. I hoped they weren't feeling under the weather and were sleeping off the effects of a dreaded illness. I called out. A noise came from the hallway.

Making my way down, I jumped as a shaggy head suddenly poked out of a doorway.

My dad let out a cry and fell back against the doorframe of his study, his hand covering his heart. 'Geez, luv, you gave me a fright. I thought you were a ghost.'

I picked up the document wallet I'd dropped on the floor. 'A ghost who calls out hello?'

'It didn't sound like that to me, more like a *woo-woo*. I've heard it before.'

'Here, in this house? How often?'

A furry eyebrow twitched. 'You'd be surprised.'

'Are you saying this house is haunted?'

'Well ... not sure I'd say that. But I do believe people leave behind an essence of themselves in places they've lived or experienced strong emotions, good or bad. Like leaving a spiritual footprint.'

I gave a weak smile. This was all too weird for me. 'So, where's Mum?'

'She's not here?'

I shook my head. 'I don't think so.'

'Oh, she's probably out back. I think she said something about working in the garden. What have you got there?' He pointed to the wallet.

'Lester Schilling gave it to me to pass on to you. Thought it might be of interest.'

'Oh, it must be the old photos of the house. Lester phoned me about them.' He held out his hand and I gave it to him. He slipped back into his room and I followed.

My study was neat and organised, whereas Dad's was like a ransacked pharaoh's tomb. Printed pages, folders, and books of all sizes lay scattered over the floor or in teetering piles on every available surface. He shoved papers off a stool and told me to sit, while he collapsed into his well-worn, high backed desk chair and opened the cardboard wallet.

As he fiddled with the contents, I studied the papers strewn at my feet. Each one held information about an ancestor, one from as far back as the middle ages. I too was interested in our family's past, but only from the time they arrived in Australia in the mid-1800s. I'd always been intrigued by the events that led someone to travel a great distance from a life they'd known and people they loved, and—in most cases—never to return.

'Well, look at this,' Dad cooed, holding up an outside shot of what I presumed was this house. 'Didn't look too bad back in 1963, did it?'

I leant forward for a closer look. The roofing was more rusted, and the verandah railings and bannisters were made of steel not wood like they were now after restoration. There wasn't any iron lacework trim on the eaves either. Still, it was a quaint little cottage for its time.

'Check out the background. Just a paddock and hills; not covered in house blocks like now.'

'Oh, look!' I pointed. 'The jasmine bush is there. Not as big as it is now, of course.'

Dad tapped a finger on the print. 'See that picket fence? It wasn't here when we first saw the house. It must have been pulled down.'

A tingle that started at my fingers and travelled up my arms, ended with a shiver when it reached my shoulders.

I pulled my phone from my bag and opened the photo app. Scrolling through images I'd taken of my study wall, I found the photo of Ben on his motorbike in front of a cottage with a picket fence. A cottage that looked remarkably like the one in the picture my dad was holding up.

'Holy Moley!' I held my phone up so Dad could see the photo. 'Is that the same cottage, or what?' I grinned.

'Well, I'll be,' he gasped. 'It certainly looks like it, and there's the exact same view in the distance. Who's this character on the bike?'

I jumped up from the stool and did a little happy dance before again showing the image to my dad. 'Let me introduce you to Benjamin Patterson, Marion Douglas's lover and past resident of this house, or visitor at least.'

'Marion's lover?'

'Or boyfriend, if you like. I prefer lover. We have to show Mum!'

I was down the hall and out the backdoor in a flash. Dad came stumbling behind me.

We found Mum on her knees beneath the spreading branches of the large apple tree, now in full blossom. She looked like she was praying, but was in fact planting bulbs, probably daffodils, a favourite of hers. She glanced up when we approached.

'Abby? What are you doing here?'

I fell on my knees in front of her. A soft breeze fluttered around us and a pink blossom landed in my mother's silver-streaked hair. I told her what we had just discovered. Dad showed her the photo from Lester, and I showed her the image of Ben, and then the one of Marion on the steps of the cottage.

She stared over my shoulder. 'Marion was here? Right here at our house?'

'Well, it wasn't our house back then, but yes, it seems that way,' said Dad, his head nodding up and down like a bobble head toy.

'I'll be damned,' Mum said, holding onto my shoulder for support as she got to her feet. 'When did she come here?'

I stood with her. 'December 1957, so says the photo I have at home.'

'She was gone by January.'

I nodded. 'Yes, she was.'

Mum took my phone and studied the photo of her cousin. She blinked a number of times and wiped away a tear, leaving a smear of dirt embedded in the folds of skin under her eye. Her bottom lip quivered as she spoke. 'She looks happy.'

I squeezed her arm. 'She does.'

Mum looked up, her eyes red. 'What did you say the young man's name was?'

'Ben Patterson. He lived with his mother, Fran, near Shadow Creek. She worked at the bakery and he worked at the mill for a time.'

Mum faced the house. 'This Ben and his mother could have lived here?'

I glanced at my father. 'Was there any information about the owners in that folder Lester gave you?'

'Not really. Just some paperwork about the house coming up for sale in 1963. It was subdivided from a bigger property known as Tulip Wood. Several hundred acres, I think it said. You can have a read of the paperwork if you like.'

'I'll do that. Maybe Ben and his mum were renting it in 1958, or else Ben and Marion were just visiting when the photos were taken. Still, we can say they were here.'

'I think I need a cuppa,' said Mum, fanning her face with a garden glove. She fed her arm through mine as we walked back to the house. 'Do you know what happened to that young man?'

My feet faltered. 'I'm not sure. I actually came to talk about that with you and Dad.'

This time, I was the one to pour the tea. As I did, I broached the subject of an 'inquisitive' stranger.

Mum held her cup with both hands. 'No, we haven't had anyone around here asking questions. Certainly not asking about Marion. I hadn't thought of her in ages, not until we talked about her the other day.'

'That's right.' Dad took a chocolate chip biscuit from the plate and dunked it in his tea. 'I can't remember the last time she came to mind.'

'What about somewhere else, in town maybe? Or at a Sunday market? Someone asking about the family.'

They looked at one another and shook their heads.

'Okay, have you seen anyone lurking around the neighbourhood, looking suspicious?' I hadn't told my parents about my run-ins with a stalker, just that I had a suspicion the giver of the necklace might still be hanging around. Now with the revelation that Ben might have lived in the house, or brought Marion here to stay, it made sense that an elderly Ben might come calling if he'd seen me around town and followed me out here.

Dad gave a shrug. Mum just looked blank.

My shoulders sagged. Maybe I was going down the wrong track with all this. Maybe the stalker was following me just because I looked like Marion, that he didn't know my family connection to her. Unease drifted over me like a heavy mist. What if the stalker was demented, like Shane had suggested? I wished I'd gotten the ute's registration number. We could have made some serious enquiries with the police.

Before leaving to find the site of the train crash, I visited the bathroom, more for an ulterior motive than a call of nature. Coming back, I took the opportunity to slip surreptitiously into each of the bedrooms and lay my hands on the VJ timber walls to test my father's theory. If Marion and Ben had spent time together in this house, then I hoped to be infused by the energy left behind by their passionate encounter. I freaked myself out a bit in the main bedroom when I was surprisingly visited by a vision of my parents entwined on their firm Sealy posturepedic mattress—not quite the scene I was expecting to filter through time and space.

I quickly said my goodbyes and made my escape.

37

11 January 1958

The tram ride into the city offers Marion the first chance to breathe since her mother's funeral the day before. There were many offers of a lift back to Stanthorpe, but she'd had enough of polite, sympathetic conversation and chose to catch a train instead. Another tram ride from Adelaide Street will take her over the river to Woolloongabba and South Brisbane station. Once on the southbound train, she hopes to catch some much-needed sleep.

Her gaze drifts to the morning traffic passing alongside and she wonders what excuse Donald has chosen for their break-up, and how his parents will take it. She hopes it isn't too outlandish, for she will also need to inform Aunt Gloria. Whatever the case, Marion is glad to be free of the absurd arrangement. She can now focus on the difficult, but necessary, task ahead of sorting through her mother's belongings. Once that is done she will pack her own things, say her farewells, and begin a new life—one she herself has chosen.

In his telephone call last night, Banjo told her that his mother has readily given permission for her to stay with them at Tulip Wood until further plans are organised. Unfortunately it will be another week before he is able to travel to Stanthorpe to bring her back. With exhaustion already threatening to overwhelm her, she must remain strong and be patient. Rubbing her forehead, she fights off another wave of nausea.

A young man and woman get on the tram at Spring Hill and sit across from her. They are obviously enamoured with one another. Snuggling close, the man continually whispers words into the woman's ear that cause her to giggle loudly. The man's dark hair and build remind Marion so much of Banjo that her eyes begin to sting. She wipes away a tear, only to have it replaced. Her chest tightens and her vision blurs. This is not good. So when the tram turns into Adelaide Street, instead of waiting until it comes to a stop closer to Victoria Bridge, she pulls the cord and alights much earlier.

Crossing the road with her suitcase, Marion enters the parkland of Anzac Square. Disturbing flocks of scrounging pigeons, she hurries past bottle trees and date palms, and memorial statues built after both world wars. Taking the steps up to the Shrine of Remembrance, she glances between its surrounding stone columns to glimpse the Eternal Flame burning in its bronze urn. Out of habit, she gives a fleeting nod of respect before crossing the street and entering Central Station.

Once inside, she finds a public telephone and places a call to Banjo's number. The wait to talk to him feels like an eternity, and she is relieved when she hears his voice.

'Yes, come to Tulip Wood,' he agrees. 'Stay the night here and travel to Stanthorpe tomorrow. You'll feel much better after spending time with me,' he jokes.

She smiles. 'Yes, I think you're right. I also need to talk to you about something important. Can you pick me up from Shadow Creek?'

'You bet. I'm just helping Mum out in the yard. You don't have much luggage, do you?'

'No, just one small suitcase.'

'Good. It should fit on the bike.'

She checks the timetable board and gives him the departure time for the next train.

'That means you should arrive around a quarter past ten, I expect.'

'Excellent. In case you've forgotten what I look like, I'll be the one wearing the heart necklace,' she says, before replacing the receiver.

A visit to the restroom is necessary if Marion wants to look her best for Banjo. A quick touch-up to her makeup and removal of pins from her hair so that it can fall less severely around her shoulders should be sufficient. And an extra splash of cologne.

As she enters and preens herself in the discoloured mirror above the basin, Marion hears someone being sick behind a cubicle door. 'Poor thing,' she thinks, noticing her own gaunt reflection gazing back as if it is she who is ill. Free of her father's control, in love with a wonderful man, and her life about to take a surprising turn, shouldn't she be glowing? Dabbing her cheeks with rouge, and adding an extra layer of lipstick, she knows it will have to do for now.

Stopping at each station, the train gradually fills with frazzled parents loaded up with hampers and picnic rugs, and squirming children. The noisy chatter sets Marion's nerves on edge, but doesn't hinder the enjoyment of the view from her open window. She leans her elbow on the frame and gazes out, finding the fresh air helpful. She thinks of Banjo, relieved that she will soon be seeing him and sharing with him her exciting news. She smiles, rests back in the seat, and drifts off to sleep.

Marion's head bangs painfully against the window frame. She wakes with a start, and finds that the excited babbling has been substituted by frantic murmurs. Rubbing her eyes, she sees passengers holding onto their seats and each other for support as the carriage rocks wildly. Baggage spills from overhead racks onto laps, and a small child starts to cry. His father soothes him.

She looks out at the bushland rushing by. The train seems to be taking the descent of the mountain range at a disturbing pace. She begins to worry, and stands with difficulty. Gripping the door for support, she peers out of its open window and spies a horseshoe bend ahead. Dread creeps over her in an icy chill. At this speed there is no way the train will be able to round the bend successfully.

Praying to the one who owns her soul, she cries out to the one who possesses her heart. Her scream is lost in the screech of iron against iron as brakes are applied too late. A mighty lurch, and then a memory of a kiss beneath falling apple blossoms is replaced by darkness.

38

It wasn't difficult to find the site of the train crash. A memorial had been erected beside the road below Archer's Lookout consisting of a large boulder surrounded by a garden of flowering bromeliads. Attached to the boulder was a brass plaque. According to the inscription, the memorial was positioned at the exact spot where the engine had ploughed into the cutting. The track had been ripped up in the 1960s and had been replaced with a bitumen road, the same one I'd taken to get here.

I followed the view of the road as it disappeared around the curve of a hillside and saw how easy it must have been for a speeding train to miss this bend and jump the track. I took in the scenery, recalling the photos taken on that fateful day. Where once there had been grassy paddocks and barbed wire fencing, there were now houses on acreages. It was quiet for a Saturday, and I closed my eyes to imagine the eleventh day of January 1958, the day Marion died.

I saw the train rounding the curve and trees alongside the track arching back from the velocity. I saw terrified faces peering from windows, and the alarm on the train driver's face just before the engine slammed into the wall of dirt. I saw the cloud of dust. I heard the crunch of timber and metal, the smashing of carriages as they rammed into one another and most of all, the terrible cries of the passengers; the injured, the dying. I shuddered, channelling a semblance of that terror, desperation, and misery. My chest constricted and a lump wedged in my throat. The mental pictures kept coming—carnage, rescue, loss, and sacrifice. A groan clawed its way out of my mouth. In response, a primordial scream that seemed to travel through time ripped apart the still, dry air, and brought me hastily back to the present.

My eyes flew open. A black cockatoo soared overhead, its wide glossy wings and yellow tail feathers in stark contrast to the pale blue of the sky. I watched as it circled and dipped, and let out a piercing, resounding call. It was joined by a screeching mob of the same; their cries chilling. I counted their number. Nineteen, one for each life lost right here where I stood. I shivered. Did the spirits of the dead still haunt this place? Or was it the essence of the horror experienced that day?

My gaze dropped to my feet. What was I expecting to see, shattered glass, splintered wood, blood? I lifted my head and viewed my car parked on the road's edge. Heat waves rippled from the bitumen and distorted its features. Wind played in the long grass, and caused the overhead power lines to sway. It was an ordinary spring day, just like that day sixty years ago.

I touched my face. My cheeks were wet from tears. Here I was, having only recently found out about my cousin yet mourning her loss as if it had just occurred. My heart broke for her and all the other lives cut short; their dreams unfulfilled. I sobbed for those who were left to continue living without their loved ones, and hoped they still remembered them. I hoped they still shed a tear.

I drove back saddened, but grateful for my life, my family's lives, for the positive outcome of Shane's health scare. It was past midday and I needed to get home to ready myself for the party.

As I accelerated, a wallaby shot out from the scrub to cut across the road in front of me. I stomped on the brake and skidded to a screaming halt, narrowly missing the marsupial as it bounded past. It stopped when it reached the tall grass and swivelled its head to face me. I returned its startled gaze. Leaning out of the window to share my concern for its safety—or more accurately, tell it where to bloody well go—I glimpsed a sign through the dense lantana. 'Woodvale Cemetery' was painted on the timber in peeling white. The sign pointed to a dirt road leading into the scrub. I was intrigued. I wasn't aware there was a cemetery out here. I was under the impression the only one in these parts was in Shadow Creek.

A phone message from Shane interrupted my plans for investigation. He and Elliott were in desperate need of steak pies from the bakery for lunch. I glanced at the painted sign. My visit would have to wait.

39

Brisbane 1958

A threatening purple cloud hovers overhead. The crowd of mourners retrieve handkerchiefs from pockets and dab fervently at eyes and brows, struggling with both their sorrow and the humidity. None could have imagined that within a week they'd be back in Lutwyche Cemetery to witness Marion being buried alongside her mother in the Douglas family plot, or that government and railways officials would also be in attendance as they have been for each victim of the rail disaster.

Standing apart from the rest, in the shade of a spreading elm, is Banjo. He shows no outwards sign of grief, yet within, misery weighs heavily. Like molten lead, it has filled every nerve, every fibre.

As the graveside service concludes, a clap of thunder breaks the stillness and heavy raindrops fall like stones. The shower increases and the bereaved swiftly disperse between rows of headstones and down narrow gravel paths leading out to the road.

Banjo fixes his eye on the mound of earth beside Marion's grave, and watches as heaven-sent drops turn it into an ugly, pockmarked pile of mud.

His two friends come alongside.

Tony places a hand on Banjo's shoulder. 'C'mon mate, it's time to leave.'

Banjo lifts his gaze. 'You go. I won't be long.'

'Okay, but don't get too drenched, you don't want to catch your death.'

Marjie elbows Tony in the ribs. He grunts, and says, 'Sorry,' before taking hold of his girlfriend's hand and dashing away with her, splashing through rising puddles.

Banjo's hair plasters to his scalp. Rivulets flow into his eyes. Marion is gone. He remembers having the same thought a few months back, when Marion told him they were over. His throat constricts. It had rained that day too. It had hurt also, but this is a thousand times worse; this time she is really gone, never to return.

He dares his feet to take him closer to the grave. Takes a step, then another until he is standing at the edge of the hole, looking down into a dazzling sea of wreaths and bouquets and single-stemmed flowers of every variety and colour. There is a pricking behind his eyes. He squeezes them shut.

'What do you think you're doing here?'

Banjo spins around.

Owen Douglas stands there, shielded from the rain by a huge, black umbrella. The revulsion he feels for Marion's father is more than he can bear yet he bites his tongue. The only movement he gives, is the tensing of his limbs. Within though, his heart pounds like a jackhammer.

The man's glare is fierce. 'How dare you come here after what you've done!'

Banjo scowls. 'After what I've done?'

'If it wasn't for you, Marion would still be alive.'

Banjo flinches. There is truth in these words. If it weren't for him urging her to stay the night at Tulip Wood, Marion wouldn't have been on that train. He should have encouraged her to head back to Stanthorpe as planned.

'She was coming out to see you, wasn't she?'

'Yes,' he admits, his gut hardening.

'You filled her head with silly notions and almost ruined our good name in the process.'

Banjo is wrenched from his self-loathing. 'Ruined your good name?' He laughs. 'That's a joke. I'd say you've done an excellent job of doing that yourself.'

The man blinks. 'I don't know what you're talking about.'

'I saw it.'

Owen's face slackens. 'What do you mean?'

'The bruises. The scar on her forehead. You hurt her.'

A grin appears. 'Accident prone, that girl. Always was.'

Banjo takes a step forward. 'You bold-arsed liar.'

A stubby finger jabs into his chest. 'And what are you, hey? A boong bastard without a decent job.'

Banjo whacks the hand aside. 'At least I don't cheat on my wife with another man, for Christ's sake!'

'Where'd you hear that disgusting rubbish? Marion? It's all nonsense. Slander.'

'Nonsense, was it? Then why is your little playmate rushing over here to see what's going on?'

Owen turns. Donald is racing across the lawn towards them.

'I'm fine, Donald!' he cries, waving him away. 'Nothing to worry about!'

'That's what you think, you old poof,' snarls Banjo. 'It won't be a secret for long.'

The balding head twists back. 'You think you can pressure me? What do you want? Money? I bet you do.' His hand disappears inside his suit coat.

'I don't want your stinking money! I want everyone to know what you really are. You're a thug who uses people and then spits them out.'

The trembling of Owen's fingers as he moves the umbrella to the other hand show he is rattled. 'And you don't use anyone for your own gain, eh? What about Marion? You used her well and truly. A bastard fathering another bastard, now that's a step up, isn't it?'

Banjo leans in. 'What did you say?'

'Oh ...' Owen's turn to laughs. 'You didn't know. Marion was pregnant when she died. The coroner mentioned it in confidence.'

Banjo's mind whirls. 'She couldn't be. She hadn't said anything to me.'

'Oops, I made a mistake. Maybe it wasn't yours after all.'

Banjo shoves the man hard in the chest. 'How dare you! There was no one else!'

Owen rights himself. 'Are you sure about that?'

'You bet I am!'

'Well then, fortunately for both of us Marion died when she did. It would have been a real problem having to deal with another black bastard running around.'

A loud crack is heard as Banjo's fist connects with Owen's jaw.

The man falls back, water splashing around him as he hits the ground, breaking the umbrella in the process. Cupping his jaw with both hands, he rolls side-to-side in the mud, gagging with pain.

Banjo shakes out his hand, satisfied that a second punch is not needed.

Donald rushes in, drops to his knees in the slush. 'What have you done?'

Banjo is unsure whether he is talking to Owen or to him. 'That's for Marion,' he says, choking back tears and striding away.

40

Shane and I shuffled up the stairs of Graeme and Julie's house, deciding not to mention our crazy roller coaster of a week and just carry on as normal—as normal as one can be dressed in Halloween costumes. We entered through a curtained doorway.

Candles flickered from within plastic skulls, eerie music wafted from hidden speakers, and fake cobwebs hung from every corner. Sitting on a leather sofa in the middle of the lounge room was a fortune teller, a werewolf, and a vampire complete with fangs protruding from blood-smeared lips.

'Oh Abby, you look amazing!' Donna gushed. 'Though I knew you would, I foresaw it in my crystal ball.' The glass sphere balanced on her lap was a Christmas snow globe containing Santa and his trusty sleigh.

'She does look great, doesn't she?' Shane grinned through a swathe of white bandages that covered his entire body, bar his eyes and mouth.

It had taken me forty-five minutes to wrap this mummy in readiness for the Halloween party, and then I had to do it all over again when Shane realised he needed to use the toilet before leaving.

I twirled, trying not to trip over the shredded hemline of my skin-tight Morticia Addams styled gown, and struck a supermodel pose. There came a ripping sound, and I felt a back seam give way. I instantly covered my exposed flesh with my shawl.

'Been to Rugs-a-Million have you, Ross?' Shane remarked, taking a seat alongside the werewolf whose costume consisted of scraps of carpeting and an ancient fur coat sewn together.

Ross gave a pout and scratched his unshaven chin. 'Hey, I did my best. At least I used some creativity. Not like Lester here. He just handed over 250 bucks at a costume store for his get-up.'

'I'm a very bithy man, I'll have you know,' Lester lisped through a mouthful of plastic teeth.

Graeme appeared through the curtaining, dressed in Frankenstein monster garb accessorised with thick-soled biker boots. He gave a wide, greenish grin, and Julie entered alongside wearing a cape and pointed black hat, and carrying a straw broom.

I took a seat next to Lester. 'Where's Karen?'

He gave a shrug. 'Thee wath thtill drething when I left.' Then he removed his fangs. 'I had to feed the kids and then drop them off at her mother's on the way over.'

'Well I hope she arrives before we start the meal,' said Donna, listening in.

Karen did eventually arrive and planted herself near her husband. She had obviously taken the easy road and found an old quilted bedspread, cut a hole in the middle for her head to poke through, and then coated her face in copious amounts of pale foundation.

'You could have made a little more effort than that,' scoffed Lester.

Karen looked exhausted and ready to cry. The smudge of kohl

under her eyes made them look even more bloodshot. 'Where was I going to get a shroud at such short notice?'

Lester pulled his cape back around his shoulders. 'We knew about this a month ago. There's no excuse.'

Karen shot him a death stare. 'And when did I have time to traipse around stores looking for an outfit?'

'There's the Internet,' snarled Lester.

She jumped up, got twisted in her bedspread, and fell into Graeme's arms. 'You got a bar around here? I need a drink.'

The next couple of hours were spent eating our way through a gargantuan dinner of zombie meat, tasting like roast pork; body parts that resembled various root vegetables; and a Chocolate Spider Mousse with Freshly Whipped Scream. This was washed down with decanters of blood red wine and sparkling body fluids.

As we finished the wine, I shared my discovery of the cemetery out near Tulipwood. Ross had a crazy idea. Seeing we were celebrating Halloween, he suggested we check out the graveyard at midnight. The guys agreed and somehow, I'll blame it on the alcohol, I decided to join them in this creepy venture.

Why we chose my VW for our covert operation is anyone's guess. Shane elected to drive, Lester nabbed the front passenger seat, and I was relegated to be the ham in the sandwich between Ross and Graeme. It was a tight fit between two hefty blokes.

Shane decided to show off his rally driving skills. Burning rubber, he sped off only to spoil his release of adrenalin by jerking the car in a series of bone jarring kangaroo hops when his bandaging got caught around the floor pedals. Finally, we were away.

The road out of town wasn't lit by streetlights so our view

consisted of that which was illuminated by the headlights. Dense scrub on either side of the road zipped by as we sped towards our destination.

'Whatever you do, don't pick up any hitchhikers,' Lester warned Shane.

'What, no fraternising with serial killers tonight?' he replied, 'Geez you're a spoil sport.'

'What about a stray zombie?' Ross enquired, 'I think they're cool.'

'Well if I see one,' said Graeme, 'I'll be happy to send you on ahead to catch it.'

'Stop!' I yelled.

Shane braked hard, and we jolted painfully. A variety of expletives filled the small interior.

'We've just passed the turn off!' I added.

Shane reversed back to the sign. We followed the dirt road I'd seen earlier that day and soon came to a halt.

'Oh, a dead end,' I remarked.

'Appropriate place for a cemetery,' Graeme said, as the headlights revealed wrought iron gates marking the entrance to a graveyard.

Beyond them was an eerie sight of tombstones in all shapes and sizes. No one moved.

'C'mon guys,' I urged, 'man up. Let's do this.'

Doors opened and we tumbled out into the cool, dark air.

'Hey look, a full moon,' Ross exclaimed, peering up into the sky and letting out a howl worthy of a Baskerville hound.

Shane passed around some torches he'd pilfered from Julie's place. 'Damn, we're one short.'

'Never mind, I have my trusty phone light.' I tapped it on and bravely led the group to the rusty gates. The creak they made as I forced them open was as spooky as the sound effects used in a haunted house thriller.

The cemetery was roughly twice the size of a tennis court, and was jam-packed with headstones leaning at awkward angles like rows of crooked teeth. Sinister stone angels stood guard over a number of the dearly departed, while pointed obelisks reached expectantly towards heaven near others. A silhouette of a crypt in the form of an ancient ziggurat stood on its own at the far side near the fencing. As I eyed a brick wall lined with brass name plaques, I realised our search could take some time.

'So, what are we looking for again?' Shane asked.

'The name Patterson would be a good start. Ben's mother Fran was very ill. She may have died while they were still living in the area.'

We fanned out amongst the granite obstacles and began our search.

Moving from site to site, I noted that quite a few of the graves belonged to members of prominent pioneer families who made their move to the area in the mid-1800s. Brave souls migrating to Australia in search of a better life only to discover that they were just replacing one set of hardships for another. I admired their gumption.

'Some of these graves are a mess,' Graeme called from the row in front of mine. 'Look, they're crumbling away. This one has a whole corner missing.' He shone his torch into the crevice. 'What if a bony hand was thrust out from some poor sap who'd been buried alive.'

'You're creeping me out, mate,' said Shane, redirecting Graeme's light so he could read the inscription on the headstone. 'Gustav Hans Schultz. 13 Jan 1886. 62 years. Struck by lightning. How bloody unfortunate is that.'

Graeme moved on to the next grave. 'Get a load of this one. It's a mass grave.'

I made my way to his aisle and read the inscriptions. 'There are a lot of infants listed. What's with that?'

'Hmm ...' Ross mused, 'All in the late 1800s I see. It's a sign of the times.' He folded his arms and nodded knowingly. 'A hard life for families in the early days. Sicknesses that we now easily ward off with vaccinations, or treat with antibiotics, were fatal back then. That's one of the reasons why they had large families.' Sounding like a commentator on a history channel he continued. 'Hygiene wasn't the best either. Did you know that almost fifty percent of all infant deaths around that time can be attributed to unclean feeding bottles?'

'Is that right?' That was news to me.

Ross nodded. 'I have an assortment at the shop. A particularly horrid-looking affair was dubbed "The Murder Bottle". It's like a glass hip flask with a nozzle, and attached to it is a long rubber tube with a teat. This invention was considered a marvel as a toddler could hold the bottle by itself and suck away. But they were the devil to clean, and bacteria bred easily.'

'That's horrible,' I frowned. 'I thought most mothers breast fed back then.'

'That went out of fashion when bottles were made accessible. Anyway, some clever fellow invented a banana shaped bottle with openings at either end which was way easier to clean, and it actually helped decrease the mortality rate.' He followed our blank stares. 'You should all come and have a look at my collection. I have a few murder bottles you can see.'

I broke the ensuing silence. 'I think I'll head over to the far corner now.'

'Yep, let's continue,' said Graeme.

Shane stumbled along behind him, let out a cry and cursed his mummy wrappings for getting caught around a stone angel's outstretched arm.

I wove my way over to a clump of headstones near the fence line. Finding it to be a family plot, I read the names of the six people buried alongside one another.

A rustling came from the bushes on the other side of the fence.

A chill slithered up my spine. Checking the distance between myself and the rest of the group, I hoped it was just a nocturnal animal on the prowl and not something more sinister.

I moved away towards a grave surrounded by fancy wrought iron edging. A stone guardian angel with broken wings and pockmarked cheeks arched over the marble headstone of Lizzie Jane Cottesloe, 71 yrs. As I gazed into the hollow eye sockets, I could have sworn I heard a sigh escape those pale, chipped lips. My hand shook. This was proving too eerie an adventure for this time of night, and I wished we'd come out in daylight. Taking a deep breath, I gave my attention to the exquisite gold lettering on the black marble.

More rustling in the bushes, but this time it was followed by a growl.

I shone my light into the foliage. Two yellow eyes glared back at me. I dropped my phone. Scrabbling in the dirt, I heard footsteps on dried leaves. My fingers found the phone. I switched on the light and spun around, my heart racing. Nothing living was revealed, not even eyes this time.

I was about to give up and return to the others when I caught sight of the stone ziggurat-styled crypt. Its gaudy design and size seemed out of place in this small country graveyard. Maybe a wealthy grazier had left instructions to have this monstrosity built in his honour. I ventured near and circled the structure.

It had a brass door that was bolted and locked shut, and a plaque above the door inscribed with 'Tarrant Family'. I fiddled with the lock out of curiosity. A noise pricked my ears. It was odd, and it was right behind me. Before I could turn and find out what it was, I was grabbed around the waist. A scream formed inside my mouth, only to come out as a wheeze as I was pulled back hard into something solid and warm. At least I wasn't being attacked by something long dead. The hot whisper that then tickled my ear assured me it was no foe either.

'I want you,' it said breathlessly.

Shane had a lot of nerve, creeping up on me like that. I could have fainted with shock, or scratched his eyes out with my long, painted fingernails. As his hands gripped my bum and squeezed, I found my fear melt away. Was he wanting more of last night's escapades? What did he think we could get away with here in this dark corner with decaying corpses listening and our friends lurking nearby?

'Now? Here?' I murmured, resting back and wriggling against him. 'I know you're keen, but do you really want to desecrate this place?'

'Mmm,' he moaned.

I grinned and turned around.

But it wasn't Shane dressed as a mummy I saw by the light of my phone. It was the chilling face of another monster entirely.

'Lester!' I squealed, pushing him back.

'Abby,' he groaned, lunging for me.

I deflected his mouth with a cheek, only to have him smother my ear with a sloppy kiss. 'What are you doing?' I gasped.

'I can't hide it any longer,' he said, 'I feel the same as you.'

I ducked my head.

He clasped me to him, enveloping me in his massive black cape. 'I've waited all night to tell you.'

I cringed within the suffocating embrace and inhaled a stale woody scent with a hint of citrus—a Giorgio Armani for sure. 'Tell me what?'

'I'm attracted to you, like you are to me. Isn't it wonderful?'

'Don't be stupid. I've never said such a thing!' I tried to twist free, but he held me fast.

'Yes, you did. The other day outside the pub.'

'I did?'

'Don't tease,' he said, tilting my chin to look me in the eye. 'You said I was handsome, and sensitive. Remember?'

Oh, God. Like a horrid flash flood, it came rushing back. It was true. I did mention something like that. 'Lester, I—'

'It's okay,' he crooned, 'I think you're gorgeous too. I always have.'

'But, I only said those things to be nice.'

'And you are. Oh ... Abby!' Lester held my face in his hands. His mouth came close to meeting mine.

'No, you don't!' I cried, wrenching away. 'Lester, you've got it all wrong. I was just being a good friend when I said those things.'

His hands dropped. 'You were? Really? I thought you were coming on to me.'

'I most definitely was not.' Even in the limited light I could see disappointment shadow his eyes. 'Have you talked with Karen about your situation?'

'No.' He now looked sheepish. A sheepish vampire. 'How could I? I haven't been able to stop thinking about you ... us ... and ...'

I wagged a finger in his stupid face. 'Lester, you've misdirected your need for affection. You grabbed hold of what I innocently said the other day and turned it into a fantasy.'

His mouth slackened. 'Is that right?'

'Believe me. You want Karen's affection, not mine.'

'I do?'

'Yes,' I nodded.

He stared for what seemed like an eternity.

'Are you okay?' I asked, worried he'd gone catatonic on me.

'I guess you're right.' He smoothed down his gelled hair. 'I guess I'm just going stir crazy. You won't tell anyone about this ... about what just happened?'

'God, no. Our secret,' I assured him. I certainly wasn't in a hurry to tell anyone I'd just been felt up by Lester Schilling behind a crypt and enjoyed it. It was going to be hard enough erasing the memory of this incident myself without having anyone else reminding me of it.

'I guess you won't keep my gift then,' he said.

'Gift?'

'Yeah. I knew you liked flowers, so I bought you a present with a pretty blossom design. Sorry, I only had newspaper to wrap it in.'

I jolted back, my mouth falling open. My brain convulsed as recent assumptions exploded like eggs in a microwave. No, it couldn't be true. Not Lester. I shook my head. 'Don't tell me you were the one who gave me the necklace.'

Lester's eyes became slits. 'What necklace?'

'The one you dropped off last Sunday morning ... early. The one with the heart pendant.'

Now it was his turn to shake his head. 'I don't know what the hell you're talking about, Abby. I gave you a bookmark. A lovely, handmade one I bought at the craft shop. I put it in the document wallet with the stuff for your dad ... the house stuff.'

'Bookmark?' I blew out a sigh of relief. Lester giving me the necklace would have been awkward ... and incredibly disappointing.

'I thought you'd sneak a look inside and find it. I wrote your name on the paper.' He gripped my elbow. 'You didn't see it then?'

'No, sorry.'

'Did you give the wallet to your father?'

I nodded. 'Yep, I passed it on like you said.'

He pulled his hand away. 'Oh, shit!'

'Oh, shit, what?'

'I wrote on the back of the bookmark. It was a message for you.'

I scowled. 'What kind of message?'

'Umm ... er ...' I heard his shoes scrape in the dirt. 'The kind you wouldn't want your father to read.'

'Oh no, Lester. You wrote me a love note?'

'Umm ... I wouldn't call it that. It was a bit spicier ... a bit racier. Okay, it was sexually explicit, alright? I'd had a few too many chardonnays, I was feeling randy—'

'Stop!' I clutched my head in my hands. 'I get the picture. Let's just hope Dad hasn't delved that far into the wallet. I'll get it back as soon as I can.'

'That'd be a good move, believe me. Hey, did you see that brute of a dog just before?'

I flinched. 'Dog? What dog?'

'I was ... er ... relieving myself behind the crypt, and this mutt appeared out of the darkness. I nearly pissed on my Windsor Smiths.'

'What type of dog?'

'An ugly, brown, snarling type.'

I looked around, my legs beginning to wilt. 'Where did it go?'

Lester shrugged. 'No idea. It just took off.'

I grabbed his arm. 'I think we'd better get back to the others.'

When we rounded the crypt, we saw Shane waving his torch and calling us over. As we zig-zagged our way through the tombstones, we were joined by Ross and Graeme.

Shane was in front of a white marble headstone, his torchlight shining on black lettering. 'Could this be something?'

We all moved closer.

Satisfaction rose as I studied the inscription. Maybe this adventure wasn't such a disappointment after all. I took a photo with my phone.

The graveyard was suddenly illuminated in red, blue, and white flashing disco lights. The sharp 'woop woop' of a siren made all heads turn towards the cemetery gates.

A car door slammed and a silhouette appeared. Bright torchlight blinded us.

'Holy crap!' a voice screeched. The light wavered for a moment and then rose higher, and the familiar form of Senior Constable Will Feather came into view. 'What the hell's going on here?'

Graeme rushed forward.

'Stop right there, Herman!' commanded Will, his voice a little shaky. 'Arms up so I can see them.'

'Constable Will, it's Graeme Roper.'

'Wha ... Reverend Roper? Is that really you?'

He nodded, shielding his eyes from the light.

Lester pushed Graeme aside. 'Hi Will, it's Lester Schilling here, too.'

The light was now aimed at Lester. 'Are you sure?'

'Of course I'm sure.' Lester untied his cape and let it slip to the ground. 'See?'

The torchlight waved over the rest of us. 'What in God's name are you all doing out here? I got a frantic call from a woman up on the hill saying she saw lights. Thought some kids were making a nuisance of themselves. I didn't expect to find a bunch of ... of mature-aged monsters. Tell me this isn't some strange satanic ritual.'

'It isn't,' said Graeme, 'it's just a Halloween thing.'

'Yeah, nothing to worry about,' added Ross.

Constable Will moved closer, cocked his head. 'Ross Clarke? Is that you under all that fur?'

'Yep. We were just looking for a missing person.'

Will gasped. 'A missing person? Why didn't you call it in? There are standard procedures to follow, you know.'

Now it was my turn to explain. I shuffled forward, 'It's okay. The person's dead.'

'Holy shit!' Will's hand went to his shoulder, to his radio.

'Wait!' I yelled. 'We were looking for a grave. An inscription on a headstone, to be precise.'

He dropped his hand, removed his cap and massaged the furrows lining his brow. 'God-dammit. You're all bat-shit crazy. Why do it tonight?'

Graeme came alongside, patted Will on the back. 'Had a good night, got a little excited, had an idea. You know how it is? Harmless fun.'

'Well you got me out of bed. The missus won't be happy when she finds out what I was called away for.'

'How about a selfie?' said Lester.

'A what?'

'A group selfie ... with us. That might give Bev a laugh.'

Will grinned. 'Or give her a good scare. Yeah, why the hell not. It's Halloween, after all.'

He tucked his Maglite under his arm, took a mobile phone from his pocket, and snapped a pic of himself surrounded by a bedraggled bunch of very tired—yet very relieved—monsters. Then he told us to quit disturbing the peace and mosey on home. We didn't argue about that. It was early morning and we were desperate for coffee.

Shane draped a tattered arm around my shoulder as we headed back to the VW. 'Hey, what were you and old Lester doing behind that crypt?'

It felt suddenly very chilly. 'The crypt? Lester and I? Nothing we were just—'

'Did he vant to zuck your bl-a-a-rd?" he interjected, using his worst Transylvanian accent.

I laughed nervously. A memory of Lester's gaping mouth bearing down on me made me shudder.

'Cold?' Shane asked.

I nodded, and felt much better when he enfolded me in a bandaged embrace.

When we got to the car, I made sure Lester sat in the back with the other guys. The only man I wanted to be close to was my husband.

Back at the house, I was the first to rush up the stairs and through the front door.

Donna greeted me in the hallway, eyes wide with alarm. 'You lot certainly took your time. Is everything all right?'

'Yeah, it was a real hoot. I need to pee.' I headed for the bathroom.

'Don't go in there!' She warned, stepping in my way. 'Karen's inside, she's a mess.'

'What? Is she sick? Too much rich food? Too much drink?'

Donna shook her head. 'She's crying. Julie and I have been talking with her the whole time you've been away. Karen's really opened up. She's thinking of throwing in her job as Acting Principal.'

'No! Really?'

'Uh-huh. She's been struggling, trying to juggle work and the family. She says she can't do it anymore. It's even putting pressure on her marriage.'

'Oh? Lester will be pleased, I'm sure,' I said, as if this was all news to me.

Just as I mentioned his name, Lester appeared in the hallway. I thrust a finger in front of his powder-streaked face. 'You! In there, now!' I pointed towards the closed bathroom door.

Lester frowned. 'What the hell for? Remember, I went earlier, behind the crypt.'

'Karen's in there, she needs you.'

He stood dumbstruck. The only thing moving was a tick in one corner of his mouth.

'Go on.' I shoved him forward.

Lester opened the door just a crack, unleashing the sounds of sobbing within. He slipped inside and the door was instantly slammed shut.

Donna grabbed my arm. 'By God, Abby, you can be really tough when you want to be.'

The others traipsed through the front door, their costumes in all manner of disarray.

Julie poked her head around a corner. 'Coffee anyone?'

Lester and Karen were still ensconced behind the bathroom door. Everyone else was seated around the dining table.

'Who was this Frances Baxter?' Ross asked, accepting a steaming mug from Julie.

'Didn't you read the wording?' I picked my phone up from the table and found the photo of the headstone.

Donna snatched the phone from me before I had a chance to pass it on to Ross. 'According to the inscription, she was the mother of a Ben Patterson.'

'Yes,' I nodded, 'that gives it away.'

'And you reckon this Ben is our Ben,' Shane said, stuffing a chocolate Tim Tam biscuit into his mouth.

'Must be. It makes sense.'

Graeme took the phone from Ross and eyed the picture. 'Does it? She doesn't have the same surname.'

'Maybe she re-married,' offered Shane, through a mouthful.

'Well there's no mention of a husband,' said Donna. 'What happened to him? Did you see his grave?'

Shane shook his head.

'He could have died elsewhere,' piped in Ross, 'or maybe done a runner'.

'Maybe Frances left him,' Julie interrupted. 'This Baxter bloke could have been a right bastard.'

'Or she could have even been a single mum,' said Donna, 'and happened to be living out this way because she was ostracised by her family for having a child out of wedlock.'

'Well, whatever it was,' said Graeme, staring at my phone's screen, 'Ben got on with his life. The inscription mentions he had a family.'

'Yes, it does,' I said. 'He found love again.'

We all looked to the doorway at the sound of hurried footsteps.

Karen appeared, her face flushed a very healthy pink. Lester was at her side; his perfect hair now tousled. 'Sorry, but we're off now.'

'Got to get home', Karen added, readjusting her dishevelled shroud.

'But why?' cried Julie, 'Aren't the kids at your mother's?'

Lester winked in my direction. 'Yes, that's why we're going home.'

'Thank God for that,' I sighed, reaching for the last Tim Tam and watching them scoot away.

41

Tulip Wood 1958

Fran Baxter holds the slender trunk of the young apple tree upright while Banjo's boot presses the earth around the base. Honey circles them, yapping and sniffing at scents unearthed by the tilled soil.

'This is a good thing,' Banjo's mother encourages. 'It will always remind you of Marion.'

He lashes out. 'I don't need a bloody tree to remind me of her!' Then regrets his show of anger.

Planting the sapling has helped in a strange way. Memories, good and bad, have come with each shovel-full of dirt and now, as he waters the soil, he prays that the tree will grow strongly; that it will take on the life that Marion lost and greet each new day in her stead.

His mother squeezes his arm reassuringly. She has been a great help during this difficult past week. Knowing that she too had experienced a grief as profound as his has brought him comfort, and he'd allowed her to soothe him like when he was a child. When he'd sobbed, she'd held him and cried along with him. When he'd vented his anger, she'd listened. When he'd remained silent, she'd left him alone with his grief. His love and respect for her has grown tenfold. How could he have survived this darkness without her? He regrets that Marion and his mother had never met, for he is sure they would have gotten on like a house on fire.

'I'll go make us a nice strong cup of tea,' she says, and walks back towards the house.

Banjo drops the empty bucket and wipes his muddied hands on his trousers. Staring at the sapling, he imagines it as a fully-grown tree laden with delicious fruit. Maybe by then the ache in his soul will have lessened. He closes his eyes and once again attempts to picture Marion's face, undamaged and intact. Since the crash, he's struggled to do this without a photo of her in his hands. His dreams at night have also been haunted with gruesome images and he's taken to drinking himself to sleep. He's aware of his mother's disapproval, but so far, she hasn't taken him to task. They both know it will pass, at least Banjo hopes it will.

With hesitation, he brings to mind their picnic in the orchard beside the creek. He recalls the excitement of the day and how his heart had drummed with expectation. He pictures Marion sitting before him surrounded by apple blossoms; remembers her outfit, her slender figure, and the soft curls in her hair. Yet when he tries to recall the freckled nose, the vivid green of her eyes, and the fullness of her smiling lips, the image is instantly replaced with a gory mess.

Dropping to his knees, Banjo pummels the ground with his fists while tears stream from his eyes. Slumping back, he rocks back and forth, groaning, and feels Honey lick his hand in an effort to ease his suffering. A gentle breeze hisses through the trees and swirls around him. Tender breaths caress his cheeks, play with his hair, cool his skin. His heart slows and calm returns, until a word is carried to him in a gust of wind.

'Banjo,' it seems to whisper.

The beating in his chest accelerates.

He hears it a second time and looks around; left, right, behind. Other than Honey sitting quietly beside him, he is alone. He waits, but all he hears is the rustling of leaves, the buzzing of insects, the rattling notes of a honeyeater. The garden is just as it was. Empty.

'I'm going crazy,' he cries, and pushes himself up to his feet.

42

It was morning. A ray of sunlight streamed through a gap in the bedroom curtains and lit Shane's face as he lay snoring and drooling onto his pillow. At least he hadn't had any trouble sleeping off the shenanigans of the Halloween festivities, whereas I'd woken from a dream an hour before and hadn't been able to settle back down. I leant back against the bed's headboard and stared once more at my phone and the photo of the headstone engraving.

Frances Ellen BAXTER
31 May 1915 – 5 Jul 1961
Mother of Ben Patterson
Grandmother of Jamie & Ken
Sister of Martin
Lovingly missed

Who had Ben married? I hoped she was a nice person—one who understood his loss and gave him the love he needed. I hoped theirs was a happy marriage. I also wondered if she'd called him Banjo. A thought surfaced.

Searching an Internet site of archived newspaper articles, I typed in Frances's name followed by the year of her death. A bereavement notice appeared at the top of the list. Opening it up, I was thrilled to see that the name and date of death matched the details on the headstone. The notice also mentioned Frances's brother and his wife, and her son and his family. According to what I read, Ben had married a woman called Selena. I looked up. *Selena*. Not such a common name these days.

A sudden noise broke through my line of thought. I cringed. Someone was knocking on our front door.

I checked the clock. 7:25 am. Oh my God! One week ago, to the minute, I'd heard the exact same sound. This time nothing was going to stop me catching the visitor at their game. I kicked off the sheet and got out of bed.

Not bothering to peek out the window, I rushed out of the room to the front door. Flicking the lock, I grabbed hold of the knob, took one deep breath, and wrenched open the door.

The breeze was strong, but there was no moisture behind it like last Sunday. No fog, no mist, and nobody hightailing it back up the driveway either. I was disappointed and disturbed. Who had made that noise?

'Hello,' came a voice to my left.

My head turned. There was a person sitting on the wicker chair, holding a duffle bag.

'Gemma!' I cried. 'What are you doing here?'

'Well, that's a nice welcome, Mum,' she said, stretching and giving a mighty yawn.

'I thought you were still up north?'

She got to her feet. Though suntanned and gorgeous as usual, she looked exhausted. 'Had enough. Caught an early flight back from Cairns, and an Uber ride from the airport to here. Cost a fortune.'

I looked around. 'Where's Max?'

She pulled a face. 'Who cares.' Then brushed past me and walked inside.

I shut the door behind us. 'What happened?'

Gemma dropped the bag onto the floor and removed the hair tie that had caught her long blonde tresses into a ponytail. 'Seems he was wanting more of a nanny for his kids than a girlfriend. Kept banging on about all the ways I could help out once I moved in with them. That wasn't the type of relationship I had in mind. I dumped him when we got back to Cairns. Couldn't get home fast enough.'

'Oh ...' I said, struggling to find the right words in response to this news. 'I told you so', 'Thank you, Jesus', and 'Yippee' probably wouldn't have gone down too well. I just gave a smile. 'Glad you're home safely. Are you hungry? I could make you something.'

She shook her head and yawned again. 'Nope. Think I'll go straight to bed for a few hours sleep. I so missed my mattress.'

Dragging her bag behind her, she headed down the hall.

'Wait!' I hurried after her. 'Bree is in your bed.'

Gemma halted outside her room. 'Bree? In my bed?'

'She stayed over last night.'

'Great. Now I'll have to sleep on the lumpy mattress in the guest room.' She opened her door a smidge and peeked inside, then scowled. 'Mum, there's no one in my bed.'

I pushed the door wide open. Gemma's bed was just as I'd seen it the day before, made up and undisturbed. Not one wrinkle could be seen on the bed cover. My whole body slumped. I thought I'd made my stipulations clear to Elliott.

Stomping over to his bedroom, I cracked open his door. Bree was in his bed, fast asleep and breathing deeply. Elliott, meanwhile, was curled up in his sleeping bag on the floor, just as deep in dreamland. Okay, so they weren't in bed together, just sharing a room. One thing I'd learnt these past few days was the importance of trust. I had to trust that no funny business had taken place, or if it had, then I had to trust my son had used protection. I shut the door and crossed the hall.

Gemma was already kicking off her sandals and pulling back the bed cover. 'See you in a few hours,' she said, slipping between the sheets.

'We can talk then, if you like,' I offered. She just nodded and told me to close the door.

I found Shane still asleep, so I grabbed my phone and headed up to the loft.

43

Tulip Wood 1958

That night in bed and unable to sleep, Banjo once again attempts to visualise Marion's face.

To ease himself into the task, he starts at her feet—small with painted toenails, a light pink. Then narrow ankles and shapely calves, leading up to firm thighs yet to be blemished by age. Narrow hips, though with the gentle curves of a woman. Stomach —firm, flat, and dinted in the centre by the cutest shell of skin. The swell of breasts that fit so perfectly in his hands and respond readily to his touch. At her sides are slender arms lightly dusted with fine hair, and graceful, long-fingered hands sporting delicately shaped nails. His eyes fly open. The bedroom is thick with darkness, but in his mind he sees the bloodied arm as it slipped through the gap in the wreckage; the hand pale with death, the diamond and sapphire ring sparkling through the cloud of dust.

A thought stabs him.

He sits up, swings his legs over the side of the mattress. Why was Marion still wearing that ring? He hadn't had time to grasp this fact before now, what with all that had followed since the train crash. He is bewildered. Marion said she would be returning it to Donald. And then there were the fingernails. He can see them, bitten, chewed short. That wasn't like Marion at all. He brushes hair from his brow, sticky with sweat. Was she distressed by her mother's death, or was it something else, something more troubling? The baby? He reaches under the bed for a hidden bottle of whisky.

The bedroom is now bright with early morning sunshine. Rays of light sneak under the curtains as they billow from an energetic breeze. Banjo pushes himself up and drops his feet to the floor, knocking over the empty bottle. Kicking it under the bed, out of sight, he lets out a groan and rubs his temples with his thumbs. A glint catches his eye. Sunlight has found something in the corner of the room. It is the silver clasp of Marion's red handbag, which has been sitting untouched behind the door since being brought back from the crash site. Her small suitcase was passed on to her aunt after he'd made sure there was nothing inside he wanted to hang on to. Sadness slams into him at the realisation that Marion will no longer have need for these items.

He thinks of all the other personal items that were strewn amongst the wreckage and now forever separated from their owners. How many were collected by family members or loved ones only to be stared at with hearts breaking, just like his? The heart necklace! Marion mentioned she was wearing it that day, yet it wasn't with her body. He swats away another ghastly vision. What if it fell amongst the wreckage? Maybe it was found and taken back to the police station with other unclaimed belongings. He has to find out for sure.

~

The bitumen road into Shadow Creek is shimmering with heat haze. As Banjo parks the motorbike outside the police station, he removes his helmet and leather jacket and slings them over the handlebars. Though he only has to walk a short way before entering the small weatherboard building, it feels as if the sun is targeting him alone, like Flash Gordon blasting a ray gun.

He steps aside for an exiting woman before entering the station and discovering that, though the ceiling fans are going full pelt, it is still as warm as an oven inside. At Banjo's appearance, a middle-aged constable comes to the counter.

'It's a hot one, isn't it?' the man says, pulling his starched collar out from his neck, and giving it a few flaps. 'How can I help you, young fella?'

'I was wondering if I could look through the unclaimed items from the train crash. I saw a policeman collecting stuff on the day.'

'You were there, were you? Shocking, absolutely shocking it was. Were you a passenger on the train?'

'No. But I knew someone who was. Someone very dear to me.'

'They all right?'

Banjo shakes his head.

The policeman reaches over the counter and gives Banjo's shoulder a squeeze. 'Sorry to hear that, mate. Terrible business. I'll get the items for you.'

Banjo waits as the man disappears through a door and returns a few minutes later with a large cardboard box, which he drops onto a long trestle table. Two more boxes are retrieved and placed either side of the first.

'You can come around here and go through them.' He points to the half door at the end of the counter.

Banjo undoes the latch and walks into the main area.

'Interested in any of the kiddies' toys?'

'No. No toys.'

The policeman takes one box down from the table and opens the larger of the two remaining. 'Clothing in here. Hand luggage and odd bits and pieces in the other.'

'I'm looking for a necklace,' Banjo says with a hint of urgency, 'A heart pendant on a silver chain.'

The policeman's lips pucker as he considers this. 'Nope, can't say I've itemised such a thing. How about I leave you to sort through all this. Oh, yes ... I must advise that nothing is to be taken away until forms have been completed and I've gotten your details. Standard procedure, you understand. Let me know if you need any help.'

Banjo thanks him and begins the task of sorting through the clothing, while the constable sits at his desk and fiddles with a tiny hand held motorised fan.

Inside the first box are hats, jackets, and an odd assortment of shoes. One work boot is smeared with what he assumes is blood. It is a heart-wrenching exercise, but no necklace is found. He then opens the second box containing two Gladstone bags, a satchel, a drawstring beach bag, and a handbag with a bamboo handle. He opens each one and checks inside, just in case. Again nothing. Two shoe boxes at the bottom are found to contain smaller items such as cigarette lighters, powder compacts, lipsticks, books, spectacles, and some jewellery, but not Marion's necklace. He replaces the lids and thanks the policeman, who in turn offers an apology for not having the item Banjo is looking for.

Returning outside, he again rubs his temples. His headache is growing. If the necklace wasn't collected with the other things, could it still be at the crash site? If so, it will be like trying to find a needle in a haystack. He knows he is clutching at straws, but if he doesn't give it a go, the weight on his mind will not be relieved.

44

1958

The sun is now directly overhead. Its hot breath blows brittle leaves from straggly ghost gums, turning them into whirling eddies of lifelessness. Seven days ago, this site was a scene of carnage, a hive of desperate activity. Sounds of rescue, cries of the hurting, and moans of the dying assaulted the air. Now it is as quiet as a graveyard. An eerie presence lingers. The shattered carriages have been removed and the train track cleared and repaired, yet flattened grasslands, hundreds of tyre tracks, and a gouged hillside give evidence of the catastrophe that had taken place a week before.

He props up his bike in the shade of a tree, and removes his helmet and jacket. Walking the track, he slowly follows the trail of residual debris—splintered wood, iron shavings, and glass shards that glitter like jewels in the sunlight. His feet drag. It's stinking hot, and flies drawn to the sweat on his arms and face won't leave him alone. He swats them away with limited effect. What is he doing? Is he going mad?

The litter of fragments eventually peters out and then ceases completely as he nears the horseshoe bend. He scans the gravel and his hope of finding the necklace vanishes. It has all been a stupid waste of time. His shoulders slump. He should have his head examined. He eyes the foliage on either side of the track and his attention is suddenly drawn to something peculiar.

On the track's right side, there is a gap in a thick brush of lantana. Thin, prickly branches are snapped and bent at odd angles. A few have been broken off completely as if something has forced its way through. Could a train have lost some of its load, or hit an animal and sent it careering into the scrub? Curiosity compels him to slip down the embankment and view it more closely.

Squatting, he pushes his way through the brush. Small birds 'peep, peep' and dart away at his intrusion. Clothing is snagged and flesh is pricked. As the foliage thickens he drops to his knees and shuffles through. Branches crunch under his weight, poke him in the eye, imbed fine needles into his hands. Within the gloom, he sees something out of place. It is caught on a low branch. Reaching forward he tugs it free and discovers it is a torn piece of material, white embossed linen. It is stained with what looks like dried blood. So, not an animal then, a person. He has a grim thought that this could have been someone from the train crash. He shakes his head. No, this area was too far away from the site of impact. Somebody has been here, though; somebody with an injury and a need to escape. He tucks the material into a trouser pocket and struggles on.

At last, he breaks through the lantana into a small clearing in the middle of a forest of tall trees. It is shady and cool here, with sunshine streaking down through spaces in the leafy canopy. He stands and brushes dirt and leaves from his clothing. Climbing over the large trunk of a fallen tree, he comes across a path worn through the bracken on the forest floor and follows it. Not far along, it meets with a dirt road where tyre tracks can be seen winding their way uphill. He has a strong urge to see where they lead.

It takes a good fifteen minutes to reach the destination of the tracks, a weathered timber cottage sitting on a cleared property on the side of the hill. Banjo peers back down the rise. Through the forest of trees he catches glimpses of the terrain below. A glint of reflected light from sun hitting iron proves a section of the train line is visible from up here. Viewing the cottage again, he sees no stirring of life, just the movement of leaves on tall trees. The only sound being the whip crack call between a whipbird and its mate. He ventures closer.

A bark and a flash of grey.

Banjo pulls up with a start as a sturdy cattle dog hurtles towards him. As if colliding with an invisible wall, it jerks to a halt just a few feet away. He sees that it has been tethered to a house stump by a chain. The barking stops and is replaced with a growl from between razor-sharp teeth.

Banjo holds up his hands. 'Hey girl! Settle down!' He backs away, trying to show calm even though his heart rate has doubled.

He makes his way around the side of the cottage, passes a sizeable shed, and comes to a back yard. It is covered in pumpkin vines. Green and grey globes are glimpsed beneath wide leaves. There is also an outback toilet—a dunny. The door is ajar and he can easily see that no one is seated on the wooden box inside.

He walks over to the cottage porch and up the steps. The back door is open. He knocks on the doorframe, calls 'hello'. There is no answer. He leans through the doorway into a kitchen and spies two plates, two bowls and two teacups stacked on the cupboard by the sink. He steps inside.

Calling out again, he walks through the house. It doesn't take long. Through a doorway comes a sitting room cluttered with odd pieces of furniture, all worn and in need of repair. On them rest stacks of newspapers, and bits and pieces of machinery. The room smells of grease and dust. Leading off from this are two sparsely furnished bedrooms. To him it looks like no female has lived here for quite a while. It is a man's abode devoid of charm and colour, nothing like the house kept by his mother.

The room on the right is in disarray. If he was Sherlock Holmes he may have deduced that there had been a struggle in here. But considering the rest of the house Banjo surmises this may be the normal state of things. As he starts to move away, he notices an item on the floor between the door and a wardrobe. It is a piece of cloth. When he picks it up, he sees that it is a ripped woman's blouse. This surprises him. What surprises him more, is that it seems to be made from the same material as the piece he found in the lantana. He pulls it out of his pocket. Yes, a perfect match. He can even make out where it has been torn from the left sleeve.

Banjo rushes back through the house and out into the yard. The dog barks from under the house but doesn't appear. He goes over to the shed. One side of the double door is open and he peers inside. It is dark and takes a while for his eyes to adjust and see that the interior is filled with all manner of junk and farming equipment, but no vehicle. Whoever lives on this property has gone.

He hurries to the front of the cottage. Careful to keep his distance from the dog's run, he stares down the drive. What if the tyre tracks were, in fact, leading away from the property, not to it? He jogs downhill until he reaches the beginning of the bracken path. The road continues from here but disappears around a bend. He decides that if he's going to search any further, he'll need his bike.

Crossing the clearing and returning through the lantana tunnel, Banjo reaches the train track and finds his Triumph still waiting for him in the shade. The sun is dipping lower. Once it drops behind the mountain range, it will be more difficult to follow any leads. He mounts the bike and travels to the glade via a different route, this time through a paddock. He finds the bracken path and then the dirt road where he stood not long before. This time he heads to the right, around the bend.

About a mile along, he spots a vehicle and slows. It is a truck pulled over at an odd angle. The tyre marks leading up to it show that it braked hard and then fishtailed to the road's edge. He comes to a stop and sees that the truck has collided with a gum tree and the bonnet is smashed beyond easy repair. Stepping from his bike, he opens the driver's door to check inside. It is empty, though there are red smears on the steering wheel and dark droplets on the seat. A touch with a finger confirms that it is blood. It seems the driver has slid in the dust, run the truck into the tree, and been injured. He checks the back tray. There is nothing there but soil and traces of dried vegetation. He glances around. No injured person is lying by the roadside. What should he do now?

Shutting the car door, Banjo sights strands of hair caught in the deteriorated rubber trim. They glint a deep copper in the dying light, and when he touches them, they curl around his finger in a way that causes his breath to catch in his throat. His head snaps to the left, in the direction he'd just come. His mind spins like a whirlpool. His stomach knots. He doesn't understand, but knows he needs to get help, contact the police. He climbs back on his bike.

Further down the road he passes a painted sign nailed to a fence post that reads: 'Nell's Guest House. Bed and Meals. 500 yards'. Gripping the throttle, he flicks his wrist, and the bike speeds ahead.

Nell is friendly and in her fifties. She smiles widely as he approaches the front counter and asks to use her phone. She sees his concern and enquires as to the problem. He says it is an emergency, that someone has crashed a truck down the road and may be hurt. She says not to worry, that she is aware of this and has it under control.

He asks what she means by that. She says the person is safe and being cared for. His nerves tighten and he asks if it is a man or a woman with auburn hair. Nell's smile disappears. She tells him to leave it alone. He says he can't. His fingers curl. His voice rises. He demands she tell him more. She asks him to settle down. He slams a fist on the counter. The brass counter bell jumps and jingles and she urges him to leave, tells him he can't see her.

His eyes widen. 'Her? Where is she?' he growls.

The woman's eyes jerk to the right, in the direction of a hallway.

He swings himself over the counter and pushes her out of the way.

'No! Don't!' Nell shouts. 'Leave her alone!'

He rushes down the hall, is hit on the back of the head by a flying counter bell.

'I'll call the police!' she warns.

'Do that!' he answers.

Coming to a door, he swings it wide. The room is neat, pretty, and vacant. He opens a second and freezes. His knees buckle and a skyrocket explodes within his chest.

45

11 January 1958

Peering out of the carriage door window, Marion is horrified by the view of the sharp bend up ahead. She clutches the window frame for balance and prays earnestly. The train lurches. The carriage door swings open. Losing her grip, she plummets into rushing air. The shoulder of the track races up to meet her and she smashes hard against gravel. Sliding down an embankment, she rolls into a wall that bites. Then blackness.

Terrible sounds bring her back to a level of consciousness. A groaning, hissing monster. Screams so shocking they cause her to wonder if she's entered the grisly pit of hell filled with the cries of the damned. Her heart pounds, demanding she distance herself from the cacophony. With a heavy head, a jaw that can't open, and eyes glued shut by a sticky substance, she attempts to rise.

An ache in her side keeps her breathing to a minimum. Knife-stabs of pain course from her left shoulder to her wrist—the arm is useless. She moves her legs—they seem unharmed. Scrambling to her knees, she shuffles forward, her movements hampered by curtains of sharp things that poke and scratch and snap as she forces her way through. She must be in a thicket of some kind. The scent is familiar, peppery. She reaches out, pulls her hand back when it is pricked. Lantana. This does not stop her from pushing forward. Using her head and uninjured shoulder she muscles further in and away from the horrors.

Her shirtsleeve is grabbed. She cries through her teeth, and rips it free. Sweat burns her eyes; rubbing them makes it worse. Lifting a corner of her blouse, Marion wipes her face, clearing away some of the muck. Now she can see a little. Shadows haunt the thick brush. The air is stifling, bursting with odd noises—near and far—and her panic escalates. She has to get out of this fearful cocoon of branches. With extra effort she drags herself over knobby roots, her clothes and flesh tearing from stick fingers that grab and prod.

Eventually Marion is out in the open where the air is cool and smells of eucalyptus. The ground is soft. She falls against something hard—a log—and sobs from both pain and exertion. Her head feels ready to burst and she wishes for the darkness to return.

Heavy footfalls and a snorting force her to prise open both eyes. She expects to see a snarling beast—a cow, a horse—yet what she finds staring down at her is ... a scarecrow. She manages to scream before the blackness envelops her once again.

46

1958

The noises that now terrify Marion come from her own mouth. Visions of Banjo, her parents, and a stranger with leering, bloodshot eyes taunt her until the moment when the pain dulls and she is able to surface from the fog.

She is lying on a bed, in a room she doesn't recognise. Across from her is a casement window with sunshine seeping through the glass, hurting her eyes. It must be daytime. She blinks and peers down. She is wearing a man's pyjama shirt and her left arm is in some sort of sling. A sheet covers her legs. This must be another horrifying vision, for sitting at the foot of the bed is a strange looking man. She quickly shuts her eyes, but a pressure on her knee makes them open again. The scarecrow is still there.

Marion squints. He is indeed real. The man is young—about her age—though thin with wiry hair sticking out from under a wide brimmed hat. His face is coarse and splashed with freckles, and either side of a huge misshapen nose are eyes, pale and veiny. Marion shudders and moves her legs away from his touch.

Fleshy lips part to reveal a mouth crowded with yellowed teeth. 'Back in the land of the living, are ya?' His voice is surprisingly high. 'Still feeling crook?'

Marion nods, holds her throbbing head with her hand. 'It hurts ... everywhere.' Even the act of talking is painful. The movement of her jaw sends arcs of pain up the left side of her face. 'What happened? How did I get here?' she asks through clenched teeth.

'I found ya. You was in the bush.'

'The bush? What was I doing there?'

'You was dinged up. I strapped ya up a bit. I 'spect you'll mend, directly.'

Suspect? What does that mean? The effort of conversation makes her dizzy. She squeezes her eyelids together.

'Hungry?' he asks.

She is about to answer with a 'no' when her stomach responds with an audible growl.

'Back in a jiffy,' the man says, rising from the mattress. He shuts the door behind him when he leaves.

Forcing through pain, Marion sits up. When the room ceases to spin, she glances around. Other than the bed, there is only a mirrored wardrobe and a bedside table with a lamp on it. As she gingerly swings her legs over the side of the mattress, the sheet falls away and she gasps. Her limbs are covered in dark purple bruising, and deep, bloodied scratches rake her skin. She is at a loss as to what has happened to her, or how she has come to this place.

A noise from the other side of the door. The man is talking to someone he calls Molly, and Marion is relieved to know that a woman lives here. The door opens and the man enters balancing a steaming mug and a plate of buttered bread on a wooden tray. Marion's hand shakes as she takes the mug and lifts it to her lips. It is a watery beef stew and, though rather bland, she scoffs it down.

'Thank you,' Marion says. 'Please thank Molly too.'

His eyes narrow, 'Molly?'

'Yes,' she nods towards the doorway, 'I heard you talking. Maybe you could send her in. I'd like to meet her.'

'Oh, ya will,' he grins, 'ya will.'

Fatigue soon draws Marion back to a much calmer sleep.

This time it is the ache of a full bladder that wakes her. The room is now in darkness and the night sky is seen through the window. She switches on the lamp beside the bed. Cautiously rising from the mattress, she stands, suddenly aware of a thickness between her legs. Lifting the oversized shirt, she discovers she is wearing a pair of men's Y-front underpants lined with a hand towel. Molly has fashioned her a nappy of sorts. How often had it needed to be changed? Embarrassed, she doesn't hesitate to remove the towelling.

Shuffling past the wardrobe, Marion catches her reflection in the mirror. What she sees is shocking. A monster looks back at her. She moves closer. The left side of her face is distorted by swelling, and the flesh encircling her bloodshot eyes is bruised dark purple. Her hair is wild and crusty. Marion swallows hard. It looks as if she's been beaten. Why can't she remember what had happened to her? She has to get home. Must contact Banjo, Aunt Gloria, or at least someone who can help. After finding a toilet, she will ask to use the telephone.

She opens the door and steps into a hallway. Turning left, she staggers—every muscle screaming—through a cluttered sitting room. Drawn into a lit kitchen, she scans the room. So far, she has seen no person and no sign of a telephone. Her apprehension increases.

The back door is wide open. Hesitating, she then steps out and onto a small porch. It is dark out here, but the moon is full and gives enough light for her to discover that bushland surrounds the cottage. The sizeable yard is criss-crossed by leafy vines bearing spherical objects, and silhouetted in the moonlight is an outhouse. She takes a step. A breeze brings with it an odour of cigarette smoke, and her heart kicks up a notch. She is not alone.

Three steps take her down to a cement path, but before she can call into the darkness, a growl is heard. A dark shape rushes out of the shadows. She screams and stumbles back against the railing.

'Molly! Stay!' a voice yells from the side of the cottage.

A speckled grey cattle dog halts in front of Marion. It begins to whimper, its tail between its legs.

The man appears in the arc of light coming from the kitchen. 'Whatcha doing?' he asks, flicking his cigarette onto the grass.

'Molly is a dog?' she cries, staring up at him.

'Yep.' He moves closer. 'Where do ya think you're going?'

'I need a toilet.'

'Use the pot.'

'What pot?'

'The one under the bed.'

She points. 'But there's a toilet out here.'

The man scratches his head and mumbles, as if calculating a difficult equation. Then grabbing Marion by the hand, he leads her across the yard she discovers is overgrown with pumpkins. It is a vegetable minefield.

'Make it quick,' he says, yanking the door open by its rope handle.

Marion manages better than expected, and when she comes out again the man is waiting for her.

'Inside, now,' he urges, giving her a shove.

As they weave their way back to the porch steps, Marion wonders why the man is so annoyed. She only wanted to do what normal people do, and this trip has saved him some washing. He should be grateful for that at least.

'Is there any chance I can have a wash?' she asks, hopefully.

He scowls. 'A bath?'

'Yes. I need a good wash.'

He cocks his head, eyes her, and snorts through his nose. 'Righto.'

The bathroom is off the kitchen, and while the tub fills, Marion rests on a wooden stool. Walking about has taken its toll and she is exhausted. Her left arm is stiff and any further attempt at movement results in her wincing with pain, so the man aids her in removing the cloth sling. He is less agitated now, and informs her that the shoulder was dislocated.

'You put it back in?' she says, surprised.

He nods and tells her to hold it at an angle, close to her chest.

When the bath is ready, he leaves her, shutting the door behind him.

Marion struggles to wriggle out of the shirt, yet one quick tug brings the underpants falling to her ankles. Easing herself over the side of the tub, she slips into the heated water. There is a washcloth and a cake of soap on the bath edge and both look clean. Washing carefully, she is shocked by each bruise and welt marking her body. Searching her memory for answers, she once again draws a blank. The last thing she can remember is saying goodbye to her Aunt Gloria and catching a tram into the city. What came after was a mystery. Sliding down, she soaks her hair.

The warmth of the soapy water is soothing and she finds herself drifting off to sleep.

She opens her eyes. The water is barely warm. The bathroom door is ajar and the man is seated on the stool.

'Want a hand?' he says, with a twitch of a wiry eyebrow.

'Get out!' Marion cries, slipping further under the murky water.

Thick lips form a sickening grin. 'I've seen ya starkers before, ya know.'

She cringes, suspecting as much. 'I said, get out of here.'

The man grips the sides of the stool with both hands and shuffles forward until he is right next to the bath. His veiny eyes travel over her. His breath labours. He rubs his palms over his trousered thighs. 'You have soft skin. I like touching it.'

Nauseated, Marion turns her body towards the wall. 'Please leave,' her voice trembles, 'I don't want you here'.

Rough fingers trail down her spine. She jerks away, pressing against the far side of the tub.

'You were nicer before,' the man whines.

Her head whips around. He is leaning over the edge of the bath; his hand in the water, stirring, splashing.

'Get lost, you idiot!' she screams.

He squints. 'I looked after ya ... all by myself. You coulda died out there.'

'Out where?' she demands. 'What happened? You have to tell me.'

He glares, then removes his hand from the water. Wiping it over his trousers, he rubs it against his groin and grins.

Marion turns away. 'You filthy moron. You make me sick.'

She hears a cry and the sound of the stool being kicked against the wall. Then the door slamming shut. Peering over her shoulder, she sees that he has gone. So has her clothing.

Dressed only in a towel, Marion sneaks back to the bedroom, shuts the door, and slides down behind it. Aiming to stay awake all night and bar the man from entering her room, she begins to make plans for a morning escape.

Marion wakes at daylight, furious at herself for dropping off to sleep so easily. She presses her ear against the door. There is no noise from the other side. Rising stiffly, she turns the handle, but the door won't budge. She turns it again, pulls hard. The door has been locked. Moving over to the window she attempts to open it, only to find that paint and swelling timber has sealed it shut. If only she had two good arms to force it free. A new fear takes hold. She is a captive.

Rather than drown in misery, she goes to the wardrobe. One door is locked, but the other is easily tugged open, though all she finds on the shelving is a handbag, a cloche hat, some scarves, and a slim box. The box, when opened, reveals a navy frock with padded shoulders and a white Peter Pan collar; a style she knew was popular in the 1930s. Being a couple of sizes too large makes it easier to slip into and, though the dress swims on her, Marion is glad to be wearing something other than a smelly pyjama shirt. She fashions herself a sling with one of the scarves and sits on the bed, waiting.

It isn't long before the bedroom door is opened and the man steps into the room.

His eyes widen and he almost drops the plate of sandwiches he is holding. 'Get that off!' he yells.

'I certainly will not,' Marion responds.

He grabs at the garment. 'Get it off. It's not yours.'

She beats his hand away. 'No. Get away. I have to wear something.'

He pants through his teeth. His eyes look as if they are about to pop free of their sockets.

'Whose dress is it?' she asks. 'Your mother's?'

His fat lips purse as he screams, 'Shut up! Shut up!' Hurling the plate of sandwiches across the room, he storms out of the room, relocking the door behind him.

Marion rises and collects the sandwiches thickly spread with Vegemite, stuffing them into her mouth. She feels like an animal, but is far from caring. She needs to gain her strength.

Curious as to what else is within the wardrobe, and hoping to find some decent underwear this time, Marion again pulls on the handle of the locked side. The door creaks. She plants her feet and tugs harder, hearing a 'pop'. The door swings wide at the next effort. It is empty apart from three wooden hangers, and a parcel of newsprint resting in a bottom corner.

The parcel falls open in her hands, revealing a wad of fabric. Marion recognises the pattern. It is her linen blouse, the one she must have been wearing when found. When lifted out, she discovers it is ripped and filthy and spattered with dried blood. As she gives it a shake something falls to the floor. Marion gasps. It's the necklace Banjo gave her. She drops to her knees and scoops it up, clutching it to her chest. Her heart aches so much it might crumble.

'Where are you Banjo?' she groans. 'Why haven't you come looking for me?'

Slipping it over her head and around her neck, her eyes are drawn to the creased newsprint beside her, and the photograph in the centre of the page. She spreads the page out flat. Above the photo, in bold print, is a headline.

'RAIL SMASH. 19 Dead. Dozens Injured.'

She reads the date on the top edge of the page, and then quickly scans the smaller print. Words leap out at her.

'9:45 am ... Shadow Creek line ... Archers Lookout ... train jumped the track ... carriages telescoped ... carnage ... men, women and children ... tragedy.'

Her eyes dart back to the photograph. It is a view of the smash. The train engine—or what is left of it—has crashed into a hill cutting and is on its side, along with a mess of carriages from the front section. People are everywhere. It looks catastrophic.

Sounds enter her memory. Screeching, crashing, hissing, and most horrible of all, screaming. She covers her mouth. A cry slips between her fingers and she slumps to the floor. She was there. She was on that train. She recalls the carriage door opening, the fall, the pain, the darkness; the desperation to get as far away as possible from those awful noises. Hot tears rush down her cheeks.

There is a sound of a key in a lock. The doorknob turns and the man bursts in.

'You found me near the train crash,' she cries.

He snatches the newsprint from her fingers. Crumpling it into a ball, he stuffs it into the front pocket of his overalls.

'Why didn't you call for help? Why didn't you take me back, or take me to a doctor at least? People will be looking for me. They'll be searching everywhere.'

His lips part into a smile. 'Will they?'

'Of course they will. You have to let someone know I'm here.'

He shakes his head. 'I can't.'

'Why can't you?'

'Finders keepers,' he says, placing his hand on the top of her head. 'You is mine now.'

Marion is appalled. She pulls away, but his fingers are entwined in her hair. They grip tight.

He squats in front of her, and her nose wrinkles at the

pungency of his body odour. 'You stay with me now. I'll look after ya. I done a good job so far, haven't I?'

She tries to tug free. His hold strengthens and her scalp burns. 'Yes, you have,' she says, trying to steady her voice. 'I'm grateful for that. But now it's time to take me back. That's what any good person would do.'

His face crumples. 'What if I don't want to be good?'

Yanking Marion to her feet, he pushes her onto the bed and falls on top of her.

She kicks out, knocking over the side table. The lamp shatters as it hits the floorboards.

He leans over her, licks her cheek with his tongue. His breath is foul. 'Now we can play,' he says, lifting her dress.

Marion squirms, raises a knee and aims it into his groin. He grunts and rolls away. She quickly rises, but is dragged back down by her hair.

His mouth is in her ear. 'Give me a kiss.'

She shakes her head, and then shudders as the man pulls her face around and forces his moist mouth on hers. Pulling her good arm free, she punches him in the side of the head.

He jerks sideways, but his hands find her shoulders, shakes her hard.

Marion's vision blurs from the pain. She tries to pry his hands away 'Please ... please ... let me go.' Desperation gives her an idea. 'My mother, she'll be worried sick.'

His fingers ease their hold. 'Ya mother?'

She nods, 'Yes, my poor old mother.'

His hands slide away. A sharp fingernail catches on the chain around her neck, and the heart pendant slips out from beneath the collar of the dress. The man's face suddenly softens, revealing his youth. He lifts the pendant and dangles it before her eyes.

'Did she give you this? Did your mother give you this?'

'Yes,' she lies again, 'for my birthday. We are very close.'

'Does she love you?'

'Yes,' Marion nods, 'very much.'

The man's face contorts. He drops the pendant. 'Okay,' he sighs, 'go.'

Marion stares, confused. Had she heard correctly? 'Go? You're letting me go?'

He nods and slides off her, curling into a ball on the bed like a despondent child.

She wonders if the man's mother is dead, like hers. 'You loved your mother, didn't you,' she says.

He doesn't answer.

She gets up and backs away, but he doesn't budge. She takes a few more steps towards the door, then turns and stumbles away.

Outside, in the backyard, Marion goes left, hopscotching over swollen pumpkins and vines as thick as braided rope. A dog bark brings her to a halt. Molly is under the cottage, teeth bared, hackles raised. Marion freezes. A rattle of chain. Relief. The dog cannot follow her.

Continuing around the cottage, she comes to an iron and timber shed twice the size of the cottage. A wide door is peeled back. It is gloomy inside and all manner of tools hang from hooks and rusted chains. The place reeks of grease and fertiliser. Machinery, oil drums, tyres, and assorted garden implements lay scattered on the dirt floor, while bottles of every size and shape stand at attention on timber shelving. She spies a pair of dusty boots in a wheelbarrow. Footwear will be useful if she is to travel a distance.

Rushing in, she turns the boots upside down and gives them a shake. Nothing frightening falls out. Dropping each one, she stuffs her feet inside. A clatter causes her to spin around. A kerosene tin is rolling in the dirt. Movement further back reveals a large rodent scurrying behind a bright blue, Globite suitcase. It is partly open. Drawn by a pressing curiosity, she steps over.

Though the corners have been gnawed and the surface is dusty, finger marks indicate the suitcase has recently been handled. She cautiously opens the lid and finds it is filled with women's shoes in assorted colours and styles. Sorting through them, Marion discovers they are all the same large size. Had they belonged to the man's mother? She recognises a smaller black shoe with a buckled ankle strap. The leather has been scraped in parts and the heel is loose. A check of the size in the lining confirms it is hers. Her hand recoils and she turns around.

A silhouette is in the doorway.

'I need some boots,' she says, pointing to her feet.

The man comes over; his face expressionless.

Marion attempts to walk around him, but her arm is seized. 'What are you doing?' she yells, tugging, yet unable to free herself from his strong grip.

'I changed my mind. You is staying put.'

Where is that sorrowful child now? She tries to buffet him away, but hurts her injured shoulder in the process.

'Let me go. There doesn't have to be any trouble. If you're scared I'll tell where I've been, or what you've done, then don't worry. I'll just say I've been lost in the bush for a couple of days ... all alone. They'll believe me.'

He pulls her against him, rubs his face in her hair. 'I'm lonely.'

'You're sick. You need help.'

He frowns. 'Sick?'

'In the head.'

He grabs her injured arm by the elbow and yanks down. Marion screams and she kicks out, her boot connecting with a bony shin. The man releases his hold, and she drops to the ground.

'I am not a moron!' he yells, shaking his fists.

Then, reaching high, he grips a heavy linked chain hanging from a rafter and tugs it free. Standing over Marion he swings it back and forth, barely missing her face.

She shuffles backwards in the dirt.

He follows, flailing the chain over his head like a medieval weapon. His teeth are bared and his eyes wild. His nostrils flare as he snorts.

Marion's head bangs against something solid. A glimpse shows her escape is being prevented by a row of oil drums. As the man stops in front of her, and the chain's momentum increases, Marion lifts a leg and aims her boot into a kneecap.

A loud popping sound. A shriek. The chain flies off into the shadows and clatters against tin sheeting.

While the man folds to the ground, holding his leg and groaning, Marion crawls around him. Attempting to stand, a hand clutches her ankle and pulls her off her feet.

'Ya not going nowhere!' he shouts, pinning her down with his weight.

One powerful hand seizes her throat, while the other is forced between her legs. She struggles. Clawing the dirt with her good hand, her fingers grasp the handle of something heavy. Lifting the implement high, she slams it into his head.

The man topples sideways.

Pulling out from under him, Marion raises the wooden mallet for another swing, but her attacker is motionless. Blood seeps from a smashed forehead into dark, open eyes.

She drops the mallet and stands on wobbly legs. Stumbling through the shed, she hurries out into the sunlight. Blinking against the glare, she sees an old farm truck parked in the dirt driveway.

Rushing over, she finds the key is still in the ignition. Not having driven a vehicle as big as this before, she falters before clambering inside. At least it has a column shift. A floor gear stick would have been far too difficult to manoeuvre in her condition. With effort, she tugs the door shut, catching her hair in the frame. Pulling free, she shuffles to the front edge of the bench seat so that her feet can reach the pedals. Twisting the key, the engine splutters, and the truck jerks down the long drive and onto a dirt road.

Marion gulps back a sob. Pain and dizziness threaten to deter her bolt for freedom. She has no idea where she is or where she is going. All she knows is she has to get well away from the cottage and the man lying dead in the rear of the shed.

Her concentration in driving is broken by the appearance of a scrub turkey as it darts from the bushes and dashes across in front.

She brakes hard. Skidding in the dirt, the truck slides and collides with a huge tree on the side of the road. Thrown forward, Marion's head hits the steering wheel.

When consciousness returns, Marion finds her nose is throbbing fiercely and dripping blood. Slipping from the truck, she hobbles down the road, away from the horrid nightmare.

'Help!' she cries, to an afternoon filled only with the drone of summer insects. 'Somebody help me!'

47

1958

E yes open to a gentle light. Marion rests on a cloud; her skin caressed by a lavender breeze. Wrens twitter, bellbirds tinkle, and an angel holds her hand. If this is a dream, then she never wants to wake from it. If it is heaven, she never wants to leave.

'Hello dear,' she hears, and the marshmallow world evaporates.

A kindly face comes into her field of vision, a woman's. Her mother's? No. The cheeks are too round, the hair too light. She watches the wrinkled hand as it pats hers. The fingernails are neatly trimmed, painted soft pink, while Marion's are serrated and encrusted with dirt.

'How are you feeling, luv?' Full lips smile. Soft eyes fold at the corners like venetian blinds.

Marion attempts to speak. Her throat is parched and there is a throbbing in the centre of her face. She has trouble breathing through her nose. She coughs, feeling a spasm of pain in her chest. 'I ... I'm not sure. It ... hurts.'

The woman sits on the edge of the bed, beside her. 'No wonder. You arrived here in a bad state. I've sponged off most of the blood.'

Marion cringes at the memory of her face hitting something hard. A steering wheel. She touches her nose, discovers it is bandaged.

'It may be broken,' says the woman. 'It is very swollen.'

She takes in the pretty room decorated in white lace and florals. 'How did I get here?'

'Don't you remember?' The woman's eyebrows arch. 'You came stumbling through the door, blabbering something about being trapped and having to get away. You were scared, and I could see you'd been in the wars, so I brought you back here. You fainted away as soon as you hit the mattress.'

Marion squirms as scenes flash in her mind. The dark shed, the suitcase of shoes, the attack, the mallet ... those dead eyes. 'Yes ... escape. I think I crashed a truck.'

The woman nods, deliberates, then speaks. 'I couldn't help notice your ... ah ... other injuries. Your arm; the bruising and scratches. My dear, have you been beaten ... by a man?' Marion sucks in a breath, looks away. The woman pats her hand again. 'It's all right, luv, I've seen a fair share of brutish men in my time. You're safe here. I won't let anyone hurt you. He'd have to get past old Nell here first, and that's not going to happen.' She brushes hair back from Marion's face. 'Would you like me to call the police?'

She shakes her head. That's the last thing she wants. They'd find out everything. She'd be taken away.

'Okay. I understand. How about a doctor? You really do need a proper look over.'

'No, not yet.'

The woman nods. 'Sure. We can wait. Anyone else?'

Marion considers this. No, she couldn't bear to see Banjo now. Her nerves are shot. Her mind is mush. She needs time to think things through. 'No-one,' she rasps.

'Would you like a drink, then? A cup of tea?'

'Yes ... tea.'

Nell lifts off the bed and takes a few steps towards the door. Turning back, she says, 'This is my guesthouse. I'm light on bookings at present, so you're quite welcome to stay until you've gained your strength. We can work out what to do once you're up to it.'

'Thanks ... Nell,' Marion says, feeling her eyes pool.

'You'll be fine. It takes a lot of guts to leave a bastard like that, and I'm glad you found the strength to do it. I once lived with a mongrel of a fellow who treated me badly. Who knows what would have happened if I hadn't gotten away from him.'

Marion is tempted to tell the truth, but holds her tongue. It's better that Nell believes she'd been beaten by a lover than having to hear she'd run away after killing a man.

Nell pulls the door closed behind her, then sticks her head back into the room. 'I might bring you a slice of my ginger sponge as well. Everyone says it's delicious.'

The door is shut and Marion holds her head in her hands. The pain behind her eyes is increasing, and the dizziness is returning. After the tea and cake she hopes to drift off again. At least she doesn't have to think when she's asleep.

That evening, Marion is able to eat a light dinner and manage a bath. Nell finds her items of fresh, suitable clothing, and she sleeps solidly without nightmares.

∼

In the morning, she takes an aided stroll outside to a paved courtyard, and sits for a while in the shade breathing in scents of flowering shrubs, and watching small birds take dips in a garden rock pool. Under other circumstances, the guesthouse would've been a delightful place to spend a relaxing holiday. But her time here is limited. It has to be.

When she gets the chance she'll search for the telephone, find Banjo's number in the phone book, and give him a call. The thought of him, frantic with worry, wondering why she never reached Shadow Creek, makes her anxious. He'll have to be told the truth of what happened; what she's done. Nausea rises at this thought

Nell doesn't ask too many questions, and Marion's answers aren't always the truth—she says her name is 'Mary'. They small talk about books, gardening, the weather, and Marion finds out that the guesthouse is in the hills, on a mountain range west of Brisbane. She realises it mustn't be too far away from where the train crashed, possibly just a few miles. The disaster isn't mentioned, and Marion doesn't bring it up.

After a light lunch—egg salad, and a delicious passionfruit flummery—she retreats to the bedroom for another nap.

Sounds disturb her sleep. There are shadows in the room. It must be late afternoon. She sits up, strains to listen. Voices—Nell's and a man's. They rise and fall in waves of conversation. Her heart pounds. Could it be the police? Has the man's body been found? Have they come for her?

She hears a rush of footsteps and a clatter as something hits the floorboards. The footsteps stop briefly and then start up again. They are on the other side of her door. Marion covers her mouth to stifle a scream.

The door is pushed open.

It isn't the police.

48

Another reason why the name Selena caught my attention when reading Fran Baxter's bereavement notice is that it is my mother's middle name. Mum had been given this in honour of her grandmother, Selena Theresa Australia Hughes. It was a mouthful, yet revealed my immigrant great-great grandparent's gratitude for birthing a child in a new land. Either that or they wanted to remind their first born, known as Tess, of the sacrifice made in coming out to a country poles apart—literally and figuratively—from their own birthplace in Wales.

In the loft study, I sorted through the items on my desk until I found the manila folder my dad had given me containing the updated family tree. Flicking through the printed pages, I came to a diagram detailing my maternal ancestors, and followed the branch upward with my finger.

My mother *Rose Selena Denning*, then her mother *Gloria Bourke*, then *Selena Theresa Australia Hughes*, then her mother *Alice Jane Marsh*, whose mother was *Jane Selena Gillet*, who had a mother named *Selene Pulos*.

So, evidence of a tradition that dribbled through in fits and starts like a blocked kitchen tap. I was about to close the folder, when my eyes were drawn to yet another Selena. This one took my breath and gripped it in her slender, dead hand. *Selena Marion Douglas*, born 1938 to Owen and Ruth Douglas.

I was gob-smacked. No one had mentioned that Marion was known by her second name. But then, why would they? Shane's mother was known by her middle name as well, due to Edwina not being half as appealing as Grace.

I opened the recent Internet search I'd done on my phone and re-read Frances Baxter's bereavement notice. Her son falling in love with two Selenas was too much of a coincidence. My skin goose-bumped. There was something else. Pushing up from the chair, I raced downstairs to the china cabinet in the lounge room.

Lifting out the Apple Blossom pin dish—the match for Marion's pendant—I flipped it over and read the designer's mark. 'James Kent'. I held it alongside the bereavement notice on my phone's screen. Ben's children were named Jamie and Ken. Another coincidence?

My mum answered on the second ring. I asked her if she'd ever heard of someone by the name of Selena Patterson. Her first reply was in the negative, but after a moment of deliberation she mentioned that her mother—my nana Gloria—had corresponded for a time with a Lena Pattinson. She had assumed they were pen friends, or someone nana had met on one of her yearly train trips interstate to visit Uncle Stevie.

I asked her if it were possible that this person's surname was Patterson. She told me she could find out, and told me to wait. Before I had a chance to ask where she was going, she passed the phone on to my father.

'Hi, sweetie,' Dad crooned, 'how was your Halloween party?'

'Loads of fun,' I replied. 'I think we might have unearthed something surprising.'

'Not a wife for Dracula,' he chuckled.

'Not that type of unearthing. I mean more information about Marion. Why didn't you mention her real name was Selena?'

'I didn't think I needed to. No one ever called her that. Anyway, what did you say to your mother? She's running around like a chook with its head cut off. Oh, now she's disappeared into the bedroom.'

'Dad, I'm curious. What happened to Marion's father ... Uncle Owen?'

'He died years back, in the eighties. He moved to Byron Bay at some stage, became a recluse. Your grandmother didn't keep in touch. She didn't like him at all. Called him a pervert for some reason. So ... how's Shane?'

'Shane? Good.'

'And how are you two getting on?'

What did he know about our recent situation? It didn't matter now. All was going well, very well. 'Great, couldn't be better.'

'That's good. Was Lester Schilling there last night?'

'Yes, why?'

'I ... er ... just wanted to say that I understand, Aberdeen luv ... I really do.'

My skin crawled. Bloody Lester and his idiot bookmark.

He coughed and continued. 'Years ago, there was a woman at work. We used to flirt just for a bit of fun, and then things took a turn, a not so good turn I might add. I was foolish, I—'

'Dad!' I interrupted. 'Stop! I don't want to hear it.'

'It's okay. Your mother knows all about it. I had a brain fart, that's all. Maybe that's what you and Lester—'

'No, it's a mistake, Dad! I'm not—'

'Not continuing with it?' he butted in. 'That's good to hear.

Shane will forgive you, I'm sure. Your mother did, eventually. Just come clean and—'

'Dad, you're not listening! There's nothing going on between Lester and me. He's been delusional, that's all. It's all sorted. You can chuck that disgusting bookmark away.'

'Oh, all right. If you say things are fine then ... anyway, your mum's back looking hot and bothered.'

After some shuffling noises, my mother's laboured voice sounded in my ear. 'Abby, I think I've found something.'

My grandmother, it seems, kept most of the birthday cards she'd been given in an old chocolate tin. After her death, my mum decided to hang on to them as keepsakes. Lucky she had, for amongst them were a few sent by this Lena. One still had an envelope attached, and the sender was indeed a Lena PATTERSON.

'Does this help at all?'

'You bet it does. It has to do with the Marion and Ben mystery.'

'Do you think there's a connection?'

I tried to control my excitement. 'Mum, I'm beginning to think that your cousin Marion may not have died after all.'

Mum laughed. 'Don't be silly, of course she did. I went to her funeral.'

I had to tread carefully. This would be a hell of a shock for her. 'Well, I just found out that Ben married a Selena.'

'Did he? Well, well, isn't that strange. You know, Marion's first name was Selena.'

'Yes, I know that now.'

'Oh ... so that's why you . . . no, it couldn't be. Marion died, everyone knows that.'

'Listen, Mum. Ben had two children ... boys. Their names were Jamie and Ken. James Kent was the designer of the Apple Blossom pin dish that Marion owned. That can't also be a coincidence.'

There was silence from the other end of the line. 'Mum?' I prodded anxiously.

She responded, her voice strained. 'It ... it all sounds too ridiculous. There has to be an explanation.'

I took a deep breath. 'What if there was a mix up. What if, by some miracle, she survived the train crash?'

'She would have contacted us, surely.'

'I'm thinking Nana knew something.'

'Well why didn't she say anything to me? Why did she keep such a thing a secret?'

'I don't know. The Alzheimer's?' I offered up. 'Maybe she forgot to tell you. Or forgot who Lena really was.'

There was a weird noise at the other end of the phone. Then it went dead. I was worried. I hoped I hadn't upset my mother to the point of collapse.

I decided to go see my parents and make sure Mum was okay. There might even be more information in my grandmother's keepsakes that my mum wasn't aware of.

Shane was awake now, but still in bed. I informed him that Gemma was back and I was heading off for a quick visit with my parents. He told me I could take his ute instead of the VW.

'Might ward off being stalked,' he added with a wink.

I threw on a pair of shorts and a shirt and escaped outside.

49

1958

Banjo rushes in, takes Marion's hand, kisses her face, crushes her in his arms. She winces. A laugh bubbles from her throat.

Nell appears in the doorway wielding a floor mop; eyes wide, cheeks flushed.

'It's okay, Nell,' Marion says, still smiling. 'He's not to be feared.'

'Are you sure?'

Together, Marion and Banjo answer a definite 'yes'.

Nell's face relaxes. 'Well it's lucky I haven't yet called the police. I'll leave you to it, then.' She disappears.

Banjo touches Marion's cheek, lifts her hand to his lips. 'It's a miracle. We thought you were dead.'

'Dead? Why would you think that?'

'I found you. I held your ...' He grimaces. 'You were definitely dead.'

She gasps. 'But I didn't die.'

He smiles. 'So it seems.'

'I was hurt. I was found and taken ...' She starts to tremble. 'I was—'

'It's okay, Marion.' He brushes his fingers through her hair. 'I know where you've been this last week.'

'Week? What day is it?

'Saturday. Seven days since the train crash.'

She sucks in air, searches his face. 'The train crash. Was it as bad as they say?'

His face slackens, and he gives a nod.

She falls back onto the pillows. 'I was on that train. I was heading out to see you.'

'What happened, Marion? Did you jump? Is that what you did? I followed some tracks through the bush. They weren't near the site of the crash. Did you see what was going to happen and leap from the train?'

Her tongue feels like a dried sponge. Her head is heavy, and the ache behind her eyes has returned. 'I fell from the train ... the door opened and I fell ... just before the crash, I suppose. I heard things, dreadful things, and had to get away.'

'You hurt your arm, the bruising ... bloody hell, it must've been awful.'

She leans into him. 'Yes, everything ... so awful.' She closes her eyes. Her breath is ragged. 'A man found me. A young man, but odd looking. Simple-minded, maybe. He took me back to his house, fixed me up. But then he got weird. He ... he ... ' Her fingers grip his shirtfront. 'It was horrible, Banjo!'

'Marion ... he didn't—'

'No!' She looks him in the eye. 'He tried ... but I stopped him. I killed him, Banjo. I killed the man to save myself.'

His mouth gapes and his eyes blink hard. 'You killed him?' His voice quavers. 'Are you sure? How? What did you do?'

'I smashed him in the head with a mallet. He didn't move. There was blood, and his eyes were …' She chews her lip.

Banjo takes her hand. His grips is tight. 'Where did you do this?'

'At his place, in the bush, on the hill.'

'But where? Which room?'

'Which room?' she replies, puzzled. 'What's that got to do with anything?'

'I was there, just an hour ago. I walked all through that house. There was no person there … dead or alive.'

She pulls her hand free. 'You were there? How did you … he wasn't in the house, he was in the shed. I killed him in the shed.'

'I looked in the shed. It was dark, but I didn't see anyone.'

'Did you go to the back, over near the oil drums?'

'Oil drums?' His eyebrows squish together. 'No. I didn't go inside. I didn't think there was anybody there. The truck was gone. I thought someone had taken her … you … away. I got my bike and followed tyre tracks. Came across the truck crashed into the tree. Saw the blood. Found hair the colour of yours in the door. I thought I was going loopy. I knew you were dead, but I had to find you.' He touches her cheek with the back of his hand, wraps a curl of her hair around his finger. 'We have to tell the cops, Marion. Everyone has to know you're alive. It will make the front page of all the newspapers.'

'No!' Marion falls back into the pillows. 'I killed a man, Banjo. I'll be charged with murder.'

'It was self-defence. You said that.'

'But it will just be my words. No one else saw it. There were no witnesses.'

'He kept you there against your will, didn't he?'

'He also fixed me up. Fed me. Took care of me. That's what they'll say. Why would I murder someone who looked after me?'

'For God's sake, Marion, the bastard tried to rape you!'

She raises her chin. 'How do you know?'

'You just told me.'

She points a finger in his face. 'See, just my words. I could be lying.'

He eyes her suspiciously. 'Are you?'

'Of course not! But that's what they'll think.'

'They won't, Marion. Believe me, they won't.'

'My father will.'

He slaps a hand down on the mattress. 'Bugger your father! I don't give a rat's arse about him.'

Marion sighs and closes her eyes. She shakes her head. 'When he finds out I'm alive, and hears that I killed someone out of a fear of being raped, he'll tell the police I'm lying, that I brought it on myself.' Her eyelids flick open. 'He said he'd do anything to bring me down and I know he'll use this to do it. We can't go to the police, and we can't let anyone know I'm alive.'

Banjo scowls. 'What are you saying? No one?' He gets up. Paces the floor. 'What about your aunt, the rest of your family? How can you keep this a secret? You survived the train wreck, Marion. That's a flamin' miracle!'

She rises from the bed. Her nails bite into his flesh as she grabs him by the arm. 'Banjo please, listen to me. If you love me you won't tell anyone. We have to keep it a secret. It's best we just get on with our lives. Just you and me, together.'

His head flinches back. 'That's crazy, Marion. How can we do that?'

'Well it would've been easier if I still had the money.'

'What money?'

'The money my mother had secretly put aside over the years.

Before she died, she gave an envelope to my aunt, told her to pass it on to me after ... after she went. Aunt Gloria gave it to me at the wake. Inside the envelope was a note from my mum telling me to use the enclosed money wisely. Mum warned me not to say anything to my father or else he'd come after it.'

'What happened to the money?'

'Who knows? Buried in the wreck I suppose.' She drops her hand and lets out another long sigh. 'I had it in my handbag. That's what I was eager to tell you once I arrived at Tulip Wood. We could have gone away. Started a whole new life together. But ... well ...'

Banjo scratches his chin. 'How much of a new life?'

'Two thousand pounds worth of one.'

He gives a whistle. 'It was in your handbag, you say?'

She nods.

'I have it,' he grins. 'I have your handbag. I found it in the carriage, in the wreckage.'

'You what? Where is it?'

'Back home.'

She clasps her face in her hands. 'This is incredible, Banjo. Is the envelope still inside?'

He gives a shrug. 'I don't know. I don't recall seeing one. Just hankies, a coin purse, lipstick ... stuff like that.'

'There's a secret pocket in the lining. I hid the envelope there for safekeeping.'

'Well, how was I to know that?'

She smiles widely. 'It's got to still be there. Oh Banjo, this is wonderful. We can do whatever we want now.'

'But ... what about my mum? What about your aunt?'

'Well, I guess you'll need to tell your mum, but she'll have to keep our secret. As for Aunt Gloria, I'll get in touch with her eventually.

After what we've been through I don't think it'd hurt to be a little selfish.' Excitement stirs within. 'I'll have to take on a new identity. We'll have to move away, far away, and we'll have to go soon.'

Banjo takes her face in his hands and kisses her. 'I love you, Marion. If this is what you want right now, then let's do it. I'm just grateful you're alive. We can deal with the other stuff later if we have to.'

Marion returns the kiss. 'That's good because I love you.' Her hand goes to her bare throat. 'I'm sorry. I lost your necklace. God knows where it is now. Probably back at that house ... or the shed.' She knows she could never go back there, even to find something so precious to her.

'Don't worry,' Banjo soothes, 'I'll get you another one. A proper, more expensive one this time.'

Marion has a sudden thought. 'Why did you say you saw me dead? I was missing, not dead.'

'Like I said, I saw your body.'

'But how can that be? I wasn't there. I wasn't in the train wreck. It couldn't have been me.'

'I know that now, but at the time I thought it was you. You were wearing that pink dress.'

'Pink dress?'

'The one with the flowers and all those buttons ... and you were wearing Donald's ring, for God's sake.'

A cry escapes her mouth. 'Oh no ... oh no. That poor girl.'

'What girl?'

She drops onto the end of the bed. 'The young woman I met in the station restroom before I got on the train. I gave her my dress to wear.'

'You gave some strange girl your dress?'

Marion's eyes sting. 'She was sick. She'd vomited all over her outfit. I felt sorry for her and loaned her a dress from my suitcase. It fitted her perfectly. She said she'd mail it back.'

'And why did you give her the ring? I thought you'd returned it to Donald.'

'He didn't want it. He said I could have it to pay for all the trauma I'd been through. When the girl confided in me that she was expecting a baby, and was unmarried, I felt sorry for her and gave it to her. I told her to hock it and use the money.' She wipes tears from her eyes. 'Dulcie, that's the girl's name. She took a seat in my carriage, a few rows over. It was so crowded. She was heading home to tell her parents about the baby. She hadn't seen them for ages and was really scared.'

'The baby.' Banjo lets out a long sigh. 'Then, you weren't pregnant.'

Marion pulls a face. 'Me? Of course not. Why would you think that?'

'Your father ... no, don't worry about it. It doesn't matter now.'

'She had hair like mine, and was a similar build ... I knew my dress would fit her. But her face ... couldn't you tell it wasn't me by her face? We were different.'

'Well,' he sits beside her, 'to be honest, you ... she ... her head ... it was a real mess. Let's just leave it at that. It was the dress and ring that helped me identify you. And your handbag, of course. There was also your suitcase. Anyway, we had your funeral. That was really terrible.'

'You buried Dulcie under my name?'

'Yes. Oh God!' Banjo jumps up and goes to the window. As if drawn by the fragrance of flowering shrubs, he leans out and inhales deeply. When he turns to face her, Marion sees his eyes are red and welling up. 'What have we done?' he groans. 'Her poor family must be missing her. Wondering what's happened to their daughter.'

Marion beckons him over, holds his hand. 'We'll put it right, Banjo. Once we've sorted ourselves out we'll put it right.'

He nods slowly. 'We'll head back to Tulip Wood tonight, or maybe tomorrow. You can meet my mum.'

She touches her aching nose. 'Sorry I don't look my best.'

He cups her face in his hands. 'You look good to me. You're skin is a healthy pink, and you're breathing. You'll do just fine.'

50

My head hurt from questions and answers playing an unsuccessful game of Perfect Match within. I pulled over at my favourite viewing spot and stood at the wire fencing to gather my thoughts. The sky was clear, save for a few clouds building on the horizon, and a light breeze ruffled through the long grass on the slopes. I inhaled the morning's freshness, then took my phone from my pocket and called my parents at home to let them know I was on my way.

There was no answer, so I thought I'd try Dad's mobile. I must have tapped on his name too hard for the phone slipped from my grasp. Dropping to the ground, it skidded on loose gravel and slid under the fencing. I watched in horror as it then skimmed over a patch of dewy grass and toppled over the edge of the escarpment.

'No-o-o!'

I leant forward to see where it had fallen and found there was no way I could tell from this position, so I fed myself through the barbed wire, and forced myself to kneel on the grassy knoll for a better view. Though giddy, I saw it. It was on a rock ledge a couple of metres down. I scanned my surroundings. To my left, the gradient was not as steep. With some effort, I knew I could tackle the descent to retrieve the phone.

Fighting back fear, I scrambled down over rock, shale, and spinifex to reach my destination. Grabbing my phone, and sliding it safely inside a pocket of my shorts, I prepared myself for the tricky return climb. It was at this point, as I stood on the slopes above Tickle Bridge, I realised the rocky outcrop was the one I was heading for the other day. This meant the cave could be just below, waiting for me. Amazed at the courage and dexterity given by determination, I manoeuvred further down without injury and dropped onto a ledge in front of a cleft in exposed bedrock. Ducking my head, I stepped into the shadows.

The cave wasn't quite like I'd imagined. It was the size of a four-man tent and, rather than decorated with ancient Aboriginal rock paintings, the walls bore recent graffiti markings. From the ones I could decipher, I was enlightened to the fact that, 'Colin loves Mandy', 'Darren likes boys', 'Riley is a prick', and 'Tiffany does it for $1'. A pile of ash and charcoal gave evidence that a fire had been lit there several times, though the rubbish scattered about suggested potato chips, chocolate bars, and cans of energy drink had been consumed, not food obtained from hunting or gathering. It also smelled dank and mouldy, with sharp notes of guano and obnoxious teenagers.

Disenchanted, I went back out into the light and found the views to be equally as expansive as the lookout's. If the story of the Aboriginal man was true, then he'd had a bird's eye view of the changing landscape. Contemplating this sadness, my eyes were drawn to a flash of reflected light as a vehicle made its way up the winding road. When it neared Tickle Bridge, I saw that it was an old Holden ute, the colour of a cloudy day. I shuddered and ducked back into the crevice.

What was the stalker doing this time?

I leant back out and peered below. The ute had stopped just after the bridge and the man with the hat was getting out. Rounding the front of the vehicle, he stood on the verge. What was he doing, checking out the view, waiting for someone? Then, by his stance, I realised he was doing neither. He had stopped to take a leak. I stepped back. I didn't want to be caught perving on a man with his tackle out, writing his name in the dirt.

I gave him thirty seconds, and then gave another cautious glance. He was now getting back into the ute. I knew the wiser option would have been to pay a visit to the Shadow Creek police station and have a chat with Senior Constable Will; tell him what had been going on; ask him to search for details on this particular vehicle, this particular driver, and get him to find out if the man had a history of stalking lone women. Instead, I stubbornly decided to confront the creep on my own. Dusting off skills I learned in my one and only indoor rock climbing adventure, I made my way back up to the top of the hill and Shane's ute.

It took me ten minutes to reach Tickle Bridge, and not once did I pass the stalker's ute. There were no side roads, so where could it have gone? Driving further downhill—at a faster, less cautious speed—I caught sight of the vehicle as it disappeared around a sharp bend. The sneaky bugger must have turned around and was heading back to town. I followed at a distance.

The driver didn't stop in Shadow Creek as I'd hoped, but kept going, heading out towards Tulipwood. Passing the area where my parents lived, he continued driving through the countryside towards the lower incline of the mountain range. Where the hell was he going? I couldn't spend my whole day tailing some loon. At some point soon I would need to turn back. I gave him another ten minutes.

He veered left onto a side road, then right onto a more regular thoroughfare; one I'd driven on for the first time the day before. I waited to allow a sedan to come between us before following on. We passed the train crash memorial and then, after about a kilometre, I saw the ute take a dirt road on the right. The sedan kept going straight, while I continued to tail the stalker, pinpointing my position by Archers Lookout on the ridge just above. Though this road wound sharply uphill, and I lost sight of the ute, the dust cloud left in its wake made the route easy to trail.

The terrain was very wild and bushy, though at one point I noticed a faded sign for a guesthouse hanging awkwardly from a timber post. The only evidence of this being a boarded-up cottage with an overgrown yard reclaimed by lantana. Eventually the dust cloud petered out at the entrance to a fenced property, and I parked on the roadside well away from the galvanised steel farm gate.

Winding down the window, I was greeted by the steady hum of cicadas. Tall gums and hoop pines grew all around, and the rustle of leaves on their high swaying branches showed the strength of the wind at this height. A glance over the road and through trees, revealed snatches of the bitumen road much further down. It was indeed a secluded spot. I tapped out a phone message to Shane, giving my rough whereabouts and telling him that if I wasn't home in an hour, to come looking for me. Then I got out of the car.

As I walked towards the gate, the cicada noise increased to an ear-splitting shrill. Were they warning me of imminent danger? My heart pounded a wild drum solo within my chest, yet I wasn't giving up, not after coming this close to getting some answers. I also needed to take back control of my life, even if it was just overcoming the fear of being stalked. Opening the gate, I headed up the drive.

The grey ute was parked out the front of a dilapidated timber cottage. The paintwork, stripped by age and weather, revealed wood cladding the colour of bleached bones. The iron roof was rusted a deep orange, while the busted guttering sagged and dripped moisture from bright green tendrils of hair-like moss. The house also had a definite lean to the left, which led me to believe that one good kick would send it toppling off its short stumps and crashing in a messy heap on the ground.

I crept over to the ute, noticing that the back was covered by a tarpaulin fastened so tight it could have been used as a trampoline. I wondered what diabolical equipment a stalker could hide beneath such a covering. Rope, zip ties, duct tape, assorted instruments of torture? I shivered and moved towards the driver's open window. Leaning my head in, the darkness suddenly came to life when drooling jaws snapped just centimetres from my face.

I lurched back, recognising the boofy-headed dog and its vicious, toothy snarl. It was the staffy that had accosted in the town park alongside Shadow Creek. The dog who would have mauled me to death if it hadn't been called off by a whistling phantom. So, the stalker in the ute was also the owner of the rampaging dog. Now I was truly scared. I retreated slowly and the dog dropped back below the window frame. Relief steadied my heart. I was obviously not on the lunch menu today.

I glanced at the house. It had no front porch, just a few steps leading straight up to the door. Curiosity surged. Adrenaline rushing through my veins caused my feet to make their way up the steps. Taking a deep breath, I raised a fist and knocked on the door. When no response came, I knocked a little louder. Nothing. Then, just like a reckless character in a B-grade thriller, I turned the handle of the door and stepped inside.

The first thing to hit me as I walked into the darkened hallway was the smell. I'm not sure what Tutankhamen's tomb smelt like when first opened by Howard Carter after thousands of years, but I guessed it had been much like what now assaulted my nostrils and caused my eyes to water. The second thing was the heat; it felt like I'd stepped into a pizza oven. Every window and door must have been shut. The third thing that jolted my senses was the sight of mould growing in clumps over the ceiling and walls.

To my right was an open door to a small room, the floor ankle-deep in strewn litter. The owner of this house was most definitely a hoarder as boxes, household items, newspapers, and things I couldn't even identify were scattered around the room or piled either side the lone bed. Spying a closed door to my left, I turned the knob and poked my head in.

In contrast, this room was sparsely furnished and uncluttered. A single wooden chair stood centre stage facing a wall lined entirely with newspaper print. Moving in for a better look, I discovered that every page of print gave details about a train crash. As I studied the articles, I learned that every report covered the same event—the Shadow Creek rail disaster of 1958.

Some were printed on the day of the crash. Some were from the days following, giving survivors' accounts of what had taken place. Others were written weeks later with updates of the Supreme Court inquiry into the cause of the crash. A few reports were on the twelve-month anniversary, and another ten years later to the day. These anniversary reports also included photos of the deceased, and seeing all their faces made the disaster more real. Nineteen people stared back at me. Nineteen men, women, and children who had ceased to exist that day. I picked Marion out immediately. In a studio headshot I hadn't seen before, she smiled enchantingly for the camera.

My disturbance escalated when I found an enlarged print of this same photo in a frame resting on a wall shelf. Also on this shelf was a match to the shoe that had been left on the hood of my car; though this one was for the left foot and the heel was broken. I crumpled inside. A shrine of sorts had been set up for a woman lost in tragic circumstances. Every time the man walked into the room he would be reminded of the way in which she'd died. How depressing. How sad. What kind of person would do such a thing? There was only one person I knew who would feel her absence so strongly. Ben Patterson.

I felt the pressure of an invisible weight on my neck, my shoulders, my spine. Had I been wrong in my assumptions? Had Marion, in fact, died that fateful day? I was more confused than ever. I felt shattered, then horrified. That would make Ben the stalker.

I took the framed photo from the shelf and searched anew for similarities between Marion and me. Could Ben have returned after years away and holed up here in this deserted cottage to dwell on the woman he'd loved and lost? Could seeing me around Shadow Creek have sparked a misconception that I was Marion returned from the dead?

I had to admit that at a quick glance we could be taken for sisters—one older than the other of course—or mother and daughter at least. No wonder he had been following me. He was already haunted by Marion's memory and then, desperate and delusional, he believed I was she. But why hadn't he confronted me instead of skulking around and baiting me with the necklace?

A creak of floorboards had me turning around.

A man stood in the doorway.

He was tall but with stooped shoulders. Grease-stained overalls hanging from his thin frame looked as if they'd been borrowed from a much larger man. Knobby, arthritic fingers removed a floppy, bush hat to reveal a freckled scalp dotted with tufts of wiry grey. Below this, a forehead creased by a choppy sea of wrinkles bore a pearlescent scar like a semi-circular island. When pale eyes widened either side of a tuber-shaped nose, and moist lips peeled away from stubby yellowed teeth, I gave a cry.

I recognised him. He was the old man I'd bumped into in town the other day. The one carrying a hessian sack filled with potatoes.

I took in a mouthful of fetid air. 'You're not Ben Patterson!'

The hideous smile disappeared and the man moved into the room.

'Ben ... Patterson?' he repeated, scrunching up his nose, which now took the form of a shrivelled turnip. 'Who's that?'

'Not you, that's for sure. You've been following me around Shadow Creek, haven't you?'

He turned his head to the side and spat a glob of God-knows-what onto the floor. I made a mental note not to step on that spot on my way out. It was then, as I stared with disgust at the thick blob of mucus on the floorboards, that I noticed the man was wearing a pair of women's court shoes with red bows and low heels. Very weird.

He gave a grunt. 'You came back.' He glanced down at the photo in my hand and then up to my face. 'You're old.'

Talk about the pot calling the kettle black. I was about to tell him how rude he was, when it dawned on me that he really did think I was Marion. 'How do you know me?' I asked.

He squinted, and his lips pursed like a drawstring bag. 'What?'

I continued in my role as Marion. 'Where did we meet? I can't remember. Was it in Shadow Creek?'

His eyes darted to the wall, then to the picture frame in my hand. He snatched it away. 'I found you. Fixed your arm. You liked my stew.' He returned the photo to its place on the shelf and patted the lone black shoe as if it were a small pet.

My heart kicked against my ribs. *Marion had survived the crash!* He must have found her in the wreckage. Brought her here. Looked after her. Unease stirred within. Why had he done that when there was plenty of help at the scene?

He twisted around, his gaze cold. 'You hurt me!' he growled, fingering the scar on his forehead.

Alarm took a huge bite of my innards. 'She ... I ... did that? Why would I do such a thing?'

His hands formed into fists and his mottled face began to turn red. He began to pant, blowing great gusts of air through his fleshy lips. Then he bared his few teeth and snarled, just like his feral dog.

I decided it was time to leave. As I brushed past him, he seized my arm and yanked me back.

'Don't go! I looked after ya heart.'

My heart? What was this idiot talking about?

His hand went to my throat. I flinched. A grimy finger traced around the collar of my shirt.

'The chain was broke. I fixed it. Kept it safe.'

'The necklace!' I cried.

He nodded. 'You came back. I know'd you would.'

'You saw me around town and followed my car. You knew where I lived. You left the necklace at my house.'

He stroked my cheek, and his eyes drifted over me, lingering on my chest. My skin bristled at the memory of him watching me strip beside the creek. He might be ancient, but he was still a man; a dirty old man in women's shoes. It wasn't difficult to imagine what he'd attempted with Marion—that is if it was just an attempt, an unsuccessful one, I hoped. He would have been younger then; strong, virile. Her attack on him had to have been an act of self-defence.

I stepped around him and aimed for the doorway.

He beat me to it. Gripping the knob, he slammed the door shut behind him as he exited.

In disbelief, I heard a key being fed into the keyhole on the other side as I was locked in.

I banged my fists against the door. 'No! No! Let me out!'

A rasping cackle came from the hallway. The dim-wit was enjoying himself, the bastard!

I twisted the knob, but to no avail. I spied through the keyhole. But there was no key to poke out and land on a sheet of newsprint and drag back in like I'd seen on plenty of crime shows.

Stepping back, I kicked the door panelling hoping it would bust wide open like doors always did for TV detectives. But the only result was a jarred ankle.

Shit! What to do?

I spun around. The faces on the wall seemed to laugh at me—all but one. I pleaded with Marion for help.

The window! Of course.

Hobbling over, and finding no handle on the casement and that it was sealed shut with age and swelling timber, I looked for an object to smash the glass.

The chair!

I lifted it high, ready to ram it into the glass. Yet before I could give the window a taste of my fear, there came a noise at the door —the sound of the key turning in the lock.

The door slowly squeaked on its hinges. But as it swung wide, no one was seen in the doorway.

When nothing else eventuated, I inched forward. As quietly as I could, I leant out and peeked into the hall. Looking left and then right, I found it was deserted. As far as I could tell from all the clutter piled inside, there was also no one in the room opposite. I listened some more. Nothing, other than a house gecko clicking somewhere in time with the beat of my heart. I had to get out!

Dropping the chair, I moved into the hall and made for the front door. Clutching the doorknob, I flicked my wrist. It too was locked.

I faced the interior. At the far end of the hallway was light.

That, and millions of dust motes drifting towards me on a breeze proved there was an open back door. If I was quick, I could rush out, and around the house, and down the drive to the safety of Shane's ute. Yes, I could do that. I had a few years on the elderly nut-job.

Taking off down the hall and past a chaotic lounge room, I slipped on a woven runner and stumbled against the wall. A mounted shadow box loaded with dusty ornaments rattled and then plummeted, just missing my head. All kinds of china miniatures shattered on the floor. I stepped over the shards, only to be wrenched back by my waist. Twisting around I found the spindly man right behind. His ugly excuse for a face grinned at me as I stared open-mouthed. Where had he come from?

I tugged my arm, but his grasp tightened. He was surprisingly powerful for a scrawny geriatric.

'Let me go!' I screeched.

'You're coming with me!' he yelled, his talon-like fingernails digging into my flesh as he shoved me through a kitchen and onto a back porch.

Forcing me down the stairs, he stumbled out of one of his court shoes, giving me the opportunity to wrench my arm free and make a dash across a backyard covered in overgrown vegetation.

Before I could make it to the side of the house, my foot caught in a thick vine and I tripped, crashing down on a huge pumpkin that burst underneath my weight. Rolling in slimy pumpkin pulp, my arm was caught once again, and I was dragged forward. I screamed for help, but the only one who heard my cries was the dog as it came hurtling around the side of the house to join in the attack. I managed to kick it away, but only after it had taken a few sharp nips of my shins.

Pulled to my feet, I was shunted towards a large tin shed and pushed inside. Falling hard against the rusted grill of an ancient truck, I collapsed onto the dirt floor. As I attempted to rise, the man grabbed an item from a jumble of tools on a shelf and stood over me.

I let out a shriek and fell back.

A shaft of light piercing down through a hole in the corrugated tin roof illuminated his face, turning the scar on his forehead into a shimmering pucker of flesh. From this angle it was easy to see that only a mighty blow could have caused such damage.

He raised his arm and I flinched. Held high above his head was an old wooden mallet of the type I'd seen my grandfather use for hammering in tent pegs when setting up camp for a Christmas holiday. I squealed as the man's arm came down fast.

A rush of air passed my ear.

My eyes flew open. He'd missed crushing my head by just a few centimetres. Had that been on purpose or due to his bad aim?

'That's what you did to me!' he screamed. 'I coulda died!' Then, slumping onto his knees, he broke down.

I watched in shock as convulsing sobs transformed a sinister creature into a pathetic old man. The dog joined in, whimpering along beside him.

Staggering to my feet, I took the mallet from his hand and swiftly returned it to the dusty shelf.

'I promise I won't hurt you ever again,' I said in a shaky voice, once again taking on the persona of Marion. 'As long as you promise to stop following me. No more stalking, okay?'

He ceased blubbering long enough to give a nod and a groan.

'Right, I'll take that as your word. But I'm warning you. If you break your promise, I'll have to get the police involved.'

The man's wailing increased and the dog began to howl.

Leaving the odd couple in their misery, I walked out on legs that felt as wobbly as cooked pasta and made it back to Shane's ute without being followed.

Trying to drum up the energy to drive away, I took hold of the steering wheel and contemplated my near miss. At least if I'd been injured or held captive, Shane would have come searching and rescued me, or maybe called the police for assistance. Pulling my phone from the back pocket of my shorts, I found the screen had been cracked in one of my falls, yet it was still working. Checking messages, I was horrified to discover that the one I'd tapped out to Shane, giving details of my location, had failed to send. It seems there was not enough network coverage up in this neck of the woods.

Turning the key in the ignition, I performed a messy U-turn and sped away. Halfway down the hillside, I realised I still hadn't gotten the grey ute's registration number or the old guy's name. It didn't matter. I knew where he lived. Besides, I wouldn't be having any more trouble from him. That was my hope, anyway.

51

My phoned dinged like crazy as soon as the car hit bitumen. Three missed calls and one text message, 'Where the hell are you?' all from Shane.

There was also a voice message from my father. 'Call me as soon as you can. It's urgent.' It had been sent fifteen minutes ago.

I pulled off the road and returned the call.

Dad's voice sounded high, erratic. 'Aberdeen! Oh my Lord ... we're at ... Mum and I ... we're at the cemetery.'

'Cemetery?' I spluttered. 'Which cemetery?'

'Lutwyche. We're standing in front of Ruth Douglas's grave and ... my word, you're not going to believe this.' I had a strange feeling I would. 'Marion isn't here. I mean, the grave is here, but it isn't hers. The name on the headstone has been changed.'

I held my breath. 'Whose name is on it?'

'A ... Dulcie Challinor. And get a load of this ... she died on the eleventh of January 1958. The same day as Marion.'

'The day of the train crash.'

'Yes,' he croaked.

Dad's phone must have been on speaker for I could hear the anguish in my mother voice. 'Where's Marion, Abby? Where is she?'

Good question. 'Head on home. I'll call back later. I haven't worked everything out yet, but I certainly have things to tell you.'

'Call back ... yes ... good idea. I think your mum needs a strong cuppa.'

'No, a strong bloody shandy,' I heard her say before Dad hung up.

I then phoned home.

Gemma answered. 'Where are you? Dad's frantic. He's made a booking at that new restaurant in town for midday and you're still not back.'

'Has he? That's nice. How about I meet you there. I'm only about twenty minutes away.'

'Where've you been? Dad said you went to Nana and Pop's, but Pop phoned here looking for you.'

'I'll fill you in on everything over lunch. Can you bring me a change of clothes? There's a mauve dress hanging in the wardrobe. I think it still fits. And some shoes.'

'Okay. I'll see what I can do.'

'Thanks. I'm really glad you're back, Gem.'

'Yeah ... so am I.'

Driving back onto the road, I realised I was only a few metres from the train crash memorial. As it flashed by, I dwelt on the information I had gained from the loony mountain man. Marion had survived—I knew that for certain now—and she'd probably run off after belting the man with the mallet. But where had she gone after her escape? And why hadn't she contacted her family?

The packed car park next to the new restaurant showed their first weekend was proving a success. My VW was parked on the road, which meant my family were waiting inside.

As I ran up the front steps, I read the newly painted sign hanging from the awning. 'Mulga Bill's'. The decor inside the restaurant was rustic: polished wood floors; roughly hewn timber rafters; and wrought iron tables and chairs. The front counter was lined with corrugated iron and the whitewashed walls boasted landscape paintings and memorabilia from a bygone era. It was noisy with patrons and music, and I recognised the voice of Lee Kernaghan in the rousing country song playing in the background.

Shane waved me over from a corner table.

'This is charming,' I remarked, on reaching my family.

Four pairs of eyes checked me over. Four faces grimaced.

'Where the hell have you been?' asked Shane, his eyes filled with concern.

I bit my lip. 'I ... er ... confronted the stalker.'

His jaw dropped. 'You did what!'

'I'll tell you all about it once I'm cleaned up.' I held out a hand. 'Where are my clothes?'

Gemma handed me a cloth shopping bag. 'I also put in some deodorant and a bottle of perfume.'

'And I added some make-up and some bling, Abby,' smiled Bree. I hoped it wasn't charcoal eyeshadow, black lipstick, and a nose ring.

'Before you dash off, choose a meal so we can order,' said Shane pointing to a menu board nailed to the wall. 'I'm going to give the Marinated Kangaroo Steak a go.'

'I'm having the Lamb Shank Stew and Dumplings,' Elliott chipped in. 'Bree's going with the Pumpkin and Sage Risotto.'

'Crocodile Kebabs with Wild Rice is my choice,' grinned Gemma.

I glanced at the chalked meal options and realised I was famished. 'Order me a Mushroom and Leek Pie. I'll be back in a tick.'

I wove my way around occupied tables and chairs and made my way to the front counter.

A George Clooney clone greeted me—well, a good looking and smartly dressed man with short cropped salt-and-pepper hair and beautiful teeth, anyway.

'Where are your toilets?' I asked.

He pointed to a timber partition. 'Just behind there. You can't miss them.'

I hurried around. Two doors stood in my way. 'Jolly Swagmen' was painted on one, 'Matildas' on the other. It wasn't difficult to choose which door I needed to open.

The full-length wall mirror inside proved I looked a mess. A face streaked with grime stared back at me. My arms were covered in pink grip marks, my legs with bloodied scratches, and on my thigh a circular bruise was forming. As for my clothing, my joggers were splotched with green muck, the back of my shirt with reddish rust, and the rear of my shorts had squashed pumpkin hanging from it in stringy strands.

I quickly undressed.

Wiping myself down with a damp paper towel, I dabbed on deodorant and perfume, and twisted my hair into a very messy bun. Slipping on the mauve dress, I was relieved to discover that it still fit. When I dipped my hand into the bottom of the bag for the make-up, I also pulled out a velvet drawstring bag. My heart skipped a beat as I opened it and found that the 'bling' Bree had mentioned was Marion's necklace. I held it for a moment before fastening it around my neck.

Doing my make-up and slipping on a pair of flats, I stood in front of the mirror for a final inspection and caught the reflection of the wall behind me. I spun around. Hanging on the wall was a framed oil painting of a white cottage. It had a flowering creeper growing over the porch railing and a picket fence out front. In the background was a farm paddock and a mountain range. Painted in a fine spidery hand in the bottom left corner were the words 'Tulip Wood'.

'No way,' I said, leaning closer.

In the right-hand corner was the signature of the artist. 'Frances Baxter.'

I grabbed the shopping bag, now filled with my soiled clothing, and rushed out the door.

George Clooney Mark II was playing with the till.

'Excuse me!' I called.

He closed the till drawer and glanced up. 'Oh ... you found the toilet, then.'

'Yes. Listen ... the painting in the ladies' loo, 'Tulip Wood', where did you buy it?'

He came over, rested his hands on the counter. 'I didn't buy it. It's a family heirloom.'

'An heirloom?'

He nodded. 'It was painted by my grandmother, Fran Baxter. She and my father lived in the area for a few years, and she liked to paint local scenes. Tulip Wood was their home for a time.'

'You've got to be freaking kidding me!' I gasped, dropping the bag and gripping the counter edge for support. 'And you would be?'

He pointed to his chest. I read his name badge and let out a cry.

He smiled. 'Yep, James Patterson, just like the author. Though

I'm not raking in the squillions he makes from all his books. Not yet, anyway. My family calls me Jamie.'

'And you have a brother named Ken.'

His eyes narrowed. 'Yes, I do. How did you know that?'

I breathed in deeply, then out again. 'We could be cousins.'

'Really?' His eyes lit up. 'Wait till I tell my son. He's a little busy at present.' He nodded towards the seating area.

As my eyes moved over the crowd, a patron looked up and gave me a wink. It was Stoney Maloney and he was seated with an attractive older lady with a mass of bleached blonde hair and bright red lips. He gave me a double thumbs-up and I realised he'd been successful in asking Doris out. My focus then moved to a young man standing alongside our table. He seemed to be having an animated conversation with Gemma.

'Your son's a waiter here?'

'Good God, no. Don't let him hear you say that.'

As he said this, his son glanced up. James waved, catching his attention, and the young man ambled over.

Checked trousers; white double-breasted tunic delicately splattered with meat juices; shaggy dark hair sticking out in curls from beneath a black chef's bandana.

'He's the chef?' I remarked with surprise.

'Yep, sure is.'

As he neared I took special note of his purposely-scrappy beard, and smouldering brown eyes. Hello, Jon Snow. Julie was right; he was gorgeous. I had a strong urge to ask him if winter was coming.

'Watcha want, Dad? I need to get back into the kitchen.'

James drummed his fingers on the counter. 'I wanted you to meet … sorry, I didn't catch your name.'

'Abby Eaton,' I said, unable to take my eyes off his handsome progeny.

'Okay. Abby here, says we might be related.'

'Is that right,' said his son, giving me a once-over.

'Yes, on my mother's side. My mother had a first cousin, Marion Douglas ... or I should say, Selena Marion Douglas.'

I glanced from father to son. For a moment, it seemed my words meant nothing to either one of them.

Then James smiled. 'That's my mother.' Leaning over the counter, he gave his son's shoulder a playful punch. 'Whattaya know, young Benji! We have a cousin!'

The young man grinned at his father, then at me.

I sucked in air. He had a gap between his top two front teeth—a diastema—just like his grandfather.

'Holey Moley!' I exclaimed. 'I have to know. Are Ben and Marion ... er ... Selena ... still alive?'

James laughed. 'They certainly are. Dad was the one who suggested the name for the restaurant. He's a Banjo Paterson fan. *Mulga Bill's Bicycle* is one of his favourite poems.'

'Nana Lena offered up some of her recipes for the more traditional meals we serve here,' said Benji, 'though, of course, I always add a new twist.'

I scanned around the restaurant. 'Are they here? Did they come for the opening?'

Both men shook their heads.

'They live in Tasmania. Hobart,' said James. 'It's a bit of a hike for them.'

'Maybe we'll have better luck coaxing them up for Christmas,' added Benji. He started to move away. 'Sorry, I need to get back to the kitchen. Catch you later, cuz,' he grinned, flashing a familiar smile and disappearing.

James had to answer the phone, but before he took the call, he mentioned that we should get together soon, when it was less busy. I agreed, and finally made my way over to my family who were already tucking into their meals.

'Were you just hitting on both the manager and the chef?' asked Elliott.

I pulled out my chair and flopped down. 'No, not at all.'

'Good,' said Bree, 'because you wouldn't be getting anywhere with the chef. He's got the hots for Gemma.'

I stared at my daughter. 'Really?'

She gave a shrug and blushed. 'Hey, did anyone else think he looks a little like—'

'Kit Harington?' I butted in. 'Yes, I've noticed. He seems quite a catch.'

Gemma quickly changed the subject. 'Didn't you say you were going to fill us in on where you've been all morning?'

I took a mouthful of pie. It was still warm. 'I don't know where to begin. There's just so much to tell.'

'Well, before you start,' said Shane, sliding an envelope across the table towards me, 'open this.'

'What is it?'

'Just open it,' he urged.

I did. Inside were two printed airline tickets, several accommodation vouchers, and a swag of tourism brochures. 'What? But ... how?'

'I've pulled out of buying the motorbike. You were right. It was a selfish act. The money should be used for our holiday. How does three weeks travelling around Tasmania sound? It's the Apple Isle, you know.' He pointed to the heart pendant and the apple blossoms standing out against the mauve of my dress.

I seized Shane's face and kissed him hard, right there in front of the kids. I'm sure he thought I was just showing my gratitude for him changing his mind about the bike. What he didn't yet know, was that this gift of a holiday in Tassie would enable me to return the necklace to its rightful owner, and discover firsthand the true facts surrounding Marion and Ben's love story.

'Oh ... and I noticed that the dress shop across the road has a sign in the window,' Shane said, with a grin. 'Seems they're closing down soon and the premises will be up for lease. I think you should consider opening your own bookshop in town. I'm sure we could work something out financially. With your know-how, I reckon it could be a real winner.'

My mouth fell open. One week ago, my world had imploded. Now it was expanding in ways I never thought possible. One by one, those juggling balls were returning to the air, and life looked as if it would soon be back on track.

'First, let me bring you all up to speed on my morning adventures,' I said to an eager audience of four.

52

Tulip Wood 1958

The rear garden at Tulip Wood is stippled with light and shadows. The scent of jasmine is strong.

'Such a clear night sky,' says Marion. 'Oh … I think I just saw a shooting star!'

Banjo gazes upward. 'Are you sure it's not Sputnik 2? Or should I say, Muttnik.'

Marion slips her arm through his. 'It's not returning yet is it? I've sort of lost track of time.'

'No, not for another three months. Longer than Sputnik 1.'

'I feel so sorry for the little dog.' She sighs. 'Fancy being stuck in that thing and orbiting around and around. I couldn't imagine Honey taking it very well.'

Honey rubs her wiry body against Banjo's leg. He tickles her under the chin and the little tail thumps a steady beat on the dewy grass. 'Especially when she'd only survive a week.'

'A week?'

'That's what they've reported. Laika was never going to come back alive anyway. If by some miracle she'd gone the distance, she'd have been incinerated with the satellite on re-entry.'

'I didn't know that. How are they ever going to send a man into space and have him return safely.'

'They will. They'll work it out. The future holds no bounds.'

She rests her head against him. 'Like ours.'

He nods. One more night at Tulip Wood and then they leave to begin a brand-new life. He glances over his shoulder towards the kitchen window and the silhouette of his mother. 'Mum has coped rather well with our plans, don't you think?'

'I think we talked her round. Maybe once we're settled she'll decide to come stay. I'd really like that.'

'Yep, as Henry Lawson said in one of his poems, "Tis the hope of something better that will save us in the end". Thanks to the money in your handbag, we should be as right as rain.' He gives Marion's arm a squeeze. 'I was thinking the name Meredith could work.'

She pulls away. 'Meredith? I was thinking ... Selena.' Banjo's scowl is noticed and she gives his arm a slap. 'It's my real name, you know.'

He chuckles. 'My foot, it is.'

'It's the truth. I'm Selena Marion Douglas.'

'You're kidding me.' He sees her shake her head. 'Geez, just when I thought I knew all about you.'

She elbows him in the ribs 'You haven't even scratched the surface, buddy.'

'Well then, Selena Douglas, I look forward to getting to know you.'

'We'll have plenty of time to do that, Banjo me old mate, because I'm not planning on going anywhere without you ever again.'

He takes her hand, so small in his. 'We'd better get married then.'

Her eyes sparkle in the moonlight. 'Yes, I think we'd better.'

'Is that an acceptance?'

She laughs. 'I guess it is.'

He lifts her hand to his mouth and kisses the finger that will one day—very soon, he hopes—bear his ring. 'We should celebrate. Maybe Mum will let us open one of the bottles of wine she brought back from her last visit with Uncle Marty.'

'Wine that tastes fruity and spicy, like the one we had in the orchard that day?'

That day. Only a few months back, yet it feels like a lifetime ago. 'I reckon so.'

'Good,' she smiles, 'I quite liked that one.'

'And I liked what it did to you.' He wraps his arms around her. 'I warn you though. If the wine goes straight to your head again and you get a little frisky, I won't be acting like a gentleman. It's not often you discover that the one you loved and lost has risen from the grave.'

'Well it's not often you find out you were dead,' she says, snuggling into him.

A tender breeze picks up. It circuits the garden, drifts into the yard.

Banjo watches the quiver of leaves on the recently planted sapling and imagines its roots taking a firm hold in the soil. Even though they may not be here to see it, he hopes the apple tree will have a long and fruitful existence, just like theirs.

He kisses the top of Marion's head and breathes in her scent— the sweet fragrance of life.

ACKNOWLEDGMENTS

My writing journey for this book has been a long and winding one —yet what a ride! My heartfelt gratitude goes to:

My tribe, Writers Rendezvous Dayboro, for motivating and encouraging me in all of my writing ventures. You warm my heart.

Editors Lauren Daniels and Peta Culverhouse for your wisdom, keen eyes, and insights into worthwhile storytelling.

The team and readers at BetaBooks.co who gave such helpful feedback and advice.

Author and writing companion, Carleton Chinner, for paving the way and sharing your knowledge; and author and best writing buddy ever, Jane Ireland, for the fun and laughter, and narrative problem solving—I raise my vanilla latte to you. Thanks for the not-so-gentle nudging to step outside my comfort zone.

My extended family. While writing this story, we shared many joys and a number of sorrows. I can't thank you enough for your love and support, and for walking with me through this crazy life.

To Ron & Dawn West and Jack & Marj Stevens—the most amazing parents and role models of love. I miss you every day.

To Rachel, Hayley, & Ryan—my greatest achievements! You three are my delight and inspiration.

Lastly, this story would not have made it to print if it wasn't for David—my cheerleader, coach, character stand-in, sustenance maker, and life-partner. Your untiring patience and belief in my ability got me here. Love on & on.

ABOUT THE AUTHOR

Vicki Stevens lives on the rural fringe of Brisbane, Australia, with her husband and an abundance of inquisitive wildlife. An avid short story writer in several genres, her keen interest in genealogy inspires her to write evocative and suspenseful family history mysteries. *Shaking Trees* is her debut novel and the first book in her Abby Eaton Mystery series.

For more info:
www.vickistevens.com.au

facebook.com/VickiStevensAuthor
instagram.com/vickistevens.au

www.ingramcontent.com/pod-product-compliance
Lightning Source LLC
Chambersburg PA
CBHW030349120726
47901CB00007B/1963